Danger is the most powerful aphrodisiac…

WICKED DESIRE

"Marriage, to the right woman, is the beginning of a life of love."

She raised a brow. "My, you are romantic tonight."

"Casanova would be envious." He pulled her into his arms. "If he had seen you tonight, he might well have changed his mind about marriage. And considered me a very lucky man."

"Then we are well matched." She gazed up at him. "For I am a very lucky woman." She paused. "Although I have been remiss in not making certain you know how very much I love you."

"I have been remiss in that myself."

She smiled into his blue eyes. "You are my hero, Adrian Hadley-Attwater." Evelyn slid her hand around the back of his neck and pulled his head down to hers. "My knight," she murmured against his lips . . .

Books by Victoria Alexander

THE PERFECT MISTRESS

HIS MISTRESS BY CHRISTMAS

MY WICKED LITTLE LIES

Published by Kensington Publishing Corporation

My Wicked Little Lies

VICTORIA ALEXANDER

ZEBRA BOOKS
KENSINGTON PUBLISHING CORP.
http://www.kensingtonbooks.com

ZEBRA BOOKS are published by

Kensington Publishing Corp.
119 West 40th Street
New York, NY 10018

All Kensington titles, imprints and distributed lines are
available at special quantity discounts for bulk purchases for
sales promotion, premiums, fund-raising, educational or in-
stitutional use.

Special book excerpts or customized printings can also be
created to fit specific needs. For details, write or phone the
office of the Kensington Special Sales Manager: Attn.: Special Sales Department. Kensington Publishing Corp., 119
West 40th Street, New York, NY 10018. Phone: 1-800-221-
2647.

Zebra and the Z logo Reg. U.S. Pat. & TM Off.

ISBN-13: 978-1-4201-1706-6
ISBN-10: 1-4201-1706-8

First Printing: February 2012

10 9 8 7 6 5 4 3 2 1

Printed in the United States of America

*This book is dedicated with great affection and
gratitude to Joan Wright.
You welcomed me into your family all those years
ago and became much more than a relative;
you became a cherished friend.
I don't say it enough—thank you!*

Prologue

My Dear Sir,

I am at once eager and filled with regret to write this missive to you as it shall be my last. No doubt, Sir Maxwell has informed you of my decision to leave my position. In truth, I never thought this day would come. I never imagined leaving this life which has been, in most ways, quite remarkable and, in all ways, extraordinary. And yet, I have grown tired of excitement and weary of secrets.

I have lived these past five years in service to my queen and my country. While I admit, it may well be selfish, the time has now come to live in service to myself, as it were. I long for nothing more than that which most women want. A husband, a family, and a place in the world where one knows one belongs.

I have met a wonderful man and I shall spend the rest of my days trying to make him happy. Which is not the least bit daunting as he has pledged to do the same for me. It sounds dreadfully ordinary, doesn't it? And yet, I have never been so eager and, yes, excited.

I have always thought those who say they have no regrets seek either to deceive others or to deceive themselves. Yet, as I cast my thoughts back upon these last years, I find few regrets. If I knew at the beginning what I know now, I daresay, I would have chosen the same path although perhaps I would have been more clever. Or possibly not. Regardless, it has been a grand adventure.

As this is my last communiqué, I feel I can be completely candid. I have only one true regret, Sir. I wish we had met, just once, face-to-face. I confess, I have often thought of that, wondered if I would know you the moment I saw you. Or recognize the sound of your voice. Silly, of course, as I have never seen you nor heard you. But through the years I feel I have come to know you although, in truth, I know nothing about you at all. I have imagined, in the late hours of the night, a meeting between us. The gaze of your eyes, wise and, no doubt, seductive, meeting mine. The corners of your mouth curving upward in amusement. The sound of your laughter. I have imagined the feel of your hand around mine as we danced across a crowded ballroom floor.

But who knows? You are a man of many secrets. Perhaps we have danced together. Perhaps you were the short, balding gentleman I danced with at the French ambassador's ball. Or were you the flirtatious Italian count who compared my eyes to the stars in the heavens? I shall never know and that is, no doubt, for the best.

I sit here now with a smile upon my face. I fear I have let my fancy take flight in this final note. Odd, that finality brings such freedom. But one does wonder about the road not taken, the quest not pursued, the last chapter of the book left unread.

You have my gratitude, Sir, for all you have taught me, for your guidance and friendship.

Travel safe, my dear Sir.

With ~~warm affection~~ love,
Eve

He stared at the note for a long moment. The hand so familiar, the words so final. But then that was the way of endings and beginnings, at once sad and exciting. Still, one needed to put the past behind before one could turn toward the future.

He drew a deep breath and picked up his pen.

My Dearest Eve,

Your note brought a smile to my face but then your notes often have. I shall miss them. As this last exchange seems to be one of confessions, I have some of my own.

You have astounded me through these years with your cleverness and your courage. I look upon you with great pride. Your decision to leave is a true loss to your country and yet no one can fault you for your choice. You have given much and it is time, past time perhaps, for you to resume the life you should always have lived. You have well earned it.

I, too, have wondered at what magic might have been found in a meeting between us. Without the barrier of po-

sition or paper. Was there fire that simmered beneath the surface of our words, or was that no more than the nature of the work we have accomplished together? No more than my own inevitable desire for a woman whose presence has filled my life even as necessity dictated she be no more than the faintest hint of perfume wafted from a page lifted to my face. Ah, Eve, the thoughts I have had.

He paused and stared at the words he had written. What was the point? There was no real need to respond. And to tell her of his feelings now might well do more harm than good. Perhaps there would come a day . . .

He sighed and placed his unwritten note on top of hers, folded them, and slipped them into his waistcoat pocket. He pushed his chair back from his desk and stood. There was much to accomplish and little time left.

Endings and beginnings . . . such was the stuff of life.

Part One

Lies of Omission

Ask no questions, and you'll be told no lies.

—Charles Dickens, *Great Expectations*

Chapter 1

Two years later, February 1886 . . .

"**Y**ou're quite mad to suggest such a thing. And madder yet to think I would consider it. You do realize that, don't you?" Evelyn Hadley-Attwater, the Countess of Waterston, rose to her feet and glared down at the man behind the desk. The man she had once thought of with the affection one felt for an annoying brother. The man she'd planned never again to see under these circumstances. "I won't do it. And I cannot believe you have the nerve to ask me in the first place."

Sir Maxwell Osgood studied her over the rim of a pipe, the smoke drifting about his head like a veil of accusation. It was most annoying.

"When did you start smoking a pipe?"

"I thought you preferred a pipe to cigars," he said mildly.

"You look ridiculous." She reached over his desk,

plucked the pipe from his mouth, and dropped it into a saucer obviously being used for ashes. "And I prefer to breathe air that hasn't been previously inhaled."

"Doesn't your husband smoke cigars?"

"Never in my presence." She narrowed her eyes. "You do understand there is nothing you can say to change my mind?"

He smiled, a slow seductive smile that had no doubt made any number of women swoon at his feet and fall into his bed. Evelyn had never been among them. She heaved a reluctant sigh and sank back into her chair. "If you're trying to charm me, it will not work."

His smile widened to a grin. "To my eternal regret."

"I fully intended never to see you again."

"Allow me to point out we have seen one another."

"Oh, certainly at the occasional social event, where we treat each other with nothing more than polite cordiality. It's not the least bit significant and can scarcely be avoided. I had no intention of ever being here again." She gestured at the room around them, a room so unremarkable as to be startling. It could well be the office of any midlevel government bureaucrat. Anyone stumbling in here unawares would find nothing whatsoever to indicate that the business of the Department of Domestic and International Affairs was not primarily concerned with treaties of trade between the more far-flung reaches of the empire and other countries. And indeed, on the first floor of the building, for the most part, it was. She met his gaze directly. "And even less intention of having anything whatsoever to do with you."

"My God, Evelyn." He clapped his hand over his heart in a dramatic manner. "You wound me deeply. Deeply and irrevocably."

"I doubt that." She snorted in disbelief. "And it's Lady Waterston."

"I thought we were friends." A hurt note sounded in his voice.

She ignored it. "Of a sort, yes, I suppose we were. But everything is different now. My life is different and I will not risk that."

He studied her for a moment, the look in his eyes abruptly serious. "His life may well be at risk."

Her heart caught. She ignored that, too. It really wasn't any of her concern. Still . . . "You said a file had been stolen."

"Two weeks ago."

"Exactly how important is this file?"

"The file consists of documents that reveal the very structure of this organization and the true identities of those involved in its governance and activities." He shook his head. "That information would jeopardize the safety of every person listed as well as the safety of their families. Who knows to what lengths those we have pursued through the years would go in seeking revenge."

She drew her brows together. So like Max to dole out pertinent details a little at a time. "You should have mentioned the importance of this file in the beginning. From what you have said thus far, I had the impression this was no more important than bureaucratic—" A thought struck her and her heart froze. "Am I on that list?"

"No," he said simply.

Relief coursed through her, replaced at once by suspicion. "Why not?"

"The only reference to you is to *Eve* and that is minimal. When you left the agency, all records regarding your true identity were expunged." He rolled his eyes toward the ceiling. Obviously this was a point of some annoyance. "At Sir's orders."

Her heart jumped at the code name of the agent she had worked with for five long years. A man she never met in person, who communicated with her only by written word. Who guided her, issued her orders, and yes, on occasion, saved her. A man who had once invaded her dreams late in the night and had made her ache for something she—they—would never know. But that was a long time ago and those dreams, that man, were firmly in the past, and there she intended to keep them. That she would react to his name was only natural and not at all important. There was only one man who filled her dreams now. The same man who filled her life and her heart. She narrowed her eyes. "Why?"

"He wished to protect you and seemed to think it was only fair to do so. Although . . ." Max huffed. "It had never been done before and, I daresay, will never be done again."

"I see." She paused. Sir's actions were as thoughtful as they were unexpected. Not that they changed anything. "He has my gratitude, of course. Regardless, this is no longer any concern of mine."

He raised a brow. "No?"

She shook her head. "No."

"I would have thought, given the many times he saved your delightful derrière—"

"I beg your pardon!"

He chuckled. "Forgive me, my dear, old habits and all." He sobered. "Now then, Evelyn—"

"Lady Waterston," she said firmly.

He sighed. "Yes, of course, *Lady Waterston*."

"Thank you," she said under her breath although she needn't have thanked him. She was now Lady Waterston, Countess of Waterston, and had been since her marriage two years ago to Adrian Hadley-Attwater, the Earl of Waterston, and very possibly the dearest man in the world.

"Forgive me, *Lady Waterston*." He eyed his pipe longingly. "It's not always easy to remember how very much the world has changed since you were last in this room."

"Not merely the world, Sir Maxwell." She pinned him with a firm look. "I have changed as well. I am no longer the helpless young woman who was forced into the employ of this agency."

"I don't recall you being forced." He chuckled. "Nor do I remember you ever being helpless."

"I was young and foolish."

"You were young but you were never foolish."

She tried and failed to hide a small smile of satisfaction. She had once prided herself on never allowing her feelings—her weaknesses really—to show to him or anyone else. Even now, secure in her position in the world and in the heart of her husband, she remained reticent to display undue emotion. "Perhaps *foolish* is the wrong word."

"Perhaps." His gaze met hers, and his eyes narrowed slightly. "You do realize that putting this in the form of a request was little more than a courtesy."

She had suspected as much. Still, she had hoped. "You can't seriously expect me to return to my previous position."

"I not only expect it, Lady Waterston, but you really have no choice."

"Nonsense. Of course I have a choice." She stood once more and crossed the room to gaze out the window that overlooked a small, private park. In spite of the fact that she had been here on no more than a handful of occasions, for nearly five years this imposing, yet nondescript, mansion on this small square in Mayfair had been the center of her world. And this man, and his superiors, most notably Sir, had ruled that world. But she had met Adrian at very nearly the same time she had grown weary of deceit and treachery, even in the name of the queen, and had left it all behind. Or thought she had. She drew a deep breath. "I have no intention of returning to this."

"Perhaps, given the critical nature of the situation, if we brought the matter to the attention of Lord Waterston . . ."

The threat hung in the air. So much for friendship.

"Blackmail, Max? Tell my husband about my past if I don't do as you wish?"

"*Blackmail* is an ugly word." He shook his head.

"And yet accurate?"

He ignored her. "There's more to it than I have said thus far."

"There would have to be, wouldn't there?" On the far side of the park, a small boy, bundled against the cold, played with a dog under the watchful eyes of a nanny. Her heart twisted and she sighed. There probably was no choice. "Go on."

"There have been threats in recent months—"

She turned toward him. "What kind of threats?"

"Those of exposure primarily. Vague, little more

than rumors, but threats nonetheless." He drew a deep breath. "As you are well aware, this agency operates under a veil of secrecy."

She gasped in mock surprise. "You mean the Department of Domestic and International Affairs is not primarily concerned with trade?"

"Now is not the time for sarcasm."

She cast him her sweetest smile and retook her seat. "I thought it was the perfect time."

"As I was saying, this is an agency that cannot function openly. If this file was made public, if it was in the wrong hands, everything we do, everything we have ever done, would be cast in the direst of lights. We have not always followed what many would see as proper procedures. Indeed, we have often operated outside the strict confines of the law in the pursuit of the security interests of this country. The repercussions of exposure could bring down the government itself, especially given the volatile nature of the current political climate. At the very least, our effectiveness would be at an end."

He paused. "As for the personal cost, the gentlemen who have headed this organization have done so at risk to themselves and their reputations. The only thing they have received in return, aside from the knowledge that they have provided an invaluable service to their country, is the assurance that their connection to this agency will never be public." He shook his head. "These men are from well-known families, they hold hereditary titles and are respected members of Parliament. Some have had the confidence of the queen herself. Exposure would wreak havoc at all levels of government."

"I understand that." Impatience sounded in her voice. "But none of it explains why you have demanded my presence. Why am I here?"

"Because you are the only one I can trust," he said staunchly.

"Nonsense. You have other agents, far more competent than I, that can certainly handle a minor task like the recovering of a file." She scoffed. "If I am the only one you can trust, then you have far greater problems than a mere missing file."

"And indeed I do." He paused as if debating his next words. "I suspect the theft of the file was arranged by someone within this organization. The file was requested by the foreign office, or so I was led to believe." He blew an annoyed breath. "Given multiple layers of bureaucracy, it's difficult to uncover specifically who requested it without revealing that it has been stolen."

She chose her words with care. "It seems to me, if one is concerned with secrecy, putting this kind of information into a single file is rather, well, stupid."

"In hindsight perhaps," he said sharply. "Do not forget this is still a governmental department, and when one's superiors make a request, one complies without question."

She raised a brow. "My, my, we are sensitive about—" A thought struck her and she gasped. "It was stolen from you, wasn't it?"

He huffed. "That's neither here nor there at the moment."

"It was, wasn't it?" She tried and failed to hide a grin.

"It's not amusing," he snapped. "I would trust no

one else with something of this importance and whoever arranged the theft knew that." He glared at her. "I was set upon by thugs and rendered unconscious by the use of chloroform." He shuddered. "Nasty stuff."

"And when you woke up?"

"When I woke up, the file was gone and I was . . ."

"You were?"

He hesitated.

"Don't stop now. If I am to be involved in this, I need to know all of it."

"Very well," he snapped. "I woke up naked in a most disreputable brothel."

She choked back a laugh. "As opposed to a reputable brothel?"

He ignored her. "It was most awkward."

"Because you have never been in a brothel before?" she said sweetly.

"One does not purchase what one has always had for free."

She stared at him, then laughed. "You have certainly not changed."

"Unfortunately, I have," he said under his breath. "Lady Waterston." He leaned forward and met her gaze. "Because you are no longer an agent and because your real name is not included in the records here, you can act without suspicion. If you noticed, I asked you here on a day when few people are in these offices. Those that are have been sent on errands. All to preserve your privacy." He paused. "In truth, what I need from you is fairly minimal."

"I can scarcely go back to being Miss Turner, an unmarried heiress with a penchant for travel and parties. Without the wealth, of course," she added wryly.

"No, but you are now Lady Waterston, who is welcome at very nearly any social event."

"Yes, I suppose."

"Your presence would be unremarkable at those events where mine might be noted. In spite of my title and my family connections, I am little more than the head of an unimportant government office concerned with minimally important trade."

She sighed. "Go on."

"I am close to discovering where the file may be located. All I ask of you is to recover it."

"That's all?"

"That's all," he said quickly although it did seem he hesitated for no more than the beat of his heart. She might have been mistaken and it had been some time since she'd trusted—or needed to trust—her instincts, but instinct was telling her now that he was not being entirely forthright.

"What aren't you telling me?"

He considered her question, obviously deciding how much to reveal. "The file contains the names of the last three men who headed this organization. The first died a few months ago."

She raised a brow. "By foul play?"

"It's impossible to say. He was elderly and appears to have died in his sleep. But you and I both know how easy it is to make death appear natural."

"Only by hearsay." She narrowed her eyes. "If you recall, I was never in a position where such measures were necessary."

"Nor will you be now." He shook his head. "It could well be coincidence especially since his death was several months ago. But it should not be discounted completely."

"Sir's name is in that file, isn't it?"

"It is."

"I would think he would wish to handle this." She thought for a moment. "Was this his idea? To bring me back?"

"He knows nothing about it."

She pulled her brows together. "Don't you think you should tell him?"

"I see no need for that." His gaze met hers. "Sir left the department at very nearly the same time you did."

"I see." Relief again washed through her. She had no desire to resume their correspondence. Sir was a road not taken and such roads were best left in the past. She drew a deep breath. "The days of my slipping into a house in the dead of night are long over," she warned. "As are my days of eliciting information by means of my charm alone."

"Understandable." He nodded.

"A certain amount of deceit will no doubt be necessary, but I have never lied to my husband and I do not intend to do so now."

"Come now, all women lie to their husbands."

"I don't." Indignation drew her brows together. "I have never had any need to."

"You've never hidden a bill from a dressmaker you did not want him to see?"

"No."

"You've never said you were going one place when you went somewhere else altogether?"

"Certainly not."

"You've never told your husband another gentleman's flirtatious manner was less than it actually was?"

"Of course not." She cast him a pitying look. "You know nothing at all about women. Most of us do not lie as a matter of course. It's not surprising that you aren't married."

"I know a great deal about women, which is precisely why I am not married. And you all lie, each and every one of you."

She ignored him. "You should find a wife. You're not getting any younger. Fair-haired men do not age well. All that boyish charm and that handsome face of yours will not last forever."

He cast her a devilish grin. "And yet, both continue to serve me well."

"You haven't changed at all." She rose to her feet and he stood. "Mark my words, one day you're considered dashing and desirable and the next you're a lecherous old goat."

He stared at her curiously. "You're happy, aren't you?"

"I have never been happier."

"You don't miss the excitement of the chase? Of unraveling a riddle? Of ferreting out information that will expose a villain?"

"Not in the least." She shrugged. "I am sorry if that disappoints you."

"And your husband, is he happy as well?"

"He has never given me reason to believe otherwise." She smiled at the thought of her husband. Adrian was everything she'd ever wanted. A good man, kind and generous, he carried his responsibilities with ease and could be depended upon without question.

That he was tall and handsome and not at all proper and restrained in their bed was an added bonus. And he loved her. What more could a woman want? "I want your assurance you will never call on me again after this. This is my final assignment."

"I can't make that promise."

"Max." A warning sounded in her voice.

"Very well." He huffed. "I shall make every effort."

"I assume you will contact me with further instructions."

He nodded. "Within the next few days."

"Very well."

She nodded and turned to leave, then turned back. "One more thing."

"Yes?"

"If this ruins my marriage, my life, I will more than likely slit your throat. Or shoot you. Do not forget, I was well trained here. And I am an excellent shot. That I have not shot anyone or never slit a man's throat does not mean I do not know how or that I will hesitate." She leaned toward him and met his gaze. "Or perhaps I will simply cut off an appendage that I know is near and dear to you."

He winced. "Come now, Eve—"

"You have my word, Max. My husband knows little about my past. If he learns—"

"And you have my word," he said firmly. "Your husband will not learn of your past association with this office from me." He smiled with something that might possibly have been genuine affection. "You have trusted me in the past. Trust me on this."

She studied him for a moment, then heaved a frustrated sigh. "I suppose I have no choice."

"Truly, Evelyn, I would never do anything to destroy your happiness."

"See that you don't." She leveled him a hard look and sent a silent prayer heavenward that he hadn't already.

Chapter 2

"Well, this could be somewhat awkward," Celeste DeRochette said calmly, peering over the spectacles she wore for effect rather than necessity.

"Somewhat?" Evelyn scoffed. "At the very least it's *somewhat awkward*. If I'm lucky, it will only be *somewhat awkward. Somewhat awkward* is the best I can hope for."

"He's not stupid, you know, your husband, that is."

"I know that." Evelyn sighed. "It would be much easier if he were." She paced the width of her sitting room.

Celeste was silent for a long moment. "You don't want to do this at all, do you?"

"Absolutely not." Evelyn brushed a stray lock of hair behind her ear. Ha! Just another indication of how distraught she was. Her locks did not stray from where she placed them. Ever. "Apparently, I have no choice. I thought it was over, in the past, behind me."

"You don't miss it, even a little?"

"No, not at all."

"Surely, there's a moment now and then?"

"Not a moment, not an instant—never!"

"Of course you don't." Celeste nodded in a thoughtful manner. As always, Evelyn wasn't entirely certain what the other woman was thinking.

Celeste had played the part of Evelyn's companion through her years of working for the department. When Evelyn had decided to leave and marry Adrian, Celeste had left with her and now served as Evelyn's secretary. And then, as now, she was her closest friend. "Do you?"

"No." Celeste shook her head, then grimaced. "Perhaps on occasion, when life seems a bit . . . dull."

"My life is never dull," Evelyn said staunchly.

Celeste raised a brow.

"Never." Her eyes widened with realization. "Is yours?"

"My dear friend. This is the life you were born for." Celeste chose her words with care. "You are the Countess of Waterston now. You have an endless number of social and charitable obligations as well as Adrian's enormous family to keep you occupied. Whereas I . . ." She shrugged. "I am your employee."

"You are my dearest friend."

"And for now . . ." Celeste cast her a warm smile. "That is enough."

Evelyn considered her curiously for a long moment and wondered if she'd seen her at all in recent years. Although not being seen, or rather, not being noticed, was what Celeste strived for. She wore her dark hair in a tight, stern knot on the back of her head. Her spectacles hid her startling violet eyes. Coupled with the drab, nondescript clothes she typically donned, one's gaze tended to pass right over her. But on any number

of occasions, Evelyn had noticed the gazes of gentlemen in particular jerking back to Celeste for a second
look. Celeste had always been good at making herself
appear to be someone she wasn't. Evelyn had long
thought her friend was a woman in hiding. Indeed, Celeste DeRochette was not her real name but she had
never shared her true name with Evelyn nor had Evelyn ever asked. Privacy was a boundary of friendship
neither woman had ever crossed. Nor had they needed
to. Evelyn would trust Celeste with her life.

They never would have become friends, they never
would have met at all, if not for the department, although they had much in common. Both women had
been orphaned at an early age, but Evelyn's father was
a viscount and she had been left the ward of a distant
relative, Sir George Hardwell. Sir George had had no
desire to be responsible for a child and had had little
interest in her. He had ensured her education at boarding schools in England and abroad and had provided a
minimal allowance when she had finished her schooling thanks to a small trust, left by her parents, now
long depleted, administered by Sir George's solicitor.
While she had dutifully corresponded with him
through the years, he had rarely responded and eventually she had stopped writing altogether. Evelyn had
often thought it odd that, at one time, the two most significant men in her life were two she had never met in
person. She had long suspected it was through Sir
George that the department had become aware of her
and her circumstances although she had nothing to
base that suspicion on. It was a feeling, nothing more.

Celeste was the daughter of an actress. She, too, had
been orphaned, or perhaps abandoned, Evelyn wasn't
clear on that point, when very young. She was passed

from family to family until she followed her mother's path and found first a home in the theater and then the department. Evelyn thought it something of a pity she hadn't continued on the stage. An expert at adopting accents, be they refined or common, Celeste was also brilliant at changing her appearance and making one believe she was someone she wasn't. Valuable skills to have when one worked for a clandestine government department yet, for the most part, wasted when one was a social secretary to a countess.

"Good Lord." Evelyn stared at her friend. "I've been dreadfully selfish."

"Indeed you have and I have permitted you to be." Celeste met her gaze directly. "But do not think for a moment I would be here if I did not wish to be. It's been most . . . refreshing. It's not a difficult job, you know. Keeping your schedule, planning your social events, assisting your correspondence. And you do overpay me." A twinkle shone in Celeste's eyes. "Why, it's almost like being on holiday."

Evelyn ignored her amusement. "But is it enough?"

"You could always pay me more."

"You know what I mean."

"As I said, it is at the moment." Celeste shrugged. "I make no promises about the future, however."

"Good. And I make no apologies for that bit of self-ishness." Celeste was as close to her as any sister might have been. Indeed, Evelyn considered her family and they did look a bit like sisters. They were of a similar height and figure although Celeste's hair was nearly black whereas Evelyn's was a determined brown. Her eyes were hazel, brown really, her friend's violet. Evelyn considered Celeste the lovelier of the two women, which bothered her not at all. They were nearly the same age as well. Celeste had turned thirty some months ago and Evelyn's thirtieth birthday was within a few weeks. "I would hate to lose you."

"I assure you, you will never lose me," Celeste said firmly. "Even if the day comes that I decide this is not how I wish to spend the rest of my life, we will always be close friends."

Still, the very idea of not having Celeste around was most distressing. Evelyn loved Adrian's family but Celeste was hers, the only family she had. She adopted a casual tone. "Adrian still has one remaining unwed brother, you know."

"The barrister?"

Evelyn nodded. "He's very nice and quite handsome."

Celeste laughed. "So you are matchmaking now?"

"Not at all." Evelyn paused. "Although it's not a bad idea. There are worse ways to spend the rest of your life than as the wife of a nice, handsome, ambitious barrister. Who will no doubt one day be a judge."

"And will therefore need a wife," Celeste said thoughtfully.

"He doesn't *need* one but a suitable wife can certainly be an aide to any man with ambition."

"And would I be a suitable wife?"

"You can be anything you wish," Evelyn said firmly.

"It's a role I have yet to play." A considering note sounded in Celeste's voice.

"A role you were *born* to play."

"I doubt that. Regardless . . ." Celeste shook her head. "Your brother-in-law has never shown the slightest bit of interest in me."

"Perhaps because he has never seen you as who you really are."

"Perhaps. And perhaps when I meet a gentleman who makes me want to be completely candid and forthright and all those sorts of things, then I will indeed marry." Celeste studied her with amusement. "You are simply offering up your brother-in-law as a sacrificial lamb. Were I to marry him, we would truly be family."

Evelyn gasped in mock indignation. "I would never encourage your marriage to suit my own purposes. That would indeed be selfish." She grinned. "But it is an excellent idea."

"It is an idea, the excellence of it remains to be seen." Celeste pinned her with a firm look. "But you, my dear, have changed the subject."

"It's not a subject I wish to discuss. Or to think about."

"And in this, too, you have no choice." Celeste's brows drew together. "What happens now?"

"Max said he has an idea as to the location of the file. He will contact me with instructions." Evelyn resumed pacing the room.

"So you wait?"

"Apparently."

"I see." Celeste watched her for a moment. "Patience has never been one of your virtues."

"Now that I have agreed to do this—although *agreed* is not the right word." Evelyn huffed. "*Coerced* is more accurate."

"You'd prefer to get on with it."

"Exactly." Evelyn nodded. "From the moment I left Max's office, I have felt that my entire life was in some sort of limbo. As if I were a leaf blown onto a pond. Too wet to blow away and not saturated enough to sink to the bottom. Suspended on the surface of the water, waiting to blow away or to sink."

"How very dramatic of you."

"But accurate nonetheless."

"Nonsense." Celeste scoffed. "Now you're merely feeling sorry for yourself."

"Perhaps."

"Admittedly, waiting is not something you do well but I don't believe I've ever seen you feel sorry for yourself." She shook her head in a mournful manner. "How have you come to such a dreadful state?"

Evelyn narrowed her eyes.

"There are a number of things you have yet to consider," Celeste said. "First of all, Sir Maxwell would not have asked for your assistance—"

"Asked?" Evelyn snorted in disdain.

"Unless he felt he had no other choice. But he is an odd and independent creature. It's entirely possible that he may recover this file without any help from you at all."

"Then why—"

"It was my experience with him that he always had several plans in reserve in case his original plan did not work. Plans B, C, and so on."

"True enough."

"And remember he only worked with you or I when Sir deemed it necessary. It was my observation that Sir Maxwell never especially liked working with, or having to depend upon, a woman. He is the kind of man who thinks women have a particular place in the world and it isn't by his side so much as in his bed."

Evelyn scoffed.

"Given his nature, there's every reason to think you are nothing more than his reserve plan."

Evelyn brightened. "There is, isn't there?"

"It's entirely plausible."

"Then why contact me at all?"

"He said there was no one else he could trust except you. I suspect he would want you to be prepared if he needs to call on you." Celeste shrugged dismissively. "Especially as he had to threaten you to gain your cooperation."

Evelyn's jaw tightened. "Do you really think he would tell Adrian about my years with the department?"

"To get what he wants?" She nodded. "Without question. Your real concern should be what Lord W's response will be when he finds out, as inevitably he will one day. Have you thought about that? You've lied to him for two years."

"I have not." Indignation rang in Evelyn's voice. "I simply didn't tell him all there was to tell about my past."

"A lie of omission—"

"Isn't really a lie at all," Evelyn said firmly. "It's not as if he ever said to me 'Evie, my dear, were you once a sort of spy?'"

"I believe the preferred term, darling, was *agent*."

Evelyn waved in a blithe manner. "Spy, agent, the word scarcely matters."

"Perhaps not. Nonetheless have you considered what the earl will say when he finds out?" Celeste shook her head. "He will find out one day, you know. Secrets of this magnitude rarely stay hidden forever."

"Oh, I intend to tell him everything one day," Evelyn said quickly. "I have given it a great deal of thought. When I am on my deathbed strikes me as the best time."

"Rather cowardly, isn't it?"

"And yet, it seems so right."

"And if he dies before you?"

"Then he shall go to his grave content in the knowledge that he had a faithful and loyal wife who loved him without reserve," Evelyn said in a lofty manner.

Celeste studied her closely. "Don't you find it curious that he has never asked about your past?"

"Not at all. He values privacy as do I," Evelyn said. "He knows about my parents, my family, my guardian. He knows I was educated properly and he knows I spent several years traveling and . . . and doing all those social sorts of things young heiresses do."

"Funded by the department."

"As all I had was the name and the background. It's difficult to flit through society as an heiress when one has no money to speak of."

"It was rather fun on occasion," Celeste said under her breath.

"Aside from the danger, the constant threat of exposure, and yes, the heart-in-your-throat fear at times."

"All part of the adventure . . ." Celeste murmured.

Evelyn was hard-pressed to argue with her. It had been exhilarating and exciting and, yes, she'd had a great deal of fun.

Evelyn had been twenty-two when she had joined the department, fresh from a two-year grand tour with the family of a boarding school friend. Her travels through Europe had changed her from a retiring girl, uncertain as to her place in the world, to a self-assured woman confident of her own worth. She'd learned as much about herself as she had about the places she'd visited. She'd always known she had a natural gift for languages but she'd had no idea she had a gift for flirtation as well. Gentlemen called her charming and delightful and enchanting. She'd been at boarding schools since the age of six, surrounded by female students and teachers. She'd never thought of herself as pretty or clever or anything at all before. Now, she was being lauded as the toast of any party, the belle of any ball. It was as intoxicating as champagne and gone just as quickly.

She had arrived back in London to be greeted by good news and bad in a letter waiting for her from Sir George. It seemed her parents had owned a modest house in Mayfair, a house she had lived in so long ago she couldn't remember. Her guardian had let it through the years of her schooling, to pay for its upkeep, the letter said. Now, however, he was turning it over to her—as it was, in truth, hers—with the admonishment that he would no longer be responsible for the building's maintenance or staff or taxes. Nor would he be responsible for Evelyn as she was of age and the money her parents had left their only child was gone. Sir George's letter suggested she would be wise to sell the house at once or marry as she had no means of support. A brief meeting with her guardian's solicitor confirmed the bad news. Even now, Evelyn's stomach still clenched at the feelings of desolation that had threatened to consume her. She had declined her friend's gracious invitation to return to the continent with her family until Evelyn could decide her future, knowing even as she did so, it was out of foolish pride. They thought she was simply alone, not penniless. Still, she had a place to live and the servants had been paid through the end of the month, which gave her very nearly three weeks to decide on her fate.

Thank goodness her social standing had not fallen

with her fortunes. While she'd never had a London sea-son, she was still the daughter of a viscount and had a large number of school friends she had kept up corre-spondence with. Two nights later, she had attended a ball at the insistence of one such friend where she'd danced with a dashing older gentleman. And while he was quite charming, she had decided then and there that she would not marry simply to survive. Although she had no idea what she would do. When the gentle-man, Lord Lansbury, escorted her onto the terrace and said he had a proposal for her, she'd had more than a moment of unease. If she was not going to become a wife to save herself, she was certainly not going to be-come some man's mistress.

She'd been seduced by then, of course, by the first man who had tried. A dreadful mistake and she knew it at the time, but she had fancied herself in love and she had learned a great deal. She'd learn to trust her in-stincts as well. So when Lord Lansbury said he had an honorable position for a young lady of her background, and a few casual questions around the room confirmed his identity and his credibility, she believed him.

The next day she went to the address on the back of his calling card, a large mansion not far from her own house. A discreet plaque by the front entry declared it to be the Department of Domestic and International Affairs. She very nearly left then but she had few op-tions as to what to do with her life and decided to hear what Lord Lansbury had to say. She met with him in the very room she had met with Max, as nondescript then as it was now. Before she knew it, she was living the life of an heiress in public all the while ferreting out secrets of those who appeared to the rest of the world to be loyal British subjects. With Celeste by her side and often with Max as well, the course of action and directions issued in writing by Sir.

Celeste was right; it had been a grand adventure. But it was long over and her life now was all the adventure she wanted. If the price for keeping it was one more assignment for the department—so be it.

"You're absolutely right." Evelyn raised her chin. "There's no need to fret at the moment. This may come to nothing at all. Max was indeed notorious for his Plan B's, C's, and so forth." She narrowed her eyes. "Annoying beast of a man."

"Excellent attitude." Celeste nodded in satisfaction. "Now, then, due to your meeting with Sir Maxwell and your subsequent distress, we are a bit behind today."

"You are exceptionally competent, you know." There was far more to being the Countess of Waterston than most people imagined. That Evelyn handled the position with ease and grace was entirely due to Celeste's efforts.

"Yet another role I play well." Celeste handed her a slim file. "This is today's correspondence, which includes a few invitations you might want to consider as well as your schedule for tomorrow. Don't forget you have a meeting of the Ladies' Literary Society as well as a dressmaker's appointment."

Evelyn nodded. "I shall deal with all this tonight after dinner."

"Then I shall be off." Celeste now resided in Evelyn's town house, which gave her the privacy to live as she pleased. She rarely mentioned how she spent her evenings, yet another area where Evelyn did not pry. Celeste would tell her what she wished her to know. "I shall see you in the morning."

Celeste bade her good day and took her leave.

Evelyn glanced at the file. Her life might seem staid and even dull to a casual observer, but it was what she had always longed for. She was part of a family with a husband who loved her and, hopefully, one day children of their own. She belonged now. She had everything she'd ever wanted and she would do whatever was necessary to keep anyone from destroying it.

Even herself.

Chapter 3

Something was wrong.

Adrian Hadley-Attwater, the Earl of Waterston, surreptitiously studied his wife over the top of the book he'd been trying to read. Evie sat at the desk on the far side of the small parlor and allegedly attended to her correspondence. Said attendance punctuated by the impatient tap of her pen and her unfocused gaze out the window and into the night. It was obvious she was distracted. He drew his brows together. His wife was never distracted. That she appeared so now was, in itself, most distracting.

Adrian had been attempting to read for nearly an hour but instead found himself watching his wife. Certainly he'd read *King Solomon's Mines* when the book had first been published several months ago, but lately he'd felt the need for a bit of adventure, even if it was fictitious. Not that life was dull or boring or tedious. On the contrary, between his duties as earl, his management of the family's finances, business, and properties, and his seat in Parliament, life—his life—was

extraordinarily full. Why, he scarcely ever had an un-
scheduled minute. If a certain restlessness had grown
in recent months, perhaps even as long as the last year,
it was no doubt to be expected. It had been two years,
after all, since his brother Richard had died and Adrian
had inherited a title and responsibilities he did not expect. Two years since he had married Evie, also unexpected but far more delightful. No doubt every man
knew a touch of restlessness after two years of a proper
and respectable life.

Evie sighed and again tapped her pen absently on
the table. His eyes narrowed slightly. Evelyn Turner
Hadley-Attwater, the Countess of Waterston, never
tapped her pen nor did she heave sighs of aimless frustration. This was not at all like her.

Perhaps she, too, felt a stirring of unrest. He was not
so foolish as to think that women, even those who had
everything a woman could possibly want, were so different from men as to be immune to boredom. Indeed,
Evie's life before they had wed had been somewhat adventurous, what with her travel and social engage-
ments and whatever. Not that they had ever really
discussed her past or his, for that matter. He didn't see
the point. They had agreed from the first that essen-
tially life had begun when they had met, that nothing
before mattered or was at all significant. It was as accurate as it was romantic. His life was empty until she
had entered it.

She walks in beauty like the night.

The poet's words flashed through his mind as they
had from the beginning. She was the epitome of grace
and charm and intelligence, everything he'd ever

wanted but hadn't known was possible until her. The poem could have been written with his wife in mind. He'd thought the same from the first moment he'd looked into her brown eyes. The first time he'd heard her laughter across a crowded ballroom. The first time he held her hand in his. Adrian Hadley-Attwater—a bit of a rogue when it came to the fairer sex—had been lost the instant Miss Evelyn Turner's gaze had met his and she'd smiled.

Of cloudless climes and starry skies.

Two years later, he was still lost.

But was she? Tonight was the first time he'd noted any difference in her manner, but then would he have noticed? He prided himself on his powers of observation, but he was extremely busy, as was she. It was not uncommon for them to go a day or more with little contact between them save in passing at the breakfast table. Business and politics often kept him out late into the night, as did her charitable events. It scarcely mattered. He had no doubt she was as in love with him as he was with her.

Admittedly, it was bothersome when his mind drifted on occasion to the fact that he was not the first man in her bed. But they'd married when she was twenty-seven, and she was, in most respects, a woman of sophistication. And his perfect match. He'd be the worst sort of hypocrite to condemn her for the same sort of activities he'd partaken of in his unmarried days, even if women were held to a higher standard. Still, it had been nice to discover she was not overly experienced although she was most enthusiastic. He bit back a grin. He doubted there was anything to compare to a wife with enthusiasm.

And all that's best of dark and bright . . .

He'd had no particular intention to marry. The world was filled with lovely women and they were most enjoyable. Besides, he had reached the age of thirty-six without so much as a broken heart. Indeed, had they never met, it was entirely possible he would never have married at all. Of course, then Richard had died and Evie had come into his life and everything had changed. Restless or not, he was a lucky man.

Meet in her aspect and her eyes.

Her gaze jerked toward him. "Did you say something, darling?"

"Not a thing." He studied her for a moment. "You seem distracted tonight, my dear. Is something wrong?"

"No, nothing," she said quickly. Too quickly. "I have just fallen behind in my responses." She heaved another sigh, even more heartfelt, as if she were trying to make a point. "I do so hate to fall behind."

"I know." He chuckled but studied her closely. "Is that all?"

"Yes, of course." She favored him with a brilliant smile that nonetheless struck him as the tiniest bit forced. Nonsense perhaps but his instincts had always been right about such things, especially her.

"You do know," he said in an offhand manner, "if there is anything wrong, you can tell—"

"You are a dear sweet man, of course I know that. There is nothing wrong and certainly nothing for you to worry about."

"Ah, well then, my mistake." He smiled and lowered his gaze to the page in front of him. He could feel her staring at him and wondered if she knew that he knew she was not being entirely truthful. It might not be obvious to anyone else but it was to him. There was the vaguest look in her eye, the slightest hint in her voice, and something in the way she sat. No, the Countess of Waterston was definitely hiding something from her husband. The question now was what.

She wasn't the type of woman to hide expenditures or exorbitant bills. Indeed, she took spending money— his money—as her due. The Earl and Countess of Waterson did need to keep up appearances. No one would ever call her frugal but she'd never been especially frivolous in her purchases. He suspected if she ever was, she would not keep it from him as she'd no doubt find it amusing.

It couldn't be an illness of some sort. One could see she was in excellent health by the glow of her skin alone. Besides, she knew full well how Richard's denial of his eroding health had taken a toll on Adrian. Evie would never do that to him.

Could his wife be feeling the same sort of restlessness gripping him of late? The need to do something. Anything. The desire for the unexpected, for a touch of excitement. The odd longing, for once, not to know what was going to happen next.

The thought struck him without warning. Wives who were restless . . . A cold hand squeezed his heart. He ignored it. What utter rubbish. His wife was certainly not dallying with another man. Other men's wives perhaps but not his. That was the worst sort of conclusion to leap to and not at all warranted. He trusted her completely, with his life if necessary and certainly with his heart.

He drew a deep breath. Evie had never done anything to make him question either her affection or her fidelity. She was not the type of woman to be led astray. That the tiniest doubt now surfaced was probably more a result of his own current state of unrest rather than anything of a substantial nature on her part. He'd never really known jealousy before yet apparently he was not immune to it. That, too, was distressing—he had thought he was a better, or at least a more rational, sort of man.

"Oh bother," she muttered, and his gaze slipped back to her. She pushed away from the desk and stood. "I'm going to finish this in the morning, which will only put me even more behind, but it can't be helped, I suppose." She brushed an errant lock of hair away from her face and frowned at the need to do so. "You're right, you know."

"I usually am." He chuckled but his heart caught. He forced a casual note to his voice. "About what?"

"I do seem to be distracted this evening. I'm not at all sure why." She frowned. "It could be the weather, I suppose. Do you realize it has snowed every month since October?"

"I had noticed that."

"A foot last month alone. And then the rioting a scant two weeks ago . . ." She shook her head. "Those poor people."

"Times are hard," he said simply. "And jobs are scarce."

"It does seem to me that if Parliament spent less

time arguing about Ireland and more discussing putting men to work, we would all be better off."

"No doubt. I shall propose it at once."

She raised a brow. "With a rousing speech on the floor of the House of Lords?"

He scoffed. "Where else?"

"You're teasing me now, Adrian, and I don't find it the least bit amusing. Poverty is rampant, children live on the streets and people have no money for food. Something should be done."

"Indeed, something should." He got to his feet. "And if I could think of something brilliant, even something adequate, a plan to solve all the ills of this country or this empire, I would put it into motion without hesitation."

She nodded in a satisfied manner, but amusement gleamed in her eyes. She crossed the room to him. "I know you would."

He pulled her into his arms. "I would try to save the entire world for you if you wished it."

"I know you would, darling. That's one of the reasons why I married you."

"Just one?"

"One of many. Another is that it's not necessary for you to actually save the entire world, only that you would be willing to do so. Besides, you're the Earl of Waterston, you don't have time to save more than a tiny portion of the world." She gave him a quick kiss, then gazed into his eyes. "Darling, if I had wanted a warrior or a savior or someone, oh, I don't know, a man of adventure, I would have married someone adventurous."

"And I'm not adventurous?" he said coolly although the comment was annoying.

"No, of course not. You're reliable and responsible and dependable and honorable."

He stared down at her. "Good God, I sound dull."

Her eyes widened. "But you're not, not in the least. You're the most fascinating man I know."

"In a reliable and responsible sort of way?"

"Not at all," she said staunchly, then paused. "Well, perhaps. But you are the kind of man one can depend upon. Not merely in times of crisis but each and every day."

"Oh, that sounds much better," he said in a wry manner.

"And you are kind and generous."

"Hmph."

"And most handsome." She smiled. "Did I mention that?"

"No." He leaned closer and brushed his lips along the side of her neck. "I can be adventurous, you know."

"Well, there are certain times . . ." She shivered. "Yes, indeed . . ."

"And exciting," his lips murmured against her skin. She loved it when he kissed her neck. "I can be exciting."

"Most exciting . . ." She swallowed hard. "I believe I shall retire now. Shall I dismiss my maid for the night?"

"Excellent idea." He grinned down at her.

"I thought so." A wicked light shone in her eyes. She pulled out of his arms and started for the door. "Coming?"

"I'll be there in a minute."

She nodded and left the parlor.

He watched her leave, then drew a deep breath. If she

was trying to distract him, he would certainly cooperate. He could use a little distraction himself. Besides, it would be wrong not to. After all, he was so reliable and dependable. Although he supposed there were worse things to be considered.

Damn it all, his wife was restless, and he absolutely refused to think that her boredom was being eased by another man. Still, it would be foolish of him to ignore this entirely. Yes, something was definitely amiss. He started after his wife. In his list of attributes she'd left out *determined*. He wouldn't rest until he discovered what was wrong.

And prayed it wasn't a man of adventure.

Chapter 4

This was absurd.

Adrian sat in a hired carriage a discreet distance from the entrance of the British Museum and watched. And waited.

It was, as well, somewhat dishonorable and definitely beneath him. One did not spy on one's wife. Especially when the wife in question had done nothing to arouse suspicion. Oh, certainly, her manner last night had been unusual, and there had been that comment about how she would have married an adventurous man if she had wished. A comment that still rankled. He, no doubt, just imagined a hint of longing in her voice. Why, he could be adventurous if he wished. She had no idea just how adventurous he could be.

And this morning, when he had asked about her day, she had listed all she intended to do but hadn't said a word about visiting the museum. Then later, when he had queried Miss DeRochette, she hadn't mentioned the museum either. Evie lived by her schedule although this could simply have slipped her mind and more than likely did. Admittedly his own mood was such that he could be reading things into her words and behavior that were not present. He would like nothing so much as he would like to be wrong. Pity he was rarely, if ever, wrong.

Regardless, he was behaving like a jealous idiot. He drummed his fingers impatiently on his knee and stared at the broad steps leading to the museum doors. In a rational part of his mind he knew and understood his behavior was ridiculous but knowing did not make it any better. Bloody hell, he'd never imagined he would ever feel jealousy. Now he wondered if it hadn't been there all along, just below the surface, waiting for the right opportunity to raise its wicked head. Regardless, he didn't like this one bit. Not the way he felt, nor his reaction to his unfounded suspicions.

It didn't help matters any that the first time Evie and he had spoken without being in the midst of a crowd of people at a ball or another event, the first time they had spoken alone, had been at the British Museum. They'd arranged to meet here, the one place one could be alone and not be the least bit improper. They had strolled past the remnants of ancient civilizations, the glories of Greece and Rome and Egypt. And surrounded by the past, he'd confirmed what he had already known about his future. About her. They'd talked and laughed and, indeed, joked about any number of younger couples obviously taking advantage of the respectable nature of the museum for relatively private assignations. Not that she was having an assignation now.

Damnation, he wished his father were still alive. He could certainly use some advice regarding women. His valet—Vincent—had always been something of a sounding board about women and any number of things when Adrian had been unmarried. But Adrian was reluctant to discuss the subject of his wife's possible infidelity with his valet.

Richard, of course, was gone and had never been married anyway. His brother Hugh was a widower, and it seemed somewhat insensitive to speak to Hugh about marital problems. Adrian's youngest brother Sebastian had only recently married and had mucked up the courtship so badly, Adrian couldn't think of a worse person to ask for advice.

One would think growing up in a household with a mother, three sisters, and a female cousin would have made him wise to the ways of women. And he'd always thought he was, with the exception perhaps of mothers and sisters and female cousins. And now wives.

No, he did know his wife. And he was being ridiculous. Whatever was bothering her, she would confide in him eventually. He clenched his jaw, and determination coursed through him. He'd wasted enough time sitting here. And what if Evie should discover him? How on earth would he explain this? She would be offended and hurt and furious and would have every right to be. No, enough was enough.

Whatever the problem was, and indeed, there might not be a problem at all that spring and improved weather wouldn't solve, it would no doubt work itself out. It was only his own boredom that made him think otherwise. Past time to turn his attention to very real problems. He had work of his own to attend to, and he would be late for a meeting if he did not stop this nonsense now. He called an address to the driver and settled back in the seat.

And even if something in the pit of his stomach or

the back of his mind screamed all was not right, he would ignore it. His life was far different now than it had been before he'd inherited his title, before he had married. Obviously, his instincts were impaired from lack of use.

And obviously, for once, he was wrong.

This was most annoying.

Evelyn absently toyed with the book-shaped locket at her throat and feigned interest in the sculptures from the ancient Parthenon displayed in the Elgin Room. Not that they weren't magnificent. She never failed to marvel at the remarkable skill of the artists who had breathed life into cold marble centuries ago. Regardless of where one stood politically or artistically or historically on the question of where these masterpieces should be housed, there was no disputing their beauty. Usually, Evelyn lost herself in admiration and appreciation of marble so expertly sculpted one could almost see the movement of fabric on bodies frozen between one heartbeat and the next. Today, however, she barely noticed. Besides, Celeste was waiting in her carriage. Both women thought caution being the better part of valor, while Evelyn would go to this meeting alone, Celeste would be nearby, as would Davies, her driver, in the event help was needed.

It had been two years since she'd played this game, and she quite resented having to play it at all. This morning a note had arrived from Max along with a small package containing the locket she was now wearing. The locket would identify her to a courier who would bring her further instructions. It was absurd.

Max could have simply sent her instructions directly but it wasn't the manner in which he worked, nor was it the way in which the department worked. It had always seemed rather unnecessary to her, but the philosophy was that the more layers added to contact, the better and safer it was for all concerned. It often meant as well that one hand rarely knew what the other was doing. Such, apparently, was the nature of a clandestine organization run by men. If women had run the department, or the government for that matter, things would no doubt be much more forthright and efficient.

She kept her gaze focused on the frieze depicting the procession of Athenian citizens but, through the corner of her eye, observed the other museum visitors milling about the room, speculating on which one would approach her. It was gratifying to realize she hadn't lost that particular skill. Indeed it did prove useful on occasion at a social event when one was avoiding an overenthusiastic gossip bent on sharing the latest on-dit or an amorous gentleman who refused to accept she had no interest in betraying her husband with any man let alone one who was obnoxious, overbearing, and old enough to be her grandfather.

She resisted the urge to tap her foot impatiently. Now that she was here, she'd prefer to have this over and done with. She would recover the missing file and then, finally and forever, this would be at an end. It wasn't going to be as easy as she had first assumed. Already today she had committed another of those lies of omission. Which weren't really lies, regardless of what anyone said. Still, when Adrian had asked about her day and she had failed to mention a stop at the museum, it had felt uncomfortably like a lie.

"I beg your pardon," a voice behind her said and she turned. An older gentleman held out a small book. "A young man at the door said you had dropped this."

She glanced at the entry.

"He was on his way out and asked if I would give this to you."

The book cover was precisely the same design as that on the locket. How clever and overly complicated. Layers, of course. "It is mine. How silly of me not to have noticed that I had dropped it." She accepted the book with a smile. "I fear I was absorbed in admiration of the sculptures."

The older man smiled. "Great art will have that effect."

"Indeed it will. You have my gratitude. I would hate to have lost this." She paused. "The gentleman who gave it to you, could you tell me what he looked like? I should like to thank him as well."

"Oh, young, light hair." The man shook his head. "Rather nondescript really."

"Of course he would be," she said under her breath.

"He seemed in somewhat of a hurry. I doubt that you can catch him."

"Then I shall have to be content with giving you alone my thanks." She cast him her brightest smile.

"It was entirely my pleasure." He chuckled. "I do not have the opportunity to do a good deed for a lovely stranger these days. But in my youth . . ." His eyes twinkled with amusement. "Good day, miss." He nodded and took his leave.

She resisted the urge to open the book and instead slipped it into her bag. It would not do to let her impatience show. After all, one never knew who might be observing her. Apparently, there was much about playing this game she had not forgotten. She forced herself to circle the room in a leisurely manner, stopping to more closely examine one frieze or another and pausing for several minutes, as she always did, at the now headless depiction of the three Fates. Perhaps it was their majesty in spite of their destruction that appealed to her; there was certainly no debating their beauty. Or more likely, it was their mystery that called to something deep inside her. Now, however, another mystery beckoned. She turned and made her way through the museum to the street.

"Well?" Celeste said as soon as Evelyn had settled in her seat and the carriage had started off.

"Well, I was given this." She pulled the book out of her bag.

"The cover . . ." Her gaze slipped to Evelyn's locket. "It matches the locket. How very clever."

"Men do like their toys."

Celeste nodded. "Indeed, but this particular toy identifies you to the courier and the book to you. And it is a lovely locket."

"If you like it . . ." Evelyn put the book on her lap, unfastened the chain around her neck, and handed the necklace to her friend. "You may have it."

"Are you sure?" Celeste took the locket. "You may need it again, for another meeting perhaps."

"Then I shall borrow it from you if necessary. I don't want it." She shook her head. "Besides, I should have a difficult time explaining to Adrian a new piece of jewelry that is as personal as a locket."

"It is personal, isn't it?"

"Max, no doubt, found that amusing."

Celeste turned the locket over in her hand. "Did you open it?"

"I tried but it's either jammed or not designed to open. Regardless, it's served its purpose." Evelyn picked up the book. "Oddly enough, the courier didn't give this to me. An older gentleman said a young man, on his way out of the museum, asked him to deliver the book, saying I had dropped it."

"Couldn't the older man have been the courier?"

"Possibly but he never once looked at the locket."

"You noticed." Celeste grinned. "I have never been prouder."

"I wasn't bad at this, you know." Irritation sounded in Evelyn's voice. "I did learn a few helpful things."

"Of course you did." Celeste's eyes widened with feigned innocence. Celeste had worked for the department far longer than Evelyn did and was far more experienced.

Evelyn ignored her. "For whatever reason, the man entrusted with this decided not to approach me directly."

"How very interesting," Celeste murmured. "One has to wonder why."

"Or not read anything of significance into it," Evelyn said pointedly. "Both answers are tempting. But for now . . ." She blew a resigned breath and opened the book.

"What is the title?"

Evelyn leafed through the book one page at a time. "*The Three Musketeers.*"

Celeste snorted. "How original of Sir Maxwell."

Evelyn paged through the first six chapters. On the seat opposite her, Celeste fiddled with the locket. Midway through the seventh chapter, Evelyn found a piece of paper, neatly folded and tucked tightly against the spine. "This is it."

She pulled the paper free, opened it, and read.

"Don't keep me in suspense. What does it say?"

"It's very brief." There were only a few lines written in Max's precise hand. "According to Max's information, he suspects Lord Dunwell to be in possession of the file."

"Why?"

"He doesn't say."

"I mean, why did he have to arrange for the theft, as I assume a viscount wouldn't hit a man over the head, take something from him, and leave him in a brothel." Celeste shrugged. "He's a member of Parliament. Wouldn't he just ask for the information?"

"One would think, but I doubt a mere request would provide the names he wants. Besides, it would make his interest known." Evelyn considered the question. "Its illicit acquisition would indicate his motives are not entirely aboveboard." Her gaze returned to the note. "It says here, if Dunwell has the file, it's likely to be among his personal papers in his library."

"I'm not sure I like his use of the word *if*."

"It gets worse." She sighed and met her friend's gaze. "Lord and Lady Dunwell are having a reception tomorrow night for the Spanish ambassador, a distant relative of the Spanish royal family, I believe. Nonetheless, we had decided not to attend."

"Oh?" Celeste raised a brow. "I was certain I had sent an acceptance of the invitation."

"Yes, well, we had planned to beg off." Evelyn shrugged. "Send our regrets with some plausible explanation. Adrian is not at all fond of Dunwell. He finds him pompous and obnoxious and overbearing. And Lady Dunwell has never been one of my favorites. She has never gotten over losing Adrian although he says he had no real interest in her. Now, however, we shall have to attend."

"How will you explain your change of heart?"

"I'll think of something." Evelyn returned her attention to Maxwell's note. "He adds here that his information might not be accurate." She raised her gaze to meet her friend's. "And isn't that just bloody well perfect."

"Lady Waterston." Celeste gasped in mock dismay. "Such language."

"My language is the least of my worries," Evelyn said sharply. "I am about to search a man's library, which probably means a locked desk—"

Celeste scoffed. "A minor difficulty."

"In the midst of a reception with any number of distinguished guests and the Spanish ambassador as well as my husband." She huffed. "Damnation."

"Speaking of your husband . . ." Celeste's manner was cautious.

"Yes?"

"And my employer."

Evelyn's eyes narrowed. "I know who he is."

"I'm not entirely certain but . . ."

"What is it?"

Celeste paused as if choosing her words. "When we arrived, I noticed a cab pull up on the other side of the street."

"And?"

"And it looked to me that the gentleman seated inside was Lord W. Of course, I could be wrong," she added quickly. "Indeed, I probably am."

"Probably." Evelyn's heart sank. Celeste's powers of observation were legendary.

"But I didn't really get a good look at the man," Celeste said. "Nothing more than a glimpse. He never got out of the carriage, and a few minutes after you went into the museum, he left."

"It doesn't strike you as odd that a cab stops at the museum, with a gentleman inside that may or may not be my husband, then does not leave the cab and instead drives off?"

"Not at all." Celeste paused. "Perhaps a little." She studied the other woman. "Do you think Lord W might have been following you?"

"Adrian?" She scoffed. "Never. To what end? Certainly, I didn't mention going to the museum, but that could well have been entirely innocent on my part. I've never given him any reason to distrust me." Although he had thought something was wrong last night. Regardless, she'd never known him to let his imagination get the best of him. "Besides, he's not the sort of man who would follow anyone, let alone his wife." She thought for a moment. "He would consider that sort of thing distasteful, even dishonorable."

"My thoughts exactly." A firm note sounded in Celeste's voice.

"Why, the very idea is ridiculous," Evelyn said under her breath and hoped she was right. "This whole situation is absurd. I am the Countess of Waterston with a very nice, proper sort of husband and a very nice, proper sort of life. I shouldn't be involved in this kind of escapade. It's mad, that's what it is."

"It seems to me we have done things far more insane than this," Celeste said in a mild tone.

"Not recently."

"More's the pity," Celeste said under her breath.

Evelyn ignored her. "I have a great deal to lose in all this."

"But much to gain."

"Yes, I suppose." Evelyn shrugged.

"You'll be saving Sir from public exposure and possibly worse," Celeste said pointedly.

"And that is the repayment of a debt that is overdue." Odd, she hadn't thought of Sir at all since yesterday. But he was indeed why she was doing this. She owed him her help. Evelyn blew a resigned sigh. "You do realize there is one more problem."

"Just one?"

Evelyn sighed. "I have absolutely nothing to wear."

Chapter 5

"The Earl and Countess of Waterston," the major-domo chimed at the top of the entry stairs to Lord Dunwell's ballroom.

"Tell me again why we are here," Adrian said out of the corner of his mouth, a smile plastered firmly on his face.

Evelyn resisted the urge to nudge him with her elbow. "Because it's good for you politically to be seen here." They started down the stairs. "Besides, I couldn't think of a plausible excuse. And a shabby excuse would only have provided fodder for Lady Dunwell. You know she has the ear of everyone of importance and can be a dreadful gossip when it suits her purposes."

"I thought that was among the reasons we weren't going to come."

"It was." She squeezed his arm. "Courage, my love. We shall no doubt have a delightful time, and regardless, the evening will be at an end before you know it."

"Hmph." Adrian scoffed but no one would have known his thoughts from the expression on his face. He was very good at this sort of thing. He greeted their hosts with a pleasant—and apparently genuine—smile. "Lady Dunwell, you look lovely this evening but then you always do."

Lady Dunwell smiled into Adrian's eyes. Evelyn tried not to clench her teeth. Beryl Dunwell was the epitome of blond, English beauty. And with his dark hair and dark blue eyes, her husband was a very handsome man. No doubt, they would have made a stunning couple.

"And you are as charming as ever, my lord." Lady Dunwell practically cooed the words. "I do hope we will have a dance together later."

"It would be my pleasure," Adrian said.

Lady Dunwell turned her gaze from Adrian, reluctantly, Evelyn thought, to his wife. "And my dear Lady Waterston." As always, her tone carried a slightly superior edge, as if Evelyn were some sort of upstart, here under false pretenses. Her gaze flicked over Evelyn's gown. "Enchanting. French?"

"Of course," Evelyn said smoothly. It was indeed French although it was not new. Damn it all. If she had originally planned to come here tonight, she would have had something new made.

Lord Dunwell nodded to Adrian and smiled in a polite manner. "So good of you to come, Waterston."

"I wouldn't have missed it," Adrian said as if he meant it.

If Adrian could be said to have a rival in politics, it would be Dunwell, although Adrian would never have admitted such a relationship existed. He found that sort of competitive rivalry distasteful. Politics, he often said, isn't always a noble profession but should be. There was little noble about Dunwell. The man was the very definition of ambitious. On occasion, Evelyn had thought Adrian could use a touch more of that himself, a bit more passion perhaps. But then he wouldn't be the man he was: calm, secure, and stable. And all she'd ever wanted.

"Lady Waterston." Dunwell greeted her with a vaguely lecherous smile. She was neither offended nor flattered. It had been Evelyn's experience that he looked at every woman who was at all attractive in that same manner. Still, one would be wise not to encourage him. "How very delightful to see you."

"Thank you for having us," she said with just the right amount of polite enthusiasm in her voice. And Celeste thought *she* was the actress.

Lord Dunwell cast her a lingering look, then turned and introduced them to the Spanish ambassador and his wife. Distinguished in appearance with an impressive mustache, the diplomat kissed her hand with continental formality. His wife, by his side, was most charming and struck Evelyn as the type of lady who would be as at home on horseback in the country as she was at a grand ball.

They moved away from the receiving line and Evelyn surveyed the room. The music had already begun and the floor was filled with dancers. More than half of the people here were those they knew but then that was always the case. It was oddly comforting to feel as though one fit in one's surroundings, as though one belonged.

"Would you care for some refreshment or would you prefer to dance first?" Adrian said.

She smiled up at him. "Do you really have to ask?"

"Silly of me, I know." He chuckled and led her onto the dance floor and into a waltz.

Dancing in his arms, Evelyn could very nearly forget everything, save the music washing through her soul and the feel of his warmth surrounding her. There was nothing in the world like dancing with her husband. She wondered if dancing, and all else between them, would always be as wonderful as it was right now. She did hope so. She fully intended to grow old dancing in his arms. "You know, you quite swept me off my feet the very first time we danced together."

"I recall it was much later that I swept you off your feet." Desire flashed in his eyes and her knees weakened. Good Lord, what the man still did to her after two years of marriage.

"Yes, well, indeed you did." She swallowed. "But that first dance was when I fell in love with you."

"Did you?" His brows drew together. "How very disappointing."

"Disappointing?" She arched a brow. "How is that disappointing?"

"I have always thought you fell in love with me the first time you laid eyes on me." He shook his head in a sorrowful manner. "I thought it was love at first sight."

She bit back a grin. "Darling, if I were to confess to that, it would go directly to your head. And you are far too arrogant already."

"I prefer the word *confident*."

"Yes, I know," she said primly. "Precisely why I chose *arrogant*."

"To keep me from becoming too *confident*?" He guided her through a perfect turn. But then they did

dance perfectly together, and had from the very beginning. As though they were made one for the other. As
indeed, they were.

"Too *arrogant*." She laughed. "Although I once
heard it said that two of the attributes most desirable in
a man are a little arrogance and the willingness to
laugh."

"I think I laugh exceptionally well." He expertly maneuvered her around another couple. "When we return
home, I should be happy to demonstrate some of my
other skills."

"Oh, I am a fortunate woman."

"Yes, you are." His tone was matter-of-fact but his
eyes twinkled. "No doubt the envy of every woman
here."

"Well, this *is* a very nice gown."

He laughed.

"Which reminds me, I'm not at all sure I want you
to dance with our hostess."

"Ah, well, I can understand that."

"Can you?"

"Indeed." He nodded. "Her gown is quite lovely as
well. The latest fashion from France, I believe."

"Your sisters and I have you well trained. But I am
not so shallow as to prefer you not dance with a lady
because of her gown." She glanced at Lady Dunwell
over Adrian's shoulder. "I don't like the way she looks
at you. As if you were dessert and she is considering
how very tasty you might be."

"I am exceptionally tasty."

"Yes, you are, but I am unwilling to share my
dessert."

"Nor does this dessert wish to be shared." He

grinned. "But Beryl Dunwell looks that way at every man."

"No, she doesn't," Evelyn said firmly. "You are the one who evaded her clutches. And she is not a woman to give up easily."

"Nonsense, she only turned her attention to me when Richard proved uninterested."

"Your sisters have told me she pursued you for several years."

"Unsuccessfully," he said firmly. "And then I met you and I was lost. Besides that was two years ago." He shrugged as best he could without a misstep. "She is now married to Dunwell, whose ambition suits her own."

"You are a better catch than Dunwell," she said.

"Yes, I am."

"You do realize there is such a thing as too much confidence?"

He chuckled.

"Women like her do not give up easily." She shook her head. "It's only been a mere two years."

He stared down at her. "Why, you're jealous, Evie."

"It is a lovely gown," she said in a lofty manner.

He laughed.

"Very well." She huffed. "I am always jealous, darling. You are a most accomplished man and quite handsome as well. Any woman would be ecstatic to have you."

"Ah, but you are the loveliest woman in the room. And I am the luckiest man."

"Yes." She met his gaze directly. "You are."

It was a joke between them, which was the luckier to have the other. Although in truth, she had always thought she was the lucky one, and no one knew that better than she did herself.

He laughed again and held her a bit tighter than was proper. Not that she minded. The music swelled around them, the whirl of dancers surrounded them, and it would all have been quite perfect. If only . . .

She responded to his banter but her mind drifted. She had found Adrian at very nearly the perfect moment in her life. He had been precisely what she'd needed then and remained so to this day. She knew without question he loved her as she loved him. Still, if he knew what she had been, the things she had done, wouldn't that love be, at the very least, tarnished? At worst destroyed?

"I have been thinking of late . . ."

He led her through another turn and she followed him without effort. Nonsense. Adrian, of all the people she knew, would understand duty and responsibility and loyalty. What he might not be able to understand was deception. Not that she had ever actually lied to him. Not in the strictest definition of the word. It was admittedly a fine point. One he might not agree with wholeheartedly. The man was the most forthright, honest person she'd ever met.

"A mistress for me perhaps and . . ."

And they had both agreed their respective pasts were behind them. Still, his past consisted of amorous affairs and roguish living and all those sorts of behaviors second sons with too much time and money and few responsibilities tended to indulge in. Certainly, he had handled many of his family's business affairs for years as he had a head for such things and apparently Richard had not.

"A lover for you . . ."

"Only fair," she said absently.

Still, he wasn't the heir, and from what she'd been told, he'd seen no need to behave as one. It had all changed, of course, when Richard died.

"I do think Lady Dunwell might . . ."

But Adrian had more than lived up to expectations. Indeed, he had taken on the responsibilities of his position as if he, and not his older brother, had been the one destined for the title. The music drew to a close and she barely noticed.

"We're agreed then."

"What?" She looked up at him.

He escorted her off the floor. "You haven't heard a word I said."

"Nonsense. I was listening quite closely. You said—" She stopped and stared. "What did you say?"

"I suggested that we might pursue new interests. Life has been rather dull of late. I was thinking a mistress, a lover." He shrugged. "That sort of thing."

"Adrian!" Shock coursed through her. "Surely you aren't serious?" At once his words popped into her head. "And Lady Dunwell? Why, I would shoot you myself before I would permit such a thing. Whatever are you thinking?"

"I'm thinking it's a sad state of affairs when a man can't command the attention of his own wife," he said wryly.

She narrowed her eyes. "You were teasing me."

He chuckled.

"It was not the least bit amusing."

"It was most amusing."

She sniffed. "Perhaps if you had named any woman

other than Lady Dunwell, there might have been some humor in it."

"That was the best part." He accepted two glasses of champagne from a passing waiter and handed her one. "You deserved it."

She raised a brow. "Because I was not paying attention to your every word?"

"Absolutely."

"You are an arrogant man, my lord."

"*Confident*." He grinned, then sobered. "You are preoccupied tonight and you are never preoccupied. I don't like it. It's disturbing."

"My apologies for disturbing you."

"I didn't mean it like that." He frowned. "But this isn't like you, and I confess I am a bit worried."

Her tone softened. "I'm certain it's the weather, Adrian. It's endless and dreary and spring is never going to come."

"Spring will come." His tone was matter-of-fact but his gaze searched hers. "It always does."

She smiled into eyes shadowed with concern. The man was most perceptive and he knew her entirely too well. She was a fool to think she could hide anything from him. Still, at the moment, it couldn't be helped. And it was time she stopped feeling pitiful and confronted the task at hand. The sooner she accomplished what was required of her, the sooner she could put the past firmly behind her forever. And banish that look of worry in her husband's eyes.

"You're right, of course. Although I do wish there were some way to hurry it along."

"The druids held rites to hurry spring." Adrian

sipped his champagne. "Under the stars. Naked, I believe."

She stared at him. "That's nonsense."

"Not at all. The druids had all sorts of rites."

She scoffed. "Not naked."

"Not that we know." He shrugged. "However, there is little of accuracy known about the ancient peoples who once inhabited this land." He gazed over the ballroom as if he were looking into the long-distant past. "I like to think most of their ritual dances were undertaken without clothes."

"Adrian!"

"You would have made an excellent druid."

"Not in this weather," she murmured.

"Especially in this weather," he said firmly. "It wouldn't be worth it otherwise." He studied her in a thoughtful manner. "Perhaps, given how the weather has affected you of late, you should try it."

She raised a brow. "You're suggesting I dance naked under the stars? In London?"

"It is something to consider." He thought for a moment. "Admittedly, it might prove awkward with the neighbors, but I do know I would appreciate it. Although, on the roof . . ."

"You are the most proper man I know, Adrian." She shook her head in a mournful manner. "And yet you have a decidedly wicked streak."

He cast her a most wicked smile.

She heaved an overly dramatic sigh. "I like it."

He sipped his wine. "I know."

She laughed. No, it would always be as wonderful between them as it was right now. She would make certain of it. As soon as she laid the past to rest. Still, as much as she was eager to find Dunwell's library, patience being a virtue she needed to cultivate, she couldn't appear too eager to leave her husband's side. They had barely arrived and there would be more than enough time to slip away later.

"Now then." She plucked his glass from his hand and passed his glass and hers to a waiter. "I should very much like to be swept off my feet again."

"Here? In front of everyone?" He shook his head. "That would be most improper. And I do think our hosts would object." He paused. "If we were discovered. If not . . ."

She laughed. "I was speaking of another dance, darling, and you well know it." She took his arm and led him back to the dance floor. He took her hand in his and she leaned close and spoke softly into his ear. "But later, I shall sweep *you* off your feet."

His brow rose. "And you claim I am the one with the wicked streak."

"We are well matched."

They danced two more sets, and while Evelyn now paid attention to every word her husband said, she also took the opportunity to study the ballroom. She'd been here once before but had no idea where the library was. In the past, she would have been provided with the plans for the house. No matter. It was simple enough to ask a servant for directions. Such a query wouldn't be considered unusual. Not that a servant would question a guest under any circumstances. But it was not at all uncommon, at a gathering of this size, for guests to wander from the ballroom, out of curiosity or in search of a moment of privacy or for a prearranged meeting for one purpose or another. If discovered, she would simply explain she was curious to see Lord Dunwell's collection as she had been told it was quite exceptional. Not that she knew what his lordship collected or indeed if he collected anything at all, but most gentlemen of her acquaintance did so. Why, even Adrian had a small but valuable collection of ancient Greek coins.

"Isn't that your cousin Portia?" she asked when the second dance drew to a close. She nodded toward the far side of the room. Portia's parents had died when she was very young and she'd been taken in by the Hadley-Attwaters. Adrian's mother considered Portia every bit as much her child as she did Adrian, his brothers, and his sisters.

Adrian nodded. "I wouldn't be at all surprised. No doubt Mother is here somewhere as well." He chuckled. "She does not give up easily."

He took her arm and they headed toward his cousin. Lady Waterston's determination to see each of her children happily wed was an ongoing topic of discussion within the family and most amusing to those siblings who were already married. The dowager countess had a list of who should be wed next and she concentrated her matchmaking efforts on that unfortunate child. Portia, widowed three years ago, was currently at the top of the list and had found it necessary to flee to Italy this past Christmas to escape her aunt's efforts.

Portia spotted them and waved.

They made their way toward her. Adrian leaned close to his wife and spoke softly. "Do you think she might have met someone in Italy?"

"Surely she would have mentioned something of that magnitude," Evelyn said. They'd seen Portia only once since her return, and that was at the wedding of

Adrian's youngest brother, Sebastian. "Why do you ask?"

"No reason really. Just an odd impression I had when we last saw her."

"Portia has never been known for her ability to keep secrets."

"No, you're right." A thoughtful note sounded in Adrian's voice. "Portia would certainly have said something." He chuckled. "If only to keep Mother from introducing her to yet another eligible bachelor."

"Good evening, Adrian. Evelyn, how wonderful to see you." Portia kissed Evelyn's cheek and spoke low into her ear. "Save me."

Evelyn widened her eyes. "From what?"

A waiter handed them each a glass of champagne. Portia downed hers in scarcely more than a swallow. "Aunt Helena, of course." She turned to Adrian. "Your mother is in rare form tonight, Cousin. Every time I turn around, she is introducing me to yet another candidate for my hand. All of whom seem to think the way to my heart is by stepping on my feet and clutching me entirely too tightly in the guise of dancing." Portia lowered her voice in a confidential manner. "One more dance and I daresay I shall be crippled for life. As my favorite cousin, I beg of you to rescue me."

"Your favorite, you say?" He eyed her skeptically. "I thought Sebastian was your favorite?"

Portia huffed. "Sebastian is my favorite youngest male cousin. You are my favorite oldest male cousin."

He bit back a smile. "And Hugh?"

"Hugh is my favorite . . ." She searched for the right word. "Barrister cousin, yes, that's it." Desperation sounded in her voice. "Now will you help me?"

"What do you want me to do?" Adrian said cautiously. No doubt growing up with seven siblings had taught him not to agree to anything they asked without sufficient information.

"Would you be so good as to drive me home?" She peered past them into the crowd. "Now if you please. Before Aunt Helena returns with yet another victim in tow." She shuddered. "I have had quite enough."

"I am sorry, Portia." Sympathy coursed through Evelyn. "But we have scarcely been here any time at all. Leaving now would be considered most impolite."

"Nonsense." Portia scoffed. "You don't even like Lady Dunwell. Not that I blame you," she added quickly.

"If you could manage to survive for, oh, say another hour or so . . ." Adrian glanced at his wife.

Evelyn nodded. That should give her enough time. "That would be sufficient, I think. Another hour wouldn't make it appear as though we were eager to leave."

"Not that we aren't," Adrian muttered, then smiled at his cousin. "And then we would be delighted to see you home."

Portia groaned. "In another hour or so, your mother will have me married with a dozen children."

Adrian choked back a laugh.

Portia glared. "It's not the least bit amusing."

"Of course not, dear." Evelyn patted the younger woman's arm.

Adrian cleared his throat. "My apologies." He studied his cousin. "I thought you wanted to marry again."

"Indeed, I do. But I wish to marry someone who is not thrust at me. As if he were a canary and I was a . . . a . . . a hungry cat!" Indignation sounded in her voice.

"I am perfectly capable of finding a husband on my own."

"Not thus far," Adrian said under his breath.

Evelyn cast him a chastising frown.

Portia ignored him, her brow furrowed in thought. "However, this is an exceptionally large and pretentious house. Perhaps I can find a peaceful place to, well, hide until you are ready to depart."

Excellent! Evelyn nodded. "And the least I can do is help you find a suitable spot."

"A parlor perhaps?" Portia thought for a moment. "Surely they have a music room? I know there's a conservatory. Or a library?"

"No," Evelyn said quickly. "You never know who might show up in a library. But a parlor is an excellent idea."

"It's rather cowardly, though, don't you think?" Adrian said mildly. "Hiding from Mother, that is."

"Yes. And I don't care." Portia glared at her cousin. "Thus far this evening I have been presented to one gentleman who was not looking so much for a wife as a mother for his herd of children and another who, well, let us simply say he was not to my liking."

"Judging on appearances, Portia?" Adrian shook his head in a disappointed manner. "I never imagined you were that shallow."

"Stop teasing her, dear," Evelyn said under her breath. The banter and teasing—some of which struck her as altogether too pointed—between the Hadley-Attwater siblings never failed to amaze her. It was as if they could say very nearly anything to one another yet it never affected their feelings for each other. She quite envied them. She hoped her children would share that same sort of bond.

"I simply want someone who stands taller than my chin," Portia said sharply. "I do not think I am asking for the moon."

"Perhaps not." Amusement gleamed in Adrian's eyes.

"As for my shallow nature, I am more than willing to debate that with you at another time." Portia cast Evelyn a pleading look. "Now, I think we should—"

"Too late, I fear," Adrian said, gazing over Portia's head.

Portia groaned. Evelyn peered around her. Helena was bearing down on them, accompanied by a fair-haired gentleman. Well, well. Portia certainly couldn't complain about the appearance of this candidate. He appeared to be an appropriate age and was most dashing as well.

"Adrian!" Helena beamed at her son. "And Evelyn. So lovely to see you both. I had no idea you would be here tonight."

"Nor did we, Mother." Adrian kissed her cheek.

"Nonetheless, I am most gratified to see you here." Helena lowered her voice. "It's a most influential gathering."

"Helena." Evelyn cast a pointed glance at the gentleman standing patiently a step behind the older woman.

"Oh dear, where are my manners?" Helena sighed. "The bane of growing older, I suppose." She turned to the victim. "May I present my son and daughter-in-law, Lord and Lady Waterston. And this"—a flourish sounded in Helena's voice—"is my niece, Lady Redwell. Portia, this is Mr. Sayers."

"Ah, yes." Mr. Sayers took Portia's hand and raised it to his lips, his gaze never leaving hers. It was as polished as it was flattering. Amusement quirked his lips. "The widow."

Portia smiled weakly. "I see my aunt has been talking to you."

"Oh my, yes." Satisfaction rang in Helena's voice. "It seems I went to school with Mr. Sayers's mother. Unfortunately, I can't seem to remember her, but then it was a very long time ago. Once again, you have my apologies, Mr. Sayers."

"None are necessary, Lady Waterston," he said smoothly. "As you said, it was a very long time ago."

"Still, it is impolite and most annoying." Helena sighed. "My memory is not what it used to be. Yet another distressing result of the passing years."

"Better than the alternative," Adrian murmured.

Helena cast her son a disparaging look.

"Lady Redwell." Mr. Sayers turned to Portia. "I would be most grateful if you would do me the honor of joining me in a dance."

"What an excellent idea." A satisfied twinkle sparked in Helena's eyes. "You have scarcely danced all evening."

Adrian coughed.

Portia hesitated, then smiled. "I would be delighted."

Mr. Sayers nodded to the others and escorted Portia to the floor.

"You really should stop doing that to her, Mother," Adrian said mildly, his gaze following his cousin and Mr. Sayers.

"She'll thank me for it one day." Helena studied the couple with satisfaction. "Don't you agree, Evelyn?"

Evelyn truly liked her mother-in-law. In many ways, she was the only mother Evelyn had ever really known.

While she was confident Helena returned her affection, it did seem wise to agree with her on minor matters. She bit her lip. "One day perhaps."

Helena glanced at her. "But not today?"

Evelyn shook her head. "Definitely not today."

"I wouldn't wager on tomorrow either," Adrian added. "You really don't remember his mother?"

Helena sighed. "Not at all. I was tempted to lie to him and tell him 'Of course, I remember your mother! Darling girl. And quite clever as well.' But that would have been dishonest as not even his name sounds familiar." She paused. "Well, perhaps it does, but it's not an uncommon name. Besides, her name wouldn't have been *Sayers* then anyway." She sighed again, this time much more dramatically, and directed her gaze toward Evelyn. "I am unfailingly honest, you know."

Adrian choked.

Evelyn had witnessed any number of occasions when her mother-in-law had, at the very least, bent the truth. She raised a brow. "Unfailingly?"

"Yes." Helena nodded. "When I am honest, I am unfailingly so."

Evelyn exchanged glances with her husband.

"You are both lucky that you are my favorites." Helena huffed. "Now, as I was saying, I can't remember his mother at all and I'm very good at that sort of thing. Admittedly, I can never seem to find where I last put my gloves, but forty years ago is quite clear. Or it always has been."

She turned her attention back to the dancers. "I'm not nearly as indiscriminate as Portia might lead you to believe, you know. I have a list of very nearly all the eligible gentlemen in London. It is only coincidence that several of them are here this evening." She fluttered her fan in front of her face. "Admittedly, I am not one to let a turn of luck go to waste."

"How fortunate for Portia." Adrian smiled.

"Indeed it is," Helena said firmly. "Unfortunately, I fear she cannot see past the fact that I am the one bringing them to her attention or her to theirs. Why, the first gentleman I introduced her to was not unattractive and charming as well. And Portia quite likes children. And the second, while admittedly a bit short, is known to be most kind and amusing and has a significant fortune."

"I am certain Portia appreciates your efforts," Evelyn said.

"You are a dear girl but it's obvious Portia does nothing of the kind." She squared her shoulders. "No matter. She will indeed thank me one day." Helena met Evelyn's gaze and chuckled. "But not today."

Evelyn laughed.

"Now then." Helena glanced around the ballroom. "I see that charming Lord Compton is alone over there. I should say good evening to him."

"Don't you think he's a little too old for Portia?" Adrian asked.

"My goodness, yes. He is entirely too old. For Portia." She flashed them her son's wicked smile. "Adrian. Evelyn." She nodded and took her leave.

"You have a unique and interesting family." Evelyn's gaze followed Helena making her way across the room.

"It's frightening, isn't it?" he murmured.

She smiled wryly. "It's rarely dull."

"One never knows what to expect next."

"I beg your pardon, Lord Waterston?" a voice said behind them.

Adrian turned and nodded. "Good evening, Lord Huntly."

"Lady Waterston." The younger man nodded toward her, then directed his attention back to Adrian. "A few of us are discussing the Irish question, and we were wondering as to your opinion on the latest developments."

"Now?" Adrian shook his head. "I don't know that this is either the time or the place."

"And yet," Evelyn said, "I could swear I have heard you say on more than one occasion that some of the best discussions of political issues occur at social events rather than the hallowed halls of Westminster."

"A word of advice to you, Lord Huntly." Adrian directed his words to the peer but his gaze remained on his wife. "Never marry a woman with a good memory. Failing that, watch carefully what you say to her."

Lord Huntly chuckled. "I shall remember, sir."

"Very well then." Adrian met his wife's gaze. "As this is at your urging, I assume you do not mind my abandoning you." A wicked light of an entirely different sort flashed in his eyes. "Unless, as you have never been reticent to share your opinions, you should like to join us."

"As enticing as you make it sound, and as much as I do enjoy a rousing debate, I believe I shall leave you gentlemen to your own devices. Besides . . ." She glanced around the room. "There are any number of people here I should like to speak with. Why, there's Lady Cavert and Mrs. Wellbourne. And your cousin may yet need my assistance." She smiled in a wicked manner of her own. "As may Lord Compton."

"Are you sure?" Adrian studied her.

"Well, he is probably capable of taking care of himself . . ." She laughed. "Of course I am. Now go." She cast him a reassuring smile. "You may rejoin me later."

"I shall count the minutes." Adrian turned to Lord Huntly. "Apparently, I am at your disposal."

"Excellent, sir." Lord Huntly beamed at Evelyn. "You have my gratitude, Lady Waterston."

She waved off his comment. "Not at all."

"We are gathered in the card room, my lord." Lord Huntly started off. Adrian cast her a resigned look and followed after the younger man. "I cannot tell you how appreciative I, well, all of . . ."

If she were a more suspicious sort, she would think Lord Huntly's arrival was entirely too convenient. But as much as she knew better than to trust Max completely, she was fairly certain she was on her own this evening. Still, someone somewhere was obviously watching over her. Adrian would be occupied for a good quarter of an hour if not longer. Perhaps there was an ancient druid god that protected women who did not wish to lie to their husbands. As she hadn't. There were people here she did indeed wish to speak to.

Evelyn circled the room, stopping to chat briefly with an acquaintance here or listen to the latest gossip there. By the time she reached the ballroom's grand entry, she had learned the ladies' receiving room was in the same wing as the library. And that Lord Dunwell did indeed have a collection of antique swords displayed on his library wall. Swords? She scoffed silently. Men were certainly transparent creatures.

Evelyn headed in the direction of the ladies' receiving room and the library beyond. All was going entirely too smoothly thus far, but she knew better than to be too confident. Too much confidence inevitably led to carelessness. Still, she sent a silent prayer of thanks toward ancient druid gods or anyone else who might be listening.

And couldn't help wonder if a naked dance of gratitude under the stars might be a small enough price to pay for success.

Chapter 6

What was she up to?

Adrian narrowed his eyes and watched his wife leave the ballroom. He'd finished his discussion sooner than he'd expected and obviously sooner than Evie had planned as well. She appeared unhurried, calm, even serene. To an unsuspecting observer, it would look as though Evie were simply off to view the rare orchids Lord Dunwell had in his conservatory. Or perhaps she was curious about the new portrait of Lady Dunwell painted by Mr. Sargent hanging in the gallery. Adrian had been thinking about having his wife's portrait painted, and he did like the American's work, even if some of it was scandalous.

Or she could be off to an assignation with a lover.

Ridiculous, of course. Why, no more than a half an hour ago, Adrian was convinced he was making a great deal out of nothing. Yes, she had not been herself in recent days. But while it was not unheard of for long winters to create a certain amount of melancholy, that answer didn't seem right. Not for her. He wasn't sure why but he knew it. He had realized in recent days, much to his surprise, that the only part of his life in which he was not completely confident was in regards to his wife. He did trust her. Still . . .

His jaw tightened and he started around the perimeter of the room. He was being a fool and he well knew it. But he was also aware he had become, well, boring in the past two years. He'd thought he was a bit staid even when they'd married. But Richard had just died and Adrian was abruptly faced with unplanned responsibilities and the realization one had to take life more seriously when one's duties changed. Now dull seemed more accurate than staid. He couldn't blame Evie for wanting a bit of adventure. She'd lived a most adventurous life before their marriage. And he'd already acknowledged a certain restlessness in himself. Not that his eye had turned in search of amorous adventures. Evie was the only one he wanted now or ever.

Not, he reminded himself, that she wanted someone else. She'd done nothing and he was little more than a jealous idiot. That, too, had surprised him. Nonetheless only a fool would fail to make absolutely certain his suspicions—absurd though they may be—were wrong.

He made his way toward the door. After all, he, too, would like to see the new portrait. His progress was continually impeded by one person or another wishing to have a word with him, and his impatience grew. When one was faced with unfounded suspicions, one was eager to prove oneself wrong. At last he reached the entry. Across a wide foyer, steps led down to the ground floor. Corridors flanked either side of the ballroom doors. He paused and considered the options.

"May I be of some assistance, my lord?" A footman

stepped up to him. Dunwell's servants were exceptionally well trained.

"Yes, thank you." The most successful fabrications tended to be those closest to the truth. "I seem to have misplaced my wife. I believe she went to look at Lady Dunwell's portrait."

"The gallery is down the corridor to the right, my lord. The family's private quarters are to the left," the servant said. "All else including the gallery, the ladies' receiving room, the conservatory, the billiards room, Lord Dunwell's library, and assorted drawing rooms are to the right."

Adrian nodded his thanks and started down the hall.

No, he could understand his wife's succumbing to the lure of adventure, the temptation of the unknown. He could understand a certain restlessness after two years of proper living. Indeed, he was feeling much the same himself.

What he wouldn't do was allow it.

Evelyn studied Lord Dunwell's desk with a practiced eye. It was obviously expensive and beautifully aged if one liked fine wood insulted by an abundance of decorative bronze garlands and flourishes as well as corner fittings depicting some sort of mythical sea creature. A sea dragon perhaps. Carved wooden waves reached up from the legs to meet the beast. Evelyn wasn't sure if it was the most amazing work of craftsmanship she had ever seen or simply the ugliest. Nonetheless, it would have been most mesmerizing and fascinating to study had she not had more pressing concerns.

Four drawers on either side flanked a center drawer over the kneehole. Often desks of this nature had one lock on the top drawer of each column of drawers that locked all the drawers beneath it at the same time. Unfortunately, each of the nine drawers on this desk had its own separate keyhole. Lord Dunwell was certainly a cautious man or a man with a great deal to hide.

She felt among the pins in her hair for the thin, flexible pick Celeste had given her. Amazing that something very nearly indistinguishable from a hairpin could be used to easily open locks. Evelyn had once had a similar tool of her own but had tossed it away with the rest of her past. Or so she'd thought. Amazing as well that a man who had a lock on every drawer wouldn't go to some effort to make them a bit more complicated. She snorted with disdain. Unless she was sorely mistaken, this would be fairly easy.

It was logical to assume that the file, if indeed it was here, would not be in the center drawer or the top two on either side as they were not as deep as the others. Still, one never knew. She knelt before the desk, inserted the pick into the center drawer keyhole, and maneuvered it until it caught on the mechanism. One careful turn and the lock clicked. She opened the drawer and quickly looked at the contents.

Dunwell was surprisingly tidy and there was nothing here save neatly arranged pen nibs, a sharpening knife, an ivory page cutter, and his lordship's crested stationery. She'd thought, on occasions similar to this in the past, that one could learn a great deal about a man from looking in his private spaces. Dunwell was organized, precise. Anything he undertook would be well thought out. This was not the drawer of a man of impulse.

Regardless of the nobility of the purpose, there was something unseemly about perusing a man's private belongings. One never knew what sorts of things a man might wish to keep locked away from prying eyes. Why, even Adrian kept his desk drawers locked although she was certain he would show her their contents should she ever ask. Not that she cared to. Adrian had nothing to hide. Her husband was very much an open book.

She made certain everything was exactly as she had found it, closed the drawer, locked it, then started on the drawers to the right. Given that Dunwell favored his right hand, he might well be inclined to store papers of importance on that side. But by the time she reached the bottom drawer, she had not found the file nor had she seen anything out of the ordinary whatsoever. She wasn't sure what she'd expected, but Lord Dunwell was apparently far duller than she had imagined.

She grit her teeth with annoyance. There were still four drawers left but an instinct she thought was long dead told her this was a waste of time. She quickly worked her way through the remaining drawers. Nothing. Either the file was hidden elsewhere in the house or Max's information was wrong. Not that he had seemed overly confident about it in the first place. She closed the last drawer and relocked it. Still, the fact that he had sent her on this wild-goose chase at all with what was obviously the flimsiest of information spoke to his level of concern about the situation. She would send word to him at once. There was no more she could do here tonight.

The library door opened and she froze. Certainly, she was concealed from sight behind the desk for the moment, but it would take this intruder no more than a few steps into the room to discover her.

"What are you doing here?"

Her heart sank. She would know her husband's voice anywhere. She drew a deep breath and started to rise.

"Why, I followed you, of course."

Again, Evelyn froze. Who in the name of all that's holy was that? Quietly she shifted to allow her to peer around the edge of the desk. She bit back a gasp.

Adrian studied Lady Dunwell coolly. "And why would you do that?"

"Why wouldn't I?" She smiled in a seductive manner and stepped closer to him. Evelyn's jaw clenched. "It's been a very long time since we have had a moment alone together."

"Has it?" Adrian shrugged. "I hadn't noticed."

Bravo, Adrian! Excellent!

"Come now, Adrian, surely you haven't forgotten." Lady Dunwell reached a long, pointed finger and lightly ran it down the front of Adrian's shirt. Evelyn clapped her fist over her mouth to prevent a scream of indignation. The hussy!

"I haven't forgotten anything," he said smoothly. "But as I recall, there was little to remember."

"Adrian!" Lady Dunwell pouted. "You wound me to the quick. I quite value the times we spent together. I have always thought it a great pity there weren't more." She heaved a heartfelt sigh. "There could have been so much more. I was a lonely widow and you were dashing and handsome . . ." She cast him a look of pure invitation. "You still are."

Good Lord!

"How kind of you to say."

Rubbish. It wasn't the least bit kind. *The woman is after you, dear husband.*

"Surely you remember? I can be exceptionally kind."

What is there to remember? And how *kind* was she? *Kind* was not at all what she had in mind now.

"No doubt your husband thinks so."

Excellent, Adrian. Remind her that she has a husband.

"Goodness, Adrian, Lionel married me for my fortune and my family connections. I know that and he knows I know it. As for the rest of marriage, well . . ." She shrugged. "My husband and I, oh, we pursue our own interests, shall we say."

"How very . . . *modern* of you both."

Modern? That was not the word Evelyn would use.

"But I fear I am somewhat more traditional," he continued. "I much prefer that my wife and I pursue mutual interests."

"For now." She smiled in a wicked manner.

It was all Evelyn could do to keep from revealing herself, vaulting over the desk, and strangling the woman with her bare hands.

"For always," he said firmly.

Evelyn's heart fluttered. Her husband was as perfect a man as one could hope to find.

"Although, perhaps . . ." Lady Dunwell studied him for a moment.

He raised a brow. "Perhaps what?"

"Perhaps I am already too late. Perhaps you are here awaiting an interest of your own."

Indignation washed through Evelyn. Not Adrian. Still, what was he doing here?

He laughed.

And why wasn't he denying it?

"I see." Lady Dunwell cast him a slow, provocative smile. "Then there is hope for me yet. I shall leave you to your *interests*." She moved to the door, then glanced at him over her shoulder. "For now." She took her leave, shutting the door behind her.

"Now, back to my original question." Adrian looked directly at Evie, and she resisted the urge to shrink back behind the desk and pretend she wasn't there. "What are you doing here?"

"I might ask you the same thing." She rose to her feet in as dignified a manner as she could manage. Wasn't it said that attack was the best form of defense?

His eyes narrowed. "I was looking for you."

"And just happened to find Lady Dunwell in the process?" she asked in a lofty manner.

"She found me."

"So it would appear. Appearances, however . . ." She shrugged.

He glared. "There is nothing between Lady Dunwell and myself."

"You led me to believe there had never been anything between you and that creature in the past save a futile attempt on her part to ensnare you in marriage."

"There wasn't," he said sharply, then paused. "Not really. Nothing of any significance anyway. Not on my part."

"And yet you never said a word."

"Why on earth would any man in his right mind confess his previous indiscretions to his wife?"

"Ah-hah!" She aimed a pointed figure at him. "Then you did lie to me!"

"I most certainly did not," he said staunchly. "It was at worst a . . . a lie of omission."

"Oh?" She stared at him for a long moment. "And as such does not count as a true lie? Is that what you're saying?"

"Yes." He nodded firmly.

"I see." She swept past him, reached the door, then turned back. "As it was a lie of omission, I can certainly overlook it."

"How very gracious of you." Sarcasm rang in his voice.

"I think so. But I do not trust that woman for so much as a single second. She has no sense of decent behavior."

"But do you trust me?"

"Implicitly."

"As well you should." He paused. "And you haven't answered my question. What are you doing here?"

"Why, I came to look at Lord Dunwell's collection." She nodded at the wall display of ancient swords. It wasn't a complete lie. She had glanced at the swords. "It's most impressive."

He studied her suspiciously. "I didn't know you were interested in swords."

"I have any number of varied interests as you are well aware. And I have always been fascinated by antiquities. Goodness, Adrian, why else would I be here?"

"You were hiding behind the desk when I came in."

"Nonsense." She scoffed. "I wasn't hiding. I had dropped one of my ear bobs and was simply retrieving it. I was just about to stand when I heard you and Lady Dunwell."

"And you were compelled to listen?"

She stared at him as if he were quite mad. "I could do nothing else."

"No, I suppose you couldn't." He glanced at her ear bobs. "I see you found it and managed to put it back on while hiding behind the desk."

"Fortunately. And again, I wasn't hiding." She touched the garnet bauble dangling from her left ear. "But I shall have to take it to the jeweler tomorrow. The clasp is apparently defective and I should hate to lose it."

His expression eased. "No, of course not."

The man was obviously suspicious. It was not at all like him. Certainly her manner had been somewhat distracted of late, but his attitude was still most annoying. She drew her brows together. "Surely you do not suspect me of engaging in something untoward?"

"Of course not," he said staunchly. "I trust you every bit as much as you trust me."

"As well *you* should." She cast him a sympathetic smile. "You look confused, darling."

He stared at her for a long moment. "This was not . . ." He shook his head. "No matter. You have become a most confusing woman, my dear."

"Well, I should hate to have become boring." She smiled in her most flirtatious manner. "You might turn to one of the Lady Dunwells of the world."

"There is little chance of that. And I daresay, you will never be boring."

"*We* will never be boring." She favored him with a wicked smile. "I shall count on you to make certain of that."

A slow smile spread across his face. "I think I've had enough of this gathering."

Desire fluttered through her. "You have the best ideas, Adrian."

He grinned and pulled open the door. Lord Radington stood with his hand outstretched. Surprise colored his face, turning almost at once to appreciation. Only a woman long in her grave would fail to be flattered. He was a handsome devil and he well knew it.

"Lady Waterston." He reached for her hand and drew it to his lips. His gaze bored into hers. The thought flitted through her mind that he and Mr. Sayers had precisely the same overly practiced manner. She didn't know Mr. Sayers, but Lord Radington's reputation with women was infamous. A reputation she had once seen the proof of firsthand but never to the extent the gentleman had wanted. As dashing as he was, she had never found him as irresistible as other women did. Or as irresistible as he found himself. He slipped a folded note into his waistcoat pocket. Triumph curved his lips. "What a delightful and unexpected surprise. It has been a long time. You are looking lovelier than ever tonight." Obviously he hadn't noticed her husband.

"My lord," she murmured.

"Radington," Adrian said curtly. And just as obviously, Adrian was not pleased to see the lothario.

"Lord Waterston, my apologies." A flicker of disappointment shone in his eyes but his tone was level. Lord Radington was well used to dealing with suspicious husbands. "I didn't see you."

"Imagine that." Adrian's eyes narrowed.

Evie stared at her husband. He had been acting rather strange of late as well.

"I was . . ." Lord Radington peered around them into the library. "I came . . ." His speculative gaze slid to Evelyn. Heat rose in her cheeks. It had been some time since another man had looked at her like that. As if he were stripping her naked right here and now. Utter nonsense. "Ah well, it scarcely matters."

"Perhaps you came to see the sword collection?" Adrian said coolly.

"Why else would I be here?" Lord Radington cast Evie another glance, then sauntered to the wall bearing the display. "Fascinating. Don't you agree, Waterston?"

"I do." Adrian studied the swords. "The broadswords are especially impressive. One could slice off a man's head with one well-placed swing."

Lord Radington chuckled. "If one wished to, I suppose."

There was a look in Adrian's eye as if he wished to do that very thing to the younger man. Surely he didn't think . . .

"Although I have always been fond of a finely honed rapier. Excellent for fencing." Adrian shrugged. "Or dueling."

"Dueling is no longer legal although it was probably common in your day," Lord Radington said with a casual smile.

"Yes, well, *in my day*, dueling was an acceptable, indeed, an expected means of defending one's honor or one's property." His eyes narrowed so slightly only Evelyn would have noticed. "Or one's wife."

Good Lord! At once Evelyn realized her husband thought she'd come to the library to meet Lord Radington. The dear man was jealous. How utterly absurd. But rather delightful nonetheless.

"Then I am no doubt fortunate it is outlawed," Lord Radington said blithely.

"Pity," Adrian said under his breath. "Do you fence?"

"On occasion." An uneasy note sounded in Lord Radington's voice, and he slanted Evelyn a quick glance as if asking for her intervention. She cast him a pleasant smile.

"Perhaps we can meet for a match someday." Adrian's polite smile very nearly masked the intent gleam in his eye.

In spite of her best intentions, Evelyn laughed. Both men turned indignant looks on her.

"What," Adrian said in a cool voice, "might I ask is so amusing?"

"Not a thing, darling." She beamed at her husband. "A random thought crossed my mind, nothing of importance." She took her husband's arm. "We have been gone far too long and I should like another dance before we leave for the evening."

He stared down at her as if he were trying to read her thoughts. "As you wish."

"Good evening, Lord Radington." She cast the man a grateful smile.

He, too, looked at her as if trying to read her mind. He nodded. "Lady Waterston."

"In my day," Adrian said under his breath as they strolled back toward the ballroom. "The man can't be more than five years younger than I."

"The nerve of the man." Evelyn bit back a laugh. She'd never imagined Adrian, who was not the least bit vain, had a touch of vanity when it came to his age. He was a mere thirty-eight and was as fine a figure of a man as she'd ever met. Still, she'd never imagined him to be a jealous sort either. Odd the things one learned when one had thought there was nothing left to learn. She chatted brightly about anything amusing that came into her head, and by the time they reached the ballroom, Adrian's mood had lightened.

She knew she should have been upset that he was

even a little jealous. And any other time she would have been. But proving she was not unfaithful, should it ever come to that, would be far easier than explaining what she was involved in. That would inevitably lead to what she had done in the past. She certainly wasn't going to do anything to encourage Adrian in thinking she was seeing another man, but for now, she wasn't going to entirely correct his erroneous assumption.

His mistake might well be her salvation.

Celeste slipped out of bed and danced out of the way of the hand reaching to pull her back.

"Don't go." Max groaned. "Come back."

"As much as I would like nothing better, I'm afraid I must be going."

"You never stay the night." He struggled to sit up. "It's insulting."

"Don't be absurd." She looked around for her clothes, discarded in their usual haste to touch and taste and partake of the pleasures they found in each other. "How on earth is it insulting?"

"You come to my home. You take liberties with my person—"

"Liberties?" She laughed.

"You have your way with me—"

She raised a brow. "Are you complaining?"

He ignored her. "And then you leave me." He heaved a sigh worthy of the most poorly trained thespian. "I feel like a . . . a trollop."

"A trollop?"

"A common trollop." He plucked at the bedcovers. "It's not at all pleasant and I don't like it one bit."

"My apologies," she said absently. Her clothes lay scattered over the floor in a haphazard trail from the door to the bed, her corset hung tipsily from the bedpost, and good Lord—was that her chemise dangling from the sconce? "Are you familiar with karma?"

"Moral causation? The idea that one gets what one deserves?"

She nodded.

His brows drew together. "Prevalent in Eastern religions, I believe. Buddhism, I think."

"Very good, Max," she said wryly. "I do so love a man who is well read."

"I am nothing if not well read." He grinned and patted the bed beside him. "I'd be happy to demonstrate exactly what else I do well."

"You are too generous."

His wicked grin widened. "You have no idea how generous I can be."

"Oh, I have some idea." She studied him for a moment. Lord, he was a handsome beast. All that blond hair, tousled now, he had the look of a small boy. If one ignored the lascivious gleam in his bright blue eyes and the evidence of his growing excitement beneath the sheet. The man was insatiable and bloody well irresistible. "Don't you find it ironic that a man like you, who has left the beds of who knows how many women, now finds himself in precisely the same position?"

"First karma, now irony." He narrowed his eyes in feigned suspicion. "Are you saying I'm getting precisely what I deserve?"

She smiled and pulled on her chemise.

"Well, I don't like it."

"Now you're pouting and it's not at all attractive." In

truth, though, it was rather endearing. Sir Maxwell Osgood was not the type of man to pout.

"Do help me with this." She looked at him over her shoulder, holding the sides of her corset together behind her back.

"I would be delighted." He stood and crossed the room. Most men tended to look better with clothes on. Max was not one of them. She never tired of looking at him naked. He took the laces and tugged them tight. "There's something about this I like."

"You were no doubt a ladies' maid in a previous life."

He bent to kiss the back of her neck and she shivered. His lips murmured against her skin. "I doubt that. Although it would have its benefits . . ."

He straightened and tied the laces, then spun her around and pulled her into his arms. "Tell me again why you won't stay."

"I tell you every time I'm here." She rolled her gaze toward the ceiling. "I have servants, you know, and I am trying to live a proper sort of life. Servants talk, and as the house belongs to Evelyn, I daresay it would only be a matter of time before she wondered what I did with my evenings if she learned I was not returning to my own bed." She shook her head. "She is my dearest friend. I do so hate lying to her."

"It's not lying, really. You said yourself she never asks what you do in the evenings."

"No, she doesn't," Celeste said slowly. "Still, she might well consider my presence with her at all a lie."

"Celeste." A warning sounded in his voice.

"Yes, yes I know." She huffed. "You and Sir thought it was necessary. But she would certainly take my leaving the department to keep an eye on her, and provide protection if necessary, as deceit at the very least."

"She will never find out," he said firmly.

"Regardless, I am going to endeavor to lie less in the future." She paused. "To Evelyn and everyone else."

"Rubbish." He laughed. "Everybody lies."

"I do so hate lying." She sighed. "Obviously I've changed."

"Two years of proper behavior will do that to you." He pulled her tighter against him.

"It hasn't been entirely proper," she said under her breath.

"Thank God." He lowered his head to kiss that sensitive spot between her ear and her jaw, and she moaned softly. The man knew exactly what to do to make her melt in his arms.

She drew a deep breath and pushed away. "That's quite enough." She cast him a chastising look. "Do you think you could at least don a dressing gown?"

"I'm tempting you to stay, aren't I?" He grinned wickedly but grabbed his dressing gown nonetheless. She found her skirts and stepped into them, then slipped into her shoes.

"Not at all," she said in a lofty manner. "I am simply concerned that you will catch your death of cold."

"I didn't know you cared."

"Of course I care." She was buttoning the last button on her polonaise when his arms slipped around her from behind.

"I'm glad." He nuzzled her neck.

"I would hate for anything to happen to you," she said brusquely, sounding rather more affectionate than she'd intended. She much preferred not to reveal her emotions.

"I want you to stay with me." He paused. "Do you realize, from the moment you first shared my bed, there has been no other woman in my life but you?"

"My God, Max." She forced a light note to her voice. "What on earth has happened to you?"

"You have happened to me." His tone was abruptly serious. "I could make an honest woman out of you."

Her breath caught. She ignored it but was glad he couldn't see her face. "Don't be absurd. You're the youngest son of a marquess. You've been knighted. I am not the sort of woman you should have as a wife."

For an endless moment he didn't say anything. Then he blew a long breath. "Perhaps."

A few minutes later she was on her way home in the cab he had, as always, arranged to wait for her, refusing, as always, to allow him to escort her. His suggestion lingered in her thoughts. He'd never mentioned marriage before; she never imagined he would. They'd been together for more than three years now, and she had long ago accepted this was all they would have.

Still, when she'd said she wasn't the type of woman he should marry, it would have been nice if, just this once, he had lied.

Chapter 7

"I would never presume to question either your decisions or your conclusions, sir, and I have done precisely as you instructed but . . ."

Adrian narrowed his eyes. It was already late afternoon and his patience had worn thin hours ago. Worse, he had no real idea where his wife was at the moment. "But?"

"But . . ." Isaiah Vincent, Adrian's valet, chose his words with care. "It would seem to me you are jumping to unwarranted conclusions."

"They're not entirely unwarranted." Adrian tried and failed to hide the defensive tone in his voice.

Vincent raised a questioning brow.

"She has not been herself."

"Perhaps not. The weather—"

"I'm tired of the weather being used as an excuse," Adrian snapped. "I have experienced the exact same weather she has and have felt no ill effects."

"You did mention you have been feeling restless of late, sir."

"That has nothing to do with the weather." Adrian waved off the comment and paced the length of his bedroom, the largest such room in the London house. It had been his father's before him and his father's father before that. As the heir, Richard had occupied rooms that were nearly as big and he'd never seen any reason to move to this suite. But then Richard had never had a wife either. A wife who had pointed out that the furnishings were sorely in need of updating. She had replaced the heavy, dark, centuries-old furniture with lighter, burled wood and carved pieces. He quite liked it, although, in truth, it scarcely mattered to him as long as the bed was comfortable and his wife was in it. He and Evie had separate bedrooms, of course, connected through adjoining dressing rooms, but as often as not, she slept in his bed. *Their bed.* Precisely as he preferred. "Before my marriage, before my brother died, when I was free to do anything I wished, as you may recall, I did."

"You did have an interesting life, sir," Vincent murmured.

"A certain restlessness is to be expected in a man after two full years of eminently proper living," Adrian said and wondered exactly whom he was trying to convince.

Vincent cleared his throat.

Adrian knew that sound. "Well?"

"Well what, sir?"

"Well, tell me whatever it is you are thinking."

"I daresay you won't like it."

"I don't expect to like it."

"Permission to speak freely then?"

"Because you haven't spoken freely up to now?"

Adrian glared. "I know exactly what you're doing, you know."

"Do you, sir?"

"You think the longer this discussion goes on, the more likely I am to come to my senses. To look at all this rationally."

"You have always been a rational man."

"Well, it won't work. Not this time. There is no need for me to come to my senses because I have not lost them." His brows drew together. "The facts speak for themselves." He ticked the points off his fingers. "Her manner has been odd of late. She went to the museum without mentioning it to me."

Vincent gasped. "Oh no, sir, not the museum."

"Sarcasm, Vincent, is unbecoming in a servant."

"I beg your forgiveness, my lord."

Adrian ignored the sarcastic note in the other man's voice and continued, "She slipped away to meet someone in Dunwell's library. Soon thereafter, that scoundrel Radington arrived, all too delighted to see my wife, I might add. The man surreptitiously slipped a note into his pocket, obviously to hide it from me, the unsuspecting husband. A note which, no doubt, arranged an assignation. And the stationery . . ." He paused for emphasis. "Was cream in color."

Vincent stared in confusion.

"My wife's stationery is cream in color," he said pointedly.

"Ah, well, there you have it then." Vincent shook his head. "Cream isn't at all a common color for a lady's stationery."

"Sarcasm, Vincent."

"My apologies, sir."

"I am simply looking at the evidence as presented and drawing an inescapable conclusion."

"Which might well be wrong."

"Bloody hell, I hope so." Adrian blew a long breath. "Surely you can understand why I have to know for certain?"

Vincent wisely held his tongue.

"Now, what were you thinking?"

"Very well, sir. If you insist." Vincent considered him for a moment. "You said a certain restlessness was to be expected in a man after two years of proper behavior."

Adrian nodded.

"Might the same not be expected of a woman?"

"Exactly." Triumph rang in Adrian's voice. "That's my point."

"However, in your restlessness, you have not turned to women other than your wife."

"Never," Adrian said indignantly.

"Then why do you expect Lady Waterston's behavior to be less honorable than your own?"

"Women are fragile, delicate creatures who do not know their own minds and are easily swayed," Adrian said staunchly.

Vincent snorted. "I would not let your wife hear you say such a thing, sir."

"I'm not an idiot, Vincent."

"Dare I say, sir, that I should like to meet the man who could sway Lady Waterston. Other than yourself, of course," the valet added quickly.

"Admittedly even I cannot often dissuade her from something she is intent upon."

"It has been my observation of Lady Waterston that she is as honorable and loyal as she is lovely."

Adrian shrugged. "I have always thought so."

"Might I suggest then, sir, that it is only your own imagination and your own restlessness that have brought you to this, no doubt, erroneous conclusion."

"I am truly hoping I am wrong, Vincent."

"Might I also say, sir, that should Lady Waterston ever discover the lengths you are going to, to prove or disprove your suspicions, she will be most distressed."

Adrian shuddered. "She'd be bloody well furious."

"And could one blame her, sir?"

"She cannot ever find out." Vincent continued as if Adrian hadn't said a word. "Especially if, as I am confident, there is nothing untoward to discover?"

The man was infuriatingly impertinent and should be discharged at once. Not that that would ever happen. Adrian truly valued Vincent's candid nature. The valet had been in Adrian's employ for more than a dozen years and knew all of Adrian's secrets. If there was one person in the world Adrian trusted without question, it was Isaiah Vincent.

"You are trying to dissuade me, aren't you?"

"It's my duty, sir."

Adrian raised a skeptical brow.

Vincent shrugged. "It's why you pay me as well as you do, sir."

Adrian scoffed. "You are paid far too well."

"And that is why I carry out your orders implicitly." Vincent paused. "Even when I disagree with your reasoning and think you are making a dreadful mistake."

"Then we understand one another."

"Indeed we do, sir."

"What have you found out?"

Vincent heaved a reluctant sigh.

"Go on, out with it."

"Very well." Vincent's brow furrowed in thought. "Lord Radington's valet is discreetly involved with Lady Helmsley's personal maid, who is the second cousin, once removed, of Lord—"

"Blast it all, Vincent." Impatience sharpened his voice. "I do not need an accounting of the dalliances of servants or their familial connections. I am well aware that news, gossip if you will, travels quickly from house to house in this town. And the best way to find out nearly anything is to tap into that knowledgeable labyrinth of servants. Precisely why I asked you to do so. Now, what have you learned?"

Vincent studied him curiously for a moment. "I have never seen you like this, sir."

"Love, Vincent, does dreadful things to a man. It wreaks havoc with even the most rational sensibilities. And a man in love with his wife . . ."

"There are worse things, sir."

"None that I can think of at the moment. Now, to the matter at hand."

"Sir, I do think—"

"You cannot change my mind so you needn't continue to put this off. Now . . ." Adrian held his breath. "I want to know what you have discovered."

"As you wish." Vincent heaved a reluctant sigh. "Lord Radington has arranged a meeting with a lady at half past four this afternoon at the Langham Hotel." He hesitated. "Room 327."

"With my wife!" Anger rushed through him, mixed with something much more painful.

"That, sir, I was neither able to confirm nor deny," Vincent added quickly.

"I shall have to kill him," Adrian said in a cool, dispassionate manner. It was most surprising as he felt neither cool nor dispassionate. Indeed, at this very moment he wanted to rip something apart with his bare hands. Preferably Radington.

"Excellent idea, sir, but might I suggest you confirm your suspicions before resorting to murder."

"Oh, I intend to." He glanced at the clock. It was nearly five. "Have my carriage sent around, Vincent." He started toward the door.

"One moment, my lord."

Adrian turned toward the valet. "You cannot stop me so I suggest you abandon the effort."

"My lord, if you insist on taking this ill-advised step . . ." He pulled a nondescript key from his waistcoat pocket. "This is a master key. It will open the door to every room at the Langham."

Adrian took the key and turned it over in his hand. "Where did you get this?"

"The night clerk has a sister who is in service—"

"On second thought, it's best that I don't know." He nodded and pocketed the key. "Thank you."

"Part of the job, sir."

Again Adrian started for the door. "Never mind the carriage, I shall take a cab."

"Sir," Vincent called after him. "Do you really think this is wise?"

"I don't know. Probably not." Adrian ignored the dreadful weight now settled in the pit of his stomach. "I do know the only thing worse than my suspicions would be confirming them."

"I am confident you are wrong, sir. Lady Waterston is not the type of woman to dally with another man," Vincent said firmly. "I would wager a great deal on that."

"I do hope you win that wager as much as I hope I am indeed wrong." Adrian pulled open the door and glanced back at the valet. "Pity, I am rarely, if ever, wrong."

It was a busy afternoon at Fenwick and Sons, Booksellers. Evelyn closed the shop door behind her and savored the warmth for a moment. She was glad to see that patronage had increased. She'd always been fond of the establishment, even though now she preferred to patronize Hatchard's. It had been more than two years since she had crossed the threshold here.

This morning she had sent Celeste to deliver a message for Max. Her friend had returned saying he would have new instructions for her this afternoon in the usual manner. The usual manner meant Fenwick and Sons. It struck her as rather silly. Couldn't he have simply given Celeste the information to pass on to Evelyn? Although perhaps he wasn't sure what she should do now and was trying to determine her next step.

She glanced around the room. The place looked the same, as it had no doubt looked for the numerous decades of its existence. She suspected the only significant change through the years would be the names and number of Fenwick sons who chose to become part of Fenwick and Sons. Shelves lined every wall, filled to overflowing in a haphazard manner, which made it nearly impossible for a customer to find what she wanted without assistance from one of the sons. Evelyn had often wondered if that might be deliberate so as to justify the sheer number of sons employed.

She approached the front desk and noticed that there

had indeed been a change. The Ladies' Reading Room, a mirror image of the main room albeit somewhat smaller and off to one side, now served refreshments. Apparently afternoon tea was most popular. Evelyn paused for a moment. Very nearly every table was occupied by two to four ladies, all chatting and obviously enjoying themselves. The oddest pang shot through her. She hadn't had tea with friends in years. Indeed, aside from Celeste and Adrian's sisters, she didn't have any friends to speak of.

When she'd worked for the department, she had played the role of Miss Evelyn Turner, which wasn't a role at all but precisely who she was. It was assumed in society that she was an heiress as well. She'd never had to don a disguise, as Celeste often had, or pretend to be someone she wasn't. No one ever imagined that the life of the orphaned daughter of a viscount was funded by a clandestine government department or that she was engaged in uncovering information and ferreting out secrets. While she would, on occasion, run into someone she'd been to school with, living a double life left no time to cultivate friendships. Nor did it seem especially wise. Now, looking at the friends sharing tea and gossip in the reading room, it seemed a dreadful pity. Perhaps, when this was at an end . . .

She approached the counter and smiled at the clerk.

"Good day," he said. "How may I—"

"I shall handle this, James." Thomas Fenwick, one of the younger sons, stepped up beside the clerk. "Miss Turner is an old and valued customer."

"Of course, sir." James smiled at her. "Good day, miss." He nodded and left her in the capable hands of this particular Mr. Fenwick.

"Good day, Miss Turner," Mr. Fenwick said with a smile. "It's been quite some time. We have missed you."

"I can't imagine why." She glanced around the shop. "You appear to be far too busy to notice the absence of one customer."

"Ah, but none can compare with you." A twinkle shone in his eyes. Thomas Fenwick had always been a bit of a flirt.

She laughed. "And you are as charming as ever, Mr. Fenwick."

He leaned over the counter and lowered his voice in a confidential manner. "I read a great deal. It's remarkable what one can learn if one is reading the right, or perhaps the wrong, books."

"Novels then? Romance and adventure?"

"Yes, indeed." He nodded. "I think it's wise to be familiar with what our best customers like to read. Besides, I quite enjoy a good novel full of smashing adventure and a gallant hero who wins the heart of a fair lady."

"As do we all, Mr. Fenwick."

He grinned. "And how may I help you today, Miss Turner?"

"It's Lady Waterston now, Mr. Fenwick," she said with a smile. "I believe a book has been reserved for me. A new edition of *The Three Musketeers*."

"Excellent choice." He knelt to rummage on the shelves beneath the counter. If anyone at Fenwick's ever wondered why one woman would need so many copies of *The Three Musketeers*, no one ever let on. Of course, she had only ever dealt with Thomas, who was, no doubt, associated with the department in some manner. She had never asked and he had never volunteered the answers. Which was, all things considered, for the best. Mr. Fenwick stood, wrapped package in hand. "Here it is."

She accepted the package, paid for the book, and chatted with Mr. Fenwick for another moment.

"Will we see you again soon, Lady Waterston?"

With any luck at all, her days of purchasing copies of *The Three Musketeers* would soon be at an end. Regardless . . . she glanced at the reading room and nodded slowly. "Why yes, Mr. Fenwick, I believe you may."

Chapter 8

Adrian stared at the door to Room 327. Perhaps it would be wiser to knock rather than use the key Vincent had supplied. He had realized on the way here to the Langham, if Evie wasn't here, as he prayed, he would be making an enormous fool of himself. Still, it was a risk he was willing to take. One could certainly recover from humiliation and embarrassment. If he had lost his wife, his heart would be shattered.

He had wondered as well if an indiscretion on her part was something he could forgive. It would be difficult, of course, perhaps the most difficult thing he had ever attempted. But if the situation were reversed, wouldn't he hope she could forgive him? Still, he wasn't entirely certain he could.

He turned the key over in his hand and debated the merits of using the key versus knocking. Knocking would be the proper thing to do. But bursting in unannounced had a certain dramatic appeal to a man in his turbulent state of emotion. Besides, due consideration did not seem to be something he cared for at the moment. No, rash, impetuous behavior was calling his name.

He slipped the key in the keyhole and rather wished he could simply kick the door in with his foot. Now that would be dramatic and most satisfying.

Adrian opened the door, stepped into a fair-sized sitting room tastefully appointed with a sofa, chairs, a fireplace, a small desk near the window, and a decorative dressing screen in one corner. He closed the door quietly behind him. He wasn't at all sure it was necessary to be quiet, although if one was going to surprise one's wife in the act of infidelity, one should ensure it was indeed a surprise. An opened bottle of champagne sat in a silver bucket on a cloth-covered cart in the middle of the room. And wasn't that just the right touch for seduction? A distinct giggle sounded from the partially opened door on the right wall.

A giggle? He was making her giggle? Adrian couldn't recall the last time his wife had giggled. Bloody hell. He clenched his fists, stepped toward the door, and regretted he hadn't brought a pistol.

The door to the bedroom opened wider. "Excellent idea." Radington laughed and backed into the sitting room, a sheet wrapped around him. His gaze still focused on whom he was addressing. Evie, no doubt. Fury flamed Adrian's face.

"I shall be—" Radington turned, grabbed the bottle of champagne, and caught sight of Adrian.

In the tiny part of his mind that still retained a modicum of rationality, Adrian marveled that any man's face could show so many emotions in such a short amount of time. Shock on Radington's too handsome face shifted to disbelief, then became caution and curiosity.

"Waterston," he said carefully.

Adrian's jaw tightened. "Radington."

"I didn't expect to see you again so soon."

Adrian scoffed. "No doubt."

"Why are you here?"

"I've come for my wife."

"Your wife?" Radington stared in confusion. "Why would your wife want you to come here?"

"No." Adrian glared. "I haven't come in place of my wife! I have come here to find my wife."

Radington stared as if Adrian was mad. "I don't—"

"Good Lord, Derrick, don't be an idiot," a female voice sounded from the other room. A voice not Evie's. Relief rushed through him, embarrassment right on its heels. "He thinks you're here with Lady Waterston." Beryl appeared in the doorway, tying the sash of her wrapper. "Don't you, Adrian?"

Adrian pointed at a very confused Radington. "He had a note from my wife last night arranging a meeting in your library."

Beryl turned narrowed eyes on the other man. "Goodness, Derrick, can you not be content with just one woman at a time?"

"I . . . I . . ." Radington had the look of a man who wasn't entirely innocent.

"Did you or did you not receive a note from Lady Waterston last night?" she demanded.

"I received a note," he said slowly. "It was not signed, and when I saw her in the library, I assumed . . ." He glanced at Adrian. "Only for a moment, mind you, that it was from her."

"Ah-hah!" An odd sort of triumph rang in Adrian's voice.

"One would think you would recognize my handwriting by now." Beryl sighed. "The note, you silly man, was from me."

"Ah-hah!" Radington smirked.

"Oh." Adrian drew a deep breath. "It appears I have made a mistake," he said with all the dignity he could muster.

"I should say so." Indignation colored Radington's voice.

"Outrage is not as effective, Derrick, when one is not appropriately dressed. Or dressed at all." She rolled her gaze toward the ceiling. "Do put something on."

Radington stared at her. "Lest you forget, this is my room."

She raised a brow.

"Very well." Radington huffed and returned to the bedroom.

Beryl crossed her arms over her chest and studied Adrian for a long moment. "I must say this is turning out to be a more interesting afternoon than I had expected."

"My apologies," Adrian said in a gruff manner. "I thought . . . that is to say, I assumed . . . well . . ."

"You thought your wife was having an affair with Derrick."

"Obviously a mistaken assumption on my part. After last night . . ." Adrian squared his shoulders. "Apparently I leapt to an inaccurate conclusion."

"Goodness, Adrian, I can't imagine your wife meeting a man in a hotel. It's far too daring for her. And I daresay your wife is too dull to have an affair."

"She is not the least bit dull."

"Not to you perhaps," Beryl murmured.

"I don't think she's dull," Radington called from the other room.

Adrian ignored him. "And she can be most daring." Was he actually defending his wife's capacity for unfaithfulness? "Too loyal perhaps but she is not the least bit dull."

"And with Derrick?" She shook her head. "I would think she had better taste."

"I can hear you, you know." Radington stepped into the doorway, now wearing a dressing gown, and frowned. "Exactly what do you mean by *better taste*?"

"My dear man, you are quite delightful and I enjoy being with you immensely. I only mean that Lady Waterston would choose someone far more discreet."

"I am most discreet." Radington glared.

"Hardly." Adrian snorted. "An afternoon meeting in a hotel is scarcely discreet."

"Well, it certainly wouldn't do to have anyone see her going into my house," Radington said firmly.

"The Langham does have a wonderful afternoon tea," Beryl murmured. "It's a perfect reason for being here."

"If one stays in the tearoom. Any number of ladies of your acquaintance frequent the tea. You could be easily spotted coming upstairs rather than to the tearoom." Adrian pinned her with a hard look. "You, of all people, know how quickly gossip of this nature can spread. In spite of your claim that you and Lord Dunwell pursue your own interests, I doubt very much that you would like him to become aware of"—he glanced pointedly at Radington—"your companion for afternoon tea."

Beryl grimaced. "That would be best, I suppose."

"A meeting like this is not without the danger of discovery," he added. Good God, he sounded stuffy. When did that happen?

"Oh my, yes." Sarcasm rang in her tone. "Who knows how many other husbands might come barging in?"

"That would be even more awkward than this." Radington shuddered.

"Difficult to believe," Adrian said wryly.

"Bloody hell, Waterston, you have become pompous." Radington shook his head. "If this is what marriage does to you, it is yet another reason to avoid it."

"I am quite happy in my marriage," Adrian said firmly.

"Tell me, Waterston." Radington considered him curiously. "You were quite the rogue in your day—"

"My day was not so very long ago, Radington."

Beryl smiled in an oddly wistful manner. "Not long ago at all really." She sighed. "Although it does now seem a lifetime."

Radington met his gaze directly. "A few years ago, you were exactly like me."

Beryl coughed.

"Hardly." Adrian scoffed. "I never carried on with ladies who were married."

"Someone has to," Radington said in a lofty manner. "But as you are older and wiser and more experienced, if not a hotel, then where?"

"My husband has a flat he thinks I don't know about," Beryl said with a shrug.

"A flat?" Radington's brows drew together in thought. "What an interesting idea."

Adrian met Beryl's gaze. "I am sorry."

"You needn't be," she said with an offhand shrug. "I'm not. We each get precisely what we want from this marriage. I have made my bed, so to speak." She flashed him a wicked grin. "Well, one of them."

"You deserve better," Adrian said quietly.

"I doubt that. But thank you for saying so." She studied him for a moment. "Even at your most scandalous, you were a good man, Adrian. You still are. Only a fool would risk losing you, and I daresay your wife is no fool. You certainly don't need to worry about her turning to a man like Derrick."

Radington's brow rose. "Because she has better taste?"

"Because if she were so stupid as to have an affair, it would be with someone who had less of a reputation." Beryl cast the man an affectionate smile. "Someone no one would suspect. Someone, oh, safe."

Radington grinned. "I am not the least bit safe."

"Precisely why I am here." She returned his grin.

Adrian stared. "What do you mean—safe?"

"I mean someone who has as much to lose as she does." Her brow furrowed. "Although I can't imagine her having an affair at all. She's quite obviously head over heels for you."

"I thought so," Adrian muttered.

Her eyes narrowed. "Then why are you here?"

"Why?" Adrian winced. "There was . . ." Evidence? Hardly, at least not when one looked at it rationally. He drew a deep breath. "I blame it all on the weather."

Her brows drew together. "The weather?"

"I don't know," he continued. "I believe I put one and one together and got fourteen."

She stared, then her expression cleared and she gasped. "Dear Lord, Adrian, you're in love with your wife."

Radington snorted. "Nonsense. No one is in love with his own wife." He paused. "Someone else's wife perhaps but not his own."

"Well, there you have it." Adrian shrugged. "I am in love with my wife."

"Love does lead men to do ridiculous things." Sympathy sounded in Radington's voice.

Beryl cast him a skeptical look. "How would you know?"

"I have been in love." Radington huffed. "More times than I can say."

"In lust perhaps," Adrian said under his breath.

"Love," Radington said firmly, then shrugged. "It simply has never lasted."

"There are reasons for that," Beryl murmured.

"I should be on my way." Adrian edged toward the door. "Once again, my apologies."

Beryl and Radington traded glances.

"I say, old man," Radington began. "I do hope you agree that the account of this afternoon shouldn't go any farther than the three of us."

"You have my word." The last thing he wanted was for his absurd jealousy to become common knowledge and, worse, for Evie to hear of it. He threw a last cautioning look at Beryl and took his leave.

On his way home he couldn't help thinking what a narrow escape he'd had when he'd realized long ago that Beryl was not the right woman for him. Not that he had ever led her to believe otherwise. She had wanted marriage to suit her own ambitions. Or so he had thought at the time. But time did have a way of coloring things. Radington's charge that he was exactly as Adrian had once been struck rather unpleasantly close to home. He had never had any illusions about his behavior, but he'd always thought he had not abandoned principles in pursuit of pleasures.

And furthermore, his wife was not the least bit dull.

Why, she was the most exciting woman he had ever met. Adventurous and courageous and amusing.

And far too clever to dally with a man like Radington. How could he have been so stupid? Beryl was absolutely right. Evie would never have an affair with a man of Radington's reputation. She would choose better than that.

Not that she had chosen. Not that she was doing anything untoward at all. Not that this wasn't entirely in his own imagination fueled by nothing save a certain preoccupation in her manner. He was making something out of nothing. He knew it and yet he couldn't seem to stop himself. He should stop this nonsense right now. Doubt fueled by jealousy and the fear of losing what he cherished most was far too powerful to overcome with mere reason. Still, hadn't he made enough of a fool out of himself already?

Apparently not. It was past time to get to the bottom of this.

He stalked into his house, barely pausing to hand his hat and coat to Stewart, the butler. "Is Lady Waterston at home?"

The servant shook his head. "No, my lord. I believe I heard something mentioned about afternoon tea but I—"

"Hah." Adrian glared at the poor man. "From now on there shall be no going out for afternoon tea."

"Yes, my lord." Stewart stared.

"We have perfectly good tea right here."

"Indeed we do, my lord," the butler said quickly. "And as Miss DeRochette did not accompany Lady Waterston, I assume tea was not involved after all."

"Excellent," he snapped and headed toward Evie's

parlor. "Is Miss DeRochette in Lady Waterston's parlor?"

"Yes, my lord," Stewart called after him. No doubt the man was even now resisting the urge to follow to discover what had put his lordship in such a rare, foul mood.

He flung open the door to Evie's private parlor. Miss DeRochette jumped up from her seat behind the ladies' desk that was her domain in the house. "Where is she, Miss DeRochette?"

Her eyes widened. "My lord?"

"My wife. Where is my wife?"

She stared. "She had some calls to make, my lord. And she was going to stop at the milliner's and select some fabric, and stop at a bookseller's—"

A lesser man might have shown some outward expression of the realization that struck him with the force of a bullet.

"A bookseller's?" he said slowly. "Hatchard's?"

He should have seen it from the beginning. Love certainly did muck up a rational man's mind.

"No, sir." She shook her head. "Fenwick and Sons."

Bloody hell, he was indeed an idiot.

Part Two

Deception

The one charm about marriage is that it makes a life of deception absolutely necessary for both parties.

—Oscar Wilde

Chapter 9

"**Y**ou simply must take your husband in hand."

"I what?" Evelyn stared in confusion and a fair amount of disbelief.

She had not yet recovered from the shock of Lady Dunwell calling on her. The woman had swept into Evelyn's parlor with the single-minded determination of a hound with the scent of fox in his nose. Evelyn couldn't recall the last time she had been at a loss for words, but Lady Dunwell's presence had done just that. Had Lady Dunwell accused her of searching her library or suspecting Lord Dunwell of nefarious acts, Evelyn could have responded with an appropriate comment. That she was at least somewhat prepared for. But as relieved as she was that Lady Dunwell's visit had nothing to do with Evelyn's assignment, this demand of the woman's left her unable to do little more than stare.

Lady Dunwell rolled her gaze toward the ceiling in exasperation. "I said you must do something about your husband." She sank dramatically into one of two matching blue brocade ladies' chairs. "He is not in his right mind."

"I beg your pardon," Evelyn said indignantly and sat on the edge of the peach-colored sofa, which nicely matched the chairs in style. "My husband is not mad. Why on earth would you think such a thing?"

"Perhaps out of his mind is an exaggeration on my part." Lady Dunwell heaved a theatrical sigh. "Do forgive me but surely you can understand my concern."

"No, I can't." Evelyn drew her brows together. "I understand neither your concern nor why you're here. Why are you here?"

Lady Dunwell narrowed her eyes in suspicion. "He didn't tell you?"

"Tell me what?"

"No, I suppose he wouldn't. The embarrassment, no doubt. Men like Lord Waterston do so hate to admit when they're wrong. Still, I did have the impression that you were one of those annoying couples who share things that are probably best not shared."

"We are." Evelyn glared. "And what was he wrong about?"

Lady Dunwell considered her for a moment. "May I be completely candid?"

"Can you be?" Evelyn said in a tone harder than she had intended.

"Oh my." It was Lady Dunwell's turn to stare. "You're a bit sharper than I had expected. I had always thought you were fairly docile."

Evelyn narrowed her eyes. "Appearances can be deceiving."

"So it would seem. I might have misjudged you." She studied Evelyn curiously. "Oh, certainly you had something of a reputation before your marriage, but it was never especially scandalous or interesting. And since your marriage, you have been the epitome of propriety."

"Thank you."

"It was not intended as a compliment."

"Yes, I know." Evelyn adopted her most pleasant smile.

Lady Dunwell's eyes widened and then a touch of what might have been an admiring smile curved the corners of her lips. She drew a deep breath. "Do I have your word you will keep this entirely between us? Except for Adrian, of course. You will want to speak to him. But will you assure me this will go no farther?"

"Yes, I suppose." What on earth did the woman want?

"Then that will have to do." Lady Dunwell paused to pull her thoughts together. "Yesterday afternoon, I was, oh, shall we say, having tea, privately, with a friend at the Langham, when your husband burst in upon us."

Evelyn drew her brows together. "Why would he interrupt your tea?"

Lady Dunwell stared as if Evelyn were the one who made no sense. "Perhaps I haven't misjudged you after all." She huffed. "The tea was a very expensive champagne. The privacy was provided by a suite, not overly large but nicely appointed. The friend was a gentleman, and while we weren't actually *pouring tea* at the moment your husband arrived, we were also not properly dressed."

Evelyn stared.

"Or dressed at all," Lady Dunwell said sharply. "Do you understand what I am trying to say?"

"Well, yes, I think—"

"I was engaged in an afternoon of fun and frolic

with a gentleman who was not my husband in a hotel room when we were interrupted by your husband." Lady Dunwell glared. "Now do you understand?"

"I understood when you said *pouring tea*," Evelyn snapped. "What I don't understand is why my husband was there and why you have come to me."

"You have to do something about him. As I said, you need to take him in hand." She met Evelyn's gaze firmly. "He came looking for you."

"For me?" Evelyn shook her head in confusion. "Why on earth would he go to a hotel looking for me?"

"Apparently . . ." Lady Dunwell paused for emphasis. The woman certainly did have a flair for the dramatic. "He does not think you are quite as proper as you appear."

Evelyn sucked in a hard breath. "He can't possibly . . ."

Lady Dunwell raised a brow.

"Absolutely not," Evelyn said staunchly. Why, Adrian trusted her as she trusted him. Certainly, he had noticed her preoccupation, and yes, at the Dunwells' reception he had shown a distinct hint of jealousy, and last night, she had caught him more than once studying her with an odd look of consideration. Of course, a touch of jealousy at a party was one thing. Thinking she was engaged in afternoon *tea* with a gentleman in a hotel room was quite another. Indignation rushed through her. "How could he?"

"No matter what else he may be, he is first and foremost a man. And men are odd and unfathomable creatures and, for the most part, not worth the effort they require. Worse, they think they are the sensible ones." She tugged at the fingers of her left glove and pulled it off. Which obviously meant she planned to stay. "And I must say, I find all this explaining has left me rather parched."

"Tea perhaps?" Evelyn said in a dry manner.

"One always enjoys a good cup of tea." Lady Dunwell removed her other glove.

"I know I shall never quite enjoy it in the same manner again." Evelyn stood, moved to the door, and asked the butler to order tea. Where were her manners? She should have thought of refreshments earlier. Besides, it gave her a momentary reprieve from the gaze of Lady Dunwell. And time to consider exactly what she had just revealed.

Wasn't it only the other night that Adrian had said he trusted her? Obviously he was more concerned about her recent preoccupation than he'd let on. But to suspect she'd be unfaithful, when she'd never so much as looked at another man, was both upsetting and infuriating. His unfounded suspicions said something rather disturbing about the man she thought she knew. And perhaps about their marriage as well.

She braced herself and returned to her seat. "So, tell me." She met the other woman's gaze directly. "Once again, why are you here?"

"I don't know really." Lady Dunwell blew a long breath. "Is Adrian here, by the way?"

"No, I'm not sure where he is." Evelyn's jaw tightened. "I don't watch him every moment."

"Perhaps you should."

"I didn't know it was necessary."

A maid knocked at the door, then entered with a tea cart bearing a tea service and a plate of Cook's biscuits. Evelyn never failed to be pleased by the efficiency of the staff, most of whom had been in service here for years.

"I realize this is your first marriage," Lady Dunwell said as soon as the maid took her leave.

"My first and last." Evelyn poured a cup and handed it to the other woman.

"One never knows." Lady Dunwell shrugged. "As to why I am here, I seem to feel some sort of obligation to you."

Evelyn scoffed. "I was under the impression you didn't like me."

"Oh, I don't." She took a sip. "But then I don't know you, do I?"

Evelyn ignored her. "And this obligation?"

"*Obligation* may well be the wrong word." She thought for a moment. "I simply feel that if my husband were going about bursting into hotel rooms, suspecting me of scandalous behavior, I should like to know. And I would hope someone would make me aware of his actions. Especially"—Lady Dunwell leveled her a hard look—"if I was innocent of anything untoward."

Evelyn bit back an immediate response as to how that was none of the other woman's concern but thought better of it. She chose her words with care. "Then you have my thanks."

"Furthermore, while I am not opposed to the sharing of gossip when I am not the subject, I should not like my husband to discover through rumor that I was caught *en flagrante* in a hotel." She shuddered. "He would not like that at all."

"I thought you and your husband were, well, independent."

Her brow rose. "What a clever way of putting it. I

like that. It's quite witty. I shall take that as my own. In spite of our *independence*, we have as well agreed upon a certain discretion."

"You needn't worry," Evelyn said coolly. "I daresay Adrian won't mention the incident to anyone. Although I can now understand why he said nothing to me."

"I hope so. But men are worse than women when it comes to talking among themselves. One says something to another in strictest secrecy . . ." Lady Dunwell sipped her tea in a thoughtful manner. "Still, he was quite embarrassed and I imagine he would not want his error to become common knowledge nor would he want the fact of his . . ." She met Evelyn's gaze. "Groundless suspicions?"

Evelyn surrendered and nodded.

"To become public as well."

"I don't like the idea of his suspicions becoming fuel for gossip either as I have done nothing to make him question my devotion." Evelyn narrowed her eyes. "And I'm not at all happy to learn he doesn't truly trust me."

Lady Dunwell shrugged in a casual manner. "Quite often men who question their wives' fidelity do so because they have something to hide themselves."

"Adrian has nothing to hide," Evelyn said staunchly. Certainly Adrian had sown his wild oats with indiscriminate abandon before their marriage, but now there wasn't a question in her mind that the Earl of Waterston was completely faithful to his wife.

"Then he loves you," Lady Dunwell said simply.

"Then he should trust me." Evelyn's jaw tightened. What had possessed the man?

"Probably, but love plays havoc with the heads of

even the most intelligent of men." Lady Dunwell selected a biscuit. "No man wants to lose what he loves.
Would that my husband be as jealous, so fearful of losing me." She paused. "No, on further consideration,
that wouldn't suit me at all."

"Yours was not a love match then?" Evelyn couldn't
resist the question even though, given all she had heard
about Lord and Lady Dunwell, she already knew the
answer.

"Good Lord, no." Lady Dunwell scoffed. "I have
never experienced love nor do I particularly wish to.
My first husband, Charles, was much older than I and
very wealthy. He already had a grown heir and all he
wanted was a wife who would look good on his arm. I
wanted to be the wife of a wealthy nobleman although
we did get on well together. Lionel, Lord Dunwell,
wanted a wife who would help further his ambitions.
He intends to be prime minister one day." She took a
bite of her biscuit. "I should like to be the wife of the
prime minister."

"You sound well suited."

"We are." Lady Dunwell thought for a moment. "I
may not love him, but I do rather like him. Perhaps I
will love him one day, but it's been my observation that
love makes women even more vulnerable than we already are." She glanced at the biscuit in her hand.
"These are excellent, by the way. I should steal your
cook from you."

"You could certainly try." Evelyn adopted her most
pleasant manner. "But she has been here for a very
long time. Why, we consider her part of the family, and
she feels the same about us. Besides." She smiled. "We
pay her exceptionally well."

"And loyalty cannot be bought." Lady Dunwell nodded. "You would be wise to remember that."

Evelyn raised a brow.

"He's not a bad sort, you know. My husband, that is." She shook her head. "Underneath all that ruthless ambition he's really a good man in his own way. He has limits and a certain code of honor, which is often at odds with what he wants." Her brow furrowed in thought. "Adrian is a good man as well."

"I have always thought so," Evelyn said under her breath.

"Good men are exceptionally rare. I like your husband. There was a time when I more than liked him. It's not often one finds a man who is as good as well as exciting." She leaned forward in a confidential manner. "Aside from politics, Lionel is not particularly exciting." She paused. "I had rather planned to keep him, you know. Adrian, that is."

"So I have heard," Evelyn said wryly.

Lady Dunwell finished the biscuit and looked at her fingers as if she would like to lick them clean. "Truly excellent."

"I shall pass on your compliments."

"Well, I've taken up enough of your time." Lady Dunwell picked up her gloves. "Now then." She rose to her feet. "I think we should be friends."

"Why?" Evelyn asked without thinking.

"I don't seem to have any female friends. I'm not sure why." She frowned. "I have a fair number of female acquaintances but no true friends."

"Oh, I daresay, Lady Dunwell, that's not—"

She laughed. "What a proper and polite thing to say, but I fear it is true. And as we are to be friends, you should call me Beryl." She pinned Evelyn with a firm look. "I suspect you don't have many friends either."

Evelyn scoffed. "I have any number of friends."

"Not so anyone would notice. Your husband's sisters perhaps, but they are obligatory friends as they are also relations." She thought for a moment. "However, if we are to be friends, you should know I have few scruples, my morals are questionable, and I am quite selfish."

"What a ringing endorsement for friendship."

"But I am unfailingly loyal to my friends. I am a friend you can always count on for very nearly anything."

Evelyn cast her a skeptical look. "I thought you didn't have any friends?"

"That's why." Beryl sighed. "Unfailing loyalty takes a great deal out of me."

"Friends do not steal their friends' cooks." Evelyn's eyes narrowed. "Or their husbands."

"Yet another argument for friendship because otherwise, make no mistake, I would have your husband in a minute if the opportunity presented itself."

"We have nothing whatsoever in common," Evelyn warned.

"Oh, I would never have a friend who is exactly like me." Beryl shuddered. "One of me in a friendship is quite enough."

Evelyn choked back a laugh.

"And I can be most amusing." She grinned. "Well?" For the briefest moment something that might have been apprehension flashed in Beryl's eyes.

It struck Evelyn that, in spite of her confident manner and scandalous tendencies, Beryl Dunwell was a lonely woman. And hadn't Evelyn recently decided she needed friends? A friendship with the notorious Lady

Dunwell might be something of an adventure. Besides, if Lord Dunwell was involved in the theft of the file, which seemed less and less likely to Evelyn, it wouldn't hurt to be friends with his wife. She'd had no word from Maxwell since she'd picked up *The Three Musketeers* yesterday and the message it contained had said little more than "wait." It was too soon to hope this assignment was at an end yet hope she did.

Even better, Adrian didn't like Lord Dunwell and she doubted that he would approve of her friendship with his wife. A woman he had obviously once had more than a passing acquaintance with. It would make him most uncomfortable. Good. At the moment, Adrian's disapproval and discomfort were excellent recommendations.

"Very well then, Beryl," Evelyn said with a nod. "You have a new friend."

"Excellent." Beryl beamed. "As your friend, and as someone with far more experience with husbands, might I offer you a word of advice?"

Evelyn's eyes narrowed. "What?"

"First of all, husbands who are irate and suspicious are frequently, not always mind you, but frequently engaged in infidelity themselves."

"Adrian would never—"

"I'm not saying he has," Beryl said quickly. "I'm just saying it is something to keep in the back of one's mind. Second, this is an enormous opportunity for any wife. Not only did your husband distrust you but he allowed that distrust to be known to others. Why, if I were not your friend, and did not figure prominently, I should be delighted to spread this story far and wide."

"It's good to have friends," Evelyn murmured.

"Indeed it is." Beryl nodded. "All I am saying is that

the magnitude of your husband's actions are such that you should not forgive him too easily. Flowers are not enough in way of apology, and even diamonds had best be of the finest quality." Her eyes narrowed thoughtfully. "You should also spend a great deal of money in a most frivolous manner."

"I had been thinking of refurbishing my town house." She glanced at Beryl. "My secretary lives there currently."

"Excellent. Refurbishing is wonderfully expensive. As are trips to the continent. New carriages." Beryl paused. "Portraits."

Evelyn laughed.

Beryl pinned her with a firm look. "Make him work for your forgiveness."

"My goodness, Beryl." Evelyn cast her new friend a slow, determined smile. "It appears we have a lot in common after all."

Chapter 10

"Why wasn't I informed of this?"

"You are no longer a member of this department." Max's manner was cool, professional. He sat behind the desk that was once Adrian's, looking for all the world like a proper government official. "What occurs here is no longer your concern."

"My wife is my concern."

"And because of your decision to expunge any mention of her true identity from the official records, she is the only one I can trust at the moment."

Adrian scoffed. "I find that hard to believe."

"It scarcely matters what you believe." Max leaned forward over the desk. "You retired from service, remember?"

"I had no choice."

"One always has a choice," Max said in a lofty manner.

"Not when one has just inherited a title, family responsibilities, and a seat in Parliament." Adrian studied his old friend for a long moment. "But you know that."

Max shrugged.

Adrian narrowed his eyes. "Just as you knew that eventually I would realize my wife was working for the department again."

"You have always been observant."

At once the pieces clicked into place. "And that realization would bring me here."

"As well as most predictable. At least to someone who knows you well."

Adrian settled back in his chair and studied the other man. "It has been a long time."

"You never call on me, you never write . . ." Max heaved a heartfelt sigh. "You have left me forlorn and abandoned."

Adrian resisted the urge to grin. He would not be disarmed this easily.

He'd been furious when he had realized the truth late yesterday afternoon. Not at Evie but at Max. No reason was good enough to drive her back to this. He couldn't blame her for not telling him herself. If their roles were reversed, he wouldn't—couldn't—tell her. Besides, as far as she knew, he had no idea of her work before their marriage.

His anger had meshed with concern followed closely by curiosity. What was so important as to necessitate Max needing Evie's help? His immediate impulse had been to confront Max at once but apparently, now that he knew what his wife was about and it had nothing to do with another man, reason had returned and prevailed and kept him from the Mayfair office until this afternoon.

"It does seem fair, doesn't it? In a universal sense, that is," Adrian said mildly. "Turnabout and all that."

Max's brow furrowed. "I am tired of people thinking my past behavior, in regards to the fairer sex, means I deserve to be ill treated. I have never deliberately mistreated a woman. Certainly, I have been inconsiderate on occasion, thoughtless perhaps, and even somewhat insensitive to their feelings. And yes, there have been moments when I have fled without a backward glance, but all in all, while I may be a bit of a scoundrel, I have never been a cad." He huffed. "And that has nothing to do with the matter at hand."

"No. Still . . ." Adrian blew a long breath. "You deserved better from me." Regret and a touch of guilt washed through him. He and Max had been friends since their first days with the department and partners for a time as well. Each man had saved the other on more than one occasion. It was Adrian who recommended Max take his place as head of the department. And Max who had understood why Adrian had wanted to eliminate all evidence of Evie's involvement and had carried out his orders, albeit reluctantly. "My apologies. We have been friends for a long time. It simply seemed wise to put everything—and everyone—involved with the department behind me. That may well have been a mistake on my part."

"I could have used your advice, now and again, in the last two years," Max said. "The benefit of your wisdom, as it were. It would have been helpful, on occasion, to talk with you. Something other than the brief, cordial greeting you manage when we run into one another publicly. Although given that you are usually with your wife, I do understand."

"You could have contacted me."

Max shook his head. "You made it clear when you left that you wanted no further involvement. Yet I didn't realize when you abandoned the department, you abandoned me as well."

Adrian winced. "I would say that is rather harsh, but I suppose it isn't, is it?"

"No, it's not. I have never thought of myself as overly sentimental, Adrian, but I was foolish enough to believe that our friendship transcended our work. Apparently I was wrong."

Adrian stared. "I don't know what to say."

"Guilt, no doubt, has got your tongue."

"Not at all," he said quickly. "Regret, perhaps, that I wasn't a better friend. Unfortunately, putting all this behind me included you. And in that, I was wrong."

Max raised a brow. "You never admit when you're wrong."

"It's not necessary as I am rarely wrong." He ignored how very wrong he had been about his wife.

Max studied him silently. In spite of his morose expression, there was a gleam of amusement in his eyes.

Adrian's eyes narrowed. "You're not wounded by my actions at all, are you?"

Max grinned. "I cry myself to sleep each and every night."

"I had forgotten how clever you are."

"I do try to disguise it. I am more than merely the face of the department, you know."

"I still consider you my closest friend."

"Hmph." Max scoffed. "In that you have my sympathy."

"I should. It wasn't easy, you know. Leaving this behind." Adrian got to his feet and, without thinking, paced the small office. Habit, of course. He couldn't count the number of times he had paced this floor. For whatever reason, he had always thought better on his feet in this room than behind the desk. He resisted the urge to glance at the floor to see if indeed there was a faint trough worn in the floorboards from the years he had spent here and instead moved to the window. The view was unchanged, the square as serene as ever. It had always struck him, gazing down on the scene, how appearances were so often deceiving. But then people tended not to see what they did not expect. It was a tenet of humanity he had often bet his very life on. He turned and met his friend's gaze firmly. "I know it's hard to believe but the life of the Earl of Waterston is not generally as exciting as the life of Adrian Hadley-Attwater, agent of the crown."

"Better known as *Sir*."

"He did have a grand time of it." Adrian grinned. "The excitement of pursuit, the constant threat of exposure, the danger of discovery. Disguises and deceptions and danger—"

"And delightful women. Don't forget the women."

"I could never forget the women." He chuckled, then caught himself. "But I have, completely. That, too, is behind me. There is only one woman in my life, only one woman I want." He shook his head. "I have no regrets about that."

"While the faces have changed here, little else has," Max said in an offhand manner. "We still have a grand time, in the service of her majesty, of course."

"Of course," Adrian murmured. Still, even if it was sanctioned by the government, there was something about operating on the edge of the rules, be they those of law or behavior, that was exciting and intoxicating. And hard to give up.

Max eyed his old friend curiously. "Tell me, Adrian, do you miss it?"

"Not at all," Adrian lied.

"Because your life of responsibility is so fulfilling?"

"Yes," he said staunchly. "It is fulfilling and extremely busy and I am most content and . . ."

Max raised a brow.

"And yes," he snapped. "I admit it. I do miss this. I didn't in the beginning but recently . . ."

"Recently?"

"Recently I have found myself impatient, on edge, restless. It led me to . . ." This was awkward to admit, even to an old friend. He drew a deep breath. "To suspect my wife of being embroiled in an affair."

"I see."

"I wasn't entirely wrong. She was involved with something she wished to keep from me." He cast his friend a hard look. "This."

"She wasn't at all pleased." Max studied him closely. "She still doesn't know, does she?"

"Good God, no." He shook his head.

"Then I assume Miss DeRochette—"

"Doesn't know either, at least as far as I know. I don't know how she could. And if she did, she would certainly tell my wife." Adrian shuddered and returned to his chair. "And then there would be hell to pay."

"From them both, I suspect," Max said mildly.

"I much prefer not even to think about it, thank you." No, the very idea that Evie might learn the man who had given her assignments and directed her activities with his often seductive words was the same man who had told her in a most romantic manner that their lives didn't begin until the moment they had met struck fear into his heart in a way no criminal or spy or villain ever had. "And it is my intention to avoid that until the day I breathe my last. Or beyond. Now . . ." His tone hardened. "Where are we?"

"We?" Max chuckled. "Welcome back."

"Only for the moment," Adrian warned.

"Agreed." Max nodded. "As I said, a file that includes your true identity as well as the names of the previous two heads of this department was stolen."

"From you." Adrian bit back a grin.

"Yes, from me." Max huffed and continued. "It may or may not be significant, but a few months ago, one of your predecessors, whose name is in the file, died. As he was elderly, I thought little of it although he was said to have been in excellent health."

Adrian nodded. "You're speaking of Sir George."

"I am." He paused. "I assume Evelyn does not know of her guardian's connection with the department."

"That's my assumption, although I can't very well ask her."

"You and your wife keep a lot of secrets from each other."

"Not at all," Adrian said. "Not since our marriage anyway. We agreed from the start that our lives before we met didn't matter."

"How very romantic of you. And extremely clever as well."

"I thought so."

"You know, one of the reasons I have not married is because I thought marriage called for complete and total honesty."

"We have complete and total honesty."

Max raised a skeptical brow.

"About the present," Adrian said firmly. "The past is another matter."

"I didn't know you could categorize honesty that way. How very interesting," Max said under his breath. "As I was saying, Sir George's death might well be nothing but coincidence given his advanced years, although I find his death, followed by the theft of the file, at the very least curious despite the length of time between the two incidents." He paused. "I did have my secretary make some inquires but he found nothing untoward in Sir George's demise. Your immediate predecessor, Lord Lansbury, thinks it is nothing more than chance and of no significance." Max's gaze met his. "I am always suspicious of coincidence."

Adrian nodded.

"Even though Sir George's death and the theft of the file are separated by some three months, I still feel it is something to keep in mind." He studied Adrian for a moment as if choosing his words. "My investigation before I involved your wife led me to believe Lord Dunwell had arranged the theft. As he is a most unimaginative man, it was reasonable to assume, if the file was in his possession, it would be in his library."

"Which is why Evelyn insisted we go to the reception," Adrian said slowly. "And why I found her in the library."

"You caught her?"

"Not exactly." He blew a resigned breath. "But her presence and the arrival of Lord Radington helped convince me as to my wife's infidelities."

"Radington?" Max choked back a laugh. "She has far better taste."

"This is not amusing."

"Not to you, perhaps." Max sobered. "You're not going to like this part."

"Because I'm so fond of the rest?" Adrian narrowed his eyes. "Go on."

"My information about Dunwell was wrong." He shrugged. "But I learned that too late to stop Evelyn."

"I see." He wasn't at all happy to learn that Evie had risked discovery for nothing. Still, it was the nature of the game. "Then you are back where you started."

"Not entirely." Max opened a drawer, pulled out a file, and tossed it onto the desk. "This is the file in question."

Adrian shook his head. "I don't understand."

"Neither do I." He shrugged. "This was delivered via Fenwick's this morning."

Adrian shook his head. "This makes no sense."

"No, it doesn't." Max stared at the file. "Although if all someone wanted was the information, they have it now."

"And might well think, with the file recovered, our investigation will be at an end."

Max grinned. "I like the way you say *our*."

"Force of habit," Adrian said absently, his mind racing. Once again, he got to his feet. "You thought initially that the purpose of the theft might be to destroy the effectiveness of the department, and the newly formed government itself, by bringing it to public scrutiny."

Max nodded.

He paced in his usual manner, noting in the back of his mind that his old office needed paint. That, too, hadn't changed. "But without the documents in the file, that is, without solid proof, the information is very nearly worthless."

"Unless," Max said slowly, "the department itself is not the target."

"Then what is?" Adrian paused. "Or who?"

Max drummed his fingers thoughtfully on the desk. "That's the question, isn't it?" He shook his head. "Whatever the answer, it's bound to be complicated. And probably clever."

"Undoubtedly."

"I'll continue my inquiries. Discreetly, of course, as my suspicions have not eased about the involvement of someone within the department." He paused. "I would certainly welcome assistance."

Adrian nodded. "Help is always appreciated."

"Two minds are usually more productive than one."

"That has been my experience."

"Your wife will be pleased to know her services are no longer necessary."

"Don't tell her," Adrian said without thinking.

Max stared. "Why not?"

"Why?" Adrian stared at his friend. It was perhaps the most absurd idea that had ever come to his mind yet it made a certain amount of sense. In recent days, Adrian had become aware of just how unsure he was of his wife's affection.

Two years ago was the last time Evie's manner had been odd. The last time she had seemed preoccupied or restless. It was minor really, no more pronounced than her recent behavior. Indeed, if Max had not been so attuned to observation and brought it to Adrian's attention and to their superior in the home office, it might have gone unnoticed. As it was, there was speculation that Miss Turner might well be working for someone else as well as the department.

Adrian suggested he meet her as himself to best determine the truth. He had quickly discovered her change in demeanor was attributable to nothing untoward at all but rather to her desire to leave the department, to leave the life of secret meetings and clandestine purposes and deceit behind her. That should have been the end of it but was, in fact, only the beginning.

Meeting her in person was scarcely a sacrifice. He had grown more and more intrigued with her through the years. And while the notes Eve and Sir exchanged were, for the most part, concerned with the business at hand, as the years went on, she revealed more of herself to him. He was more cautious than she, but he, too, revealed more than he should have. Was it any wonder then that when Adrian met Evelyn in the flesh, he knew exactly what to say, exactly what to do? She had commented more than once how it was as though they'd known each other forever. Was love then between them a surprise or inevitable? He had already been more than a little in love with her.

Then Richard had died and Adrian had no choice really but to leave the department. He had married Evie and until recently had been more than content with his choices in life. While this wasn't the first time he had wondered about his wife's feelings, it was the first time he had realized the extent of his own doubt.

But hadn't he always felt the least bit convenient? Hadn't he always wondered if she truly loved him or if he simply suited her needs? Not that she had ever actually made him feel that way. Nor had she ever given him any solid reason to question her love. But he had wondered. What man wouldn't?

And hadn't he wondered who was really the love of her life? A dashing, dangerous man she had never met face-to-face or the steady, reliable, respectable, *dull* lord she had married? Sir or Adrian? It scarcely mattered that they were one and the same. This might well be his chance to find out. Fate had presented him with the perfect opportunity, and he would be a fool to pass it up.

"I shall make you a bargain, Max." The plan formulated in his head even as he said the words.

"A bargain." Max's brow rose. "I'm not sure I like the sound of that. If I recall, your bargains always left me with more work."

Adrian grinned and retook his seat. "You have become a most suspicious man."

"It goes with the position." His eyes narrowed. "And this bargain?"

"I shall make myself available to you in whatever manner you may need my services."

Max stared. "You're coming back to the department?"

Adrian shook his head. "In an advisory capacity only." He paused. "For now."

"And later?"

"We shall see."

Suspicion shone on Max's face. "There's more, isn't there?"

"There usually is in a bargain."

Max considered him carefully. "Good God, you have that look on your face."

"What look?"

"That look that says you have come up with something terrifying but brilliant."

Adrian grinned.

"I'm not going to like it, though, am I?"

"Oh, I don't know," Adrian said in a casual manner. "I suppose that depends on how much of a bureaucrat you've become."

"More than I appear, I would say." Max sighed. "And less than I should. What do you have in mind?"

"It's, well, a personal mission, as it were."

"Oh, that sounds good."

"I should like to resurrect Sir. Only in dealings with Evelyn, mind you," Adrian added.

"You want to become Sir again?" Max said slowly. "But only with your wife."

Adrian nodded.

Max studied him for a long moment. "Dare I ask why?"

"As I said, it's personal."

"Not if you're using my department, it's not."

"It used to be my department."

"Past tense." He paused. "However, I do have a certain amount of discretion. Aside from the questions surrounding the file, it's an oddly slow period. Won't last long, no doubt." He leaned forward in his chair and met his friend's gaze. "What did you have in mind?"

"I simply want to renew Sir's correspondence with Eve." Adrian shrugged. "There's little more than that."

"I see," Max said thoughtfully.

Annoyance surged through Adrian. "What, exactly, do you see?"

"I see a man who isn't at all certain of his wife's affections."

"Rubbish." Adrian scoffed. "I trust Evelyn implicitly."

"I never mentioned trust."

Adrian's jaw clenched. "I extrapolated."

"You thought she was seeing another man."

"She was." He drew his brows together. "You."

Max ignored him. "If I recall correctly, Sir's relationship with Eve, if only on paper, had begun to get somewhat heated."

"Not at all." Adrian scoffed.

Max stared for a long moment, then chuckled.

"What?" Adrian snapped.

"You, or perhaps I should say Sir, intend to seduce her, don't you?"

"I don't intend anything of the sort." Adrian rolled his gaze toward the ceiling as if Max's charge were completely mad and not exactly what he had planned.

"You intend to try."

"I trust my wife implicitly."

"You said that." Max's eyes narrowed thoughtfully. "Nonetheless, you want to find out if her heart is truly yours or if she still harbors some affection for . . ." Max grinned. "You."

Adrian snorted. "That's absurd."

Max raised a brow.

"Very well then, I admit it." He glared at his friend. "It's insane, isn't it?"

"That's probably the appeal. There's a fine line between incredible stupidity and brilliance. One you have walked in the past. But you've always been fond of those plans that can't possibly work and yet do. One can only hope this one works as well." Max drew a deep breath. "I do, however, feel compelled to be the voice of reason."

"Go on."

"You do realize, she might well be able to forgive you not telling her that you were Sir before your marriage, lies of omission and all that, but this, this is, well, deceit."

"Regardless of what name I use, I am still her husband," Adrian said in a lofty manner.

"You are trying to trick her."

"No, I'm not. I just want . . ." He shook his head. "This question has been in my head since the beginning. I imagine I only suspected her of infidelity because of my own doubts. But I have no doubt Sir's efforts will be unsuccessful," Adrian said firmly. "And that will be the end of it."

"You can lie to yourself but I know you too well." Max fixed him with a firm look. "I never thought I'd see the day that you, Lord Waterston, are afraid."

"I'm not afraid. I have more confidence in her than I have in myself." But deep down, somewhere in the vicinity of his heart, he was indeed afraid that, once again, he was wrong.

Max shook his head. "You do realize this might be your most dangerous game yet."

Adrian nodded. "I admit, it's a gamble."

"And if you lose?"

"I don't know. What I do know . . ." Adrian blew a long breath. "Is that, in this game, the stakes have never been higher."

Chapter 11

"Have you ever killed a man?"

Celeste looked up from her desk. "Not that I can recall," she said mildly. "I have inflicted well-deserved bodily harm on one or two, but I don't believe I have ever killed one."

"Pity." Evelyn resumed pacing the parlor floor.

"Was that merely a casual inquiry or do you have something in mind?"

"Both." It was a difficult decision. Did one strangle one's husband before dinner or after? Or perhaps in his sleep. No. Evelyn clenched her teeth. That would be too easy on him. Adrian needed to know why he was about to breathe his last.

Celeste raised a brow. "Dare I ask if the intended victim is Sir Maxwell or Lord W?"

"As I haven't heard from Max in days, he is not currently at the top of my list of men who deserve to be murdered." Evelyn narrowed her eyes. "My husband, on the other hand . . ."

Celeste stared. "What has he done?"

"I am still too furious to talk about it." She cast her friend an apologetic smile. "Even with you." It was hard to keep what she had learned from Beryl to herself. Adrian's actions were not merely infuriating but humiliating as well. How did one say aloud, even to one's closest friend, that one's husband didn't trust her? No, this was between Adrian and herself, at least for the moment. Besides, Celeste might have found a way to make Adrian's actions seem less objectionable than they were, although Evelyn couldn't imagine how.

"I see." Celeste watched her pace the length of the room. "I don't believe I have ever seen you this angry before."

"I have never been this angry before." And not merely angry but hurt. How could he think so little of her?

Looking at it rationally and knowing her own lack of patience, she decided against waiting until dinner. She had already waited entirely too long, but Adrian had been gone all afternoon. Little did he know that was a huge mistake in strategy on his part. It left her with several unoccupied hours in which to grow angrier, if that was at all possible.

"Indeed," Celeste said thoughtfully. "I'm not sure I have ever seen you angry at him at all."

"Nonsense, surely I . . ." Evelyn paused in midstep and stared at the other woman. "You're right. I can't recall ever having been angry with him before."

"Don't you think that's a bit odd?"

"Not at all." Evelyn scoffed. "We are perfectly suited to one another. There is scarcely an area in which we disagree. Occasionally, we debate but I don't remember so much as a minor argument."

"It was only a matter of time then."

"Apparently. In truth, our life together thus far has been practically perfect."

"One can't ask for more than a practically perfect life." Celeste cast her a pleasant smile.

"No, one can't." Evelyn stared at the other woman. "But he's certainly not perfect, you know."

"He does seem perfect."

"Hah." Evelyn scoffed. "He reads papers at breakfast while he eats. Sometimes I find myself watching him to see if he'll put his cup back in the saucer or spill it on the tablecloth."

Celeste gasped. "No, not that."

Evelyn continued to pace. "I sleep in his bed most nights, and mind you, I quite like waking up with him, but he sprawls diagonally across the entire bed and I spend the entire night clinging to the edge in fear of falling off."

"The fiend."

Evelyn paused and lowered her voice in a confidential manner. "Sometimes, I push him harder than necessary in an effort to get some room for myself."

Celeste bit back a grin.

Evelyn resumed pacing. "He thinks the servants are there for him alone and he leaves his clothes scattered at night, but he has everything on his desk arranged precisely to his liking. Woe be it to anyone who dares to move something." She stopped. "Did you know he keeps his desk drawer locked?"

"My God, how do you put up with it?"

"The man is incredibly arrogant and thinks he is right about everything. He is efficient in matters he cares about and completely disorganized in those he does not deem important. Regardless of whether or not anyone else considers them important." She shrugged. "Admittedly, I'm not perfect either."

Celeste sucked in a sharp breath. "No!"

Evelyn cast her a firm look. "That particular bit of sarcasm is becoming tiresome."

"My apologies." The amusement in Celeste's eyes belied her words.

"I am scarcely ever ready to leave to go anywhere in a timely manner and I know that drives him mad. I refuse to have lamb served at the table." She shuddered. "I cannot abide so much as the smell of it but Adrian loves the vile stuff. And apparently"—she wrinkled her nose—"I snore."

Celeste choked back a laugh.

"He finds it amusing." She sighed. "He seems to find most of my faults amusing. It's one of his more endearing qualities."

"He's sounding somewhat perfect again."

"He's not." She resumed pacing. "I am quite content with my life as I have always assumed Adrian was as well."

"No doubt."

"Content and happy."

Celeste nodded.

"I've never been this happy."

"And it's obvious."

"My life is everything I ever dreamed of." She crossed her arms over her chest. "Including a husband I adore."

"It does sound perfect."

"In most ways it is," she said firmly. "Both publicly and privately. Why, we are on every guest list. We support artistic endeavors and museums. I am involved with any number of charitable activities. Adrian is making a name for himself in Parliament. His family has become mine . . ." She widened her eyes with realization. "We don't sound perfect at all, do we? We sound . . . *expected*. Overly proper. Too respectable. We sound bloody well dull!"

Celeste's pleasant smile didn't waiver.

"Good Lord." And hadn't Adrian said life had been rather dull of late? He had also suggested that he acquire a mistress and she a lover. He had been teasing, of course, just to see if she had been listening. Still, what if there was a modicum of truth in what he had said? What if he did think his life was dull? Worse, what if he thought his wife was dull? Admittedly, he'd had an adventurous life before their marriage. What if now he wanted something more? Could Beryl possibly be right? Did he think she had a lover because he wanted one of his own? Or already had one?

Fear now mingled with anger and hurt. Was two years too long to be happy?

Stewart appeared at the open door and knocked.

"Yes?" Celeste asked.

"Lady Waterston wished to be informed when Lord Waterston had returned." He turned his attention to Evelyn. "His lordship is in the library, my lady." He paused. "But he did say he did not wish to be disturbed."

Celeste choked.

"Thank you, Stewart." Evelyn nodded in dismissal.

"I suspect Lord W is about to be disturbed," Celeste said as soon as the butler had gone.

"Very disturbed." If her husband wanted excitement in his life, she was more than willing to provide it to him.

"I assume whatever it is you're angry about has to do with Lady Dunwell's visit."

"She brought me some very interesting information."

"That you would prefer not to tell me."

"I should tell my husband first."

"Should I wish you good luck then?"

"I don't need luck," Evelyn said firmly. "But you might say a little prayer for his lordship." She nodded, took her leave, and headed to the library. And tried and failed to ignore the distressing thought lingering in the back of her head: what if two years was all anyone had?

Evelyn straightened her shoulders and pushed open the door to the library without knocking. Adrian sat writing at his desk, directly across the large room from the door. With floor-to-ceiling shelves flanking windows and panels hung with family portraits, this was his sanctuary. On those occasions when he was away, this was where she always felt his presence. Where she always felt closest to him.

"I said I didn't wish to be disturbed," he said without looking up.

"Even from me?"

He glanced up and smiled and her heart fluttered. She loved the way he smiled. "Never from you." He covered whatever it was he'd been writing and got to his feet. His brow furrowed. "You look upset. Is something wrong?"

"Should something be wrong?" she said in a cool manner.

"I don't think so," he said slowly. "But obviously something is."

"Is there something you wish to tell me?"

"Not that I can think of."

"Or perhaps . . ." She drew a deep breath. "Something you wish to ask me?"

"To ask you?" He stared at her for a moment, then realization crossed his face and he shook his head. "No, not a thing."

She arched a brow. "Really? Nothing at all?"

"No." He shook his head. "Nothing."

"How very interesting," she murmured and casually circled the room. So this was how he wished to play this. A knife twisted in her heart. They had never played games before, not with each other. They had always been candid in their dealings with one another. She paused by a bookshelf and flicked away a small feather clinging to a book's spine. No doubt left by the dusters used by the maids. She met his gaze directly. "I thought perhaps you wished to ask me about my lover."

His eyes widened. "Your what?"

"My lover." She crossed the room toward him. "You know, the one I was meeting at the Langham."

He winced, circled the desk, and stepped closer. "Evie—"

"Did you honestly think I would do that to you? To us?"

"I didn't want to think it but—"

"But what?" She glared.

"But . . ." He squared his shoulders. "It seemed a plausible answer to your manner of late."

"My manner?" A tiny voice in the back of her mind pointed out she had indeed been preoccupied of late, thanks to the department. She ignored it. Her voice rose. "My manner?"

"It was a mistake on my part," he said quickly.

"And not your only mistake."

"Perhaps not," he said cautiously.

"Perhaps?" She glared. "Then bursting into a hotel room to confront your errant wife, who has done nothing of any real significance to make you jump to such a conclusion, was not a mistake?"

He cringed. "Well, admittedly, as you weren't there, that was a mistake as well."

Fury widened her eyes. "Because I wasn't there?"

"Well, yes. No." He shook his head in confusion. "You're twisting my words."

"That's not all I'd like to twist!"

"I am sorry."

"For which part?" she snapped.

"All of it?" He did look somewhat unsure of himself. She'd never seen him uncertain before, and under other circumstances, she might have felt a twinge of pity for him. But not today.

"You didn't trust me!"

"And I am sorry for that." He nodded. "Yet another mistake."

"Not only did you not trust me but you managed to humiliate me as well."

He frowned. "I don't know why you would feel humiliated."

"You don't? Come now, Adrian, you're smarter than that." She stared in disbelief. "You don't think letting anyone, let alone Lady Dunwell, who has never been especially fond of me, know you think I'm having an affair is not humiliating?"

"I hadn't thought of it that way," he muttered.

"Apparently you weren't thinking at all."

"I was thinking all sorts of things."

"None of them accurate!" She drew a deep breath.

"Had you considered how many of our acquaintances regularly have tea at the Langham?"

"Well, no, I—"

"And who might have seen you there?"

He shook his head. "I don't think anyone saw me."

She narrowed her eyes.

"Not that I noticed," he added weakly.

"I'm surprised gossip isn't all over the city by now."

"Oh, I doubt Lady Dunwell will say anything," he said in what was obviously meant to be a consoling manner. "How did you find out?"

"That scarcely matters at this point." She waved off the question. "How could you, Adrian? How could you think I would ever betray you? How could you hold me up to public ridicule?"

"I lost my head." He ran his hand through his hair. "Your behavior, coupled with finding you in the library and then Radington appearing, he was obviously there to meet someone and it did seem—"

"I thought your jealousy that night was rather amusing." She huffed. "But this—it's inexcusable!"

"Oh, I think it's excusable—"

"Do you really?" She glared at him. "Beyond the rest of it, if I was going to have an affair, do you think I would be so foolish as to meet a man at a public hotel? A hotel with a popular tearoom?"

"When you put it that—"

"So not only do you believe I could be unfaithful but you think I'm an idiot as well."

"I have no doubts as to your intelligence," he said staunchly.

"Oh, I am a lucky woman." Sarcasm rang in her voice.

"As for the rest of it, I was wrong, I admit it. And I

am sorry." He paused. "But you must admit you do flirt quite a bit."

She gasped. "I do not."

"You most certainly do. I've seen you. Take, for example, dinner parties. Inevitably you have the man beside you smitten by the end of the second course."

"I can be most charming." She sniffed.

"Hah." He scoffed. "You are an outrageous flirt."

"Before we were married perhaps."

"Before we were married you—"

She sucked in a hard breath. "I what?"

The charge hung in the air between them.

"You weren't exactly . . ." He paused, obviously realizing what he was about to say and thinking better of it.

It was too late. "I wasn't exactly *virginal*? Is that what you were going to say?"

"But I didn't," he said quickly. "You must give me credit for that."

"You don't deserve credit for anything," she said sharply. "And isn't that the pot calling the kettle black. Your escapades were legendary."

"I'm a man," he said staunchly. "It's different for men."

"Is that what this is all about?" Disbelief and shock gripped her. She glared at him. "Because I was not a virgin when we wed, you think I'm willing to fall into bed with anyone?"

"No, of course not," he said firmly. "Not anyone."

"And yet you did."

"Yes, I did," he snapped. "And I apologize."

She glared at him. "And that's it? You apologize and I am supposed to forgive you? To go on as if nothing has happened?"

"That would be preferable." He glared back.

"I am furious with you!"

"I can see that."

"You lied to me!"

"I did not." He paused. "When?"

"When you said that nothing that happened before we were married was important. That our lives began when we met."

"That was years ago. But I did mean it," he added quickly.

"Not enough apparently." She narrowed her eyes. "Now, not only have you thrown my past in my face—"

"No, that's not—"

"But you have used it as an excuse for why you believed me to be unfaithful."

"I know it may appear that way . . ." He stepped toward her. "But your past was the last thing on my mind."

"I'm not sure if that's better or worse." She studied him for a long, hard moment. "Do you understand that I am not only angry but deeply hurt?"

Shock crossed his face as if she had slapped him hard. Pity, it hadn't occurred to her to do so. He shook his head. "I would never do anything to hurt you."

"And yet . . ." Without warning her throat tightened. She absolutely refused to cry in front of him. She was in the right. She was the injured party. She was the one who, in very many ways, was betrayed. "You have."

"Can you forgive me?" His gaze searched her face.

"Probably." She shook her head. "But not yet."

"I see." He studied her. "When?"

"I don't know." She drew a deep breath. "I am going to spend a great deal of your money."

He nodded. "If you wish."

"I'm going to refurbish the house Celeste resides in. And I'm going to do it in a grand and extravagant manner."

"I would expect nothing less."

"And while I am doing it . . ." She made the decision even as she said the words. "I intend to live there to oversee the work."

"You're going to move out?" he said carefully.

She nodded.

"For how long?"

Wasn't he going to stop her? She shrugged. "As long as is necessary."

He studied her for a long moment. "You're not talking about the refurbishing, are you?"

"It seems we have a question of trust between us now. Or rather lack of it. I have always trusted you and thought you trusted me—"

"I do!"

Then stop me! "Not enough obviously." She chose her words with care. "Trust, my love, needs to be nurtured. And when torn asunder, rebuilt."

"But I do trust you."

"Perhaps. But I'm not sure I trust you."

"I see." He nodded in a thoughtful manner. "It's not necessary for you to go."

Thank God. He was going to stop her.

"This is your home, you shouldn't have to leave." He drew a deep breath. "I can go to my club for the time being."

Her heart sank. "No." She shook her head. "It makes more sense for me to stay at my house, to oversee the work. You understand."

"I'm afraid so." He straightened his shoulders. "Very well then."

He was going to let her go? How could he? How could she go? But if she relented now, it was as much as saying there was nothing wrong in what he had done. How he had behaved. And worse, what he had thought of her. She had no intention of spending the rest of her life with a husband who wondered about her fidelity every time he looked at her.

Anger surged anew and she turned toward the door. Nor did she have any intention of having one of those marriages where husband and wife went their separate ways. No, she would leave him to simmer in his own guilt and remorse for a few days. Then, and only then, would she forgive him. But she would indeed forgive him eventually because no matter what else happened between them, she loved him with her whole heart and soul. She was now wagering everything she held dear that he loved her every bit as much.

She reached the door and looked back at him. "One more thing in regards to my intelligence."

"Evie, I never meant—"

"While there is not a man alive I want to be with more than you, if I ever were to have an affair, I am smart enough to make certain you never know."

He frowned. "Is that a threat?"

"No, my dear darling husband." She met his gaze firmly. "It's a promise."

She was magnificent.

In spite of the heavy weight settled in the pit of his stomach, Adrian wanted to grin with the sheer delight of her. He'd seen her in the throes of passion, but this was passion of a different sort and she was amazing. God, he wanted her. How many men felt that way about their own wives? And she was his. His jaw tightened. And he intended to keep her.

He returned to his desk and sat down. She was right, of course, about all of it. He couldn't blame her for being angry and embarrassed and hurt. He was indeed an idiot. He hadn't trusted her when he should have. He should have realized right from the beginning that she was again working for the department. Certainly she hadn't told him but then she couldn't really. And she hadn't lied to him unless one counted those irksome lies of omission. It was in his best interest not to consider those important, given all that he had never confided in her.

And he never, never should have brought up her past. He winced. Especially since he knew everything there was to know about her, right down to the names of the few lovers she had had. The department had always been thorough in investigating the backgrounds of its agents.

He pulled out the paper he'd been writing on and studied his words thus far.

My Dearest Eve,

It was best that they would not share the same roof while he put his plan into effect. It would make it all much easier. As much as he had planned to ease into this seduction of words, it seemed wiser now to move quickly. He could not live without her in his house, in his bed, for long. And while Sir's efforts would be on paper, Adrian would do all he could to win his wife's forgiveness.

As stupid as he knew this deception was, it was perhaps the nature of men or the nature of love to continue under full steam straight into what could be unmitigated disaster. But he knew himself and he couldn't have this question hanging over him, hanging over them, for the rest of their lives. Until he knew for certain that her husband was the true love of her life, he would always wonder who was first in her heart. This was something she might well never forgive him for although he could argue the truth: the man who was trying to seduce her and the man she had married were one and the same. Still, she would not see it that way. Not that she would ever find out.

Unless, of course, she chose Sir. That was a bridge he would cross if he came to it.

Max was right. This was the most dangerous game he had ever played.

Chapter 12

Celeste straddled him, pinning his arms with her legs, and clapped her hand over his mouth. Maxwell came awake at once, his body tensed beneath her, poised to throw her off.

"It's me," she said to forestall his immediate reaction.

He relaxed beneath her and she removed her hand. Even in the hazy light of early dawn, she could see the gleam in his eye. "Who?"

"You know full well who." She kissed him quick and hard. "Wicked man."

"Wicked? Who is straddling whom? Not that I mind." He grinned. "This is a delightful way to awaken."

"I'm not here to delight you."

"No?" Max grabbed her and rolled over until she lay pinned beneath him, then nuzzled her neck. "Are you sure?"

She shivered. Dear Lord, the man did things to her. "I am."

"You don't sound sure." His lips murmured against her skin. "Perhaps then *I* should delight *you*."

She tried and failed to stifle a soft moan.

He chuckled. "What do you want to wager I can change your mind?"

"Goodness, Max." She did hate the breathless quality in her voice, but she didn't seem to be able to do anything about it. "I would never wager on something I am certain to lose."

"You are mad about me, you know."

I am. "Nonsense. Any woman with even a modicum of sense would not be so foolish as to be anything about you, let alone mad." She pushed him away and scrambled off the bed. "I need to talk."

"First?"

She ignored him. "I don't have much time."

"We don't need much time." He grabbed her and pulled her back onto the bed. "And you always like it when we are hard and fast and eager and hungry—"

"Stop that, you annoying beast." She struggled halfheartedly against him. Unfortunately, the man was right. She did love it when he took her hard and fast. Or when she took him with a hunger only he had ever ignited in her. He made her as insatiable for him as he was for her. And they were always ready for one another. Even now, the feel of his naked body against her fully clothed one was enough to make her ache with desire.

"You don't mean that." His hands slipped under her cloak. "I suspect I can make you scream my name in—"

"Stop it at once!" She wrenched out of his arms and slid off the bed, quickly stepping out of his reach. "I need to talk to you, and you will wish to hear this."

"There's nothing I really wish to hear except the way you moan—"

"Max!"

"Very well then." He heaved a resigned sigh. "What is it?"

"You have to do something."

"I did offer to—"

"About Evelyn." She sighed. "She has left Lord W."

"What do you mean, she has left Lord W?" Max was abruptly alert.

"Just what I said. She has moved out of the house."

"Permanently?"

"Good God, I hope not, as she is now residing with me."

"Well, that is awkward."

"Isn't it, though?" She pinned him with a firm look. "And you have to do something about it."

"Why do I have to do something about it?" he said cautiously.

"Because one could easily argue that it's your fault."

His brow furrowed. "How is it my fault?"

"Admittedly, it's not entirely your fault, but some of it is. At least, it started with you." She positioned a chair closer to the bed, far enough away to be out of his reach, and sat down. She'd never noticed before how badly in need of refurbishing the chair was, but then it was usually covered with his discarded clothing or hers. "She told me everything last night right after she swept into my house with at least a dozen bags, only enough for a few days, mind you, her maid, and an additional two other servants."

"I thought it was her house," he said mildly.

"Of course it is but it's my *home*. And she has in-

vaded. Which she has every right to do," she added.
"She is my dearest friend and I am pleased that she
turns to me but . . ."

His brow rose. "But?"

"But her constant presence will be extremely inconvenient."

"Incon—" His eyes widened. "Oh, you mean for
you and I?"

She glared. "It's not only about you, Max."

"I doubt that." He grinned.

"There are other things in my life, besides you, that
will be complicated with Evelyn underfoot. I quite
value my privacy, you know." She nodded. "And yes, it
will be difficult, if not impossible, to slip away in the
evening without having to lie to her. I am still trying to
avoid lying."

"Damnation, I hadn't considered that." He thought
for a moment. "But again, how is this my fault?"

"She confessed all to me last night." Celeste leaned
closer and met his gaze. "Her manner has been different of late because of this new assignment of yours.
She can't get it out of her head. Not the least bit surprising really. I hadn't noticed it, but then I also knew
what was afoot. At any rate, her change in manner, and
apparently an encounter with Lord Radington in Lord
Dunwell's library, led Lord W to assume that Evelyn
was having an affair."

"Did it?" Max said in what Celeste had always
thought of as his department voice. Cool, calm, and
neutral. How very odd.

"I'm not sure how he discovered this, but somehow
he learned that Lord Radington was meeting a woman
in a room at the Langham Hotel."

"Excellent spot for tea," Max murmured.

"Not only tea apparently." Celeste nodded. "Suffice it to say that when Lord W burst in upon them, the lady he surprised with Lord Radington was not his wife but . . ." She paused for effect. "Lady Dunwell."

Max laughed. "I would have liked to have seen that."

Celeste bit back a grin of her own. "I have no doubt it was most amusing unless you were one of the parties involved." She sobered. "The man has been unbelievably stupid. Evelyn naturally was upset. Furious, really, that he would think her capable of such a thing, and they had a dreadful row. The first, I think, since they married."

"And she is now residing with you."

"She's planning to refurbish my house."

"Her house," he said pointedly.

"Yes, yes. She owns the house and pays the servants. She doesn't want to sell it, and she prefers to have someone she trusts living in it rather than strangers." She got to her feet and circled the room restlessly. "I like the house the way it is." She'd paid no more attention to his one-room flat through the years than she had to his chair. She usually had other things on her mind. Glancing around now, it struck her as a typical bachelor's abode. It was large enough, which might well be the best thing one could say about it. "She spent the evening directing me to send notes to paper hangers and painters and plasterers and anyone else she could think of. I am to make certain they are delivered first thing this morning." She twisted her hands together. "She was also talking about what great fun we will have together living in the same house. We will play cards and games and attend the theater together and read aloud and . . ." She shook her head. "I've never seen her this way." She stared at him. "I don't want to read aloud."

"Oh, I'm sure she won't force—"

"This was only the first night, Max. I don't even want to think what tomorrow will hold," she said darkly. "And the day after. And the day after that. You have to do something."

"What do you expect me to do?"

"I don't know but you are the head of the department. You are all-knowing, all-seeing, all-powerful." She paused. "Or so you would like me to believe."

"I do try," he said in a modest manner.

"And you started this. You needn't have called her back to the department."

"I had my reasons."

"Perhaps." She crossed her arms over her chest. "But she hasn't heard from you in days."

He shrugged. "There's been no need, nothing for her to do really. Not at the moment."

A thought struck her and she widened her eyes. "Can't you talk to him then?"

"To who?"

"Lord W. You know him, don't you?"

"I am acquainted with Lord Waterston." Caution underlay his words. "However, I would hardly presume to tell a man, with whom I only exchange the briefest of greetings, how to manage his wife."

"Manage?" She raised a brow. "Surely you didn't mean to say manage?"

"No, of course not." He shook his head. "Never."

"No doubt." She drew her brows together. "I'm not suggesting you tell him how to *manage* her. I daresay Evelyn has never been easily *managed*, and you, of all people, should know that."

"Evelyn is a practical woman. I am sure she will come to her senses soon."

"Maxwell! *She* did nothing—"

"Or rather *he* will come to his senses soon," he said quickly. "Accompanied by copious apologies, much groveling, begging for forgiveness, and all that."

"Her work for you needs to end and soon. Then she can return to her usual manner. Her husband will have nothing to arouse his suspicions. And my privacy will be restored."

"I suspect it will be at an end soon."

"Oh?" She studied him curiously. "Are you closer to finding your file?"

"I practically have it within grasp as we speak. However, I will no longer be directing Evelyn's activities. I am turning this matter over to . . ." He paused. "Sir."

She stared. "Evelyn said he was no longer with the department."

He shrugged. "He's back."

"Bloody hell," Celeste said under her breath.

"Not exactly the reaction I was expecting."

"Evelyn was always intrigued by Sir. If she hadn't decided she'd had enough of this life . . ."

"What?"

"Nothing." She shook her head. "It's no more than an impression I've always had." She cast him a wry smile. "There is something quite intriguing and rather romantic about a man one only knows through his words. He could be anyone you imagine him to be."

"He issued you orders on occasion. Did you *imagine* him?"

She laughed.

He gasped. "You did!"

"I am a weak woman, Max." She moved closer and sank down on the edge of the bed. "With a wicked imagination."

"As long as that wicked imagination is reserved for me . . ." He pulled her into his arms. "I suppose I can live with it."

She slipped her arms around his neck and pressed her lips to his. For a long endless moment, even her imagination could not compete with the feel of his lips against hers, the heat of his body next to hers, the warm, rich, sleep-soaked scent of him. In the back of her mind she wondered what it would be like to wake up with him every morning.

Without warning, he pulled away. "I have been thinking."

"Oh no." She gasped with mock dismay. "Not that."

He ignored her. "I have given some thought to our discussion when you were last here."

"What discussion was that?"

"About making an honest woman of you."

She raised a brow. "Are you talking about marriage?"

He nodded.

"If you cannot say the word, Max, it seems to me there is little to discuss."

"I can say the word," he said firmly. "I've been thinking about your comment that you are not the type of woman I should marry."

"Oh?"

"I think it's rubbish." He met her gaze directly. "I fully intend to marry whomever I wish."

"Bravo, Max. I have never been prouder."

His brows pulled together. "You are deliberately being obtuse, aren't you?"

"Not at all." She stood, found his dressing gown and tossed it at him, then turned away. It was best for her own sense of purpose not to watch him dress. "You say you intend to marry whomever you wish and I think that's admirable. Impractical perhaps but admirable."

"I don't especially want to be admirable," he muttered behind her. "What I want is you."

She shrugged. "And you have me."

"Not entirely." He slid his arms around her waist and pulled her back against him. "Not in the eyes of the rest of the world." He rested his chin on her shoulder. "Celeste, would you do me the honor—"

She laughed. "Don't say it, Max."

"Why not?"

"Because right now, this morning, this minute." She shook her head. "This is certainly not the time and definitely not the place."

"I should think—"

"Besides, right now, this morning, this minute . . ." She pushed out of his arms and swiveled to face him. "You would not like my answer."

He stared. "I wouldn't?"

"I hope not."

"So is it me or is it marriage?"

She chose her words with care. "I have no desire to marry at the moment."

"Which does not fully answer my question." He studied her curiously. "Don't you want marriage? A family? Children and all that?"

"Oh, darling, but I do have children."

His scoffed. "I know everything there is to know about you. You have no children."

"Correction, Max," she said lightly. "You knew

everything there was to know when I worked for the department."

"We've been together for three years. How . . ." He studied her suspiciously. "Are they my children?"

She laughed. "I suspect you would have noticed if I had been with child."

"Then whose—"

"They are mine," she said firmly. "And I intend to say nothing more on the subject."

He stared.

"Speechless, Max?" She chuckled. "I never imagined such a thing."

"I have simply never thought of you as a mother." He frowned. "And I didn't realize you kept secrets from me."

"We are even then as I have never thought of you as a father." She paused. "Or a husband. Oh, and one of the differences between us is that I know you keep secrets from me."

He considered her for a long, thoughtful moment. "Perhaps it's time everyone tells everyone the truth. About everything."

"Oh dear. Are you trying to be the voice of reason?"

"Apparently."

She shook her head. "It doesn't suit you."

"Good." He heaved a relieved sigh. "I would find it extremely tiresome." His eyes narrowed. "This discussion is not at an end."

"I didn't think it was. Good morning, Max." She stepped closer, kissed him quickly, then slipped out of his flat before he could stop him. She needed to return to her house before the servants were about. Besides, it was pointless to argue. When the time was right, she would tell him about her children. And perhaps she would even consider marriage.

But whether he realized it or not, regardless of whether he cared, there would be repercussions to marriage with her. His family and friends would be appalled that not only had he married someone of questionable birth but she had been an actress as well. She wasn't sure he loved her enough to withstand that.

Indeed, right now, she didn't know if he loved her at all.

Chapter 13

"Where did all these people come from?" Celeste stared. "I was scarcely gone any time at all."

Evelyn looked up from her spot on the floor of Celeste's parlor, in the midst of fabric selections from three different linen drapers. "Goodness, Celeste, you sent for them yourself. This morning, remember?"

"Yes, well . . ." Celeste looked around her parlor in what surely was astonishment and not dismay. "I simply didn't expect all this so quickly."

"In the notes you delivered, I said I wished to proceed immediately. And as I used the words that strike joy into any merchant's heart . . ." She lowered her voice in a confidential manner. " 'Spare no expense.' This"—she waved at the room—"is the result. Over there is Mr. Henderson." She nodded at the man measuring a window. "And Mr. Wendell." Who was laying wallpaper samples over the sofa. "And Mr. Bryce." The carpet merchant was pacing off the room. "And then there's—oh, I forget the names of the others. But there are measurements being taken all over the house."

"Don't you think you should give this refurbishing further consideration?" Celeste said carefully.

"I don't see why." She got to her feet and dusted off her skirts. "I daresay, nothing in this house has been changed since my parents were alive. It's past time really." She cast a satisfied look at the activity in the parlor. "I have been remiss in not doing this before now."

"Then we should be grateful to Lord W since he is the impetus behind it all."

"And I am indeed grateful. There is nothing like spending one's husband's money in a relatively carefree manner that is most fulfilling. Even when the husband in question has always been generous." Still, Adrian used words like *economize* and *unnecessary extravagance* and *frivolous indulgence* just often enough to make this even more satisfying than she had expected.

"Even so." Celeste looked around. "You don't want to make a rash decision. Perhaps it would be wise to proceed a bit slower."

"Nonsense." Evelyn waved off the objection. "Besides I don't know how long I shall be here, and I would hate to leave you with all this undecided."

"Thank you," Celeste said weakly.

Evelyn studied her friend. Admittedly, she had not been quite as enthusiastic as Evelyn last night when Evelyn had announced her plans to completely refurbish the house but she would come around. Oh, it would be somewhat messy and inconvenient, but the end result would be well worth it. Especially since it would keep Evelyn's mind from dwelling on her husband. As it had from the moment she decided to leave, the moment he didn't stop her. And very nearly every moment since.

"Did you drop the schedule off for Adrian?" They had any number of social events upcoming, and Evelyn had no desire to attend without her husband. The last thing she wanted was to cause gossip by appearing without Adrian. But begging off from any of them would create more speculation and gossip than attending without him. There were no true secrets in London society. Fortunately, the schedule was far sparser at this time of year than it would be come spring.

"Don't you think your social obligations are something you should have talked to him about in person?"

"Not at all." Evelyn shrugged in a blithe manner. "Besides, I liked the idea of sending him a schedule with our commitments for the next month." She cast her friend a wicked smile. "It will make him wonder just how long I intend to be gone."

"And you think that's wise?"

"I think it's brilliant." In truth, she expected to be here no more than a few days before her husband insisted she return because he could not live without her. She refused to consider that he might not come to that realization.

Upon reflection, it did seem that he was not nearly as contrite as he should have been for not trusting her. As if his lack of trust wasn't especially important. Nor had he done anything to stop her from leaving. Not that he would have been able to, but he hadn't so much as protested. It was already early afternoon and she hadn't heard a single word from him. She thought surely he would have begun a campaign to win her back by now. Flowers, jewelry, even a heartfelt note of continuing apology. But thus far, there was nothing at all. Had she made a dreadful mistake by leaving? It was all most distressing. Still, she couldn't help thinking that it was better to know how little she meant to him after two years of marriage than after ten or twenty.

No. She dashed the thought from her head. She knew him as well as she knew herself. He did love her as she loved him. She couldn't possibly be wrong about that. He was no doubt simply giving her time to come to her senses. Her jaw tightened. Soon enough he would realize that bringing her to her senses would take considerable effort on his part.

"Did you take care of your errands?"

Celeste nodded. She hadn't volunteered exactly what her errands entailed nor had Evelyn asked her. Simply because they were living in the same house didn't give Evelyn the right to pry into Celeste's affairs. Celeste had always valued her privacy, and Evelyn valued her friendship too much to pry. Celeste would tell her what she wished her to know. That, obviously, was the difference between friendship and marriage. Evelyn would never doubt her friend's loyalty nor would she ever distrust her.

"We need to talk," Celeste said firmly and turned to address the others. "You there, Mr. Henderson, Mr. Wendell, Mr. Bryce." The gentlemen turned their attention to Celeste at once, but then, Celeste had a most commanding manner when she wished. Part of which could certainly be attributed to her spectacles and the way she wore her hair. "I know you are all eager to return to your respective places of business, where I am certain you will each devise an excellent list of suggestions and proposals for Lady Waterston's consideration."

The men traded glances. Mr. Henderson cleared his

throat. "I beg your pardon, miss, but we understood Lady Waterston wished to proceed as quickly as possible."

"And she does," Celeste said. "However, I am certain that you understand as well, the refurbishing of an entire house cannot be accomplished without due consideration. As she is contemplating a considerable expenditure, I suspect you would not want her to make rash decisions that she might later regret." She paused significantly. "While she would be more than willing to recommend to her vast number of friends and acquaintances work she is pleased with, I daresay she would similarly not fail to mention if she were to be disappointed."

"No, no, of course not," the three men murmured almost as one.

Evelyn resisted the urge to grin. Celeste was very good at this sort of thing.

"At this point, any final decisions on carpets or draperies or wallpaper is premature. Why, Lady Waterston has yet to decide on something as essential as which colors she prefers in which room."

"I was thinking about crimson in here," Evelyn murmured. "Or a deep rose perhaps . . ."

"Such decisions, of course, will be contingent on what you present to her." Celeste herded them toward the hall and nodded to the butler. "Hendricks, do gather whoever else is here and see them to the door."

"As you wish, miss." The butler nodded.

"And tell them Lady Waterston will be awaiting word from them as to their refurbishing ideas and concerns and, of course, the costs involved."

"Of course, miss."

Celeste cast the gentlemen her brightest smile. "I

fully expect that we shall hear from you very soon." With that, she ushered them through the parlor doors, closing them firmly behind the men.

"You do that very well," Evelyn said in a wry manner.

"It's my job." She leveled Evelyn a firm look. "I consider a critical responsibility of my position to be protecting you from yourself. And I have no intention of shirking my duties."

"Nonsense." Evelyn laughed, pushed aside the wall-paper samples, and sank down on the sofa. "I don't need protection. Not from myself and particularly not from merchants."

"Not under ordinary circumstances perhaps, but right now, as your goal seems to be to inflict as much financial damage as you can on Lord W's accounts, someone needs to keep your head on your shoulders. Especially as your actions are predicated on anger and hurt."

"Nonsense," Evelyn said again, her voice weaker than before. "Redoing this house is long overdue."

"Perhaps, although I have never noticed a problem."

"I think it's become somewhat worn."

"I prefer the word *comfortable*." Celeste glanced around the parlor. "I'm rather fond of it."

"You deserve better."

"About that." Celeste picked up the wallpaper samples, placed them on a table, then returned to sit down beside Evelyn. "You have never allowed me to pay rent—"

"I consider this part of your salary."

"And you pay the wages for the staff—"

"Come now, Celeste." Evelyn scoffed. "There's only Hendricks and Mrs. O'Mally, who is both housekeeper and cook, and one lone maid. It's a meager excuse for a staff."

"Nonetheless—"

"My husband is an eminently practical man, recent events notwithstanding." Evelyn leaned toward her friend. "If you did not live here, he would no doubt press for me to sell this house as we certainly don't need it. But this is the only thing I have left of my parents and I shall never sell it. As for the servants . . ." She shook her head. "They consider this their home. I grew quite fond of them in the years when I resided here. You know how difficult it is to find a new position. I simply could not let them go."

"Still, I should—"

"I do not wish to let this house to strangers as my guardian did nor do I wish for it to sit unoccupied." Her gaze slid around the room. Even now, she wished she remembered this room, this house. But she scarcely remembered her parents let alone where they had lived. "There is something about an empty house that has always struck me as sad and forlorn. I would hate to think of this house as being alone and unloved. You, dear friend, are doing me a great favor by living here."

"You have my thanks nonetheless." Celeste studied her for a long moment. "In the spirit of our friendship, might I suggest you start with one room rather than create massive upheaval throughout the entire house? As you said, you don't know how long you will be here."

"That makes a certain amount of sense, I suppose." She stood, crossed to the table, and studied the wallpaper. "But I need something to fill my time." She selected two samples and moved to the far wall. "I find leaving one's husband, even temporarily, leaves one feeling restless."

"You have charity work and committees of the dozens of organizations you belong to. You scarcely ever have a moment free."

"And yet I am feeling remarkably free at the moment," she muttered. Damn the man anyway. She held a damask striped pattern in shades of ivory and scarlet against the wall and glanced at Celeste.

"Too formal, I think," Celeste said. "I suspected as much."

Evelyn held up another sample. This one was entwined vines and leaves and trees in blues and greens.

"Oh, I like that."

Evelyn nodded. "So do I." She glanced at the other woman. "Suspected what?"

"That you would need something to occupy your time and your mind while you wait for Lord W to come crawling on his knees."

"I don't want him to come crawling on his knees." She scoffed. "Although I do like the way that sounds." She sighed. "If Max would give me further instructions, at least that would keep me busy."

"No doubt you will hear something soon."

"I do hope so. At least living here, I won't have to mislead Adrian as to my activities."

"That is indeed a benefit." Celeste drew a deep breath. "Might I make another suggestion? That instead of refurbishing the house, you refurbish yourself?"

Evelyn drew her brows together. "What do you mean?"

"I mean you should commission a new wardrobe."

"My wardrobe is more than acceptable, thank you."

Celeste raised a brow.

"Admittedly, I haven't had a new gown made in some time."

"And didn't you say you wished you'd had something new to wear to the Dunwells' reception rather than something that had been seen on more than one occasion?"

"I did, didn't I?" She shook her head. "It was most annoying."

"And aren't there several events on the schedule you had me deliver that scream for a new gown, including a gala Venetian masquerade?"

Evelyn waved away her comment. "Oh, I have a costume."

Celeste ignored her. "Beyond your obvious need for a complete new wardrobe—"

"It will be dreadfully expensive," she murmured. Not that expense was a consideration at the moment. Indeed, dreadfully expensive was most appealing.

"If the purpose of this exercise is to punish Lord W for his transgressions—"

"I'm not sure *punish* is the right word—"

"Then it seems to me, as Lord W has not been in this house since your marriage, while he will see the bills for the refurbishment, it will scarcely have a lasting impact. However—"

"However, if I am wearing my purchases, it will certainly remind him of the error of his ways every time he sees something new. And remind him as well of what he has that he does not wish to lose." Evelyn grinned. "That is brilliant, Celeste."

"Just another one of my duties." Her friend returned her grin. "While I was out, I made an appointment for later today with your favorite dressmaker. She has the latest patterns from Paris and is most eager to get started." Celeste shrugged. "I might have mentioned that you wished to spare no expense."

"Excellent." Evelyn laughed. "Still, this house does need work, but one room at a time is a good idea." She moved back to the table, placed the samples in her hand with the others, then studied them all. "I would hate to inflict the result of rash decisions upon you. After all, you are the one who lives here."

A brief knock sounded. Celeste moved to the door and pulled it open.

"There was a delivery for Lady Waterston." Hendricks strode into the room bearing a large bouquet of red roses in a vase. Relief washed through Evelyn. "I took the liberty of putting these in water for you." He set the vase on a table, and presented a card with a flourish. "My lady."

"Thank you, Hendricks." Evelyn took the card, waited until the butler had left the room, then turned to her friend with a satisfied smile. "I had begun to think my husband had decided not to pursue my forgiveness."

"Obviously you were wrong."

"Thank goodness," she said with a sigh. "I was starting to wonder . . . never mind. There are times when one is grateful to be wrong."

Celeste moved to the flowers and inhaled. "There is nothing like the smell of roses. And two dozen will fill the room with this delicious scent in no time."

"I have always been fond of red roses. But of course, he knows that." She opened the envelope, pulled out the card, and read the sparsely worded note. Her heart sank.

"Well?" Impatience sounded in Celeste's voice. "Is

he appropriately apologetic? Does he declare his undying love? Is he begging you to return home?"

"Not exactly," Evelyn said slowly, her gaze still on the well-remembered handwriting on the card in her hand. "These aren't from Adrian."

"Then who?"

She looked up and met her friend's gaze. "They're from Sir."

Chapter 14

Celeste's eyes widened. "Sir? Are you certain?"

"Of course I'm certain," Evelyn snapped. Disappointment sharpened her voice. "My apologies. I didn't expect this." She drew a calming breath. "Aside from the fact that it's signed *Sir*, I would recognize his writing anywhere. He favors his left hand, you know." Evelyn studied the note.

"You said he was no longer with the department."

"Apparently he has returned," she murmured. Good Lord, she never imagined she'd read a note from Sir again. At once, she was thrust back to the days before Adrian when a note from Sir would stir excitement within her and more than a little curiosity. Even, on occasion, a touch of desire, a measure of longing for someone she would never meet, never know.

"Well," Celeste said. "Are you going to tell me what it says or shall I snatch it out of your hand and read it myself?"

"It's brief and is in the manner of an introduction or

a reintroduction, I suppose." She read aloud, "'*My dear Eve, I have returned to my previous position to take charge of the current situation. You will receive your instructions from me from this point forward.*'" She glanced up. "There's little more than that."

Celeste's eye's narrowed. "But there is more, isn't there?"

She nodded and continued to read. "'*I must confess, I have missed you and look forward to renewing our acquaintance.*'"

"And?"

"And it's signed: '*Yours with great affection, Sir.*'" She blew a long breath. "Oh, this is just perfect."

"Perfect?"

"The last thing I need right now, the last thing I want, now or ever, is Sir back in my life." She paced the room.

Celeste watched her carefully. "You were rather taken with him."

"Of course I was taken with him. What living, breathing woman wouldn't be taken with him? He was mysterious and exciting and courageous. In my mind, he could be anything I wished him to be. A great hero." She rolled her gaze toward the ceiling. "A great lover."

"I see."

"No, dear, you don't." She wrapped her arms around herself and continued to pace, trying to find the right words. "I was taken with him in the way in which one is taken with the swashbuckling hero of a romantic novel. Like d'Artagnan or Sir Lancelot or Edmond Dantes or Robin Hood. One can dream about him all one wishes, but he has no more substance than a fictional character." She met the other woman's gaze.

"He's not there to take you in his arms. To tell you all will be well. To kiss you under the mistletoe in front of his entire family. To laugh with you and cry with you and make certain you know, even if he never says the words, that he will hold your hand until the moment you breathe your last. This"—she held out Sir's note— "is nothing more than a game. Great affection—hah! I don't want his great affection. I want . . ."

"You want your husband," Celeste said simply.

"Yes, I do." She paused. "The beast."

Celeste stared. "You really do love him, don't you?"

"It's not very fashionable, is it?" She managed a wan smile. "Did you doubt it?"

"*Doubt* is not the right word exactly." Celeste thought for a moment. "He came into your life at precisely the right time, when you needed someone solid and respectable and secure. It did seem that he was somewhat, oh, convenient."

"He was in many ways. But there is so much more to it than that." Her mind wandered back to the days when she had first met Adrian. "The first time I met him, the first time we danced, it was as if we had known each other forever. As if he was the one I had been waiting for my entire life. Halves of a whole, as it were. Nothing in my life has ever seemed so right, so destined if you will, as being with him."

"Oh my." Celeste shook her head. "I must say, I find I am quite jealous."

Evelyn cast her a wry smile. "You, too?"

"One could argue . . ." Celeste chose her words with care. "That great love can lead a man to great stupidity."

"I have never doubted his feelings for me. How could he doubt mine?"

"Men are idiots," Celeste said firmly. "One never knows what they are really thinking if indeed they are thinking at all. They claim to be rational, sensible creatures and yet they will jump to all sorts of irrational conclusions."

"Why hasn't he sent me a note? Why hasn't he asked me to come home?"

"You've barely been gone a full day and you are well aware of his schedule. He's hardly had time to miss you."

"Nonetheless"—she waved at the roses—"these should be from my husband. Not from a . . . a work of fiction."

"Hopefully, with Sir back, this business with the department will be at an end quickly."

"One can hope." Evelyn glanced at the card in her hand. "You know, toward the end, these notes between Sir and I became quite flirtatious."

"It does seem bad timing that he has entered your life again now. Given the situation with Lord W." Celeste studied her cautiously. "Do you fear you will be tempted?"

"Tempted? By a man I have never met in person nor ever expect to meet?" She shook her head. "No. In my last note to him I said he was a road not taken. I shall always feel a certain curiosity about him, but I have no regrets as to the path I have chosen. There is only one man I want in my life. And if Sir were to come to my door right this very moment, tall and dashing and handsome and everything I ever thought he might be, that is exactly what I would tell him."

"Tall and dashing and handsome?" Celeste grinned. "Then I would be grateful if you passed him on to me."

Evelyn laughed. "Agreed. And you may consider these roses yours as well. I want nothing to do with them. Now." She set her jaw firmly. "Apparently, I have an appointment with a woman who is more than willing to assist me in unnecessary extravagances and frivolous indulgences. At an outrageous price." She cast her friend a wicked smile. "I am quite looking forward to it."

Celeste laughed.

"Oh, and while I'm gone, I would be most appreciative if you could recall the details of the bodily harm you have inflicted on men in the past." Evelyn narrowed her eyes. "That just might be a good thing to know."

"You have to apologize," Max said firmly.

"I have." A cool note sounded in Adrian's voice. The two men sat in a secluded corner in the dim recesses of Adrian's club, a far better place to meet than at the Mayfair house. The old friends had once spent a great deal of time here and no one would comment, or even notice, Sir Maxwell Osgood and Lord Waterston engaged in quiet conversation late in the afternoon.

"Not well apparently. Your wife has moved out."

"I do not intend to allow that to continue for long. It is nothing more than a temporary state of affairs." Not temporary enough, however. Evie had barely been gone a day and already he missed hearing her voice, her laughter, having her beside him in his bed. He found it difficult to sleep if she was not there. Although her absence was not the only thing interfering with his sleep. This scheme he had devised, and all the ways it could go horribly wrong, preyed on his mind. Plus, there was the fact that, depending upon the strictness of one's own moral standards, his plot could be considered the tiniest bit wrong. "How do you know about that?"

"It's my job, remember? I know all sorts of interesting things." Max raised his glass. "And any number of things that are quite dull."

"All-knowing, all-powerful," Adrian said under his breath.

"You know better than anyone that's not true." He chuckled. "Although I do like to maintain certain illusions."

"Anything new on the file?"

"Since yesterday? Come now. Something like this takes time." He paused. "Our man at Fenwick's says the file simply appeared behind the counter. He saw nothing out of the ordinary. I daresay, anyone could have put it there."

"So until there is a new development, we are at a standstill?"

"Frustrating to be sure, but it is the nature of the game."

"Always has been." Adrian sipped his whiskey.

"Regardless, I hate waiting for someone else to make the next move." Max studied him over the rim of his glass. "Speaking of the next move, what is yours? Or should I say Sir's?"

"Sir sent Eve roses and a note."

"Did he?" Max nodded in a thoughtful manner. "And what about Adrian? Did he send flowers to his wife?"

Adrian stared.

"A token of his affection perhaps?" Max's brow furrowed. "A letter of abject apology declaring his love and vowing to make her happy for the rest of her days?"

"Bloody hell," Adrian muttered.

"Perhaps you are incredibly stupid after all." Max snorted. "What were you thinking?"

"I was thinking about how to pursue her as Sir without being too obvious. Damnation." He tossed back the rest of his whiskey and signaled for another. "It completely slipped my mind that ongoing groveling was called for."

"By her husband."

"Yes, by her husband," he snapped. "Although I do not grovel."

"You know even the most loyal of women, even those most in love with their husbands, might be lured into temptation by a mysterious stranger if their husband is not appropriately attentive."

"I fully intend to be appropriately attentive, I have simply not yet begun." He winced to himself. This failure on his part was a huge mistake. How could he have been so stupid? He didn't want to force her into the arms of another man, even if the other man was him. "It's probably best to give her a day to realize her anger was out of all proportion to my crime."

"Oh yes, because that's what women do." Sarcasm sounded in Max's voice. "They come to such realizations without any assistance. It's not as if they dwell on a man's transgressions, exaggerating misdeeds out of all proportion, although in your case I am not sure exaggeration is possible. No, that would be irrational."

"Evelyn has always been a rational sort," Adrian said under his breath.

Max stared in disbelief. "You used to be so clever when it came to women. Good God, man, what has happened to you?"

"Marriage is what has happened to me." Adrian clenched his teeth. "It makes fools out of even the most intelligent of men. I tell you, Max, it is far easier to deal with a flock of women than one single wife."

"Only if one loves the wife in question."

"That does indeed complicate everything." He thought for a moment. "I shall have flowers delivered as soon as I return home. I have a conservatory, you know. And first thing tomorrow I shall select an appropriate—no—an extravagant piece of jewelry—something symbolic and meaningful—to be accompanied by a note."

"It had better be an excellent note."

"Oh, it will." Adrian cast him a smug smile. "I have always been skilled with the written word."

"I thought it was Sir who was so skilled," Max said wryly.

Adrian ignored him. "I shall pour out my heart to her. I want her to have a choice."

"It seems to me she had a choice once and she chose you."

"Did she choose me or did she choose the life I offered?"

Max stared. "Surely you're not talking about wealth and position?"

"No," he said quickly. "She is not the kind of woman to barter the rest of her life simply for wealth.

But security and family and belonging, that appealed to her."

Max nodded. "She has no family, no one to turn to, and certainly no financial resources." He chose his words with care. "But it was my observation that the true reason she chose you was love."

"That's what I am counting on."

"It's not too late to stop this right now."

Adrian raised a brow. "Are you being the voice of reason again?"

Max grinned. "I am trying."

"My wife's decision to reside elsewhere, though, does mean this has to be done quickly." He shook his head. "The longer she stays away, the more she will become used to living without me." He drew his brows together. "I do not intend to lose her."

"And yet—"

"I will not lose her," Adrian said firmly. "And considering this all in a realistic manner, I can't really. If she were to choose Sir, I will simply have to confess that I am Sir and we can continue on from there."

"You are mad." Max snorted. "Do you mean to tell me that you truly think that she will not be furious when she discovers that you originally met her as yourself to determine if she were working for someone else? And that said fury will not be exacerbated by this ruse you are perpetrating on her now?"

"She will forgive me," he said with a confidence he didn't quite feel.

"Are you sure?" Max leaned closer and lowered his voice. "You do understand you run the risk of losing her altogether?"

"I won't." He drew a deep breath. "If—when—she

chooses me, my doubts will be at an end and she will never know the truth of it all."

Max settled back in his chair. "Because secrets of this nature never come to light?"

"This one won't."

"And if it does?"

"I will move heaven and earth to get her back."

"And I cannot dissuade you from continuing?"

"No."

"Very well then." Max sipped his whiskey. "I have been giving this plan of yours some thought."

"And?"

"And it seems to me Sir cannot accomplish this attempted seduction through words alone."

Adrian studied the other man. "What did you have in mind?"

"It might well be time for Eve and Sir to meet in person."

Adrian nodded. "My thoughts exactly."

"To that end, I have come up with a couple of options. Scenarios if you will."

"As have I." Adrian narrowed his eyes. "Go on."

"You don't want her to be able to see your face, of course."

"It would be best to avoid that."

"Yet you do want to be able to speak to her." Max thought for a moment. "Under some sort of pretext, Sir could send her away, to Paris perhaps—"

"She does like Paris," Adrian murmured.

"Where, in the dead of night, he—or rather—you could appear in her darkened hotel room, awaken her, and attempt to seduce her."

"Now who is mad?" Adrian stared. "I can't believe you would suggest such a thing."

Max frowned. "Why not?"

"Just off the top of my head, mind you, I can think of any number of reasons why not." Adrian ticked the points off on his fingers. "First of all, I am not going to send my wife to Paris without me. It's a most romantic city."

"I have had some memorable moments in Paris." Max grinned in a wicked manner.

Adrian ignored him. "Second, breaking into her room in the middle of the night would no doubt terrify her. She's never heard Sir's voice, remember. Third, while she was rarely placed in potentially dangerous situations, we did give her a fair amount of training. I doubt I could surprise her in her sleep without her inflicting some bodily harm on me, which would be difficult to explain later. Finally, and perhaps most important, I suspect my wife would be clever enough, when traveling alone, to keep a firearm by her bed. She still owns a pistol." He frowned. "I have no desire to sacrifice my life for this plan. Especially not in France."

"It was only a suggestion." Max huffed. "And admittedly, perhaps not my best. I am not used to plots that involve wives rather than villains. You do understand the idea of planning a seduction designed to fail is a concept that's foreign to everything I believe in?"

"I know this is a challenge," Adrian said in a wry manner. "But surely we can come up with something better."

"It's that whole business of not seeing your face that makes it so difficult." Max paused. "There is an advantage, though, to Sir now being the one giving her instruction."

"We should be able to use that."

"What if we set up a simple meeting . . ." Max's eyes

widened. "Why not use the confessional at the church in Battersea Park?"

"It wouldn't be the first time I've met with someone at that church while pretending to be a priest," Adrian said thoughtfully. "Although there is nothing to stop her from leaving her side of the confessional and surprising me. It's just the sort of thing she would do." He shuddered. "That would certainly muck things up."

"No." Max's brow furrowed. "It would be better if she were tied up. Oh, and blindfolded."

"It is my understanding that Catholic priests do not generally bind and blindfold those wishing to confess their sins," Adrian said mildly. "That might attract unwelcome attention."

"It would be awkward. Still . . . I've got it." Max raised his glass. "Kidnapping. It's perfect. We have her kidnapped, tied up, blindfolded of course, possibly gagged, and stored somewhere out of reach."

Adrian stared in disbelief. "I am not going to *store* my wife."

"I'm not suggesting permanent storage." Max scoffed. "Simply someplace where she can be held without discovery long enough for Sir to speak with her without her seeing his face." Max took a deep swallow of his whiskey. "I tell you, it's brilliant. We can have her put in the empty warehouse cellar on the docks. You know the place. We haven't used it for some time but we still own it." He paused. "Certainly, it tends to flood with the rising of the tide, but she will be rescued long before that happens."

"Admittedly, that is better than startling her in the dead of night in a hotel in Paris. But I don't think so. I don't like the idea of putting her in any kind of danger."

"She won't be." Max shrugged. "We'll have her rescued the moment you're done speaking with her. Sir—you—will tell her you have to go but someone will be along shortly. A few minutes later, I will have someone assigned to save her." Max paused. "Even better, I'll save her. Or Miss DeRochette can rescue her."

Adrian raised a brow. "Miss DeRochette? But she's not with the department anymore either."

"Not actively. Remember, her last assignment was to provide protection for your wife should that become necessary. Thus far it hasn't." Max paused. "She has never been officially released from duty, however. I thought it wise."

"How interesting," Adrian murmured. "Still, it scarcely matters. I suspect, at this point, her loyalty lies more with my wife than with the department."

"One would think. So . . ." Max met the other man's gaze. "Unless you can come up with something better, I think a kidnapping has a great deal to commend it."

Adrian rolled his gaze toward the ceiling. "I am not going to have my wife kidnapped and stored in a flooding cellar."

"She would be rescued before it floods, but I do see your point. However, I still think it's a good idea and should not be discarded entirely."

"I don't know. There's entirely too much that can go wrong."

"Rubbish. I would use my best men. We do know what we are doing when it comes to this sort of thing."

"It bears further consideration, I suppose," Adrian said thoughtfully. "As long as appropriate precautions were taken."

"As they would be," Max said firmly. "Then, unless you have a better plan—"

"I do have something of an idea." Adrian thought for a moment. "Evelyn provided me with a schedule of our upcoming social events. A schedule that covers the next month." He glared at the other man. "A full month. She expects to be gone an entire month. Can you believe that?"

"You thought she was having an affair and surprised an unsuspecting couple in a hotel room. You didn't trust her and you embarrassed her." Max cast him a pitying look. "If I were you, I would be grateful that a month is all the penance you have to pay."

"Apparently, it's not. She is refurbishing the house Miss DeRochette resides in as well, at great expense no doubt," Adrian muttered. "I don't want her gone for a month. I don't want her gone at all. I—" A thought struck him and he stared at his friend. "How did you know that?"

"Know what?"

"About the hotel room incident."

Max cast him an all-knowing smile. Adrian knew that smile; he had perfected it.

"Just tell me this is not common knowledge. It has not become fodder for gossip." He blew a long breath. "The only thing saving me from certain disaster is that this mess has been kept quiet."

Max laughed. "I do so enjoy it when you are not in complete control. And no, it is not commonly known."

"I'm glad one of us is amused." He sipped his whiskey. "As I was saying, Evelyn sent me a schedule of our social obligations. There is a Venetian masked ball, some sort of gala for some charity or another, in three days."

"And you are expected to attend?"

"According to the *schedule*." He grit his teeth.

"You were always a master of disguise. This couldn't be more perfect for you than if you'd sent out the invitations yourself." Max considered him curiously. "Why didn't you mention this earlier?"

"I thought perhaps you might have had a better idea as this sort of thing is what you do every day." He chuckled. "Obviously I was wrong."

Max sniffed. "My ideas were excellent and most creative. Even you agree kidnapping is brilliant—"

"I'm not sure *brilliant* is the right word."

"Even more brilliant, I'd say, if you, as Sir, disguised in Venetian dress, were to rescue her. Women can scarcely resist a hero."

"That's rather complicated, isn't it?"

"Your idea is . . ." Max shrugged. "Simple."

"And as such is practically infallible."

"I can think of any number of ways in which it might go wrong," Max said in a lofty manner. "Horribly wrong."

"Name two."

"Better yet, three." Max cleared his throat. "One, your wife expects you to attend this gala. She will not take it well should you beg off."

"And I would prefer not to add to my list of sins." Adrian drew his brows together. "Obviously both Adrian and Sir will attend."

"Two, even at your best, it would be difficult for you to be two people at the same time in the same place."

"Admittedly, it will be a challenge." Adrian waved off the comment. "But manageable nonetheless."

Max snorted. "And three." He set his glass on the table and met his friend's gaze. "There was no one better than you at disguise. You could fool anyone, anywhere. Even people you had met." He leaned closer. "But Adrian, this is your wife. She knows you as well as you know yourself. She knows how you walk and stand and dance. She knows the looks in your eye and the smell of your soap. I think in an incense-scented church or a dank cellar you might be able to deceive her, but in her own world?" He settled back in his chair. "I'd wager you can't fool her."

"I fooled her when we first met."

"Not really." Max shrugged. "She'd never met you in person. I don't think you can do it."

"Of course I can do it." He scoffed. "She'll never realize who Sir really is. People never see what they don't expect to see." Especially women who didn't think their husbands were adventurous.

"Would you care to wager on it?" Max said mildly.

Adrian narrowed his eyes. "What kind of wager?"

His tone was abruptly serious. "In exchange for my assistance in this absurd endeavor of yours, you agree to come back to the department in an advisory capacity."

"Only on a temporary basis."

"If I am right, if you cannot fool Evelyn, I want you to make it permanent."

"I can't—"

"I'm not asking you to resume your previous position. I understand why that isn't possible." He met Adrian's gaze firmly. "But you were part of this department for nearly fifteen years, heading it for the last five. Your experience and expertise are invaluable. I have to confess, it is not the same without you. We could use you back. I could use you."

"I don't—"

"We have always been at our most brilliant when we have worked together. When we have puzzled out a solution together, combined your ideas with mine. As we have today. I want to be able to call on you, not every day, of course, but frequently. As an advisor, nothing more than that," Max added quickly.

Now was not the time for Adrian to admit that he'd already been thinking along those lines. "And if I am successful?"

"Of course, you will no longer need to doubt your wife's feelings for you, which should be winnings enough."

"And all I want. However . . ." Adrian shook his head slowly. "That's scarcely sufficient for a wager between the two of us."

"And . . ." Max heaved a resigned sigh. "The department will never call on you or your wife again."

"I see." He considered his friend thoughtfully. "Do I have your word that you will not do anything to assure your winning this wager?"

"Absolutely." He nodded. "While under other circumstances, I would do whatever I thought necessary to win a wager, the stakes for you are already high enough." Max smiled ruefully. "As your friend, I almost hope I lose."

"Almost?"

"You can't ask for more than that from me." Max grinned. "It's the nature of man, I think. Even while hoping a bomb will not detonate, one can't help but look forward a bit to the spectacle of the explosion itself."

"Not all of us," Adrian murmured, his mind already contemplating the details of accompanying Evie to the masquerade and being there as Sir to flirt with her. Pity, he couldn't get the image of an exploding inferno consuming everything in its path out of his head. "Not all of us."

Chapter 15

Evelyn's gaze shifted from one bouquet to the next. The floral displays sat side by side on the table in Celeste's parlor.

"I can't leave you alone for a minute, can I?" Celeste strode into the parlor.

"Nonsense, it was far more than a minute." Evelyn smiled at her friend. "I daresay you were gone nearly an hour."

"I was gone *merely* an hour. Long enough apparently for you to fill the house with strange men." Exasperation sounded in Celeste's voice. "Again."

"That would be Mr. Merryweather, Mr. Knowles, and Mr. Lloyd," Evelyn said absently, her gaze returning to the flowers.

On the left side, an explosion of tulips and hyacinths and other spring flowers filled a large bowl to overflowing. It was most impressive. Somewhat more sedate, but no less impressive, was the elegant vase of two dozen red roses.

"Why are they here?"

"They're measuring the bedrooms. I stopped at their establishments yesterday when I was finished at the dressmaker's." Evelyn glanced at her. "You may send them on their way with the same speech you gave the others."

"I thought you were only going to refurbish one room?"

"Only one room at a time," Evelyn said. "But it struck me last night, as I was failing to get to sleep, that refurbishing my wardrobe instead of this house means there is nothing to oversee." She shrugged. "And no need to stay here."

Celeste considered her for a moment. "Therefore, you could return to your husband."

She nodded. "I could."

"And his punishment would be at an end."

"I'm not punishing him," Evelyn said in a lofty manner. "I am simply giving him the uninterrupted opportunity to see the error of his ways."

"Is it working?"

Evelyn clenched her teeth. "Not thus far."

Celeste's gaze slid to the floral arrangements. "I know the roses are from Sir. I'm assuming the other flowers are from Lord W?"

"They arrived this morning along with a brief note about spring. Quite lovely really." She recited from memory, "'*My dear Evie, I send these in hope they bring a touch of spring to your heart as you have always brought it to mine.*'"

"That is lovely."

"My husband is a man of few words." Too few really. The sentiment expressed in his note would have been quite perfect if it had come when she had been attributing her preoccupied manner to the weather. As it was, after two days and two endless nights without him, it simply wasn't enough. "And apparently his continued apology, his declaration of being unable to live without me, his vow of undying love, his assurance that he will trust me without question for the rest of our days . . ." She gritted her teeth. "Those are words that he is either unable or unwilling to say."

"Still," Celeste said quickly. "Lord W must have gone to a great deal of trouble to obtain spring blossoms at this time of year."

"We do have a conservatory, you know," Evelyn said wryly. "And a gardener quite proficient at forcing blooms."

"Regardless, it was most thoughtful, as was his sentiment." Celeste waved at the roses. "It's not as if he simply had a florist deliver something as *expected* as two dozen red roses. That takes no particular effort whatsoever nor is it especially original."

"No, it isn't. And yet, one must give credit for quantity and persistence."

"Persistence?"

"The roses in the front entry are the ones from yesterday. These came while you were out."

Celeste grimaced. "From Sir?"

"Complete with another note." She picked the note up off the table and handed it to Celeste. "Read it."

" '*My dear Eve*,' " Celeste read. " '*Thus far there is little new in regards to the missing file. Therefore, at the moment, your services are not needed.*' " She glanced up. "This is good."

Evelyn snorted. "Keep reading."

Celeste's gaze returned to the note. " '*However, until this situation is resolved, be prepared to be called upon at any time.*' " She frowned. "Oh dear."

"'Oh dear' is something of an understatement." Evelyn scoffed. "Go on."

"I'm almost afraid to," Celeste said under her breath, then continued. "'*Still, while the lack of progress is always a source of frustration, I cannot help but be grateful as it enables me to not merely renew our acquaintance but broaden it.*'" Celeste gasped and met Evelyn's gaze. "Does he mean what I think he means?"

"I'm afraid to guess precisely what he means."

"Is he mad then?"

"Given my experiences of late, I am beginning to believe all men are mad. And not merely annoying." She gestured at the note. "There's more."

"I can see that." Celeste winced. "Good Lord." She drew a deep breath. "Where was I?"

"We had just broadened our acquaintance."

"Yes, of course." She searched for the words. "Let's see . . . '*Do not think this is a casual desire on my part. You have filled my thoughts these past two years.*'"

Evelyn groaned.

"'*In your last note you said you regret that we had never met. That, my dear lovely Eve, may well be the greatest regret of my life. Yours always.*'" Celeste raised a stunned gaze to meet Evelyn's. "'*Sir.*'"

"Charming, isn't it?" Evelyn said in a wry manner.

"Oh, my God, yes." Celeste sat down on the sofa beside her and stared. "It's not merely charming but might well be the most romantic thing I have ever read. Not meeting you is the biggest regret of his life? Why, it's intoxicating and nearly irresistible."

Evelyn shook her head. "Not to me."

"Are you sure?" Celeste glanced at the note in her hand.

"Absolutely."

"But there was a time—"

"That time is past," Evelyn said firmly.

"You're not the least bit, well, moved by his words?"

"Moved?" She scoffed. "What is there to be moved by?" She plucked the note from Celeste's hand and waved it. "Admittedly, these are fine words. '*My dear lovely Eve*,' '*Yours always*,' '*greatest regret of my life*,' but they have no real meaning." She tossed the note back onto the table. "The man has always hidden behind the veil of secrecy required by his position and our work. Now, after all this time, *now* he chooses to tell me of feelings that, quite frankly, make no difference to me." She thought for a moment. "One does have to wonder what he wants."

Celeste chose her words with care. "It sounds as though what he wants is you."

"Nonsense. It doesn't sound that way to me at all. More than likely, his return to the department and his renewed communication with me have brought about . . ." She searched for the right words. "Feelings of sentiment, which are probably no more than momentary aberrations." She met her friend's gaze firmly. "And I think you are reading far more into this note than is really there."

"Oh, I daresay—"

"This regret of his that we have never met in person is no more significant than if I were to say I regret never having had the opportunity to ride an elephant or sail the blue waters of the West Indies or dance naked on a rooftop under the stars."

Celeste raised a brow. "Dance naked on a rooftop?"

Evelyn waved away the comment. "It was an example."

"Of regrets."

"I have any number of regrets every bit as frivolous as that," she said in a lofty manner. "However, as I am not on my deathbed, I am confident that someday I shall ride an elephant or sail blue waters or even dance naked under the stars."

Celeste stared. "I had no idea."

"Why? Because I have taken so well to the eminently proper life Adrian and I live?"

"There is that."

"My life is everything I have ever wanted it to be." She aimed a firm look at the other woman. "And my husband is very nearly everything I have ever wanted. Oh, certainly . . ." She smiled in a dry manner. "Bringing spring to his heart is not quite as eloquent as not meeting me being the biggest regret of his life. Still, he is a man of substance, not shadow, a living, breathing man who, in spite of his shortcomings, which do seem to increase with every passing day, has my heart. Blast him. There is nothing I can do about that, nor do I wish to do anything about it." She blew a long breath. "I just wish I was as certain of his feelings."

"He did send you flowers."

She cast her friend a withering look. "The conservatory, remember."

"Are you doubting him?"

"I am trying not to, but he is not making it easy for me. This all started with my legitimate anger at his actions but now . . ." She shook her head. "And I've been gone for two nights now. Two nights!"

"Seems like an eternity," Celeste murmured.

"Doesn't it, though?" Evelyn made a disparaging gesture at Adrian's flowers. "And this is the only effort he's made to get me back."

"Well, he does think you're here to oversee the refurbishing."

"Then he is not nearly as intelligent as he appears," she said sharply.

"Perhaps, as you are giving him the uninterrupted opportunity to see the error of his ways," Celeste said slowly. "He is giving you time—"

"To come to my senses?" Her jaw clenched and she looked at her friend. "I am the injured party, am I not?"

"Of course you are."

"Do you know what I really want from him?"

Celeste shook her head.

"I want him to show the same passion in winning me back that he did in the pursuit of what he thought was my betrayal." Even as she said the words, she knew the truth of them. A truth she hadn't realized until just now. She sighed. "Is that too much to ask?"

"Not at all," Celeste said staunchly, then paused. "But perhaps you are expecting too much of him. Lord W has never struck me as a particularly passionate sort."

"Oh, but he is. He is a very private man, restrained and controlled. He doesn't show his emotions easily." Evelyn got to her feet, stepped to the table, and bent to inhale the fragrance of hyacinth and tulip. "He is passionate about his work in Parliament. He thinks this country can be better and he feels a great responsibility to that end. He is passionate about his family. He would do whatever was necessary to protect them. And he is—was—passionate about me. About us." She turned back to her friend. "But now he has let me go and thus far has not made much effort to win me back."

"You could always return home."

"No, I can't." She shook her head. "It would be like saying that it's perfectly fine for him to distrust me. That he did nothing wrong. Why would I return to a man who doesn't seem to care if I am there or not?"

"Oh, I don't believe—"

"No." She shook her head. "If we don't have trust between us, what do we have?"

"You have never trusted him with your past."

"That's an entirely different thing." She shrugged off the comment. "He was the one who said our lives before we met weren't significant." She smiled wryly. "I suspect that was more to save him from recriminations than anything else." She met her friend's gaze. "I think, though, that I would tell him now if he asked."

"Because you trust him?"

"With my past, with my future . . ." She sighed. "With my heart. Damnable man." She paused for a long moment. "And I trust that he loves me. And hopefully, he will soon realize that himself before . . ."

"Before what?"

"Before I am forced to take measures to make him realize how much he does care."

"What kind of measures?" Caution sounded in Celeste's voice.

"I don't know yet." Evelyn narrowed her eyes. "But I shall think of something."

"What are you going to do about Sir?"

"Nothing." She shrugged. "There's nothing to do. His note did not require a response, and I see no need to send one."

"But—"

"But if I am right and you are reading too much into his words, then no response is necessary. If I am wrong, then no response is the wisest course."

"No doubt." Celeste nodded. "Still, he says he wishes to broaden your acquaintance."

"Be that as it may, as long as he doesn't show up on my doorstep, it is not something I am going to concern myself with."

"I beg your pardon, Lady Waterston." Hendricks appeared in the doorway. "You have a caller."

Evelyn and Celeste traded uneasy glances.

"I am sure she will wish to see me," a familiar voice sounded behind the butler.

Relief washed through Evelyn and she stepped forward. "I am always delighted to see you, Helena."

"Dearest girl." Adrian's mother swept into the room like an avenging angel, sympathy on her face. She took Evelyn's hands in hers. "How are you bearing up?"

"Quite well, I think," Evelyn said cautiously. "And you?"

"I am most distraught." She heaved a dramatic sigh. "Most distraught. I came to see you today and was told you were here." She released Evelyn's hands and turned to Celeste. "Ah, Miss DeRochette, you are looking lovely as always."

"Thank you, Lady Waterston." She glanced at Evelyn. "If you will excuse me, I have matters to attend to elsewhere in the house." She nodded at Helena. "Good day, Lady Waterston."

"My dear." Helena watched Celeste take her leave. "What beautiful eyes that young woman has. If she would discard those spectacles and do something more attractive with her hair . . ."

"As much as I always adore seeing you . . ." Evelyn narrowed her eyes. "Why are you here?"

"Why, I've come to find out what that beast has done."

"That beast?"

"My son. Your husband."

Evelyn chose her words cautiously. "Why do you think—"

"Goodness, Evelyn, I must have left his father a dozen times or more over the course of thirty years. He would drive me quite mad and then refuse to accept that he was in the wrong. It's all that inherent aversion to excessive emotion. It's most annoying and it is in the blood, I'm afraid."

"I haven't left Adrian," Evelyn said slowly.

Helena raised a brow.

"I am simply overseeing the refurbishing of this house."

Helena glanced around and smiled pleasantly. "It seems to be going well."

"It hasn't actually started yet."

"Of course it hasn't." She paused. "You do realize that by giving him a reason—a rational reason like refurbishing—for your absence, you mitigate the need for him to expend any effort to bring you home?"

Evelyn drew her brows together. "What?"

"Perhaps I am not being clear." Helena sat down on the sofa and patted the spot beside her. Evelyn obediently joined her. "By telling your husband you need to reside here to oversee refurbishing, he might well think that's really why you are here. And not because of any vile transgression on his part. I assume there was a vile transgression?"

Evelyn started to deny it, then sighed. "Yes."

"And he is aware of it?"

Evelyn narrowed her eyes. "Oh, yes."

"But you didn't say that's why you were leaving?"

"Well, no. I thought—"

"Evelyn, dear, you have only been married for two years. This is the sort of lesson in the handling of husbands that only comes with experience." She studied her curiously. "I suspect you have never had a serious disagreement before, have you?"

Evelyn shook her head.

"Then this type of mistake is to be expected." She thought for a moment. "You see, right now, there is no need for him to shower you with gifts and pledge his undying love and, yes, grovel, because in his dear little head he can convince himself you are gone for a purpose. That purpose being to supervise work here and not because you are furious with him. You are furious, aren't you?"

Evelyn nodded. "I was."

"But you miss him and so you are less furious?"

Evelyn hesitated.

"I thought so." Helena nodded. "And now, because he has made no true effort to make up for his misdeeds, you are starting to wonder if he cares at all. And perhaps wonder if you have made a dreadful mistake?"

"Something like that," Evelyn murmured.

"It's exactly like that and there is no time to waste," Helena said firmly. "Believe me, I speak from experience. The longer you allow this to drag on, the worse it will become."

"Are you saying I should go home?"

"Has he begged you to return?"

"No." Annoying beast.

"Then you do not return until he does so. To surrender at this point would be to give him the upper hand. Once given, it is nearly impossible to regain, and you will spend the rest of your lives together being someone less than the very confident, competent, strong woman he married. And that will make neither of you happy." She met her daughter-in-law's gaze firmly. "No, if your grievance is legitimate—"

"And it is."

"Then you do my son a disservice by not permitting him to realize the value of what he has and the very real possibility he might lose it. And realize as well that it is worth fighting for. He does love you, you know."

"I thought so," Evelyn said under her breath.

"Do not mistake stubbornness for a lack of affection." She heaved a heartfelt sigh. "Unfortunately, the men in this family have a great deal in common. They are nothing short of wonderful through the course of the pursuit, but once married, they do tend to rest on their laurels."

"Oh no, Helena, I can't believe . . ." Evelyn paused. "Do you really think so?"

"I think your refurbishment is an excellent excuse for not demanding that you come home."

"I hadn't thought of it that way. But I am certain he understands that refurbishing is not the true reason for my absence."

"Nonetheless, as it is a relatively legitimate reason, Adrian might not even realize you are still angry." Her brows drew together. "Did you leave in a huff? Tossing recriminations and pointed barbs in your wake?"

"Well, I did say . . ." She winced. "Not really."

"Oh dear, that is a problem."

Evelyn stared. "Why?"

"Dear girl, you simply *must* pay attention." Helena huffed. "Unfortunately, Adrian is a very busy man and you have only been gone for what? Two days now?"

Evelyn nodded.

"Not nearly long enough if you are redecorating an entire house and entirely too long if you're not. But as I am confident he is an intelligent boy, he should fairly soon come to the realization that perhaps you are not simply gone to refurbish and he must take action if he is to win you back." She smiled. "Although I do see he has sent flowers. Only a first step, mind you, but sending both tulips and roses is certainly a step toward the right direction."

"Oh, the roses aren't . . ." Evelyn started without thinking.

"Not from Adrian?" Helena raised a brow. "I see."

"They're Miss DeRochette's," Evelyn said quickly. It wasn't entirely a lie. She had given Celeste the first two dozen and fully intended for her to have these as well. "I believe she has an admirer." In truth, she had no idea if Celeste had admirers or not. She'd never said a word. But then there were all sorts of things Celeste kept to herself.

"I would be surprised if she didn't," Helena said firmly.

"As would I," Evelyn murmured. She hadn't thought about it before but it would be surprising if Celeste didn't have a gentleman in her life. In truth, it would explain quite a lot. When this was all resolved, with the department and Sir, with her husband, she would make a concerted effort to find out her friend's secrets. Or at least encourage Celeste to confide in her.

"Now, as I have come to give you advice, I had best get on with it." Helena met her gaze directly. "First, do not return home until he has won your forgiveness in a matter satisfactory to you."

Evelyn bit back a smile. "You said that."

"It bears repeating," Helena said firmly. "Second, if

he does not do something soon, oh, a grand gesture of some sort, I would think, you must determine a way to inspire such a gesture. But it is very important he thinks it is his idea."

"Do you have any thoughts as to what that might be?" A wry note sounded in Evelyn's voice.

"I can't do this all myself, you know." Helena cast her a chastising look. "I have given you the benefit of my wisdom; the rest is in your hands." She got to her feet, Evelyn following a beat behind. "I said you cannot allow this to continue overly long and that, too, bears repeating. You want to stay away long enough for him to realize he can't live without you but not so long for him to get used to living without you." She smiled in a satisfied manner. "Although I doubt that is possible. You know, I never really thought Adrian would marry at all. And then he met you. You, my dear, are the love of his life. Don't let him muck it up."

"I shall do my best." Evelyn paused. "Don't you want to know what he did?"

"Oh my, yes. Why, I am simply burning with curiosity, but I'm not going to ask." She shook her head. "I know it's not something insignificant and frivolous because you are far too sensible to be upset over something that doesn't matter. And if it is something as dreadful as another woman, I might not be able to forgive him for being such an idiot. Nor do I think you would forgive him. Besides, even the most stubborn Hadley-Attwater man would know it would take far more effort than one mere bouquet to atone for that sort of transgression. No, I suspect he has done something far greater than a minor sin and somewhat less than eternal damnation."

Evelyn nodded. "Somewhat."

"Now, then, I must be on my way."

"But I haven't offered you refreshments. Tea or something . . ."

"Yes, dear, I noticed. It is an obvious measure of how distraught you are and can certainly be forgiven this once." Helena's eyes twinkled. "But do not forget I have six other children who expect a certain amount of meddling on my part. I do so hate to disappoint any of them."

Evelyn laughed. "Are you making the rounds then?"

"I had planned to call on Portia next." She narrowed her eyes thoughtfully. "That girl has some sort of secret, and she has since she returned from Christmas in Italy. It's quite shocking really as she has never been able to keep a secret. One does wonder what she is hiding. There doesn't seem to be anything I can do in regards to Bianca and her husband." She leaned closer and lowered her voice in a confidential manner. "She and her husband have been estranged now longer than you and Adrian have been married, not that I blame her." She rolled her gaze toward the ceiling. "I never trusted that man. While there has never been a divorce in the family and I am certainly not encouraging such a thing, her husband is the finest excuse for divorce I have ever seen." She shrugged. "It's none of my concern, of course."

"Of course," Evelyn murmured. Not that Helena had ever let that stop her.

"There is nothing I can do to help Miranda mend her heart. Someday, she will stop mourning her husband, but while two years is enough for many people, she is not yet ready to get on with her life. Soon I think.

Hugh tends to avoid me." She met Evelyn's gaze. "You do know, now that Sebastian has married, Hugh is at the top of my list."

"I thought Portia was at the top?"

"My goodness, Evelyn." Helena smiled in a wicked sort of way. "I would never manage to accomplish anything if my children knew exactly what I was thinking."

Evelyn grinned.

"Now then, my dear." She took Evelyn's hands and gazed into her eyes. "Do not hesitate to call on me if the need arises. I consider you no less a Hadley-Attwater than any of the others. You are as much my daughter as Diana and Bianca and Miranda and Portia."

Evelyn swallowed the sudden lump in her throat. From the moment she married Adrian, Helena had become the mother she'd never truly known. "Thank you."

"No thanks are necessary, dear girl." She kissed her cheek. "I assume I shall see you tonight?"

Evelyn stared. "Tonight?"

"Oh dear, this misdeed of Adrian's must have been rather more significant than even I have imagined for you to forget." Helena's brow furrowed. "Diana is having the family for dinner tonight."

"Yes, of course." It was, after all, on the schedule she'd had delivered to her husband. Admittedly, it had slipped her mind.

"It's the first time we shall all be together since Sebastian and Veronica's marriage." She leveled Evelyn a firm look. "I expect to see you there."

"I wouldn't miss it."

They chatted for a few more minutes, then Helena took her leave.

Evelyn's gaze returned to Adrian's flowers. It wasn't at all like her to forget a social obligation, especially a family event. Obviously, this difficulty with Adrian was more distressing than she'd realized. She cherished being a part of this family far too much to take it for granted. She should probably send Adrian a note of reminder.

No. She turned and started up the stairs to her bedroom. He had the schedule. And he knew his family well enough to know any failure on his part to appear would be remarked upon. Her pulse quickened at the thought of seeing him. It had been only two days and yet it seemed forever. She did hope he knew her well enough to know she would attend. Still, given that he had suspected her of having an affair, she wondered if he knew her at all.

And as he had made little effort to get her back, she wondered, as well, if she knew him.

Chapter 16

What on earth was wrong with him? Adrian paced the width of Diana's foyer. And where was his wife?

He had considered appearing unannounced at her house to escort her here tonight, then thought perhaps it might be best to meet on what could be termed neutral territory. Not that he expected her to fly into a rage or berate him in front of his family. In truth, their argument had been remarkably civilized. Of course, from the moment she'd brought up leaving, his mind had been churning with the details of how her absence would only make his deception as Sir easier. He grimaced. He had always considered himself an intelligent man. Apparently, in that, too, he was wrong.

He'd arrived at Diana's a few minutes early on the off chance that, for once, Evie would not be late. What he hadn't considered was that he would be in the entry, waiting for his wife, when each and every member of his family arrived. Fortunately, no one seemed to take

his explanation that he'd had a late meeting and he and
Evie had agreed to meet here as at all unusual.

At least, greeting the various members of his family
had kept him occupied. He couldn't remember the last
time, if ever, he had known this kind of apprehension.
A man shouldn't feel apprehensive about seeing his
own wife. But damnation, he was nervous.

Admittedly, a man also shouldn't suspect his wife of
infidelity because she failed to mention a trip to a museum. And a man should make more of an effort to win
her forgiveness than with a lone bunch of spring flowers. Good Lord, he was doing a better job at, well,
courting her as Sir than he was as himself. Still, she
hadn't responded to Sir's latest communication, which
was gratifying. He should stop this nonsense right now.
Go on with their life together, an excellent life, as they
had before. But he'd never yet abandoned a quest, and
if he knew nothing else about himself, he knew if he
didn't answer this question now, it would haunt him for
the rest of his days. Perhaps, if he hadn't started this
course, if Max hadn't called Evie back into service, if
he hadn't let his uncertainties convince him there was
another man, he could have lived with his doubts about
Sir. He had thus far, after all. But now, he would wonder who she truly loved every time she looked at him,
every time he took her in his arms. Uncertainty would
gnaw at him. He fully intended to spend the rest of his
life with her, and she deserved better than that. As
did he.

"If you wear a path in my floor, I shall have to box
your ears at the very least." Diana stood in front of the
closed doors to the parlor.

"Do not treat me as if I am one of your children." He

drew his brows together. "How long have you been standing there?"

"Long enough, I would say." Her tone softened. "She will come, you know."

"Of course she will." He scoffed. "I am not the least bit concerned."

"You look concerned."

"Rubbish, I have nothing to be concerned about. Our arriving separately was a simple matter of expediency."

"Yes, I believe you mentioned that. Every time someone new arrived." She smiled in a manner that a casual observer might call pleasant. Said observer would have missed the knowing look in her eye. Diana was the oldest of his sisters and the closest to him in age. Adrian recognized that smile.

"What are you thinking?" he said in a sharper tone than he had intended.

"I'm thinking you look rather pathetic. There . . ." She studied him, then aimed a pointed finger. "Around the eyes."

"Don't be absurd." He shrugged. "I simply haven't been sleeping well."

She nodded. "Guilty conscience, no doubt."

"What do you mean?" He narrowed his eyes. "What do you know?"

"All sorts of things I would wager you don't."

"And what might those be?"

"Well, let me think. Hmmm." She tapped her chin with her forefinger. "For one thing, I know Mother tried to pay a call on Evelyn today."

"Oh?"

"Imagine her surprise to discover your wife was no longer living in your house."

"She is overseeing the refurbishment of a house she owns. It is convenient for her to stay there while she does so."

"Where exactly is this house?"

"Mayfair."

"And your house?"

He gritted his teeth. "Mayfair."

"My, that is convenient," she said. "I also know Mother did indeed pay a call on your wife."

His stomach twisted. "Did she?"

"She most certainly did. Which is how I know exactly why you and Evelyn are arriving separately."

"Who else knows?"

She cast him a pointed look.

He winced. "Everyone?"

"Everyone who has already arrived. And as only Evelyn and Hugh have still not appeared, I would say yes, everyone in the family, with the exception of Hugh, of course, knows you and your wife are no longer residing together."

He groaned.

"Dare I ask what you did?"

"Why do you think I did something?"

She raised a brow.

"Doesn't Mother know?"

"Quite remarkably, she says she didn't ask." Diana shrugged. "I don't know what has gotten into her. She said it was no one's concern but yours and your wife's."

"*Our* mother said that?" He narrowed his eyes in suspicion. "Are you sure this is our mother?"

"She does look like our mother. But it's not at all like her." She shook her head. "Still, you shouldn't question it, just be grateful."

"I am." He breathed a sigh of relief. Although, as

there wasn't a single member of his family who didn't let curiosity overcome good judgment, this reticence on his mother's part would no doubt be short-lived.

Across the foyer, a footman opened the door and laughter could be heard a scant moment before Hugh and Evie appeared.

"I had no idea being a barrister could be quite so humorous." Evie's lips curved with amusement.

"It's relatively staid for the most part and usually extremely serious." Hugh chuckled. "But you would be surprised at the sorts of things people come to me with." He caught sight of his brother and grinned. "I was just regaling your wife with tales of my dull profession."

"Not so dull apparently," Diana said.

"Admittedly, it does provide some moments of amusement." Hugh stepped to his sister's side and kissed her cheek. "I was afraid I was going to be late, but I met Evelyn outside as she arrived." He handed his coat to the footman, then turned to help Evie with her wrap.

"My apologies, Diana. Are we late?" Evie asked.

"Not at all." Diana smiled. "I have learned long ago with this family, while I may say dinner is at eight, I don't plan on seating everyone for at least a half an hour after that. Oh dear." Her brows pulled together in mock concern. "Now you know my secret."

"What secret?" Evie's eyes widened innocently. "I didn't hear a thing. And I certainly didn't hear a brilliant idea that I fully intend to make use of myself."

Diana laughed.

Hugh glanced from Adrian to Evie and back. "I must say I was surprised when Evelyn arrived without you. Is there something—"

"Adrian had some sort of political thing to deal with," Diana said smoothly. "As he didn't know when he might be finished, he and Evelyn agreed to meet here. Now then . . ." She took Hugh's arm and steered him toward the parlor. "Everyone else is in the parlor and I'm sure Adrian and Evelyn need a moment to themselves before joining the rest of the family."

"Of course." Hugh cast Adrian a curious look, then turned his attention back to his sister. "Tell me what is on the menu this evening. I do hope you are serving that wonderful . . ." The parlor doors closed behind them.

"I was wondering if you would be here tonight," Evie said coolly.

"Miss a family dinner? I am not so foolish." He shook his head. "Diana and or my mother and probably all the females in this family would track me down and berate me without mercy for failing in my responsibilities as head of this assembly. Besides . . ." He grinned. "It was on the schedule."

"Yes, it was," she said firmly. "I am most appreciative that you did not ignore it."

"Never." He took her hand and raised it to his lips. "You look breathtaking tonight." She was wearing a peach-colored confection, which made her dark eyes even darker. He had always loved that dress and yet he'd probably never told her. What a fool he was.

"Thank you."

"Did you know that gown is a favorite of mine?"

"I had no idea. But if I had . . ." Her eyes twinkled with amusement. "I wouldn't have so much as considered wearing something else." She pulled her hand from his and studied him. "You look dreadful." Her brows drew together. "Are you ill?"

"I'm somewhat tired." His gaze met hers. "I find it is difficult to sleep without my wife by my side."

"Ah well, that is a problem." She smiled pleasantly.

"How goes the refurbishing?"

"Not well." She shook her head in a mournful manner. "It's going to take much longer than expected. Why, I have yet to have so much as a single room painted."

"Then you don't know when you'll return home?"

"I have no idea."

Bloody hell, he couldn't stand another minute of this. He reached out and pulled her into his arms. "What can I do to make it go faster?"

Suspicion shone in her eyes. "What are you doing?"

"I'm doing what I have wanted to do since the moment you walked in the door." He gazed into her eyes. "You are quite irresistible, you know. And I have been unable to resist you from the moment we met."

"Oh no, you don't." She shook her head but made no effort to pull away. "You are not going to charm your way out of this."

"Why not?" He grinned. "I can be most charming."

"Yes, I remember." She stared. "But . . ."

"But I have not exerted my considerable charm on you as of late?"

"I'm your wife, I don't expect you to be at your most charming every minute."

He chuckled. "Well, it does take a certain amount of effort."

"This is not amusing." She glared. "I am still furious with you."

"As well you should be." He nodded in a sober manner. "My behavior was inexcusable."

"Indeed it was."

"I was a thoughtless beast."

Her eyes narrowed. "Yes, you were."

"I never should have doubted you."

"No, you shouldn't have."

"And I shall endeavor to do better in the future."

"And?"

"And?" *And what?* His mind searched frantically for something else. "And I apologize?"

"And?"

"And . . . Blast it all, Evie." He huffed and stared into her eyes. "I can't sleep. I can't think. I am very nearly worthless. I miss you!"

"Do you?"

"I sent flowers."

"And they were lovely." She paused. "As was your note."

"I meant every word of it." His gaze searched hers. "There is no spring in my life, in my heart, if you are not there."

She stared, then drew a deep breath. "It sounds so much better when you say it rather than write it."

"Then I shall say it more often." He paused. "I have been remiss, I think, in not letting you know how important you are to me. How my life is empty if you are not in it."

"Then you should not have let me go," she said firmly, but her arms slipped around his neck nonetheless.

He pulled her tighter against him. "I know, I was an idiot."

"Yes, you were."

"You could stop agreeing with me." He frowned

down at her. "Thus far I am a thoughtless beast and an idiot." He shook his head. "I don't know how you can bear me."

"I am a woman of great fortitude," she said in a lofty manner.

"Yes, you are. And you are mine." He bent his head and his lips met hers. She tasted as she always did, as she had since their first kiss. Of unknown spices and dimly remembered sweets and yesterday and tomorrow and forever. Familiar and comforting and yet still, always, exciting. Desire curled within him as it always did, from the first moment with her. As he knew it always would. What a lucky man he was to be in love with his wife. He deepened his kiss and she responded. And her own passion echoed his. Finally she sagged against him. He raised his head and smiled. "And I am a fortunate man."

"Yes." Her voice had that lovely, breathless quality which only made him want her more. "You are."

"Have you forgiven me?"

"I am considering it." She drew a steadying breath.

He could still take her breath away. He tried and failed to hide a satisfied smile.

"You needn't look like that." She pushed weakly out of his arms. "It will take more than a bunch of flowers and a mere kiss to earn my forgiveness."

He drew his brows together. "Mere?"

"Don't be arrogant, darling. It was an exceptional kiss."

He grinned. "I know."

"Exceptional kisses are one of the reasons why I married you."

"I know that, too."

"I am still furious with you."

"I know that as well." He nodded. "And I expect nothing less."

"Admittedly, I might be somewhat less furious than I was originally."

"Then I am making progress." He paused. "Would a diamond bracelet make you less furious and help earn your forgiveness?"

"Adrian." Her brow furrowed. "I am not that shallow. You cannot atone for your sins with a mere bauble."

"It's scarcely mere," he said under his breath.

"Furthermore, my forgiveness cannot be bought."

He gasped in mock horror. "I never imagined it would. I simply thought, as your birthday is approaching, a gift in advance would not be inappropriate."

She studied him for a long moment. "You are a sly and wicked devil, Adrian Hadley-Attwater."

"But I am your sly and wicked devil."

"Yes, you are." She tilted her head to one side and considered him. "Well?"

"Well what?"

"In the spirit of, oh, giving you due credit for your edging closer to amends . . ." She held out her hand. "I am willing to accept a gift in advance of my birthday."

He bit back a satisfied grin. "How very gracious of you."

"I think so. Besides . . ." She shrugged. "It would be rude not to accept. And one should never be rude when diamonds are involved. Well." She glanced pointedly at her outstretched hand.

He patted his waistcoat pocket, then grimaced. "I seem to have left it at the house."

"No doubt," she said dryly. "And I assume I need to return home to receive my bribe? Or rather, my gift?"

He nodded. "And the matching ear bobs."

"Why am I not surprised?" She rolled her gaze toward the ceiling. "We can continue this discussion later. Now, however, we should join the others. I'm certain your mother has told the rest of the family that we are in the midst of a dreadful row and I am no longer living under your roof."

He chuckled. "She wouldn't be my mother otherwise."

Evie started toward the parlor doors, then paused; her tone abruptly sober. "I am still angry with you, and hurt."

"I know," he said quietly.

Her gaze met his, and he wasn't sure he had realized until that moment how very much his lack of trust had hurt her. He ignored the thought that if she ever learned of his deception as Sir, she would be hurt again and far worse. His determination to keep that knowledge from her strengthened.

"I will make amends for my behavior, Evie, you have my word. If it takes the rest of my life."

"Oh, darling." A slow smile spread across her face. "It will."

It was an excellent dinner, which had nothing to do with the skills of Diana's cook and everything to do with the glances Adrian traded across the table with his wife. Good God, he felt as if they'd turned the clock back two years and he had to start at the beginning. He had to win her heart again. Still now, as then, he was confident of success.

Dinners, with the entire family in attendance, had become something of a tradition now that all of his sib-

lings were adults with lives of their own. Every other
month or so, Diana and her husband, James, or Adrian's
mother or his youngest sister, Miranda, or Portia, both
widows who had homes of their own, or Bianca, who
still resided in the house she had shared with her estranged husband, or he and Evie would host the gathering. As Sebastian was now married, he and Veronica
would take their turn as well although it might be wise
to ease her into it as she had little family of her own.
Still, her relations had joined the Hadley-Attwaters this
past Christmas at Sebastian's new country home, and
Veronica had handled the large number of guests with
ease, all things considered. Hugh, as a widower, was
never expected to have the family for dinner, which he
had long joked was one reason to remain unwed.

"Evelyn," Bianca said, in a tone far too innocent to
be legitimate. "Do tell us what you are doing with your
house."

"Quite honestly, I'm not sure yet." Evie sipped her
wine thoughtfully. "Thus far I have had a small army of
linen drapers and paper hangers and painters and I've
lost track of who else traipsing through the house taking measurements and assessing what needs to be
done. They are supposed to come back to me with suggestions and ideas and, hopefully, solid plans for refurbishing."

"The house was your parents', wasn't it?" Miranda
asked.

Evie nodded. "My guardian leased it out for years,
but I lived there after my school years until I married
Adrian. My secretary resides there now, which is most
reassuring." She shook her head. "I hate the thought of
it being unoccupied."

"Understandable." Diana nodded. "Are you replacing the furniture as well?"

"Most of it, I think," Evie said. "I don't remember the house at all from my childhood, but I suspect any really good pieces vanished years ago. I have no idea if they were sold to help pay for my schooling or simply disappeared with the various tenants. What remains is sadly out of date and quite worn. The toll taken on it by tenants, you know."

Portia glanced at Adrian. "This must be a somewhat extravagant undertaking."

"But worth it." He smiled at his wife. "One can never go wrong with an investment of this nature. The house itself will be far more valuable, and new furnishings will be beneficial should Miss DeRochette ever decide she prefers to live elsewhere or marries and we decide to let the house again."

"Which I wish to avoid," Evie said firmly. "Unless it was to family or friends."

"Very wise of you, dear." Helena nodded her approval.

"Didn't your guardian die recently?" Hugh asked.

Evie nodded. "A few months ago, in November."

Helena's brow furrowed. "Why didn't I know this?"

"My apologies, Mother," Adrian said smoothly. "We might have failed to mention it."

Helena aimed a pointed look at her oldest son. "How could you fail to mention a death in the family?"

"The fault is mine, Helena," Evie said quickly. "Sir George was so distant a relative, I have never even been certain how exactly we are related. Indeed, I never met the man in person."

Helena stared. "Good Lord, I had no idea."

"Apparently, when Adrian and Evelyn married, you

failed in your usual inquisition." Diana favored her mother with a pleasant smile.

James choked back a laugh.

"Nonsense." Helena scoffed. "I was well aware of Evelyn's background. I was vaguely acquainted with her parents. I knew of her education and her travels and her reputation." She glanced at Evie. "Neither perfect nor especially blemished. Frankly, I was so taken with Evelyn, I thought she was the perfect match for Adrian, that there was no need for an *inquisition*. Furthermore . . ." She leveled a hard glance at Diana. "I do not conduct inquisitions. In the best interest of my children I may, if the situation warrants it, make casual inquiries."

Hugh snorted. Portia's brow rose. Miranda took a quick sip of wine while Bianca bit her lip. Veronica hid her smile behind her napkin. James tried and failed to suppress a grin. Sebastian and Adrian didn't even try. His mother was an expert at ferreting out information, especially when it came to prospective spouses for her children. He had long thought she would have made an excellent agent.

"My apologies, Mother." Diana's eyes sparkled with laughter. "I don't know what I was thinking."

"Obviously you were thinking of someone else's mother." Helena huffed.

For a long moment, no one said a word, then laughter erupted around the table. Even his mother was hard-pressed to hold back a smile.

"Sebastian." Helena turned her attention to his youngest brother. "How is the work at your house coming along?"

Sebastian had bought a large, centuries-old house in the country several months before he had met and married Veronica. While it had proved the perfect house for a family gathering at Christmas, his guests had agreed among themselves there was still much work to be accomplished.

"Thanks to my wife, it's coming along quite well," Sebastian said with the air of a man who was at last settled and happy.

"It's going to be magnificent. We have already made plans for restoring the gardens once spring finally comes." Confidence sounded in Veronica's voice. "Of course, we have discovered the brickwork needs attention and the plumbing is not as sound as Sebastian had thought and . . . oh dear." She turned toward Evelyn. "Whatever you do with this house of yours, do not make the mistake of listing all the work that needs to be done. It can be overwhelming and will make you want to throw up your hands in surrender."

Evie laughed. "I shall keep that in mind."

"Veronica," Portia began. "I was wondering if you had heard from . . ."

The conversation ebbed and flowed around the table with topics leapfrogging from acquaintances misplaced to the endless winter weather to Hugh's marital status to Portia's sojourn in Italy and whatever else struck anyone's fancy. It was, as always, fast and a touch furious with hardly anyone waiting until someone else had finished before launching into another topic. For a newcomer to their ranks, it could be quite intimidating, which was why Adrian had not introduced Evie to this family tradition until after they had wed. But Evie had fit in at once and indeed had reveled in the exchanges between siblings, even when, on occasion, disagreement erupted into accusation and recrimination. They were certainly not perfect, after all, as any one of them would freely admit. Nor were they reticent to express their opinions on how any of the others should live their lives. Evie had told Adrian once, after one of these dinners, this was how she had always imagined families to be but thought it far-fetched that the same people who could debate at the top of their lungs and argue vehemently would, in the next minute, laugh together and defend one another without hesitation.

"I heard the most amusing story today," Bianca began, when the dishes from the last course had been removed and the meal was drawing to a close.

"Gossip, Bianca?" Portia frowned in a forbidding manner. Veronica choked back a laugh. Years ago, Portia had gotten it into her head that the Hadley-Attwaters were entirely too proper to indulge in questionable activities such as gossip. And while they were an eminently proper family in many ways, his mother and sisters had refined gossip to a form of art. Which was probably what made it acceptable.

"I wouldn't call it gossip," Bianca said loftily. "It's more in the category of news, I would think. Besides, this came to me very nearly firsthand."

Diana raised a brow. "Very nearly?"

"Well, secondhand." Bianca thought for a moment. "Or perhaps third."

"Is it a good story?" Miranda asked.

Bianca nodded. "Very good."

"Go on then." Veronica leaned forward. "Do tell us."

"Very well." Bianca glanced around the table as if to confirm everyone's undivided attention. "It seems Lady Dunwell is having an affair."

Adrian's stomach lurched.

Hugh snorted. "That's scarcely news."

"That's not the amusing part," Bianca said. "Apparently, Lady Dunwell was involved in an afternoon tryst at the Langham Hotel."

Portia gasped. "I have had tea at the Langham." She turned a scandalized gaze toward Veronica. "You and I have met for tea at the Langham."

"I daresay Lady Dunwell wasn't there for the tea," Miranda said under her breath.

"They do have a lovely tea," Veronica said in an aside to Sebastian.

"No doubt," he murmured.

Helena leaned over and patted Portia's hand. "I'm sure it doesn't affect the tea, dear."

"As I was saying," Bianca continued, "Lady Dunwell was in a room with her paramour—"

"Who was he?" Diana asked.

"This is completely inappropriate. And at dinner." Portia sniffed. "Aunt Helena?"

"You're absolutely right, it is inappropriate." Helena nodded.

Portia smiled in an altogether too sanctimonious manner.

"However, as we have no guests, no one outside the family who would judge our scandalous behavior. And as we are all simply dying of curiosity . . ." Helena nodded at Bianca. "Who was the man in question?"

Bianca smirked. "Lord Radington."

"That's not news either." Hugh scoffed.

"Lord Radington?" Evie's eyes widened. "*Lord Radington?*"

Bianca nodded.

"But he's so . . . so . . . obvious. His reputation is deplorable. I can't imagine any woman in her right mind . . ." Evie's gaze fixed on her husband. Adrian tried not to flinch. "Why, his manner is entirely too practiced, and to my taste, he isn't even especially attractive."

"Oh no, not *especially*." Miranda shook her head.

"But rather a lot really," Diana murmured.

"Nonsense." Evie pulled her gaze from his and was, at once, completely controlled. "I can't believe Lady Dunwell doesn't have better taste."

"Have you met Beryl Dunwell?" Veronica said under her breath.

"Of course I have met her." Evie nodded. "Indeed, I consider her a friend."

"You what?" Adrian said without thinking. Friendship between Evie and Beryl did not strike him as a sound idea. He had learned long ago, when dealing with women, one should never allow the past to collide with the present. He assumed, if the present was a wife, it was even more important to avoid such a collision.

"She is my friend," Evie repeated firmly.

"How very interesting," Miranda said.

"Really?" Diana stared. "Beryl Dunwell? I wouldn't think the two of you would have anything at all in common."

"Oh, you would be surprised," Evie said with a pleasant smile.

"I think you would be an excellent influence on Lady Dunwell," Helena said staunchly. "She could certainly use a good influence. You and Adrian behave most properly."

"Did you hear that, darling?" Evie leaned forward slightly and looked into his eyes. "Your mother has no doubts as to our proper behavior. She *trusts* that we will not do anything foolish and scandalous."

"Yes, yes." Bianca gestured impatiently. "You and

Adrian are most proper, Lady Dunwell is a strumpet, and Lord Radington is a scoundrel. Be that as it may, it's not . . ." She paused in the manner of an expert storyteller. "The best part of the story."

"Oh, do get on with it then, Bianca." Impatience sounded in Portia's voice. Her eyes widened with the realization of what she had said. "Not that I'm at all interested," she added quickly.

James grinned. "I find I am rather interested."

"As are we all," Diana said. "Out with it, Bianca."

"The best part," Bianca continued, "is that, apparently in the middle of, well, the *act*, who burst in upon them unannounced?"

Bloody hell.

"An irate husband," Bianca said with a flourish in her voice.

"Lord Dunwell?" Hugh raised an incredulous brow.

"I can't imagine Lord Dunwell being outraged." Veronica turned to her husband. "He is no better than she is."

Sebastian had spent much of his adult life traveling the world and had only returned to England for good last autumn. He stared at her. "How do you know all this?"

"Oh, one hears things, here and there." Veronica cast her husband a wicked smile. "You would be surprised at the things I know."

Sebastian chuckled. "I have been thus far."

"That certainly is anticlimactic," Adrian said. Past time to change this subject. "Lady Dunwell and Lord Radington." He scoffed. "Nothing surprising there." He turned to his youngest brother. "Sebastian, have you started your new book—"

"I'm not finished." Indignation sounded in Bianca's voice. "There's more and it's even better."

"I'm afraid I have to agree with Portia." Adrian shook his head. "This is most definitely gossip and I don't think—"

"Nonsense, darling." Evie's gaze pinned his. "Everyone wants to hear the rest of the story. I know I am fairly consumed with curiosity." She glanced at Bianca. "Please, don't stop now."

"Thank you, Evelyn. As I was saying, an irate husband interrupted them. However . . ." She paused. "The husband in question was not Lord Dunwell!"

Adrian held his breath.

Sebastian stared in confusion. "Does Lady Dunwell have more than one husband?"

"She did, dear," Veronica said, "but her first husband is dead. Goodness, even Lady Dunwell only has one husband at a time."

Diana frowned. "Now I am confused, Bianca. What are you trying to say?"

"The husband who burst in upon them was not looking for Lady Dunwell but rather for *his* wife. Who he apparently thought was with Lord Radington," Bianca finished with a satisfied grin.

For a long moment everyone stared.

"Oh my," Miranda said.

"And at the Langham." Portia shook her head.

At once laughter again engulfed the table.

"And the name of this outraged but obviously mistaken husband?" Evie asked.

"Oh." Bianca visibly deflated. "I'm afraid I don't have that. All I know is that he and his wife have an impeccable reputation and there has never been any talk regarding infidelity about either of them."

Relief washed through Adrian.

"Probably for the best." Helena nodded. "That you don't know his name, that is."

"One wonders if it wasn't a mistake on the part of the husband," Evie said mildly. "Given their reputation."

"Can you imagine such a thing?" Diana shook her head. "I would be furious if my husband burst into a hotel room looking for me. If he didn't trust me."

"Fortunately for me . . ." James cast an affectionate look at his wife. "I trust you implicitly."

Diana smiled with satisfaction. "As well you should."

"Still," Adrian said slowly, knowing full well any comment on his part was probably a mistake yet unable to stop himself. "One also has to wonder if the wife's manner didn't lead the husband to suspect something was amiss."

Evie's expression didn't change but anger flashed in her eyes. "Certainly, men jump to irrational conclusions all the time on the flimsiest bits of circumstantial evidence."

Hugh frowned. "I don't."

Bianca snorted. "You're not married."

"If, of course, the wife is innocent," Miranda began.

"And one does have to wonder about that as well," Portia pointed out.

"But if the wife has done nothing untoward, how terribly humiliating for her," Miranda continued. "For anyone, let alone Lady Dunwell, to know your husband doesn't trust you, it's very nearly unforgivable. I would be furious as well, and I daresay, my forgiveness would not be easily gained."

"I don't know why you are all assuming the wife is innocent," Hugh said. At once, six pairs of indignant female eyes pinned him. "Although she probably is," he added quickly.

"Nonetheless if a man loves his wife . . ." Sebastian chose his words with care. "Isn't a certain amount of jealousy to be expected on occasion?"

"But if a man trusts his wife as well as loves her," Veronica said, "wouldn't he confirm any doubts he might have by, oh, I don't know, asking her outright rather than letting his suspicions build until he finds himself bursting into the wrong hotel room?"

"I do wish you would all stop using the word *burst*," Adrian said sharply. "It conjures up images of splintered doors and madmen persecuting innocent wives."

"*Burst* is how it was told to me." Bianca's brows drew together. "Whatever is the matter with you?"

"You'll have to forgive your brother," Evie said smoothly. "He has not been sleeping well of late."

"Poor dear," Helena said with an overly innocent smile.

"My apologies," Adrian muttered and took a long swallow of his wine. Even if the incident at the Langham was now fodder for gossip, the identity of the irate husband was apparently not public knowledge. Yet. With any luck, it never would be. And if there was one lesson he had learned through years of clandestine operations, while luck could not be counted on, luck often made the difference between failure and success.

"Veronica." Evie turned to his sister-in-law and

smoothly changed the subject. "Have you seen the new exhibition at the Grosvenor Gallery?"

"Not as of yet." Veronica shook her head. "But I have heard nothing but the most wonderful . . ."

Within moments the conversation had turned to art, which would inevitably lead someone, probably Bianca, to the latest gossip concerning the artistic community in London. There was always something scandalous in the air, and Bianca was extremely fond of art. And scandal.

She was good, his wife, but then Adrian knew that. While he was grateful for her intervention, one look in her eyes told him the conversation had not helped his cause. And how could it? With every female present expressing her opinion as to the unforgiving nature of the unnamed husband's sins. It was obvious the conversation served to remind her why she was so angry and hurt. As heartened as he was by his talk with Evie this evening, and their kiss, it was clear even diamonds would not lure her back to his house, or his bed, tonight.

When it came to his wife, at least at the moment, his luck might well have run out.

Chapter 17

"**D**are we ask what vile crime you committed?" Hugh asked casually after the ladies had left the gentlemen to their brandy.

"Why do you think I have committed a vile crime?" Adrian said.

"You do understand . . ." Sebastian chose his words with care. "Mother told us you and your wife have had some kind of falling-out."

"And that she is now living in that house of hers," James added.

"So, as Evelyn has always struck us as most level-headed and not at all the type of woman to blow things out of all proportion . . ." Hugh studied his older brother over the rim of his glass. "It's only natural to assume the crime you committed was most vile."

"However," James added quickly, "as she attended dinner tonight and we noticed no overt rancor between you—"

"Although there were a few harsh looks," Hugh said under his breath.

"We also assume your crime was not so vile as to involve another woman."

"I would never be involved with another woman." Indignation sounded in Adrian's voice. "I gave up other women when I married."

"Most men do." James nodded. "Or they say they do."

Adrian narrowed his eyes.

"However," James added quickly, "a man whose wife has three protective brothers and who values his life would never stray." James's firm gaze slid from one brother to the next. "Nor would a man who is more in love with his wife now than on the day they wed."

Sebastian chuckled. "Excellent answer."

James shrugged. "Nothing but the truth." He grinned. "But it was good, wasn't it?"

Hugh raised his glass to his brother-in-law. "You, James, are a lucky man." He turned to his brothers. "As are the two of you."

"No argument there," Sebastian said with a smug smile.

Adrian sipped his brandy and wished his sister allowed cigars in her dining room.

"So . . ." Hugh studied his brother with what Adrian had always thought of as his assessing barrister look. "Are you going to tell us what you did or shall our imaginations run amok?"

Adrian forced a cool smile. The last thing he wanted was to share his idiocy with his brothers. "Run away."

James shook his head. "My imagination is not up to a challenge like this. I shall leave that in the hands of the author among us."

Sebastian chuckled. "And while I can think of any

number of sins that are significant but not unforgivable, it's probably best to keep them to myself."

"You are wiser than you look," Adrian said.

"He would have to be." Hugh laughed.

"Perhaps, as we are discussing my wisdom," Sebastian began, "I might be of some assistance. In regards to the handling of wives, that is."

Adrian scoffed. "You've been married, what? Scarcely a month?"

"And yet . . ." Sebastian's eyes narrowed in a crafty manner. "I have already learned a great deal."

"If I were to solicit advice from any of you it would be James." Adrian nodded at his brother-in-law. "He's been married forever."

"Not forever." James scoffed and sipped his brandy. "On occasion it may feel like forever . . ."

Hugh chuckled.

"But well worth it all in all." James thought for a moment. "It hasn't been entirely perfect but then what is in life? What it has been is good and it continues to be good."

"Our life is good," Adrian said staunchly.

"No doubt." Hugh paused. "Then this difficulty of yours—"

"A momentary aberration," Adrian said firmly. "I expect it to be resolved in no more than another day or two."

"I see." James studied him. "Then you have apologized, vowed never to do whatever it is you did again, groveled—"

"I do not grovel," Adrian said sharply. "I'm not sure I even know how to grovel. But I have apologized, more than once."

"Then all you can do is continue to apologize," James said. "And wait."

Sebastian nodded. "For her to come to her senses."

Hugh snorted. "You really haven't been married very long."

"The last thing you want to do is tell a wife to come to her senses," James said firmly. "Especially when you are in the wrong, as I assume Adrian is."

"So it would appear," Adrian muttered.

"Nothing infuriates a wife more than the implication that she is irrational, even if she is." Warning sounded in James's voice. "You may trust me on this. I am speaking from experience."

"But you're suggesting I wait?" Adrian shook his head. "I would much prefer to take some sort of action."

"Perhaps you should reconsider groveling," Hugh murmured.

Adrian ignored him. "I was quite optimistic before dinner. We spoke when she arrived and I believe she was very close to forgiving me." He glanced around the table. "I was quite charming."

"No doubt. However, it might have been wise, all things considered," Hugh said, "if you had refrained from coming to the defense of the outraged husband in the tale Bianca told."

"Oh, she did not like that." Sebastian grimaced.

"Nor did any of them." James sipped his brandy. "They are much like herding beasts in that respect, banding together to protect one of their own."

"If I recall correctly, you were once quite skilled at seduction," Hugh said. "Of course, you might well have lost those skills."

Adrian raised a brow. "Those are not the kind of skills one loses." He paused. "Although admittedly, they may well be rusted from lack of use."

"Perhaps you should try seduction. I daresay she won't be overly critical." Hugh shrugged.

Adrian narrowed his eyes. "Thank you for your confidence."

"You have my complete confidence," Hugh said staunchly. "You won her once, you can do it again. Proceed as you did when you first met. Flowers, romantic notes, that sort of thing."

"I have." Adrian huffed. "I am."

"I know this is not what you want to hear, but in situations like this, not that we actually know the situation, time really does heal all wounds." James leaned forward and met Adrian's gaze. "You say she was softening toward you?"

"It seemed so." Of course, that was before she had been reminded of his misdeeds.

"Then continue what you have been doing. Remind her of why she married you in the first place, exactly as Hugh suggested." James thought for a moment. "Perhaps take her to a fine dinner. Or escort her to a ball. Dancing is an excellent means of working your way back into a woman's heart."

"Aren't you going to that charity ball tomorrow night?" Hugh asked.

"It's on my schedule," Adrian said wryly.

"We are planning to attend," Sebastian said. "According to Veronica, it's to be a Venetian masquerade complete with costume and masks." He grinned. "There is nowhere more romantic than Venice and nothing as enticing as flirtation behind a mask."

"You can be anyone behind a mask. Who you really are." Hugh cast them a wicked smile. "Or someone else entirely."

"There is that," Adrian said under his breath. And hadn't he already realized that? Wasn't that why he had decided the masquerade was the perfect place for Eve and Sir to finally meet in person? Although perhaps he hadn't considered the consequences of *romantic* and *enticing* in terms of Sir. Nor did he wish to. But *enticing* and *romantic* might serve a man wanting his wife back quite well. "It's something to consider."

"I'd say it's a plan." Hugh raised his glass in a toast.

Adrian shrugged. "I would scarcely call it a plan."

"Oh, it's definitely a plan." Sebastian nodded. "Believe me, I know plans and this one sounds most effective."

"So for one more night, you allow your wife time to consider how much she misses her charming husband," James said.

"Women always want that which is not too easily had." Sebastian nodded in a sage manner. Perhaps he had learned something about wives after all. Or more likely, he simply knew women.

"And tomorrow night, helped by Venetian splendor and a night of dance and romance. Tomorrow night, old man . . ." James, too, raised his glass. "You shall seduce your wife."

"They should have family dinners more often." Max's fingers traced lazy patterns over her naked abdomen, trailing up to her breasts and then drifting lower to her stomach.

"But as it will not continue forever, I need to be on

my way." Celeste propped herself up on her elbows and glanced down at his hand. His touch teasing and tantalizing and more than sufficient to make her forget her responsibilities. Desire once again tightened within her. She ignored it. "Whatever are you doing?"

"I am writing you a note."

"Pity I can't read it."

He leaned forward and kissed her stomach. "Shall I read it to you? It's very interesting."

For a moment desire warred with duty. "Next time you may read it to me." She sighed. "Now, however, I should be off. I wish to return home before Evelyn does."

She started to sit up but he pulled her back down.

"You're not going anywhere yet." He threw his leg over hers, shifted to straddle her, then captured her wrists with one hand and held them over her head. He bent and nuzzled the side of her neck. "You love it when I do this."

"I hate it when you do that," she lied and he knew it. How could she hide it? The way her treacherous body writhed beneath him . . . the breathless note in her voice . . . "Stop it this instant and release me."

He murmured against her skin. "You and I both know if you really wanted me to stop, you have ways of accomplishing just that." He raised his head and grinned down at her. "Painful and most effective ways."

"You would be wise to remember that."

"It is never far from my mind." He released her wrists and straightened but continued to sit with his knees on either side of her hips. He gazed down at her. "I miss you."

She laughed. "I doubt that. I am here nearly every other night."

He shook his head. "But you never stay the entire night."

"There are reasons for that."

"I know." His tone was abruptly serious. "I want you here every night. I want you here when I awaken in the morning."

"Max." She sighed. "If you are talking about marriage again—"

"I am."

"I told you I am not the type of woman you should marry."

"And I told you I shall marry whomever I please." He moved off her and slid off the bed. He grabbed his trousers and pulled them on.

She sat up and pulled the sheet up around her. "If you are putting on clothes, this must be serious."

"It is." He buttoned his trousers and looked at her. "I am tired of this."

"Nonsense." She ignored the touch of fear that flickered inside her. "You are the least tired man I have ever met. Indeed, *insatiable* is a more accurate term than *tired*."

He grinned. "Thank you." His expression sobered. "But I am tired." He waved at the bed. "Of sharing nothing aside from this." His gaze met hers. "I want more."

"There isn't any more, Max," she said softly, hoping he didn't notice the catch in her throat. "Not for us."

He stared at her for a long moment. "You may well be the most stubborn woman I have ever met."

"Then we are well matched as you are the most stubborn man."

"And I have never failed in achieving what I want."
His eyes narrowed. "You will marry me, Celeste."

She raised a brow. "If that is a proposal, it's rather
high-handed of you."

"It's not, a proposal, that is." He shook his head.
"Only a fool would ask a question he knows the answer
to, if that answer is not what he wants. I will not ask
you until I know you will say yes."

"Then I hope you are a patient man." She wrapped
the sheet around herself and slipped out of bed, glancing around, as always, for her clothes. "As I cannot
conceive of that happening."

Without warning, he grabbed her and pulled her into
his arms. "You love me, you know."

She stared into his eyes for an endless moment and
considered denying it. At last she sighed in surrender.
"Yes, I suppose I do."

"Good." A slow, satisfied smile spread across his
face. "Someday, very soon now, you will agree marriage is the best gift we can give one another."

"Really?" She forced a light tone to her voice. "And
I have always considered emeralds to be the best—"

"I want you in my bed every night and every morning." He gazed down into her eyes. "I want to introduce
you to my family, my friends. I want to dance with you
at grand balls and picnic with you in public parks. And
I want you by my side on the day I breathe my last."

"Goodness, Max," she said weakly. "All that?"

"All that and more. I want you to be the mother of
my children." His tone hardened. "And I want to be the
father to your children."

"It does tend to work better that way."

His eyes narrowed. "You know what children I'm
talking about."

"I should have expected you would not let that go." She pulled out of his arms, spotted her undergarments, and crossed the room to collect them. "I knew it was a mistake to mention them." She pulled her chemise on over her head.

"Why was it a mistake?" His brows drew together. "I rather like children, you know. I was a child once myself."

"Once?"

He ignored her. "You should have told me about them."

"What? And keep you from the joy of solving the mystery yourself?" She continued to dress as he talked. "I knew you would although I had thought you would be too distracted by that file business to turn your attention to this so quickly. How is that situation?"

"There is nothing new in regards to the file. And you are changing the subject."

"But I do it so well." She wrapped her corset around her midsection and turned her back to him to enable him to assist her. It struck her that it was the sort of thing a husband might do for a wife. "Very well, then. Do tell me what you have discovered."

He stepped closer and started tightening her laces. "What I have learned is that some two years ago, around the time you allegedly left the department, which I am now seeing in an entirely different light, by the way."

"Are you?" She bit back a smile.

"I am indeed." He tugged at the laces. "Upon reflection it now strikes me that, while I was prepared to convince you to leave the department to be at Evelyn's side should she need you, little persuasion was necessary. I had always thought you liked, no, reveled in this life of secrecy and danger and triumphs that are never made public."

"It was great fun," she murmured.

"Instead of objecting, if I recall correctly, you thought it was a grand idea. You said . . ." He tugged again. "It was time to have a more settled kind of life although, I must confess, I had never thought of you as the type of woman who wished for *settled*."

"We all have our secrets, Max."

"Apparently. As I was saying, that is, when you, for lack of a better word, *inherited* five small children, three girls and two boys. Now ranging in age from four to eight."

She glanced at him over her shoulder. "And do you know their names as well?"

"Of course I do," he said, giving her laces one last tug, then tying them tight. "Beth, Kate, Wills, Emily, and Daniel." He finished with her laces, then wrapped his arms around her and pulled her close. "You do know I have four brothers and two sisters?"

She nodded.

"I have always wanted a large family." He paused. "Five seems an excellent place to start."

"Do you know about their mother?"

"From what I have been able to discover . . ." He paused and she braced herself. "It seems she might have been your sister."

"In many ways she was." She pulled her thoughts together. She had never told this story, not even to Evelyn, never thought she would. Now she wondered if she had mentioned the children because she wanted this man to know. Perhaps it was a test of sorts. Of trust possibly. Or love. She drew a deep breath. "When I was a child, after my mother died, I was passed from one family to another. Some might have been relations, I really don't know."

"I'm sorry." Genuine sympathy sounded in his voice although she was sure he already knew this about her background.

"Don't be. It was far better than being on the streets. Often, it was no better than being a servant. But the last family I was with, they lived in a village an hour or so from London." She rested her head back against his shoulder, and his arms tightened around her. "They were very kind. They had three children of their own but that didn't stop them from taking in the rest of us. Altogether there were eleven children in that tiny cottage." She smiled at the memory. "There was little money but it was the happiest time of my life.

"Laura was their daughter and my age. We were very close, much like sisters, until I left to try my hand in the theater and she married." She paused to collect her thoughts. "They're all gone now. Her parents died, oh, some ten years past and her brothers were killed, one in Africa the other in India. Laura and I had lost contact with one another, but a little over two years ago, I received a letter from her through one of the theaters where I had once performed.

"I went to see her, of course. She was in a dreadful state." Even now, the memory of the hovel where Laura and her children resided threatened to overwhelm her. "Her husband had died a few months earlier. She was ill and knew she hadn't much time left. Days, as it turned out. Daniel was only two, Beth was six. She asked me to take care of her children when she died."

"And you have," he said quietly.

"In some ways it's the repayment of a debt but it's

more than that." She thought for a moment. "I remember her parents once saying children should not be tossed away like so much rubbish. I would have been thrown away if not for them." Her tone hardened. "I could not let that happen to Laura's children."

"So, now you lease a modest house in Chelsea with a small staff to care for the children. You spend all you earn on their support. And on those nights that you are not with me, you are with them."

"You are clever, Max." She twisted in his arms to face him.

"Clever enough to know what I want."

"You only want marriage because you can't have it." She pushed out of his arms and looked for her skirts.

"I can have it and I will."

"Then you should find someone more acceptable to your family, your friends, your position." She located her skirts and stepped into them.

"I don't want someone more acceptable, I want you."

"What a way you have with words, Max," she muttered, pulling up her skirts.

"Bloody hell, Celeste, I don't care what anyone else thinks. I want you and I want you as my wife."

"Max—"

"I have been with no one but you, nor have I wanted anyone but you, for three years." He glared. "That alone should be evidence of my intentions."

"Max—"

"I know I just mentioned marriage recently but I have been thinking about this for some time now. I am tired of"—he waved at his room—"of living my life alone." He studied her. "I am quite well off financially, you know. I am well able to support a fine house and a wife and more than five children. I have a substantial inheritance I have yet to touch save for some sound investments. In truth, I could be considered a wealthy man."

"Oh, well, then, if you are rich, I should marry you at once," she snapped and continued dressing.

"I'm not saying you should marry me because I have money." He glared. "But because you love me. You admitted it a few minutes ago."

"And when I did so, your response, if I recall correctly, was *good*!"

"Because it was good to know, finally, after all this time, that you love me! I was glad, and *good* seemed appropriate." He huffed. "I would hate to be in love alone."

She narrowed her eyes.

"I love you. There I said it. I want to spend the rest of my life with you. And you . . ." He grabbed her and pulled her back into his embrace. "You want that, too."

She shook her head. "Max—"

"There's no need for an answer." He pulled her tighter against him and kissed her hard and fast. And took her breath away. "I said I wouldn't ask until I knew I would get the answer I wanted. Now." He released her and stepped back. "You should be on your way."

"Yes, I should."

He moved to the window and looked out. "Your cab is waiting."

"Thank you."

"But one day soon, Celeste DeRochette, I will not send you home because one day soon your home will be with me." His smile belied the serious look in his eye. "Married or not."

"Wicked man."

His laughter trailed behind her as she closed the door and she grinned. If nothing else, the man was amusing. No, he was much more than amusing. He was . . . all she'd ever wanted but never dared to hope for. Even if one didn't consider his fortune or position, he was still the kind of man women dreamed of. He was clever and kind and funny, and she could not think of anyone she would rather spend her life with. Not that she had ever truly thought she would marry at all.

She stepped into the carriage and settled back for the brief ride home. Was she being unfair to him? Or to herself? Was he brave enough, strong enough, to marry a woman his family and friends considered beneath him? Wasn't that the surest way to destroy what they had? She'd never had her heart broken before; she had always guarded against being hurt. Could she trust Max with her heart? With the rest of her life? With her children?

With every turn of the carriage wheel, she wondered at the very idea of being married to the man she loved. Of living together in the same house with her children—their children.

And wondered as well if it was his courage she questioned or her own.

Adrian wasn't the only one who had difficulty sleeping alone.

Evelyn tossed and turned and couldn't get all that had occurred tonight—and worse, all that hadn't—out of her head. Blast it all, she wished Celeste had been here when she'd returned home and not out wherever it was she went at night. At some point, her dearest friend was going to have to trust her with her secrets. It would have been nice to discuss the evening with someone rational. Evelyn hadn't felt even remotely rational since Max had demanded her return to the department. She did wish the bloody man would come up with something solid in the search for the file. Waiting was more difficult than any kind of action and preyed on her nerves.

Then, of course, there was Adrian. She had been within moments of forgiving him and throwing herself bodily into his arms. Blasted man did that to her and had from the first time they'd met. It was all well and good to talk about soul mates, but in reality she truly was incomplete without him. They were halves of a whole. Even after they had heard Bianca's latest gossip and she had realized his bursting in on Beryl and Lord Radington was public knowledge and even after his sisters had recognized the monumental sin that had been committed, she had still considered returning home tonight. After all, he had been most charming at the beginning of the evening. And whether he noticed or not, he certainly had ignited that spark of desire within her.

She had been entirely truthful when she'd told him she didn't expect him to be charming all the time. But tonight, it was as if they'd gone back to the first days of their meeting when he was indeed charming and romantic. Not that he wasn't always fairly charming and somewhat romantic, but they had been married for two full years and things between them had become more comfortable than romantic; he was more affable than charming. And she was . . . content. But tonight it had been as if he were trying to make her fall in love all over again. And she was.

She sat up, punched her pillow, much harder than was necessary, then flopped back down. Not that it would make any difference. Her husband apparently thought his cause had been lost thanks to the conversation at dinner. She had hoped he would insist on driving her back to her house, which would naturally lead to him making improper advances in the carriage, which she had been fully prepared to subtly encourage. And in the throes of increasing desire, she would scarcely notice that he had the driver take them to their house instead of her house. Indeed, she had suspected it would take hours of bliss in his bed before she would realize where they were. Then, after chastising him soundly for taking advantage of her passion-drugged state, she would relent. After all, as she was already home and in his bed . . . And her legs would once again entwine with his, his naked body would heat hers, the feel of his hands exploring and caressing and teasing would take her to a place of sheer sensation. His mouth pressed to hers, their breath mingling, their tongues tangled . . . The taste of him on her lips, the smell of him surrounding her, the feel of him moving inside her . . .

Good Lord. She groaned and rolled over. What was wrong with the man? Right now they could be, *should* be, together. Surely he realized he'd had her very nearly in the palm of his hand before dinner. He was not a man to give up easily, yet after the gentlemen had rejoined the ladies and the family had begun to take their leave, he'd said he had matters to discuss with Hugh. But he had suggested he escort her to the masquerade. She agreed and then he had, pleasantly enough, bade her good night, looked for just a moment as if he wished to kiss her again, then directed their

driver to take her to her house. Why hadn't he realized
that the evening as she had imagined it would have allowed them both a certain measure of victory? She
would have come home without feeling that she had surrendered, and he could have savored at least a semblance
of victory. Damn it all, she wanted him to win her!

And if Adrian's actions, or lack of them, weren't
enough to drive her mad, she had returned home
tonight to find another note from Sir.

*My dear Eve, it had read. I regret to say there is
nothing to report regarding the whereabouts of the stolen
file. Therefore, I shall soon recommend your obligation to
this department be terminated.*

Well, that was something at any rate. But unfortunately the note had not ended there.

*As much as I know it is highly inappropriate to use
these missives for personal purposes, if you recall, this is
not the first time. Admittedly, your life is much different
now than when we last worked together, as you are now wed
to another. I should apologize for my presumption but I
cannot regret at last putting my feelings to paper. When it
comes to desire, dearest Eve, I am no different than any man.*

Oh, that was more than she wished to know.

*You have not merely filled my thoughts these past two
years but my dreams. Dreams of the two of us together,
lost in one another. Dreams I can neither ignore nor deny.
Dare I hope to one day see them fulfilled? Yours, Sir*

Wonderful, just bloody wonderful. And what in the name of all that's holy did he mean by *see them fulfilled*? How absurd. While his notes in years past had, on occasion, been most flirtatious, this was, well, *more*. Was Sir bent on seduction? Surely not. Although *see them fulfilled* did sound suspiciously like seduction. Not that it mattered. She was, after all, married now and happily so in spite of present circumstances.

Still, it was more than a little gratifying to know there was a man who dreamed of her and wanted her and perhaps even intended to pursue her. A man who, admittedly, had once filled her own dreams. A man who, had he made these declarations long ago, might well have won her heart.

She heaved a heartfelt sigh, rolled onto her back, and stared unseeing at the shadowy ceiling. Odd that on a night like this when she was unable to sleep and erotic images and desires filled her head, they weren't for a man of adventure and excitement and mystery. But for the man who drove her quite mad and didn't always realize what she wanted or even when he had won. The man who could still make her tremble with desire and melt her with his kiss and take her breath away.

The one man, the only man, who always would.

Chapter 18

If one didn't know better, one might have thought one was indeed at a glittering ball in Venice a century ago. Masked guests garbed in silks and satins, powdered wigs, and sparkling jewels crowded the Effington House ballroom, the London home of the Duke and Duchess of Roxborough. The duchess had graciously offered to host the masquerade as the event was, after all, for the benefit of charity. The huge ballroom itself was as festive as its guests. Urns were filled to overflowing with greenery and blossoms, no doubt from the Effington greenhouses. Gas lighting was eschewed in favor of candles, in the spirit of eighteenth-century Venice, and candlelight flickered from candelabras and sconces and centerpieces. It was, all in all, a setting enchanting and magical and romantic.

If, of course, one was in the mood for enchanting and magical and romantic. And not in the mood to strangle one's husband in his sleep.

Evelyn accepted a glass of champagne from a passing waiter and surveyed the room. She had been here for a good half hour thus far and had barely managed to make her way much past the doors of the ballroom, the crowd was so thick.

When their carriage had arrived at her house this evening, there was no Adrian, simply a note saying he would be late but would join her here. One would think if one was trying to win back one's wife, one would make an effort to, oh, make an appearance when one said one would. She hadn't attended an event like this without an escort since before she was married, and even then, Max or Celeste or someone else from the department unknown to her was somewhere in the vicinity. Odd how two years of marriage changed things. She used to feel quite confident on her own. Tonight she was vaguely ill at ease. Incomplete perhaps. Not that it really mattered. She was probably acquainted with most of the people here. Of course, her gaze skimmed the crowd, no one was recognizable behind the masks and clothing of the Venice of a long past age. But then, her spirits brightened, neither was she.

Still, even if one could not properly identify individuals, one could tell a lot about a person, especially men, by what they chose to wear at an event like this. What they chose to hide and what they revealed.

She noted a fair number of men whose satin waistcoats were matched in fabric to that of a woman's gown. Obviously those were married or betrothed couples who were either too stupid to realize how predictable such a display was or the gentleman was too under the thumb of his wife to protest or simply didn't care. Or the couple was too much in love to be completely anonymous for one mere night. She pressed her lips together. She had come perilously close to ordering a matching waistcoat for Adrian when she had ordered her own gown. He would have laughed, but he would have worn it to please her.

Then there were those gentlemen who wore the knee britches and brocade coats of a century ago with a confident air and a swagger in their step. No doubt, somewhere inside, those gentlemen regretted that men now wore black and white for formal occasions instead of the peacock hues of their predecessors. Those would be the Lord Radingtons of society who never doubted their charm or skills with women. In contrast were those men wearing very much the same style of dress who appeared, in their manner of movement, to be ill at ease in garb that was not what they were accustomed to wearing. Evelyn suspected they had no lack of confidence under ordinary circumstances but now felt somewhat silly.

Amid the brightly colored silks and satins were those gentlemen who had chosen the very Venetian white bauta mask, covering nearly the entire face and muffling the voice. Coupled with the traditional black tricorn hat and hooded black cloak, the effect was one of total anonymity as well as mystery. Who knew what face was behind that mask and what that gentleman might be hiding?

As for the women, Evelyn hadn't seen one yet who was wearing a full mask. Most wore some sort of half mask, simple or ornamented with gems and feathers, that covered only the eyes, as did she. But then women as a whole tended to delight in the donning of extravagant gowns and hairpieces and wanted to look as alluring as possible. She certainly did. There was something about wearing the cream and gold, satin and lace confection in the style of the last century she'd had made for this occasion that was most intoxicating. Its daringly low bodice coupled with her powered wig and cream satin mask could very nearly make her believe she was someone else entirely. Someone desirable and alluring and even a touch wanton. And wasn't that the nature of a masquerade? Evelyn would have wagered there wasn't a woman here who didn't wish to look like the most delectable Venetian courtesan of the past. And why not? Behind a mask, you could be anyone at all. She sipped her champagne and smiled to herself. And perhaps tonight, she would be.

"Darling, you look exquisite tonight." A woman in an extravagant red and gold gown appeared before her. Her powdered wig was as extreme as her dress. Her mask was gilded and jeweled, her fan gold lace, and her bodice so low Evelyn feared what might happen if she leaned forward. Even so, Evelyn couldn't help feeling a prick of envy. While she was quite pleased with her own appearance tonight, and in truth thought she had rarely looked better, the woman before her was nothing short of magnificent. Indeed, she was a vision of a Venetian enchantress, if only in a man's dreams.

"As do you but then you always do," Evelyn said lightly as if she knew who was behind the mask. Although the voice was vaguely familiar.

The red courtesan studied her, then laughed. "You have no idea who I am, do you?"

Evelyn considered a polite lie. After all, if they had met on the street and Evelyn had been unable to recall her name, she certainly would have pretended otherwise. But this was a masked ball, and under these circumstances, not realizing someone's identity was something of a compliment. She shrugged in a helpless manner. "My apologies but I have no idea who you are."

The courtesan sniffed. "So much for friendship."

Evelyn stared for a moment, then laughed. "Beryl, of course. I should have realized at once."

Beryl fluttered her fan and cast her a smug smile. "Because no one else you know could possibly look as glorious in the garb of a seductress?"

"Well, yes, that." Evelyn grinned, leaned closer, and lowered her voice. "And the fact that only you would wear something so daring."

"Daring?"

"Your bosoms, dear." Evelyn nodded at the other woman's bodice. "Another quarter of an inch and you will pass daring and slide right into tomorrow's gossip." She adopted a falsetto voice. "My goodness, did you see Lady Dunwell's bosoms spring free from her gown? And at a charity event, no less. The woman has no sense of propriety."

"Oh dear, I hadn't thought of that. But as you didn't recognize me, no one else will." She cast Evelyn a wicked smile. "I shall have to take off my mask should my bosoms escape their confines. I would hate for gossips not to have the correct information." Beryl glanced down at her impressive display of décolletage. "Although I would think my bosoms would be recognizable to any number of people even with my mask on."

Evelyn stared. "You really have no sense of propriety at all, do you?"

"I certainly hope not." Beryl huffed. "I have put a great deal of effort into my wicked reputation, and I should hate for it to have been a waste."

Evelyn laughed. Good Lord, Beryl was scandalous and immoral and destined, no doubt, to come to a bad end. Still, there was something Evelyn quite liked about her. Perhaps it was because she was so unlike anyone else she knew.

"But how did you know who I was?" Evelyn said. "I thought I was quite cleverly disguised."

"Ah yes, about that." Beryl glanced from side to side although with her mask on it was difficult to tell. "I shall explain but not here." She plucked Evelyn's glass from her hand and passed it to a waiter, then took her arm and steered her toward the entry.

"Where are we going?"

"Somewhere we won't be overheard."

"Why?"

"I may not care about my reputation, but I do have concerns for yours. You are such a proper sort." She heaved a heartfelt sigh. "And I am such a good friend."

Evelyn stifled a smile. "So I see."

"I told you I would be." They passed through the entry to the ballroom, then Beryl paused and glanced around. "The ladies' receiving room is down that corridor so we shall take this one instead."

Beryl headed down the hall, Evelyn by her side. Not at all easy given the width of their respective gowns. "Why are you being so mysterious?"

"I'm not being mysterious, dear, I'm being cautious. It's not nearly as much fun. And as I am, well, certainly not older but definitely wiser, I feel you would benefit from my advice."

"Do you?" Evelyn bit back a grin and silently thanked the department. In spite of her work for them, and any number of questionable activities, she had emerged with a public reputation which, while admittedly not spotless, was, as her mother-in-law put it, not especially blemished. Respectable enough to marry an earl. Her brows drew together. Where was he anyway?

Beryl pushed open a closed door and peered inside the room. "This will do."

Evelyn followed her into a fair-sized salon, tastefully appointed for both comfort and style, but then she would expect nothing less. "I must say your secrecy has quite piqued my curiosity."

"Secrecy is essential when one plays these sorts of games."

Evelyn narrowed her eyes. "What sorts of games?"

Beryl ignored the question and closed the door behind them. "As you know, there was a time when I had my cap set for Adrian."

"And?"

"I only mention it because I do know the type of man he is. It's of no significance really." Beryl shrugged. "You were his choice after all."

"When we met . . ." Evelyn chose her words with care. "Adrian said nothing that happened in our lives before then mattered."

Beryl stared. "Why, what a dear, sweet liar the man is."

"He is not." Evelyn huffed. No matter how annoyed she might be with her husband, she did not wish to hear anyone else speak ill of him.

"Goodness, dear, a man only says nothing in your pasts matters when he has more to hide than you do." She studied her for a moment. "Unless I'm mistaken."

Evelyn's stomach tensed. "Oh?"

"Well, I had thought you were extremely proper and I do know Adrian worships the ground you walk on—"

"Does he?"

"Of course. He tried to catch you *in flagrante delicto*."

Evelyn raised a brow. "And that means he worships me?"

"Not all husbands make the effort," Beryl said with a casual shrug. "Only a husband who truly cares or one who views his wife as nothing more than a possession would go to the trouble of tracking down his errant—"

"I was not errant!"

"Wife. Adrian has never struck me as the sort who would think of his wife as something he owns."

"No, he's not."

"I told you I know the type of man your husband is. You do realize how lucky you are?"

"Yes, I do." Evelyn pulled her brows together. "What on earth are you trying to say?"

"I'm trying to say that you should not follow in my footsteps."

Evelyn stared. "I should not what?"

"You have far too much to lose," Beryl said firmly.

"I have no idea what you are talking about."

Beryl studied her for a long moment. "You don't, do you?"

"No." Evelyn huffed. "And I thought you were going to tell me how you knew who I was."

"It all ties together, dear." She paused. "Are you certain you don't know—"

"Would you please tell me what you are going on about," Evelyn said sharply.

"You really don't know." Astonishment sounded in Beryl's voice. "How very interesting."

"Beryl," Evelyn snapped. "Out with it."

"Patience, my dear friend." Beryl grinned in a wicked manner. "Oh, this is delightful."

"Beryl!"

"Very well then." She heaved a dramatic sigh. "If you insist on taking all the fun out of it."

"And I do."

"I knew what you were wearing because you were pointed out to me."

"I haven't told anyone what I was wearing tonight." Evelyn shook her head in confusion. "Who on earth could have told you?"

"I have no idea." She shrugged. "He was wearing one of those white masks with the black hat and cloak. Why, you couldn't even see his hair." She thought for a moment. "He was tall, though."

"And this mysterious gentleman pointed me out to you?" Evelyn said slowly.

"Well, he had to, of course."

Her breath caught. "He did?"

"He did if he wanted me to deliver this to you." Beryl plucked a folded note from between her breasts although where she found room to hide something out of sight was beyond Evelyn. Beryl presented the note with a flourish.

Evelyn reached for it but Beryl pulled it back.

"You know nothing about this or who this man might be?"

"No." Evelyn held out her hand. "Now, give it to me."

"And you are not planning an assignation with a mysterious stranger at a masked ball?"

"Most certainly not!"

"No one can feign that kind of indignation." Beryl grinned and handed her the note. "I'm glad, you know. Aside from your recent difficulties, you and Adrian are very nearly the only truly happily married couple I know. Oh, certainly I can name any number of couples who are content, but you have always struck me as genuinely happy. As such, you are an example to the rest of us." She paused. "Well, not to me but to others." She handed Evelyn the note. "Don't do anything to muck it up."

"I have no intention of mucking up anything." Evelyn stared at the note in her hand.

"Well?" Beryl said impatiently. "Aren't you going to read it?"

Evelyn turned the note over in her hand. "I'm not sure."

"If you're afraid, I'll read it." Beryl reached for the note. "It's bound to be interesting."

"Oh no." Evelyn took a step back and shook her head. "I'll read it." She unfolded the note and knew, even before she saw the distinctive hand, who it was from.

At long last, the time has come. Dance with me, Eve.

"What does it say? Is it signed? Who is it from?"

Evelyn forced a light laugh. "I do hate to disappoint you, but it's nothing of significance. It's not signed, but the handwriting is that of an old friend. He's simply trying to be mysterious."

"An old friend?" Beryl studied her closely. "An admirer?"

"Not at all." She shrugged. "Simply someone I haven't seen in, oh, forever."

"That's all?"

"He does wish a dance."

Beryl sucked in a sharp breath. "Evelyn Waterston,

you're lying to me. How can you lie to your dearest friend?"

"I'm not lying," Evelyn said firmly. Indeed, Sir could well be considered an old friend, and as she had never seen him in person, *forever* was not entirely inaccurate. "It is from an old friend. He does wish a dance and it's not the least bit important." She refolded the note and tucked it into her bodice, realizing she had far more room to hide notes than her friend did.

"Are you going to dance with him?"

"As I have noted any number of gentlemen in white masks and black cloaks, and it's impossible to know which one he is . . ." She shrugged. "If a gentleman so attired asks for a dance, I see no reason to refuse."

"Won't Adrian mind?"

"Not in the least." She scoffed. "I dance with other gentlemen all the time at events like this. It is a ball, after all. Besides . . ." She paused. "Adrian has yet to arrive."

"He isn't here?" Surprise sounded in Beryl's voice.

"He was delayed. I do expect him at any minute." Nor was that a lie. She had thought he would be here by now.

"My, that is interesting," Beryl murmured.

As much as she didn't know her *dearest friend* well, she did recognize that tone. "What is interesting?"

"Adrian, who has been known to be jealous, is not yet here. And a gentleman who is completely disguised, with a mask that even muffles his voice, an old friend or so he says, has asked you to dance. And . . ." She paused. "This man knew how you were dressed."

"What are you getting at?"

"It seems to me, a masked ball presents the perfect opportunity to test a wife's loyalty. What if"—she paused dramatically—"your admirer is, in truth, your husband?"

"Don't be absurd." Evelyn scoffed. "Adrian would never do such a thing." Besides, she knew exactly who the note was from. Still, why not allow Beryl to suspect Adrian? It was certainly easier than explaining the complete truth.

"The same way he would never burst into a hotel room where he thought he would find you?"

"He doesn't like the word *burst*," she said under her breath.

"No doubt." Beryl thought for a minute. "There's really only one way to find out."

"And what way is that?"

"Why, we shall return to the ballroom." Beryl opened the door and waved Evelyn through. "And you shall dance with every man in a white mask and black cloak until you find your *old friend* or your husband."

"I couldn't possibly." Evelyn scoffed. "There must be dozens of men in that costume in the crowd."

"Then you have no time to waste." Beryl started down the corridor. "Come along."

"You do understand that usually I wait for a gentleman to ask me to dance."

"Good Lord, dear." Beryl sighed and glanced at her over her shoulder. "This is a masquerade. For the most part, no one knows who anyone else is. Anonymity makes anything possible. You can be anything you wish and tonight you are the epitome of a Venetian courtesan. A mere flick of your fan and any man in his right mind will fight for just one dance with you. You do look exceptionally fetching tonight."

"Yes, I do." And if she was at last to meet Sir in person, exceptionally fetching was the very least she wanted to look. She cast her friend a smug smile that belied the emotions churning within her.

Apprehension battled with anticipation. Once she had wanted nothing more in the world than to meet him, to speak to him, and yes, there had been a time when she had wanted more. A time when he had filled her dreams, fueled her desires. Now, the time had come. What would he be like? On one hand, she felt he was indeed an old friend that she knew well. On the other, he was no more than a shadowy figure from her past and she knew nothing about him at all. Was the unease that now lodged in the pit of her stomach fear that he would be less than she'd expected? Or did she fear he might be so much more?

And more to the point, how would she feel when meeting him at last? Would those nearly forgotten feelings return? As much as she loved her husband, was that love enough to overcome the temptation of a man she had truly known only in her dreams? A man who now wrote of his own dreams of the two of them together?

She drew a deep breath. She would prefer not to meet Sir at all, but it seemed she had little choice. Regardless, she was not the same woman she had been when she left the department. Then, she would have leapt at this opportunity. Then, she had no idea what love truly was. Then, she had nothing to lose. Now she knew love was the only thing in life worth fighting for. And no matter how adventurous or romantic or intriguing Sir might be, there was only one man who held her heart. Not at all adventurous and not overly romantic and very much an open book. But she loved him and she had had no doubt he loved her and would until they breathed their last.

"There's nothing to be done about it then," Evelyn said more to herself than to her friend. "I shall simply have to adopt my most flirtatious manner and dance with mysterious men who are, no doubt, quite dull without their masks."

"Excellent." Beryl nodded her approval. "And do keep in mind, behind your mask you can be anyone you wish."

"And as I can be anyone I wish tonight . . ." Resolve surged through her and she lifted her chin. "I believe I shall be me."

Chapter 19

What was Evie thinking?

Adrian narrowed his eyes behind his mask and continued to observe his wife from a discreet distance, in a nearly concealed alcove, tucked along the side wall of the ballroom. Since she and Beryl had returned, Evie had done nothing but dance with one gentleman after another. Each and every one dressed in the exact same costume he wore and each and every one dancing a bit closer and holding her just a little tighter than he considered appropriate. Of course, they didn't know who she was and she didn't know who they were. Not that it mattered. Seeing his wife in the arms of one man after another, chatting and laughing and obviously being most flirtatious, was more than a little disconcerting. As was the fact that she was obviously looking for Sir.

It was Beryl's fault, no doubt. It might well have been a mistake to give her his note to deliver to Evie although it had seemed a good idea at the time. He had seen Beryl and Dunwell arrive and had recognized their carriage. Of course, even if he hadn't, he would have still recognized Beryl regardless of any disguise. It had been a long time but he had seen those lovely breasts before. Besides, Beryl, given her own nature and the dubious fact that Evie now considered them friends, was more likely than anyone else to deliver his message without condemnation. Although she was also more than likely to encourage his wife to dance with every white-masked man in the room.

No. If there was any fault here for anything, it lay with him. He wasn't a man used to being wrong and he wasn't a man to make mistakes. But recently, it seemed he had made any number of mistakes and he had indeed been wrong more often than not.

He shouldn't have started this, and he shouldn't have continued it. He should never have let the idea that she married him because he was convenient fester in the back of his mind. He should never have allowed doubt to lead him to believe she would be unfaithful. He certainly should not have let his emotions overtake his head. He should have had far more substantial evidence before—he groaned to himself—*bursting* into a hotel room to confront her. He should have trusted her. Even when he failed to do so, he should have begged, pleaded, groveled to keep her in their house, where she belonged.

And he should have told her he was Sir right from the beginning. Now, he never could.

And now, this needed to end.

The music drew to a close and Evie took a step away from her partner. The gentleman in question might not have realized it, but to Adrian's eyes, it seemed she did so with a subtle air of relief. Good. He made his way through the crowd toward her. He still had no idea what he would do if she proved amenable to *Sir's* advances and hoped—no—prayed he would not have to find out.

He was still several yards away when she caught sight of him and froze. As if she knew it was him. But which him, an annoying voice in the back of his head asked. He ignored it. For no more than an instant he wondered if she indeed recognized him, then discarded the notion. Beryl hadn't recognized him and he had always thought her surprisingly perceptive. While it had been some time since he had donned any sort of disguise, he was confident tonight's was nearly perfect. The traditional Venetian garb was designed centuries ago to provide anonymity. The mask muffled his words, but he had also adopted a change in the timbre of his voice, a feat not as easy as it had once been. And with cork wedges in his shoes, he was a good two inches taller. No, Beryl hadn't recognized him and neither would his wife.

He stopped in front of her and nodded a bow. "I believe this is our dance, Lady Waterston."

She stared up at him. "Is it?"

The masquerade made this deception possible, but damnation, it would have been good to see her entire face.

"It is indeed. I believe you were looking for me."

She laughed lightly. "And I believe you flatter yourself. Why, I don't even know who you are."

He held out his hand. "Don't you, Eve?"

She gasped, then almost at once composed herself. She placed her hand in his. "It's a pleasure to meet you at last, Sir."

"The pleasure is entirely mine." He chuckled. "Shall we dance, or would you prefer to seek a setting more private?"

"I'm not sure that is either wise or proper."

"And yet tonight, no one would know who you are."

A smile curved her lips. "I would."

"If I recall, you were never overly concerned with propriety before."

"That was a different time and I was a different person." She shook her head. "Then I had nothing to lose."

"Ah yes, you married a respectable man with wealth and position."

Her smile tightened. "I did not marry my husband for his money or his name although I see nothing especially wrong with that. It's the nature of the world."

"Then why did you marry him?" He held his breath.

"The music has begun, Sir." She nodded at her hand still in his. "Even a man completely unrecognizable and one of any number of courtesans here tonight would be commented upon if we continued to stand with my hand in yours."

"Then a dance it shall be." He took her in his arms and they started off to the tune of a sedate waltz, fortunately for him. He was not as accustomed to the wedges in his shoes as he had once been, and a livelier tune might have been his undoing. Still, they danced together well, but then they always did. She was, after all, his partner. He gazed down at her. "Have you thought of this, Eve? Of dancing together? Of being in my arms?"

"Would you prefer complete honesty, or shall I be polite?"

"There have never been secrets between us." In spite of the kaleidoscope of dancers, of brightly colored silks and satins, swirling around them, it seemed as though they were quite alone. Caught up in their own world.

"No, I suppose there haven't been." She drew a deep breath. "There was a time when I thought of you a great deal."

He nodded. "Our work, of course."

"It had nothing to do with that. I will confess, I did once dream of dancing in your arms."

"And of my lips pressing to yours?"

"I would be less than honest if I denied it. And yet . . ." She shook her head. "Those thoughts ended the day I met my husband."

"Was I so easy to forget?"

"Oh, I have never forgotten you. I daresay I never will."

"Then . . ." He tried to pull her a little closer but she gracefully resisted.

"You and the department were my life for five years. I could scarcely forget that." Her smile returned. "It was a glorious adventure, a grand journey, and I am, oh, grateful, I suppose, to have experienced all that I did. However . . ." A firm note sounded in her voice. "I am more grateful for what I have found now."

He steered her through a turn, made somewhat more difficult by his shoes, but nearly perfect. Apparently, some skills were not entirely lost.

"But you haven't answered my question." Again he braced himself. "Why did you marry him?"

"It's not an easy answer but I suppose things like this seldom are." She fell silent for a long moment. "I wanted a man exactly like my husband. Someone solid and settled and respectable. An honorable man who cared about those things that seem ordinary—home and family and permanence. Apparently the answer is easy after all," she said thoughtfully. "When I met Adrian, I realized I didn't want a man exactly like him.

I wanted him." She cast him a brilliant smile and his breath caught. "And I still do."

"And yet," he said cautiously, "he is not here with you tonight."

"He will be." She sighed. "Sir, my husband is charming and intelligent. And yet, like any man, he can be an idiot as well. But make no mistake, he is my idiot and I love him with every fiber of my being."

His heart thudded. "I understood you were no longer under the same roof."

"Not for long." Determination showed in the set of her chin.

"Oh, are you going to forgive his transgression then? Not that I know what it is," he added quickly.

She laughed. "I'm surprised you don't. I thought you knew everything."

"I do try." He shook his head in a mournful manner. "But I am sadly out of practice."

"Oh dear, you shall shatter my illusions about you," she teased.

"I would hate to do that." He paused. He should stop this now. He knew what he needed to know. And yet . . . "Do you love him enough to forgive him?"

"I love him too much not to. Besides . . ." A thoughtful note sounded in her voice. "One could argue a great sin could be the result of great love."

"Is that what you think? That you share a great love?"

"Not at all." The smile on her face was that of a woman in love. With her husband. With him. What a fool he had been. "It's what I know."

"Then love is all, is it?"

"Oh my." She studied him for a moment. "You're one of those men, aren't you?"

"What men?" he said cautiously.

"One of those men who proudly and arrogantly proclaim they have never been in love." She leaned closer and spoke low into his ear. "Those are the ones who have the worst of it, you know, when it does happen."

"Do they?" He bit back a smile.

"Mark my words, Sir."

"Well, I am not one of those men. I have been in love but she loved someone else." He held her a little tighter and this time she did not resist. But there was a distinct air of farewell in her manner. God, he was a lucky man.

"I see." She nodded slowly. "I shall have to assume you are not speaking of me. Because if you aren't, we shall both be terribly embarrassed that the thought even crossed my mind. If you are, well, then I should have to make certain you understand that your feelings are not returned."

"Not even a little?"

She laughed. "Oh, certainly a little." She shook her head. "But not enough."

The last strains of the waltz ended and they drifted to a standstill. He released her with reluctance and slowly escorted her off the dance floor.

He drew a deep breath. "Thank you, Eve."

"No, Sir, thank you. I have long felt you were a book whose ending I had failed to read. I have always hated not finishing a book." She cast him a brilliant smile. "I can now close the book and set it away on a shelf with other books."

He gasped in feigned dismay. "Left to the ravages of mold and rot and worms?"

"Not at all. Set carefully aside to be cherished and

kept safe always." She smiled in a wry manner. "But never to be read again."

"You have no regrets at the turns your life has taken?"

"My life is as I always wished it would be. No, I said I would be honest and that isn't entirely honest." She paused. "In truth, Sir, my life is better than I ever imagined it could be, which has nothing to do with my husband's money or position and everything to do with the kind of man he is. Good and kind and clever and amusing. And while he may not have your adventurous spirit, he is the most exciting man I have ever met. At least he is to me. He has my heart and I could not live my life without him."

His heart twisted. "Then you have no regrets."

"Only a fool or someone quite perfect would have no regrets. I am not at all perfect, and I do hope I am not a fool. But my regrets are, for the most part, insignificant." She smiled. "I do regret that the only true mystery of my life will never be solved. That I will never know who you are. That I will never know if you are someone I see frequently at events like this. If we have exchanged idle conversation perhaps. Or if you are someone I pass and nod a greeting to in the park. I regret that I will never know your face."

"I could be dreadfully ugly, you know," he warned.

She laughed. "I doubt that but it doesn't matter." She tilted her head and gazed up at him. "Will you grant me a favor?"

"Anything."

"Someday, when you are very old and gray and you know the end of your days is near, will you send me one last note? Will you solve that mystery for me?"

"I would be delighted." He chuckled. "It will be something to look forward to in my declining years."

"A very long time from now, I hope."

"Still, one never knows how much time one has left."

"No, we don't, do we?" For a long moment she stared at him, then she smiled. "Farewell, Sir."

"Farewell, my dear Eve."

She turned and a moment later he had lost her in the crowd. But not for long.

She married him because she loved him. She may well think him an idiot, which admittedly he had been of late, and not adventurous and a man who cared about ordinary things, but she loved him and that was all that mattered.

He made his way through the throng to a side door, slipped out of the ballroom, and hurried to a salon he had found earlier in the evening where he had hidden what he would need to change from Sir. As he had the clothing he would wear to appear as Adrian on under the cloak, it was a simple enough matter. It would take him only a few minutes to discard this costume, change his shoes, and put on a different mask. Then he would return to his wife and take her in his arms.

And never let her go again.

She had to get home.

Evelyn hurried through the milling guests toward the exit. She had to see Adrian now, this very instant. She had wasted enough time allowing him to be foolish. And indeed, one never did know how much time one had left.

She asked a footman for her cloak and requested her

carriage be sent for. It was odd to have at last met Sir, even if she had still not seen his face. Once she had longed for this, wanted him to say the sorts of things he had come perilously close to saying tonight. But now . . . she shook her head. Now, it simply didn't matter. And now, she had to admit, if only to herself, that some of her apprehension had been in part a fear that, upon meeting him, desires she had thought long gone would return. That they hadn't was both a relief and an affirmation. She'd had no doubt about her love for her husband, but she had wondered if she might be tempted by a man she had once wanted but never had. Now, at last she knew.

Her carriage arrived quickly. She directed Davies to take her home, then settled back in her seat. She did hope Adrian wasn't already on his way. She would hate to pass him on the streets.

There was nothing she had said to Sir about Adrian and her love for him that she hadn't already known. But somehow, saying it all aloud, saying it to someone else, made her realize how very deep her love for him was. How much he really meant to her. And how lucky she truly was.

Adrian was the love of her life. Now she wondered if he understood that. All the things she had said to Sir, she should say to her husband as well. She always thought he knew how important he was to her but perhaps not. There was not now, nor would there ever be, any reason for jealousy or suspicion. He needed to know that.

And tonight she would make that very clear. Before she took him to his bed. Or perhaps, she smiled in a most wicked manner, afterward.

The carriage came to an abrupt stop. Davies's raised

voice could be heard along with at least one other. What on earth was going on? She huffed in impatience. She needed to get home as soon—

Without warning the carriage door jerked open. Before she knew what was happening, hands grabbed her and a gag muffled her screams. A rough sack was thrown over her head and pulled down over her shoulders, binding her arms against her. She caught no more than the briefest glimpse of men in masks. Men in masks were the bane of her existence tonight. She felt herself pulled out of the carriage and struggled all the while. It was futile and she knew it. Still the occasional grunts from her captors when her foot connected with some part of them, hopefully, extremely sensitive parts, was most gratifying. Within moments, she was transferred to another carriage and it took off at a surprisingly sedate pace. No doubt to avoid notice.

Fear threatened to overwhelm her but she pushed it aside. Now was not the time to become a fragile female. Besides, fear could be crippling and she needed her wits about her.

Obviously she was being kidnapped but to what end? Ransom? Adrian would certainly pay anything to ensure her safety. But there were other reasons for taking a woman against her will on the streets of London that were far more vile. Her jaw clenched. Those women were never heard from again.

It struck her that her captors were most efficient. They scarcely said a word. And when they did, they kept their words too low for her to make out what they said or recognize their voices. They were clever, these kidnappers of hers. They had obviously done this sort of thing before and were, just as obviously, well trained.

It seemed an endless time but it was surely not long at all before the carriage stopped. She was lifted out of the vehicle and carried for a brief time. It was useless to struggle. They were obviously much stronger than she. Her mind would be of greater use in terms of her escape.

Boards creaked with every footfall. There was a distinctive smell in the air and the sound of water slapping against wood. Of course, they were on the docks. She scoffed to herself. How very predictable. Unless they were taking her to a ship. Panic welled within her, and she fought against it. Admittedly, even as an agent, she had never been kidnapped, but she knew that neither fear nor panic would serve her now.

The thug carrying her stumbled and muttered an unintelligible curse. Before she knew what was happening, she felt herself flying through the air. She braced for impact and prayed she would not land in the water. In these skirts she would surely drown within moments and she would much prefer not to die that way. But she hit the dock with a jarring thud, her head smacking against something hard. And in the instant before blackness claimed her, the most absurd thought flashed through her mind.

This was not at all how she had planned to spend the rest of the evening.

Chapter 20

Damnation, where was she?

It had taken Adrian far longer to return to the ballroom than he had planned. Apparently, the secluded room he'd chosen to shed Sir's costume appealed to more than men wishing to change from one persona to another. He'd almost been discovered by a couple seeking a spot for a private moment with barely enough time to dive behind a sofa. Damnation. He had once headed a clandestine organization. Now he was reduced to hiding behind furniture. Fortunately, the unidentified lovers—he never did get a look at their faces, and their voices were unfamiliar—did not linger. Apparently, they both had to return to their respective spouses.

Still, even with the delay, he was in high spirits. And why wouldn't he be? All his doubts had vanished with Evie's words.

Nearly an hour later, his mood had dimmed. Where was his blasted wife anyway? He was ready—no—eager to sweep her off her feet. And he was willing to wager he could do a far better job of it as himself than he had as Sir. If, of course, he put the same amount of effort into it. And from now on, he would. It had been rather fun really, attempting to lure his wife into seduction. He resolved to remember that.

He continued to circle the ballroom until he found himself near the main doors. It wasn't easy. He swore there were more people here now than there were when he'd left the room as Sir. And somewhere in this crush was Evie. From here perhaps he could get an overview of the entire room.

"You look like a man who could use something more substantial than champagne," a familiar voice said at his side. "But I fear this is all they are offering tonight." Max handed him a glass.

"I'm surprised to see you here." Adrian accepted the glass gratefully. His friend looked the perfect picture of a Venetian rake, Casanova perhaps, in a bronze-colored coat coupled with a heavily embroidered waistcoat, brown knee britches, and half mask. Adrian had thought his own costume with its blue coat, cream waistcoat, and dark britches to be very nearly too extreme, but next to his old friend, he felt like a wren beside a peacock.

"Why wouldn't I be here?" Indignation sounded in Max's voice. "I am not an earl but I am still socially acceptable. Even, dare I say, in demand. I am considered a most eligible bachelor, you know."

Adrian laughed. "How did you recognize me?"

"I have my ways." Max grinned. "But I'm surprised to see you here as well. I thought you and Evelyn would be home by now."

"We would be if I could find her."

"Then all went according to plan tonight?"

Adrian grinned. "Better than I could have hoped for."

"Excellent." Max breathed a sigh of relief. "Although I am surprised you managed it without assistance. I expected to hear from you."

"Nonsense. I had no problems at all. Not that I anticipated any."

"Your confidence is most impressive."

"And well deserved. You did lose your wager, by the way." He chuckled. "Between the mask, hooded cloak, and wedges in my shoes, she had no idea it was me."

"To my eternal regret." He raised his glass to his friend. "And your eternal happiness."

"You should find a good woman yourself, Max."

"I believe I have," Max said thoughtfully.

Adrian's brow rose under his mask. "Have you?"

"That's neither here nor there at the moment." Max paused. "I must admit, even I had a few misgivings about tonight's plan."

"Why? I knew it would work."

"Well, you did admit it was brilliant."

"Simple, Max." Adrian nodded sagely. "Simple and uncomplicated is always best."

Max stared at him. "There was nothing simple about it. It required a fair amount of coordination."

"Max." Adrian shook his head in confusion. "What are you talking about?"

"What are you talking about?" Max said cautiously.

"I'm talking about my plan to speak to Evelyn here tonight as Sir," Adrian said sharply.

"Oh." Max grimaced. "Am I to gather then that you didn't get the message I had delivered to your house earlier this evening?"

"What message?" A horrible thought occurred to him and his stomach twisted. "Max," he said slowly, "where is my wife?"

"You said it was a brilliant idea."

"Max." A warning sounded in Adrian's voice.

"I thought we had decided—"

"We decided nothing of the sort." Adrian turned, strode through the entry doors, across the marble floor, and down the steps leading to the Effington House grand entry. He pulled off his mask. He had no time for such nonsense. "I thought I made my position very clear about this."

Max, too, discarded his mask. He was right at his side. "Bloody hell, Adrian. I thought we had agreed."

Adrian crossed the foyer. "She is my wife. I would never agree to that." A footman opened the doors and Adrian continued into the night without pause.

Max grabbed his arm and pulled him to a stop, lowering his voice. "Yes, but you asked for my help and right now you work for me." His tone was hard. "If this goes awry, the blame will not be placed on you but on me. This is my responsibility because this is my department and I used its resources for personal reasons."

For the first time Adrian realized Max was not merely the face of the department; he was, in truth, its head. "Regardless, she is *my* wife." He ordered a footman stationed by the street to hail a cab. "Where is she?"

"Where we discussed," Max said sharply. "The warehouse cellar at the docks."

Fear stabbed him. He ignored it. "And the tide is rising."

"I would never place her in any real danger. The

water probably won't reach as high as her knees." Max scoffed. "The worst that will happen is that she'll get a little wet. A bit cold perhaps."

Adrian narrowed his eyes. "I can think of any number of other things that can happen to her in a cold, dark cellar with water rising around her."

"But they won't," Max said firmly.

"My lord," the footman called. "Your cab."

Adrian took a step. Max again grabbed his arm. "Aren't you going to change back into your costume? Back into Sir?"

"There's no time. I have to rescue my wife, remember?"

"I instructed a lantern to be left by the main warehouse door. Here." Max released him and withdrew a key from his waistcoat pocket. "This should do for the lock. I didn't think it was wise to leave the building unlocked. Simply a precaution, nothing more than that."

"I should beat you senseless for this." Adrian snatched the key from his hand and started toward the street.

"As if you could!"

"Hah!"

"And when you find her? Then what?"

"I have no idea," he said over his shoulder, hurrying toward the cab. He directed the driver to take him to the docks, then fairly leapt into the small carriage. Adrian leaned forward in his seat, as if he could urge the horses faster by strength of will alone.

Max was right. Evie was in little physical danger.

The real danger here was to their marriage and their future and the rest of their lives.

*   *   *

Celeste stared in disbelief, then stepped out of the shadows. "I thought you barely knew him."

"Celeste!" Max's eyes widened. "What are you doing here?"

"I came to find you. To get your help."

"My help?" Caution sounded in his voice. Oh, he was a crafty devil. "What do you mean?"

"Evelyn's driver said he was beset by thugs, tied up—not well, I might add, which I now find much more significant than I did a moment ago—and she was abducted. When he freed himself, he went to Lord W and, when he wasn't at his house, came to mine." She narrowed her eyes. "And I came to you."

"Quite right." Max nodded. "I shall take matters in hand from here."

"I suspect you've done quite enough already."

"Oh?" Max's expression was noncommittal, neutral as it were. This wasn't the face of Max, the man she loved, but rather of Sir Maxwell Osgood, head of the department. "Exactly how much did you hear?"

"More than you would like, no doubt." She studied him for a long moment. Even with all she had heard, it was still difficult to accept the truth. "Enough to know Evelyn's kidnapping was a sham." Anger surged through her. "Lord W is Sir, isn't he?"

"This is not the place for this discussion." He grabbed her arm and steered her toward the row of waiting carriages.

"You bloody bastard," she said under her breath.

"My birth was completely legitimate and I have the papers to prove it." They reached his carriage and he fairly tossed her inside. "I may be any number of things but bastard isn't one of them."

"I wasn't talking about your birth."

He issued directions to his driver, then climbed in beside her. "Yes, my love, I realize that."

"Sir is Lord W."

"Yes, he is."

"And he has been lying to his wife for the past seven years."

"I wouldn't say that." He shrugged. "She has only been his wife for two. Before that—"

"And you have been lying to me," she snapped.

"One could look at it that way, I suppose. Although in truth, you never asked, did you?"

She shook her head in confusion. "Never asked what?"

"You never asked me if Waterston was Sir. You never asked me if Evelyn was marrying the man she had worked for. The man you both worked for." Even in the scant light in the carriage, she could see his eyes narrow. "The man you both dreamed of."

She gasped. "You are twisting this about entirely. You are in the wrong here."

"No, I'm not. At least not for the most part. It's the nature of the department. Agents know only what they need to know. It was never necessary for you to know Waterston was Sir."

"Perhaps." He did have a point. One she could scarcely argue with. "But when Evelyn married—"

"She left the department. As did Sir. As, for all intents and purposes, did you."

"Still—"

"There is no *still* about it. I have never lied to you. There are things I have never told you because it was not necessary to do so. If anything, I am guilty of lies of omission, which I feel no need to apologize for as those were dictated by the nature—"

"Yes, yes, I know." Celeste waved away his words impatiently. "The nature of the department."

She considered what he had said and was hard-pressed to argue the point. Indeed, she had never asked about the man Evelyn had married, had never thought to ask. Why would she? In spite of his reputation with women, Lord W was of good family and had recently inherited a title. One could tell simply by looking at him that he would rise to the occasion. And he had. Nor would one ever have suspected his randy bachelor days concealed a life far more serious. And indeed, hadn't they always lived by the rule that people never saw what they did not expect to see?

"Admittedly, you have a valid point."

"I usually do."

"But," she said pointedly, "since you called Evelyn back to the department, you have to admit you have not been entirely honest with me."

"But"—his tone echoed hers—"you have to admit I did not actually lie to you either."

"You led me to believe—"

"Which is not the same as lying."

"I am still furious with you."

"Now who is lying?"

"You had my dearest friend kidnapped!"

"Yes, but I never lied about it." He shrugged. "It needed to be done."

"Why?"

"Waterston needed to know how his wife felt about him. Whom she would choose if given the choice."

She stared in disbelief. "You mean a choice between Lord W and Sir?"

"Yes."

"But they are one and the same."

"But she doesn't know that."

"And you helped him."

"He is my friend. He has saved my life on more than one occasion. It seemed little enough repayment." For a long moment Max didn't say a word. "Besides, I wanted him back."

"What do you—" The answer dawned on her and she sucked in a hard breath. "You never truly needed Evelyn at all, did you? You just brought her back to get her husband."

"It was rather clever."

"It was rather vile."

"*Vile* is a harsh word."

"And yet appropriate." She huffed. "What happens now?"

"Now?" He shook his head. "Nothing, it's over. Waterston is on his way to rescue his wife. And that's the end of it."

"She needs to know the truth."

"Not from us," he said firmly. "It's between the two of them now and we should leave it to them."

"Yes, we should." And she firmly intended to do so until the moment she saw Evelyn. "Then you will not tell him I know his secret?"

"Oh, well, he should know that—"

"No." Her tone hardened. "You tell him that I know the truth, and I swear by all that's holy, you'll regret it."

"Are you threatening me?"

"I prefer to think of it as a promise."

He considered her carefully. "But he is my friend."

"And I am the woman you claim to love." She paused. "The woman you wish to marry."

"I see." He thought for a moment. "Nonetheless it does seem to me that I owe greater allegiance to a man who has saved me in the past than to a woman who may or may not marry me."

She gasped. "Oh, you are a wicked man."

"But I am your wicked man or at least I want to be."

Celeste thought for a moment. "And your allegiance to, oh, say a fiancée? Would that be greater than to a friend?"

"Without question." He paused. "But only if said fiancée truly intended to marry me and was not just getting her way."

She nodded slowly. "I can agree to that."

"When?"

"When what?"

"When will you marry me?"

"I don't know. Eventually."

"Celeste."

"Very well then. Sooner rather than later, I suppose." She huffed. "This is not the place to be discussing the rest of our lives. Where are you taking me anyway?"

"We are going to my flat, where you will spend the entire night," he said firmly. "I wish to celebrate with my fiancée."

"But I should be home when Evelyn—"

"I suspect she will not return tonight either."

"Well, then . . . but your flat." She wrinkled her nose. "I can think of far better places to celebrate. I'm not at all fond of it."

"Nor am I. Tomorrow I shall look for a house." He paused. "A large house, big enough for a wife and a dozen children."

"I only have five."

"For the moment."

"Oh," she said weakly. The idea of a dozen children

was not particularly attractive. Still, the best days of her life had been spent in a family with eleven children. But seven, maybe even eight, children might be quite lovely. It was certainly a point of negotiation.

"Then we are agreed," he said. "You will marry me and I will not tell Waterston you know he is Sir."

She heaved a resigned sigh and noted she didn't feel quite as resigned as she'd thought. She was in truth, a little, well, happy. "Agreed."

"And you will keep his secret."

"I said I agreed."

"No doubt she will know the truth tonight at any rate." He shook his head. "I don't know how Waterston will pull off this rescue without telling her everything."

"The truth is often best," she said in a sage manner.

And Evelyn really did need to know the truth. One way or another, Celeste was determined she learn it. It would be nice if Lord W did indeed tell his wife everything. While she didn't feel she had exactly lied to Max about her intentions, he might well feel differently. Still, she owed Evelyn a great deal and she deserved to know the truth.

Even if it destroyed them all.

Bloody hell. He'd forgotten how dark it was here. At least the nearly full moon cast a bit of light.

Adrian deftly slid the key into the lock on the warehouse door and slipped into the building. Where was that blasted lantern? It should be to one side . . . He felt cautiously with his foot until it struck metal. He bent down and found a matchbox beside the lantern. Quickly, he lit the lantern, then headed toward the stairs for the cellar. It had been more than two years since he'd been in this building yet nothing had apparently changed. While it was used as well for legitimate storage, its true purpose had always been for whatever use the department had for it. It was a most convenient place to store anyone the department wanted out of sight for a while. Tonight, from what he could see, it was empty.

Under other circumstances, he would be more cautious, but these were not other circumstances; he knew exactly what to expect. What he didn't know was exactly what he would say. Surely something brilliant would come to him. Or anything at all. It was time, past time really, to confess everything to her. But he would prefer to avoid doing so tonight. How did one tell one's wife he had deceived her from the first moment they met? Or that he had tricked her tonight? Or that her being held in a cold, wet cellar was his fault?

He held the lantern up and made his way down the narrow stairs. They were bordered on one side by the outside wall and a second wall on the other side. Built years ago at the discretion of one department head or another, it provided both protection and a stealthy approach. "Evie?"

"Adrian?" Her muffled voice sounded from somewhere below him. "Adrian!"

"Where are you?"

"I have no idea. Follow my voice."

He reached the bottom of the stairs and stepped into no more than an inch or so of water.

"I can't see you. There's a sack over my head." She sounded more irritated than scared. Good.

"Keep talking." He continued in her direction for a few steps more until her figure emerged from the shadows. She was tied to a wooden chair, a sack pulled down over her head to her waist.

"Thank God you found me."

"I'm here." He set the lantern down, grateful the water was too low to extinguish it, and began untying her wrists. "Just another minute. Are you hurt?"

"No, they were fairly careful. Of course, they dropped me once." She squirmed. "Please hurry. This sack smells dreadful, there's a disgusting gag that has slipped down my chin and my feet and my skirts are wet."

"Hold still," he said in a sharper manner than he'd intended. "I can't get you untied if you continue to wiggle. These knots are difficult."

"Do forgive my impatience," she snapped. "I've been tied up here for . . ." She thought for a moment. "Well, I have no idea how long. I hit my head when they dropped me and lost consciousness for a time. Not long, I think."

Guilt stabbed him. "Are you sure you're all right?"

"Fine, really, or I will be once you get me out of this. Is Davies hurt?"

"No, he was unharmed."

"Good." Relief sounded in her voice.

"There." He pulled the rope from her wrists, then eased the sack up over her head.

She drew a deep breath, yanked the gag free and stared up at him. Her wig was askew, her face smudged, and there was a nasty bruise to one side of her forehead. "Oh, darling, there was a moment when I thought I might never see you again."

"No possibility of that, Evie, ever." He bent to untie her ankles. The rope was wet and the knots harder to work free.

"How on earth did you find me?"

He braced himself. "About that, I—"

She sucked in a hard breath. "You paid the ransom!"

"The ransom?" Of course. Relief washed through him. She had quite logically jumped to the conclusion she was being held for ransom.

"Good God, Adrian, how much was it?"

"No price is too high for you, my love." He winced to himself. It wasn't exactly a lie. If she had truly been abducted, he would have paid anything to get her back.

"Still, I do want to know what the current rate is for wives."

"It's not of any significance at all. There." He pulled the ropes away from her feet, then straightened and grabbed her hands. "Do you think you can stand?"

"Certainly. I haven't been here that long. At least I don't think I have. To be honest, I have completely lost track of time."

He pulled her to her feet, and she threw her arms around him and buried her face in his neck. "Oh, darling, you have saved me. Without any hesitation or concern for your own safety. Those thugs could still be here. This could have been a trap for you. The Earl of Waterston is worth far more than his wife."

"Never. You are priceless to me. You are my wife." He held her tightly. "My love."

She raised her head. "Then take me out of here."

"Excellent idea." He picked up the lantern with one hand and kept his other arm around her. "I have a carriage waiting."

Her wide skirts were weighted down by the water, and it took longer than he would have liked to leave the warehouse. Even though he knew she—they—were in no danger, he had a distinct feeling of dread. A feeling he hadn't had in years and one impossible to ignore. Surely it was due to nothing more than having a taste once again of a world of intrigue he had long left behind. Still, he refused to let his guard down until they were safely in the carriage and very nearly home.

"Adrian." She snuggled against him and he tightened his arm around her. "I think you were extraordinarily brave tonight."

Again guilt pricked at his conscience. "I only did what was necessary."

"I have always known you would do anything for me, but I have never considered you an adventurous sort. Not the kind of man who charges into danger. That you did so, for me . . ." Her voice caught. "You saved my life."

"I would have no life without you."

For a long moment she didn't say a word. Then she sighed. "There are things I need to tell you. Things you should know."

He stared down at her. "Do you love me?"

"With all my heart."

"Then that's all I need."

"I want to go home." She reached up and kissed the side of his neck. "To our home, our bed."

"Yet another excellent idea. But I should warn you." He smiled. "Regardless of refurbishing in the future, I do not intend to allow you to ever leave again."

She laughed. "You will not allow me?"

"No. Even if it means a certain amount of pleading and"—he winced—"groveling, there will be no more leaving."

"Yes, my lord," she said in an obedient manner that didn't fool him for a minute. "I do still want to know my price."

"And as I said, you are priceless."

"And so, my dear husband, are you." She reached up

and pressed her lips to his, and desire at once welled within him. But then it always had, always would, with her.

He was under no illusions that their life would be perfect from this point forward. Neither of them was perfect after all. And certainly at some point, he would have to tell her he was Sir, but not tonight.

Tonight, the love of his life had confirmed in no uncertain terms that he was the love of hers. The world, the future, had never looked brighter.

Chapter 21

It would have been most awkward to tear Adrian's clothes off the moment they stepped into the house. Evelyn wanted—no—needed to reaffirm life and love. Besides, she had missed him more than she could say. But the servants would surely notice. Although tonight they might well have forgiven such an overt display of affection. The relief on the faces of the staff was evident when they arrived.

They were all most solicitous and obviously pleased to see her alive and well, if somewhat disheveled. Her maid accompanied her to her room, and while she helped Evelyn out of her ruined gown, another ran a bath. As much as she would have loved to soak for hours, she had no intention of lingering. Quickly she washed the scent of dank cellar and docks away and pondered the odd evening. At long last she had met Sir. She had put into words how very much her husband meant to her, and she had been abducted by thugs who obviously knew what they were doing. She was, in addition, rather proud of herself for keeping panic and fear at bay. There had been moments when it hadn't been easy.

Her kidnappers had been most efficient, and if the one carrying her hadn't tripped, she would have been completely unharmed. They had obviously contacted Adrian without the least hesitation, possibly even before she had been left in the cellar. There was no doubt in her mind: they were fast, they were organized, and it was clear they had done this before. If she had been inclined to admire nefarious acts, her kidnappers would have won her admiration. The only thing that could have gone wrong would have been for Adrian not to pay the ransom. She might well have been selected in the first place because it was assumed Lord Waterston would pay without question, as, of course, he had. She wondered if she had other acquaintances who had been in this position. If so, it was something the department might well want to look into. She still wanted to know what she had cost her husband, but he would tell her eventually.

Her maid helped her into her pale blue dressing gown, Adrian's favorite, then Evelyn dismissed her for the night with her gratitude. It was nice to have people who cared for you. She'd been more than a little touched by the concern of the entire staff. And more than a little impressed with her husband.

She'd never thought her husband was weak in any way, but she'd also never imagined he was the type of man to plunge headfirst into danger. Before tonight, if asked, she would have said he'd give due amount of consideration to all the eventualities and, perhaps, would orchestrate her rescue rather than leaping into it himself. It was a side of him she'd never seen, never truly imagined. She couldn't have Sir and, in truth, didn't want him, but it struck her now that, when called upon, Adrian might well have a touch of Sir in him. It was most exciting.

Evelyn tightened her wrapper, stepped through the dressing room connecting her room to Adrian's, and pushed open his door. He had taken off his blue coat and his shoes and was in the process of untying his complicated cravat. She walked over to him and pushed his hands away. "Allow me."

He grinned. "With pleasure."

"Did I tell you how dashing you looked in your costume?" She kept her gaze on the cravat. It was as tricky to untie as her ropes had apparently been. "I felt as if I was being rescued by a hero from another century. Or perhaps someone less noble who would carry me off and have his way with me."

He chuckled. "Casanova perhaps?"

"Definitely Casanova." The cravat loosened. "Although I don't believe he ever married." She pulled it free. "And I think he said something about marriage being the tomb of love. Or the death of love. I can't recall."

"Then he was a fool. Marriage, to the right woman, is the beginning of a life of love."

She raised a brow. "My, you are romantic tonight."

"Casanova would be envious." He pulled her into his arms. "If he had seen you tonight, he might well have changed his mind about marriage. And considered me a very lucky man."

"Then we are well matched." She gazed up at him. "For I am a very lucky woman." She paused. "Although I have been remiss in not making certain you know how very much I love you."

"I have been remiss in that myself." A shadow darkened his eyes. "If anything had happened to you . . ."

"But nothing did, thanks to you." She smiled into his blue eyes. "You are my hero, Adrian Hadley-Attwater." She slid her hand around the back of his neck and pulled his head down to hers. "My knight," she murmured against his lips. And then his lips claimed hers and passion erupted between them.

Desire gripped her, gripped them. They tore at his clothes and he was soon naked. He yanked free the tie of her dressing gown and it fell open to reveal her as naked as he. He cupped one breast in his hand and kissed and sucked until she trembled and clung to him. He shifted his attention to her other breast and she moaned at the sensations surging through her. Slowly he sank to his knees in front of her, his mouth trailing a path of fire from between her breasts and lower, down her stomach, and lower still. Until he parted her legs, his hands running up the insides of her thighs. Her breath caught in anticipation. Dear Lord, what the man did to her. What he made her feel.

He spread her legs and caressed her. She moaned softly with his touch. Her dressing gown slid off her shoulders to her elbows. She was already slick with need and wanting him. His fingers slid over her and exquisite sensation washed up from his touch. Her breath quickened. He opened her with his fingers, then leaned closer and blew softly. She shivered and waited. Her eyes closed, her head dropped back, and she gripped his shoulders.

The first flick of his tongue brought a gasp of delight from her. There was a great deal to be said for marrying a man of experience. A man who knew the most sensitive parts of a woman and knew precisely what to do with them. How to pleasure a woman until she thought she would surely not survive such delight. His tongue caressed her, and her hands tightened on his shoulders. He teased and tasted and sucked at her until her hips rocked toward him of their own accord. She ached and wanted and yearned. Blood pulsed in her veins and she wondered if he could feel her throb against his mouth.

"Oh, God, Adrian . . ."

She raised her head, opened her eyes, and stared down at his dark head between her legs. It wasn't the least bit proper; indeed, it was no doubt a great sin. But, oh, what a heavenly sin. If eternal damnation was the price for this, it was well worth it.

Her muscles tightened. Her world narrowed. She existed only in the feeling of his mouth, his tongue, his teeth. Tension coiled within her. He had brought her to release with his mouth before, but tonight she wanted to pleasure him as much as he did her.

"Adrian," she whispered and reluctantly pushed him away. He glanced up, his eyes dark with passion, his lips glazed with her. "Come to bed."

"Now?" He raised a brow.

Laughter bubbled through her. She moved to the bed and let her dressing gown slither to the floor behind her. She glanced at him over her shoulder. "Yes, darling, now."

He rose to his feet, and her gaze wandered over him. She'd never been particularly enamored with the naked male form, unless it was carved from marble. But from the first time she had seen her husband *sans* clothing, she'd been most impressed. With his broad shoulders, hard-muscled chest, and flat stomach tapering to narrow hips, he could have easily modeled for any marble statue. Her gaze slipped to his cock. She swallowed. That, too, was most impressive.

He laughed and heat rushed up her face.

"I like that I can still make you blush." He stepped to her, nuzzled the side of her neck, then tumbled onto the bed and pulled her down with him.

"Don't be absurd." She scoffed. "I do not blush."

"It looked like a blush."

"Don't be so arrogant, darling." She shifted away from him, then threw one leg over his and straddled him, her knees on either side of his hips, his cock nestled behind her. "I was flushed, not blushing. It's an entirely different thing."

"Is it?"

"You sound skeptical." She wiggled her derrière against his cock and he gasped. "I don't think women who blush do this." She leaned forward and circled his left nipple with her tongue, then nipped at it gently. He shuddered beneath her. She smiled with satisfaction and moved her attention to his right nipple, holding it with her teeth and flicking her tongue over it. He groaned and she sucked hard at the tiny nub.

"Evie . . ."

She straightened and smiled wickedly down at him. "Well?"

His smile matched hers. "You were blushing."

She shook her head regretfully. "Stubborn beast."

She lowered herself forward to lie on top of him, hooking her legs around his, his cock hard between her legs. At once, his arms wrapped around her and he met her mouth with his. Their tongues dueled and tangled, hungry and eager, urged to devour one another by passion and need.

She pulled away and slid slowly down his body, trailing kisses and tiny bites, feeling his erection pressing against her. Against her stomach, between her breasts, until it sprang free, begging for her touch. She settled between his legs and stroked him in a teasing manner until he moaned and fisted his hands in the sheets.

"Do I blush?"

He could barely hiss out the word. "Yes."

She propped herself up on one elbow and slowly licked the head of his cock. He shuddered. She drew him into her mouth and sucked, raking her teeth lightly over the underside, reveling in the taste of him. The feel of him in her mouth. The sheer power of knowing she could do to him what he did to her. The throbbing ache between her legs increased.

"God, Evie, oh God . . ." He writhed beneath her. "I can't . . ."

She raised her head and gazed up into his passion-glazed eyes. "Yes?"

He gasped. "You don't blush."

She flicked her tongue over the top of his cock. "Are you sure?"

"Lady Waterston, you try my patience." Faster than she would have thought possible, he sat up, pulled her into his arms, and abruptly, she was no longer on top. He grinned, positioned himself between her legs, and rubbed his cock against her until she whimpered and arched upward, reaching for him.

He eased himself into her with a measured deliberation he knew drove her mad. In the back of her mind, she was grateful Sir had asked if she'd married Adrian for his money and not for this. It wouldn't be the least bit proper to admit such a thing and she did so hate to lie. He slid deeper and she dug her heels in the back of his knees and urged him on until he filled her.

He thrust into her again and again, and her hips rolled against him, meeting him, welcoming him. They moved together in a rhythm at once familiar and exciting. A dance they had perfected together to his satisfaction and hers. She lost herself in the hot, hard feel of him inside her. In delicious sensation and unrestrained pleasure. In growing need and tension, winding tighter and tighter. His thrusts grew harder, faster. Her hips moved in tandem with his. She was no longer a being of substance but a creature of raw emotion, demanding and insistent and wanting all he had.

She clutched at his shoulders and he strained against her. Until at last he thrust hard and shuddered and groaned in that way he had, claiming her, possessing her. Her muscles tightened around him and then she, too, plummeted over the edge with wave after wave of ecstasy crashing through her, over her, engulfing her. She arched upward and her body shook against his and she clung to him. And slowly the bliss of her release faded, leaving a lingering sense of well-being and satisfaction and joy.

He lifted his head and smiled down at her. "Welcome home, wife."

She laughed weakly. "It's good to be home, husband."

"And this"—he kissed her nose—"is where I intend to keep you."

"In your bed?"

"I was thinking my house, but that is an excellent idea." He shifted and rolled to his side, then propped himself up on his elbow and studied her. "A truly excellent idea."

She laughed. This—he—was home and it was perfect. He was hers and she was his, and she would never let him question her love again.

"I shall send for my things in the morning."

"What an excellent idea." He grinned. "But what of your refurbishing? I thought you wanted to live there to oversee it."

"You did not."

He chuckled. "Not for a moment."

"The house is no more than a fifteen-minute walk from here. I can be there in no time at all, really, to check on the work. I might need to reconsider exactly what I intend to do there. Celeste is fond of it as it is. Besides . . ." She paused. "You obviously paid a great deal last night for my safety, and frankly, I feel a bit guilty undertaking huge refurbishing costs at the moment. Also there is a new wardrobe I may have failed to mention."

He laughed. "You are not to blame for anything that occurred last night. Spend whatever you wish," he said magnanimously.

"My goodness, Adrian." She studied him curiously. "You have never been miserly but this is overly generous. Whatever has come over you?"

"You have." He drew a deep breath. "It was brought home to me last night how very much you mean to me. I have always known I loved you. I have always known I did not want to live without you. But last night, there was the possibility that I might well lose you forever." He shook his head. "It is not a possibility I ever want to confront again. All I want now is to devote the rest of my life to making you happy. And if you want to spend outrageous amounts—"

"Even frivolously?"

"Especially frivolously, I shall not say a word."

"Perhaps I should be kidnapped more often."

"Perhaps." He nodded. "But only by me."

"Oh?" She raised a brow.

"Tie you to a chair."

"Adrian!" She laughed.

He nuzzled her neck. "Have my way with you."

"Oh my." She swallowed hard. "And will you ask for ransom then?"

"Never." He growled against her neck. "I have you and you'll be mine forever."

"That, my darling kidnapper"—she drew his lips back to hers—"is a bargain."

It was well past noon when at last they awoke for the day. Or rather, when she rose from their bed. If Adrian had had his way, they would never leave his bed at all. Evie looked for all the world like a woman who had been well and truly loved. He chuckled. As indeed she was.

It did seem the world was somewhat brighter today; his mind was certainly sharp and clear. Amazing what settling a few doubts could do for a man. Evie had gone into her room to dress and he was about to call for Vincent when a knock sounded at his door. Vincent, no doubt. There was nothing like being confident of the love of one's wife and servants who anticipated a man's every need to make a man feel he was in command of his life.

And life was good.

"Come in."

Vincent entered the room carrying a tray bearing a steaming pot of coffee. Adrian much preferred coffee to tea in the morning. Or afternoon, as it were. Vincent set down the tray and closed the door behind him. "Good day, my lord."

Adrian grinned. "And an excellent day it is, too, Vincent."

"Then I gather all went well last night, sir?" Vincent poured a cup and handed it to him.

"Better than I had hoped for." Adrian took a sip. Excellent. It always was but today it tasted even better than usual.

"And Lady Waterston is none the worse for her ordeal?"

Adrian shook his head. "That was an error, Vincent."

Vincent's brow twitched. "In judgment, sir?"

"No," he said sharply. "In communication."

"I see." The valet moved to the wardrobe and opened its doors.

Adrian narrowed his eyes. "What, exactly, do you see?"

Vincent selected Adrian's clothes for the day. "You would never do anything to place Lady Waterston in danger."

"Never," Adrian said indignantly.

"Of course not." Vincent laid Adrian's clothes out on the bed. "One more thing, sir." He stepped to the tray, picked up an envelope Adrian hadn't noticed, and handed it to him. "A message arrived for you a few minutes ago from Sir Maxwell, I believe."

Adrian accepted the envelope. "And was there a message last night as well?"

Vincent nodded. "It was on the table near the front entry. It arrived after you had left, but its arrival was not brought to my attention. I was not aware of it until moments before you and Lady Waterston returned to the house. At that point, it seemed moot."

"You read it then?"

"It has long been part of my job to relay Sir Maxwell's missives when you are not present." Vincent cast him a vaguely disapproving look. "Unless you prefer that I no longer do so."

"No, of course not. We have always worked well together."

"I took the liberty of placing it in your desk drawer." Adrian breathed a sigh of relief. "Thank you."

"Will there be anything else, sir?" Vincent's noncommittal expression was that of a perfectly trained valet. Adrian knew better.

He rolled his gaze toward the ceiling. "Out with it. What are you thinking?"

"May I—"

"Yes, yes, speak freely."

"If I recall correctly, sir, while Lady Waterston's activities with the department were not as extensive as yours, or mine either as your second, she did receive training in the handling of firearms."

"And?"

"And she was quite proficient if I remember correctly." No more than the hint of a smile touched Vincent's lips. "Something of a natural gift, I believe."

"And?" Impatience sounded in Adrian's voice.

"And should she find out the truth about last night and everything else from any source other than you, I would not put it past her to shoot you." Vincent's eyes narrowed no more than a fraction. "And she is an excellent shot."

"I intend to tell her everything," Adrian said staunchly. "Not today perhaps but soon."

"Of course, sir."

"I will."

"I don't doubt it, sir." He paused. "Will there be anything else?"

"No, you may take your leave." Adrian drew a deep breath. "Vincent?"

"Yes, my lord?"

"I know you thought our days of intrigue were over, but they may not be. Oh, nothing like before. I would be more of an advisor than anything else and only on rare occasions. Still, I would require your assistance as always." He studied the valet. "Would you be amenable to a bit of a change?"

"My allegiance is to you, my lord, and without question I would do my job as you see fit." He paused. "Might I add you are not the only one who has experienced a bit of restlessness of late. However . . ."

Adrian raised a brow. "However?"

"It is one thing to engage in secretive activities when one is free to do as one wishes. Quite another when one has a wife."

"I said I will tell her."

"Yes, of course, sir." Vincent nodded but Adrian knew the valet didn't believe him for a moment. Nonetheless, Adrian fully intended to tell his wife everything. When the right moment presented itself. "Then if there's nothing else, sir?"

"No, thank you, Vincent."

Vincent nodded and took his leave. Obviously only action would prove to the valet Adrian's good intentions. His attention turned to the note from Max. No doubt his friend wanted to apologize for last night's debacle in hopes Adrian would agree to consult with the department. Obviously, as proven by recent incidents, the department needed him. Adrian chuckled. Although Max would be more inclined to twist the situation and imply Adrian needed the department.

He opened the envelope and read the brief, curt message. His jaw clenched.

"Bloody hell."

Chapter 22

It was amazing how a little danger and rescue by one's very courageous husband could prove most intoxicating to one's spirits. Evelyn couldn't remember when she had been quite so euphoric. Why, she felt like she was in the first throes of love. She wasn't, of course, although apparently love reaffirmed was every bit as exciting as love newly discovered.

Adrian had been called away to a meeting but had kissed her quite soundly before he left with a promise to continue today what they had so thoroughly enjoyed last night. And again this morning. There was a great deal to be said about finding one's soul mate, and they were indeed made for one another. Evelyn smiled in a manner that an observer could only describe as satisfied. Body as well as soul.

She was grateful to have him and, indeed, grateful to be alive and well with nothing to show for her ordeal save a bruise on her forehead and a ruined gown. Still, there were two things about last night that continued to plague her. One she couldn't quite put her finger on. It lingered in the back of her mind, just out of reach. No doubt it was nothing of importance. Still, it was bothersome.

The other was the amount of the ransom. No matter how often she had asked last night, Adrian had refused to tell her the amount. It was a point of pride with him, she supposed, although that was really rather silly. She was the one who had been abducted, after all, and she would very much like to know what she was worth. She paused in midstep. Perhaps he had bargained with them. Offered less than they had asked. Good Lord! Had he acquired her at a discount? No, surely not, nor did it matter. Besides, the entire episode had taken place much too quickly for there to have been any sort of negotiations.

She headed toward Adrian's library. With any luck at all, the ransom note would be lying forgotten on the desk. Her husband certainly had far more on his mind when they had returned home. She pushed open the door and crossed the room to the large, mahogany desk. It had been well cared for and the years had aged it gently, adding a warm patina. It was the kind of piece that stayed in a family for generations, linking one to the next. Indeed, it had been Adrian's father's and his father's before that. And with any luck at all, it would one day be their son's.

There was nothing on the desktop save a desk set: matching inkwell, blotter, pen tray, letter rack, paper knife, and small box for holding odds and ends. Bronze with a decorative, embossed Greek key design, the set was more a work of art than mere craftsmanship. She had given it to him as a wedding gift because of his love of Greek antiquities. He had given her a choker of perfect pearls.

Evelyn sat down in Adrian's comfortable leather chair and considered her options. He would surely show her what he had locked in his drawers should she ask. Her husband had nothing to hide, after all. Still, for whatever reason, he did not wish to reveal the amount of the ransom, and she knew herself well enough to know that that fact alone would eat at her until she uncovered the truth. Besides, once she knew the amount, she saw no reason to let him know she knew. If he wanted to keep what he'd paid for her safety his secret, she would allow him to do so. Once she found out, of course.

She studied the desk carefully. Like Lord Dunwell's, each of the drawers had its own separate lock although the chances were the same key would open every drawer. She could certainly open the locks although it did seem, well, somewhat distasteful to pick the locks on her own husband's desk. Not that he would know. Not that he had anything to hide. But it would be easier to find the key.

She flipped open the bronze box. It was empty. Why on earth would one have a box for trinkets if one had no trinkets in it? Very well then. Where would her efficient, organized husband hide a key? She felt under the top desk drawer, in all the nooks one might conceal a key, then bent down and looked under the desk and under the chair as well. Nothing. She looked under the pen tray and the blotter, picked up and examined the empty letter rack—again why have one if you didn't use it?—as well as the paper knife. She looked under the inkwell, then carefully removed the ink-filled glass insert. Nothing. She resisted the urge to stick a pen in the ink to see if perchance there was a key at the bottom.

Nonsense. What was she doing? Her husband had nothing to hide. Although for a man with nothing to hide, he certainly did take care not to leave his key lying about. He was simply prudent, that's all. Still . . .

In two years she hadn't had the tiniest desire to look in her husband's desk. Now, something inside her was demanding she do so. Something that had nothing to do with the amount paid for her ransom. Besides, without knowing it, he had turned this into a challenge.

She drummed her fingers on the blotter thoughtfully. Where would a man like Adrian Hadley-Attwater hide a key? He'd always liked puzzles and obviously hiding his key was his idea of an intriguing puzzle. But who did he think would try to work it out? It was a most interesting question although probably of no real significance. No, this was no doubt a game her husband was playing, if only with himself.

Her gaze slid around the room. Past the shelves with their neatly arranged volumes. Past the family portraits and the tall windows until she focused again on the items on the desk. The inkwell, the blotter, the box, the tray, the rack, the knife. Absently, she traced the Greek key design on the blotter corners. The bronze glowed dully in the sunlight. It really was a lovely set . . .

At once the answer struck her and she laughed. Oh, he was a clever beast, that husband of hers. She rose to her feet, moved to a bookshelf, and pulled out a wooden case designed to look like a book. Adrian had four such cases, each with two layers of ancient Greek coins nestled in padded holders. But this case held his favorites. She brought the case to the desk and opened the lid.

Here there were coins of gold and silver bearing the

likenesses of gods or goddesses, or the symbols of city-states. Some of the coins were more than two thousand years old. Adrian had been collecting them since he was a boy. Today, his collection was invaluable. Odd, that he would have his coins simply sitting on shelves, yes, disguised as books but still not overly protected, yet the key to his desk was well hidden. She never would understand the minds of men.

She carefully lifted out the first layer of coins, then the second. She resisted the impulse to laugh in triumph. A key lay in the bottom of the case and she promptly picked it up. When she was finished, she would put the case and its contents back together, precisely as it had been. She had no desire to have her husband learn she'd been, well, snooping.

Evelyn decided to try the middle drawer first. She sat down, inserted the key, turned it, and pulled open the drawer. She studied the neatly arranged contents but resisted the urge to touch. It looked like nothing more than correspondence. Still, it would be the perfect place to store a ransom demand.

A familiar handwriting caught her eye, and she picked up a note lying on top of the others. How strange, it was from Max. She didn't think he and Adrian were more than passing acquaintances. Quickly, she scanned the note. It made no sense at all. Confusion drew her brows together. It sounded as if Max had arranged her abduction so that Adrian . . . Surely, she wasn't reading this correctly.

Carefully, she paged through the remaining correspondence until she found one in her own hand. How very sweet of the dear man, to have saved a letter from her. She picked it up.

My dear Sir, I am at once eager and filled with regret to write this missive to you as it shall be my last . . .

This was absurd. This was the last letter she had written to Sir. She riffled through the rest of the letters. Why, these were all notes she had written to Sir. And here. She grabbed another page. This one was in Sir's distinctive hand and unfinished.

My Dearest Eve, Your note brought a smile to my face but then your notes often have . . .

She'd never read this before. How would Adrian get this?

I shall miss them. As this last exchange seems to be one of confessions, I have some of my own . . .

What on earth? Why would Adrian have her notes to Sir? And why would Adrian have a half-written note from Sir?

If he had seen you tonight, he might well have changed his mind about marriage.

That was it. The detail she couldn't put her finger on. While Adrian had seen her gown when it had arrived, he had not seen her dressed in her costume last night. But Sir had.

The oddest thought struck her. Surely not. What a ridiculous idea. It couldn't possibly be true.

A man only says nothing in your pasts matters when he has more to hide than you do.

More to hide? Abruptly the truth slammed into her and her breath caught.

Adrian and Sir were one and the same?

Tiny details from their life at once made sense. Why she felt she'd known him forever when they first met. Why he saw no need for her to tell him of her past. He already knew very nearly everything there was to know about her past. He was a huge part of it!

She narrowed her eyes. Last night he had tried to seduce her as Sir. Tried to get her to say Sir was the man she loved. Worse, he had interrogated her!

Why did you marry him?
Do you love him enough to forgive him?

She gasped.

He implied she had married him for money and position!

There have never been secrets between us.

Hah! There had apparently been secrets between them from the moment they met face-to-face! And all of them his! How could he have kept this from her? How could he—

The door to the library opened and Celeste poked her head in. "There you are. Stewart said you might be in here."

"And indeed I am," Evelyn said through clenched teeth. If she'd thought she had been angry when he'd burst in on Beryl and Lord Radington, that paled in comparison to this. The man had been lying to her for two years! She drew a deep breath and carefully replaced everything she had taken from the drawer exactly as she had found it.

"I have something to tell you." Celeste closed the door and crossed the room to the desk.

"I have something to tell you as well." Evelyn studied the arrangement of the desk drawer, satisfied it was precisely as it had been, then closed the drawer and locked it.

"What are you doing?" Celeste's brow furrowed.

"I am engaging in, oh, let's call it *revelation*." She placed the key in the bottom of the coin case.

"What?" Celeste shook her head. "Never mind."

"You cannot imagine what I have discovered."

Evelyn replaced both layers of coins, closed the case, and crossed to the bookshelf.

Celeste snorted. "It cannot possibly be as shocking as what I have learned."

Evelyn slid the case into its space on the shelf, turned to her friend, and drew a deep breath. "Adrian is Sir."

At the very same moment Celeste announced, "Sir is Lord W."

Evelyn stared at her friend. "How did you—"

"When did you—"

"Just now." She nodded toward the desk, "My notes to Sir are in his desk. When did you—"

"Last night," Celeste said, "I overheard Lord W and Max. I came to the masquerade to find Max because Davies reported your abduction. An abduction orchestrated by Max and your husband."

"Ah-ha!" Evelyn scoffed. "It's no wonder the men who took me seemed so professional. They obviously worked for the department. My only question is why?"

"It's my understanding that Lord W had decided it was time for Sir and Eve to meet in person."

Evelyn narrowed her eyes. "Oh, he had, had he?"

"This part is a bit confusing but apparently Max thought kidnapping was the plan while Lord W thought Sir would simply meet you at the masquerade." Celeste shook her head. "I'm not entirely clear on how it was all supposed to work, but then Max didn't seem very clear about it all either."

"And yet I find it very clear."

"Do you?" Caution sounded in Celeste's voice.

"Oh yes." A grim note sounded in her voice. "Last night's was not the only masquerade."

"Evelyn—"

"'*No price is to high for you, my love.*'" She paced the room. "That's what he said. '*I would have no life without you,*' he said. '*If anything had happened to you,*' he said." She resisted the urge to clench her fists and scream. "Apparently the greatest danger I was in was from a head cold as result of wet feet!"

Celeste studied her. "What are you going to do?"

"I don't know." Evelyn thought for a moment. "But it should be something appropriate. Something involving, oh, I don't know, deception?"

"You could simply be honest with him and tell him you know the truth," Celeste said slowly.

"Yes, because he is so adept at honesty himself," she snapped. "Oh, no. Honesty is entirely too easy for Lord Waterston. Or *Sir*, for that matter. Besides he has forfeited the right to honesty from me." She glanced at the other woman. "Will Max tell him you know the truth?"

Celeste shook her head. "Absolutely not."

"Are you sure?"

"There's not a doubt in my mind."

Evelyn studied her closely. "There's something else, isn't there? What else have you not told me?"

"Nothing of importance." She rolled her gaze toward the ceiling and sighed. "I am seriously considering marriage."

Evelyn stared. "To whom?"

Celeste winced. "To Max."

"Why?" Evelyn scoffed. "He is no better than his friend."

"Given that you have been quite happy with his friend until recently and you will, no doubt, be quite happy in the future if, of course, you both survive, that is not a bad endorsement. Besides . . ." She shrugged. "I could do far worse."

"You could do far better."

"Yes, but I don't seem to want far better, I seem to want him." Celeste shook her head as if she couldn't believe it herself. "It makes no sense, it's completely impractical, totally irrational, and he's never seemed the kind of man one would wish to keep around forever."

"And?"

"And nonetheless, I do."

"You might wish to reconsider," Evelyn said grimly.

Celeste stifled a smile and turned to answer a knock at the door. Evelyn paced. The other woman was right. She and Adrian would be happy in the future if they survived this. In doubt, however, was whether they could survive.

It was as if their entire marriage had been nothing but a sham. Yes, she had long felt guilty for keeping the truth of her past from him, but as he already knew all, it seemed to her that was no longer even a lie of omission. Whereas his lies were ones of . . . of . . . deception!

"Stewart says you have a caller." Celeste paused. "Lady Dunwell. She's in the red salon."

"How perfect for her," she muttered and started for the door. "And what perfect timing she has."

"You're not going to confide in her, are you?"

"I'm furious, Celeste, not insane. Regardless of anything else, revealing my husband as the former head of a secretive government department is something I would never do." She narrowed her eyes. "However, there are few women I know that are cleverer than Beryl Dunwell when it comes to seduction. Or, I suspect, settling a score."

"Well," Beryl said the moment Evelyn stepped into the room. "Who was he? What happened?"

"You were right after all." She shrugged. "It was Adrian."

"Really?" Beryl's eyes widened. "Odd, I don't remember him being that tall."

"He's grown."

"That would explain it," Beryl murmured, then shook her head as if to clear it. "How terribly romantic of him to try to seduce you as another man."

Evelyn froze. "Another man?"

"A masked stranger, of course." She studied Evelyn carefully. "Whatever is the matter with you today?"

"It was a very late night."

"Yes, of course." She stared for a moment, then realization dawned in her eyes and she nodded. "Oh, now I understand."

"Understand what?"

"I could be wrong, of course."

"One can only hope."

"Well, a man who bursts into a hotel room to catch his wife in a compromising position and then flirts with her incognito, well . . ."

"Well?" Impatience rang in Evelyn's voice.

"He's a man who needs to be taught a lesson." Beryl nodded firmly.

"My thoughts exactly."

"Do you have a lesson in mind?"

"Not yet." Evelyn studied the other woman for a moment. "I was hoping you might be able to help me come up with something."

"Perhaps." She paused. "Although I have always found a good biscuit to be most conducive to clever planning."

"I have already ordered tea and biscuits."

"Oh, you are a good friend."

Evelyn bit back a smile. "I do try."

"Now then." Beryl settled on the sofa and thought for a moment. "Whatever you decide, it should fit the crime."

She nodded. "I have already thought of that."

"But you don't want to be too harsh with him."

"Why not?" Evelyn drew her brows together. "Harsh is the very least of what I want to be."

"No doubt." Beryl considered her cautiously. "Oh dear, you are that angry then?"

"That angry and more."

"I see." She paused. "Still, I would hate to see you take any step that he might consider unforgivable."

"Then we would be evenly matched."

"Yes, of course," Beryl murmured. "Last night, I said you and Adrian were an example to the rest of us."

"But not to you."

"I do think of myself as being above that sort of thing," she said in a lofty manner, then sighed. "Apparently, I was wrong."

"You?"

"I find it difficult to believe myself but . . ." Beryl drew a deep breath. "I have decided to reform."

Evelyn raised a brow.

"It might not be permanent, mind you," Beryl said quickly. "But I do intend to try."

Evelyn stared. "Why?"

"Other than those pesky questions of morality?"

Evelyn nodded.

"I am quite envious of you, you know. Oh, not because you have Adrian," she added quickly. "But because of what you and Adrian have." Her brow furrowed. "I am not used to feelings of envy or jealousy. I find them quite distressing." She heaved a resigned sigh. "Nonetheless, your life has made me consider mine." Her gaze met Evelyn's. "He's a good man, you know. A bit pompous, overly ambitious perhaps . . ."

Evelyn shook her head in confusion. "Who?"

"My husband, of course, Lionel."

"Oh, I see."

"He's certainly not a saint. His morals are no better than mine but . . ."

"But?"

"But, well, I think he deserves better." She raised her chin in a resolute manner. "As do I."

Evelyn stared.

"And as I cannot change husbands, I have decided to work with what I have," she said firmly. "As has he. We had a long talk last night. We have both agreed to forgo liaisons with others. He is going to give up his flat and I . . ." She smiled weakly. "I shall never again visit Room 327, or any room, at the Langham or any other hotel." She met Evelyn's gaze. "Do you think I can do it?"

"I daresay you can do anything you set your mind to," Evelyn said firmly.

"You would say that, you are my friend. Still . . ." Beryl smiled in a sheepish manner. "I am grateful for your confidence." She paused. "And your friendship."

"And I am grateful for yours." She cast the other woman an affectionate smile. It seemed the day was to be filled with revelations. Who would have thought Beryl Dunwell . . . "Beryl," she said thoughtfully. "Room 327?"

Beryl cast her a knowing look.

"Is that the room where Adrian discovered you?"

"It's a lovely suite," Beryl said firmly. "Nicely appointed with a comfortable sitting room." A regretful expression crossed her face. "Extremely comfortable."

"I see." Evelyn thought for a moment. "The punishment should fit the crime, don't you think?"

"The punishment?" Beryl's brow furrowed, then her eyes widened with understanding. "Why, Evelyn Waterston, we do have a great deal in common." She smiled in a wicked manner. "Do you need any assistance?"

"No, but I am grateful for the offer." Evelyn's smile matched her friend's. "I'm quite certain I can manage this myself."

Adrian's jealousy had started this and it seemed only fitting that jealousy play a part in ending it.

It struck her this was the dénouement of a play between them that had started years ago. A play in which the unwitting heroine, having at long last uncovered the wicked masquerade perpetrated on her by the hero, no longer had to choose between two competing heroes but, as they were one and the same, could have them both.

Of course, first she would make him pay.

Both of him.

Part Three

Ruse

Oh what a tangled web we weave,
When first we practise to deceive!

—Sir Walter Scott, *Marmion*

Chapter 23

Adrian blew a long breath. "How?"

"His throat was slit," Max said calmly. "He was found floating in the Thames this morning."

"I see." He met the other man's gaze firmly. "This puts the theft of the file in an entirely different context."

"As it does Sir George's death." Max nodded. "There are any number of ways to kill an elderly man without making it apparent he was killed. Lord Lansbury's death, however, leaves no question."

"Let us say for a moment that Sir George did not die of natural causes. His death was in November. The file was stolen in February." He thought for a moment. "If Sir George was murdered, great pains were taken to make it appear natural. Yet no effort at all was made to hide the nature of Lord Lansbury's death."

"Which might well mean whoever is behind this is running out of time," Max said.

"My thoughts exactly." Adrian drew his brows together. "A deadline of some sort?"

"That would make sense." Max chose his words with care. "With Lord Lansbury's death, there is reason to believe the theft of the file and Sir George's death are connected." He met Adrian's gaze. "Agreed?"

Adrian nodded. "Carrying that assumption to a logical conclusion: two of the last three heads of the department are now dead. One might conclude, therefore—"

"That you are next."

"Perhaps," Adrian said slowly. "But to what end?"

"Revenge is the obvious motive." Max shrugged. "Against the department most likely. Or the government in general. It might well be personal although there's no connection between you, Sir George, and Lord Lansbury."

"Except," Adrian said slowly, "for my wife."

"Given recent events, it's obvious why she is the first thing that would spring to mind. But she has no link to Lansbury."

"Isn't he the one who first approached her about working for the department?"

"As he recruited both of us and any number of others, I doubt that's significant." Max shook his head. "Besides, he left the department within days of her arrival. I don't think they spoke more than twice, if that. The tie between them is practically nonexistent. The stronger connection is that you, Lansbury, and Sir George are all former heads of this organization."

"Which would seem to indicate revenge as a motive." Adrian considered the matter. "If the goal was to disrupt the department or even bring it to public exposure, thus embarrassing the government, the more appropriate throat to slit"—he cast his friend a humorless smile—"would be yours."

"Thank you for putting it into perspective," Max said wryly. "Still, all we have at the moment is a file that was stolen and returned that included the names of three former heads, one of whom was already dead, who may or may not have died naturally, and another who was definitely murdered. And you."

"And I am alive and well. Extremely well." His thoughts drifted back to last night. "Better than I've been in quite some time."

"You have my heartiest congratulations. Now, however, we do need to keep you alive."

Adrian shrugged. "I'm not especially worried."

"You should be."

"Nonsense. First of all, we have no idea if our conclusions are remotely accurate. We may well be stringing together pieces that do not fit the same puzzle."

"Still, I would think caution is advisable." A warning sounded in Max's voice.

"Perhaps. Second . . ." Adrian ticked the points off on his finger. "Sir George was elderly and we are not sure he was killed. But, given his advanced years, he could scarcely fend off an attacker. Third, Lansbury thought Sir George's death was nothing more than co-incidence and was therefore not concerned about his own safety. I would wager the man took no particular precautions. I, however, am well aware of the potential danger and shall certainly be on guard."

"Nonetheless—"

A knock sounded at the side office door. Adrian cast Max a sharp glance.

"My secretary, Mr. Sayers."

"Oh?" Adrian raised a brow.

"I can't do this all by myself, you know." Max huffed. "There have been a lot of changes in two years.

More accountability and much more paper. Reports, files, expenditure accountings. We are not all as overly efficient as you are."

"I didn't say a word." He bit back a smile. He had preferred to handle the bureaucratic nonsense that went along with the job himself. It was one less person to have to trust. "I didn't see him when I came in."

"His desk is in the small office to the side of the stairway, connected to mine."

"The room that used to be for storage?"

Max nodded in a satisfied manner. "There is a series of hidden mirrors that allows him to see who is approaching."

"How very clever," Adrian murmured.

"Come in," Max called.

A fair-haired, vaguely familiar young man entered the room, an envelope in his hands. "A woman delivered this a few minutes ago for you, sir. Most attractive, spectacles, striking eyes. She said it was urgent." He stepped to the desk and handed it to Max. "Shall I wait for a reply, sir?"

"I shall let you know if a reply is necessary," Max said.

"Of course, sir." He glanced at Adrian. "Pleasure to see you again, my lord."

"Mr. Sayers," Adrian said cordially.

"If there is nothing else, sir?"

"That will be all for now." Max waited until the young man had taken his leave and closed the door behind him. "Do you know him?"

"We met at the Spanish ambassador's reception," Adrian said. It was good to know Evie had not been entirely on her own in that venture. Leave it to Max to make certain there was help there should she need it. "My mother was thrusting him at my cousin."

"A much more dangerous assignment." Max chuckled. "He is well placed socially and he was not there at my direction."

So much for Max assuring Evie's safety. "You trust him?"

"Implicitly. He joined the department shortly after you left. His references were excellent and his record is outstanding. I moved him into this position about a year ago," Max said, opening the envelope. He pulled out a folded piece of paper, and another smaller folded note fell out. He read the message, then met Adrian's gaze. "This is interesting. It's from your wife and apparently this . . ." He picked up the smaller note and handed it to Adrian. "Is for you."

Adrian quickly unfolded it.

My Dearest,

Upon reflection, I fear I might have been too hasty last night. I was not entirely honest about my regrets as well. Today I find I cannot get the thought of your lips pressed to mine out of my head. I shall be in Room 327 at the Langham Hotel this afternoon at 4:00.

The door will not be locked.

Yours,
Eve

Adrian stared at the well-known hand in stunned disbelief.

"Well, what is it?"

"My wife is arranging an assignation." He could

scarcely believe his own words. "With Sir!" How could she?

"I thought you said things went well last night."

"I thought they did." Again he stared at the note. "And in the same room I discovered Lady Dunwell." He narrowed his eyes. "I knew that friendship was a mistake."

"What are you going to do?"

"What can I do?" He clenched his jaw. "It would be rude to refuse so delightful an invitation."

Max stared. "But who, precisely, is going to accept said invitation?"

"There's no way around it. I shall have to tell her the truth."

Max winced. "After last night, she will not take it well."

"She would not take it well before last night." He glared at his friend. "She's invited that blasted man to a hotel room!"

"She's invited *you* to a hotel room," Max said pointedly.

"She doesn't know that."

"With any luck," Max said under his breath.

Adrian stared. "What do you mean?"

"It's entirely possible she recognized you last night."

"No." He shook his head. "She had no idea. I am certain of that."

"Perhaps . . ." Max chose his words with care. "You should reconsider. It might be best to ignore this—"

"Ignore this? How can I possibly ignore this?" Adrian stood and paced the room. "My wife has invited a man to join her in a hotel room. It's not something one ignores."

"Even so—"

"And this time when I burst into that hotel room, I will be in the right!"

"Which makes it all so much better." Max got to his feet and met Adrian's gaze. "But the question to consider now is whether you really want to be."

"I don't." His tone hardened. "But it appears I am."

"I think it's a mistake."

"Not my first."

"If you are going to do this, you'd best be on your way." Max shook his head. "It's already after three."

"And I would so hate to be late." Anger sharpened his words. He nodded and took his leave.

As much as this time he was indeed in the right, he was truly the injured party. Adrian wondered, during the brief ride to the hotel, if perhaps his friend was right. The rational, logical thing to do would indeed be to ignore her invitation and confront her when she returned home. Such a confrontation would inevitably mean confession on his part, but it would give her the chance to say she had known who he was at the masquerade last night. And she was now trying to teach him a lesson. Even if they both knew it wasn't true, it would serve to salvage the situation somewhat. But she'd had no idea when they'd danced together that he was Sir. That was one thing he was not wrong about.

And rationality had nothing to do with this. He'd been irrational from the moment he'd allowed his doubts to surface. The last time he'd gone to the Langham to confront her, he had as well carried the hope with him that he was wrong. Now, he knew he wasn't. A heavy, leaden knot hung in his chest, apparently his heart. So this was the feeling of true betrayal. He had brought it on himself, he knew that. Yet that knowledge made it no easier to bear.

Odd, how the betrayal of one's wife wiped all else from one's mind. The implications of Lansbury's death and everything else bore further consideration. But not now. Now, he had a wife to confront. Something suspiciously like fear curled inside him.

Once again, he avoided the Langham's elevator and sprinted up the stairs. He reached the room and for a long moment stared at the brass numbers on the door: 3-2-7. It was not too late to stop this, Max's voice whispered in his head. No, it was too late. And once he stepped into that room, nothing between them would ever be the same again. He had never in his life questioned his courage before, yet at the moment, courage threatened to fail him. Regardless, one did what one had to do.

He drew a deep breath and opened the door. The sitting room appeared empty. The door to the bedroom was closed. She was probably in the other room. No doubt already in the bed. His stomach twisted.

"I do hope that's you, Sir." Evie's voice came from behind the screen. "Otherwise I shall be most dreadfully embarrassed."

Without thinking, he adopted the lower tone he had used as Sir and resolved to keep his comments to a minimum. "Good afternoon, Eve."

"Do sit down, I won't be a minute."

There was a chair positioned facing the screen. It struck him as a most theatrical setting. For a moment, hope fluttered in his chest. Perhaps, this wasn't at all what he thought it was. He sat down.

"As you wish."

"I have been giving a great deal of thought to our conversation last night."

An article of clothing popped up from behind the

screen, then drifted down to settle on the top of the screen. Her bodice? She was undressing? All hope shattered.

He swallowed. "Have you?"

"Indeed I have. I must admit, your comments came as a complete surprise." Skirts flew upward, then settled over the screen. "And something of a revelation as well."

His tone hardened. "Did they?"

"Oh my, yes. In all those years that I was dreaming of you, I never imagined you might dream of me as well."

"Didn't you?"

She laughed, a sound that would have been most delightful under other circumstances. "Not for a moment. I had hoped, of course."

A stocking flipped over the top of the screen.

"Did you?"

She heaved a heartfelt sigh. "Every day." She paused. "And very nearly every night." A second stocking joined the first.

"It's only natural, I suppose," he said in a grudging manner. And wasn't that, too, his fault? Hadn't he been falling in love with her long before they'd met in person? Hadn't Sir's notes become more flirtatious through the years? Could he blame her now for reaching for something she'd long wanted but had never had?

"I have to confess, I wasn't entirely honest last night. My regrets go beyond never having seen your face."

"Do they?"

But damnation, now she was a married woman! She wasn't supposed to want anyone but him. It scarcely mattered that the object of her desire and her husband were one and the same. She didn't know that!

"I do wish they didn't but I can't seem to help myself. You are the man I have always wanted."

His jaw tightened. "But what of your husband?"

"Oh, Adrian is a dear, sweet, darling man." A corset joined the rest of her clothes. Good God, did she intend to disrobe entirely? "And I shall always be fond of him—"

"Fond of him?" His voice rose. "I thought you shared a great love?"

"Yes, well, that was before."

"Before?"

"Before I knew of your feelings."

He sucked in a shocked breath. "You said he was charming and intelligent and amusing."

"And he is. But he's not the least bit adventurous. Not overly exciting really, he can even be dull at times, although he is very nice," she added quickly.

"Nice?" She thought he was dull but nice? *Nice?*

"And while I have recently discovered there is more to him than I ever imagined, he is not you, is he?" Her chemise flew upward from behind the screen as if to emphasize her words. "As much as I hate to admit it, he does pale somewhat in comparison to you. But then most men do."

Adrian choked. "Do you intend to leave him then?"

"Divorce, you mean?" She scoffed. "I should hate to give up being the Countess of Waterston. I quite like it, you know. As well as all that lovely money." She sighed. "I don't think anyone who has always had money can appreciate what it's like not to have any at all. Oh no, I have no intention of giving that up."

"I thought you didn't marry him for his money?"

"I didn't but it certainly made him much more appealing."

He struggled to keep his voice level. "If you're not going to leave him, what do you intend?"

"Why, I intend to have you both, of course." She laughed lightly. "Any number of women I know have lovers as well as husbands. It seems to work out quite well for all concerned. I see no reason why it won't do as nicely for us."

"I can think of any number of reasons," he snapped.

"My goodness, Sir, I didn't expect you to be quite so stuffy about this."

"I have no intentions of sharing you with another man." *Even if that other man is me!*

"Well, you can't have me all to yourself. It simply wouldn't be fair."

"Fair?" he sputtered.

"We do want to be fair. Adrian deserves no less." She paused. "He's quite a decent sort, you know, even if he isn't adventurous—"

"Would you stop saying that!"

"Why?" Her tone was harder than before. "It's true, isn't it?"

"No, it's not true." Anger brought him to his feet.

"Perhaps it's time for the truth then?"

"Past time, Evie." At the moment he didn't care what her reaction to his revelation would be. He drew a deep breath.

A knock sounded at the door.

She huffed in exasperation. "Do get that, would you, Sir? I'm not entirely presentable."

"Perhaps you should have considered that before you disrobed," he said sharply.

"I wasn't expecting anyone else," she snapped.

This was not a good time for interruptions. They were moments from settling everything between them once and for all. He stepped to the door and yanked it open. "Yes?"

Two shockingly large men stood in the doorway, dressed in hotel uniforms. "Sorry to bother you, my lord."

"Is there a problem?"

They traded glances. "You could say that."

The shorter man shouldered his way into the room and nodded toward the closed bedroom door. "She must be in there." He strode across the room, grabbed a chair, and wedged it under the bedroom doorknob.

At once, Adrian realized these men were not who they appeared. If he hadn't been so angry, he would have recognized the truth the moment he opened the door. Before he could act, the taller man grabbed him from behind and clapped a rag over his face. Bloody hell, he knew that smell. He struggled against his captors, but in spite of his best efforts to hold his breath, the chloroform acted quickly and he felt himself slipping into oblivion. And prayed Evie would remain hidden and safe.

And prayed as well he would see her again.

Evelyn counted to ten before leaving the safety of the screen. She had seen everything through the cracks between the screen's panels. The hardest thing she'd ever done in her life was to keep still when they'd dragged her husband out of the room. Every instinct urged her to act but she knew better. She was no match for those brutes. Fortunately, the clothes she had tossed over the screen were those she had brought for the purpose and she was still fully clothed. Now, she needn't waste time dressing.

It was obvious: this kidnapping was real. The distinctive sweet smell of chloroform lingered in the air. It no longer mattered what he had done or how angry she was with him, she was not about to let him disappear from her life or this world forever. One look at the thugs who had taken him told her they would not be gentle and there would not be much time. Determination hardened within her. She would not let Adrian go without a fight. But this battle could not be won alone. She would need her friends.

Whether as Sir or Adrian, her husband had never failed her. And she would not fail him now.

Chapter 24

She slammed opened the door to Max's office. "I'm assuming this is not another perverted attempt to . . . to . . . well, I don't know to what. Adrian has been abducted!"

Max got to his feet and stared. "Adrian, your husband?"

"Yes, Adrian my husband." She narrowed her eyes. "Or should I say Sir, your cohort."

"I have no idea what you're talking about," he said in a lofty manner. "I say, Evelyn, you can't come barging in here, making accusations and—"

"I came as soon as I got your note." Celeste appeared in the doorway.

Max's eyes widened with surprise. "Miss De-Rochette."

"Sir Maxwell," Celeste said coolly.

"Oh, come now." Evelyn rolled her gaze toward the ceiling. "You needn't continue this pretense. I know it all."

"All of it?" Caution sounded in Max's voice.

"All of it," Evelyn said in a hard tone.

"You told her?" Max glared at Celeste. "You agreed not to say a word."

"Did I?" Celeste raised a brow. "I don't recall agreeing to any such thing. And if I did"—she shrugged—"I lied."

"That's neither here nor there at the moment," Evelyn snapped. "The more pressing problem is my husband has been abducted. I have no idea if the intended victim was Adrian or Sir. The men who took him barely said a word."

"Took him from where?" Max asked.

"The Langham."

"Ah yes, Room 327," Max murmured.

"Indeed." Evelyn clenched her teeth. "Who could have done this, Max?"

"And more to the point . . ." Celeste said. "Why?"

"We think it all ties into the theft of the file." He glanced at Evelyn. "As you know, it reveals the names of the last three heads of the department. Lord Lansbury was found dead this morning."

Evelyn's breath caught with fear. "And the other man?"

"He died a few months ago. Initially, we thought it was due to natural causes; now we are not so certain." His gaze met Evelyn's and he winced. "That was Sir George."

She stared. "Sir George Hardwell?"

Max nodded.

"My guardian?" Evelyn's voice rose. "He was a head of the department?"

Celeste gasped. "Good Lord."

"I am sorry, Evelyn," Max began.

"Don't be." She waved away his comment. "There

was no affection lost between us. I never even met the man. It does, however, explain why I was approached by Lansbury to join the department."

"He probably knew you'd make an excellent agent," Max said staunchly.

Even Celeste cast him a skeptical eye.

"What he knew was that working for the department would take care of my financial instability and he could wash his hands of me," Evelyn said. Odd, she probably should feel some sort of remorse for his passing or even bitterness at his treatment of her, but there were no feelings at all for this man who had cared so little about her he never even met her in person. "That's of no concern now at any rate."

"We suspect, Adrian and I, that is," Max said, "that as the file revealed the true identities of the last three heads of the department, whoever is behind this has some sort of grudge against the department or against Adrian, Lansbury, and Sir George personally."

"That makes no sense." Celeste shook her head. "Between the three men that would be a personal grievance that goes back, oh, nearly thirty years?"

Max nodded. "Which is why we think it's more likely the purpose is to cripple the department or embarrass the government or expose—"

"I don't care! It doesn't matter! What is wrong with the two of you?" Evelyn glared at the others. "All that matters is getting Adrian back. And I would much prefer to have him back alive."

"That's exactly what we are trying to do," Max snapped.

"Evelyn, dear." A reassuring note sounded in Celeste's voice. "The more we know about the why, the better we can determine the who. Which will hopefully lead us to where Adrian is being held."

If he was still alive. She dismissed the terrifying thought. "Yes, of course."

"Max," Celeste said thoughtfully, "you don't know for certain the circumstances of Sir George's death?"

"I had my secretary make inquiries." Max shrugged. "He found nothing unusual."

"Perhaps there was something that was insignificant at the time," Celeste said, "that now might prove important."

He cast her an admiring look. "Quite right." He turned to the side door, opened it, and frowned. "He's not at his desk at the moment. Odd, he usually tells me when he goes out."

"Max," Evelyn said slowly. "Only Celeste knew I was meeting Sir today. Who here knew about my meeting with Sir at the Langham?"

"Only Adrian and I. No one else."

"The man I delivered Evelyn's note to." Celeste met Max's gaze. "Might he have read it?"

"Mr. Sayers?" Max shook his head. "I doubt that."

"But if he read the note, he would know Adrian was to be at Room 327 at four o'clock," Evelyn said slowly.

"Rubbish." Max scoffed. "I trust the man completely. He's been with the department for years. His record is spotless."

"But doesn't he have access to all the records?" Evelyn asked. "If one wanted to make oneself look as trustworthy as possible, it would be a simple matter to change one's own record. And he had access to the file."

"And as it was he who allegedly looked into Sir

George's death," Celeste began, "couldn't he make his report to you say whatever he wished?"

"Beyond that," Evelyn continued, "you thought from the beginning the theft of the file involved someone within the department."

Max stared at the women.

"Max." Evelyn met his gaze directly. "No one else could have possibly known about the meeting at the Langham. No one."

"Bloody hell." Max's expression hardened. "We might be wrong, but it's all we've got at the moment."

"As you are the only one of us who knows him, think, Max." Celeste's brow furrowed. "Where would he be holding Lord W?"

"He has a key to the warehouse," Max said slowly. "And aside from last night, we haven't used it in quite some time. But that strikes me as too obvious."

"It's only obvious if we know Sayers is the culprit," Evelyn said sharply. "Now, what shall we do?"

Quickly they devised a plan. Max left the office for a few minutes to send for some of his men and issue orders. They would meet them at the docks. It was all going entirely too slowly for Evelyn, but it couldn't be helped. Max wasted a few more minutes trying to convince the women not to accompany him. He certainly should have known better. They had once been trained agents, after all. And neither she nor Celeste would sit calmly at home and wait. It was not in the nature of either woman. There was entirely too much at stake.

"Oh, you'll need this, I suspect." Celeste pulled a small pistol from her bag. "I have mine as well."

"Yes, thank you." Evelyn hefted the gun in her hand. It had been two years since she'd held the revolver. A

Webley bulldog, it wasn't as light as something more appropriate for a lady, but it was small enough to fit in a pocket. Besides, she rather liked the weight of it. Of course, she had to hold it with two hands but that only served to make her aim more accurate. With its checkered wood grips, it was a most practical firearm. She glanced at Celeste. "Loaded?"

Celeste cast her an indignant look. "Of course."

Max groaned.

"She's very good with it, Max." Celeste nodded in a smug manner. "As am I."

"And when was the last time either of you practiced?" he snapped. "It's not like riding a horse, you know. You can't get back on it and suddenly remember how to ride."

"Nonsense, Max," Evelyn said absently, still reacquainting herself with the revolver. "It is exactly like riding a horse. One never forgets this sort of thing."

Within the hour, all was ready and they prepared to leave.

"One more thing." She aimed Max a hard look. "If at all possible, I would prefer not to let Adrian know I know he's Sir."

"Very well." He threw his hands up in resignation. "I won't ask why. I don't want to know. I'll just be grateful if we all survive the night in one piece. And frankly, I'm not as worried about Adrian's welfare as I am that one of you might accidentally shoot me."

"Accidentally, Max?" Celeste grinned. "I certainly wouldn't worry about an accident."

"No, Max. If I fire this pistol . . ." A grim note sounded in Evelyn's voice. "It will not be an accident."

* * *

Every minute that passed brought Evelyn one minute closer to being a widow.

Max and Celeste continued to discuss the situation in low tones, probably to ease her apprehension. She did learn Lord Lansbury's throat had been slit, which did nothing to allay her fears.

Evelyn tried to hold the ticking clock in her head at bay, but as she sat in the carriage, on the endless way to the docks, the direst thoughts filled her head. And clutched at her heart.

She tried as well not to think about the possibility they might not find Adrian, that he might not be at the warehouse. Or the chance Sayers was not the culprit and the real villain was still unknown. She clung to the hope that their assumptions were correct. They had no others.

Still, she could not ignore the fact that if they were wrong about any of it, they might be very wrong. And it would be too late. She knew they were moving as quickly as possible, but it did not seem nearly fast enough. Evelyn had never especially been one for prayer, but at the moment, prayer was all she had. And she begged God not to let her husband go to his grave thinking she had betrayed him.

It was still twilight when they arrived at the docks. Max's men had arrived before them and had already caught the two thugs who had taken Adrian. They confirmed he was in the warehouse cellar and admitted things had not gone smoothly. It had taken his abductors much longer to transport Adrian than had been planned. But as far as they knew, he was still alive with Sayers, apparently in the same room where Evie had been held. Thank God.

Max, Celeste, and some of his men were to enter the

warehouse by a back entry and then descend a back stairway. It meant they would be on the far side of the building and would have to make their way toward the front. Evelyn would retrace Adrian's steps from last night, again with several men accompanying her. It struck neither she nor Max as a particularly clever plan. Confrontation with Sayers might be disastrous, but the element of surprise might well serve their cause. And what would be more surprising than the unexpected appearance of Lady Waterston? With any luck at all, it would distract Sayers long enough for Max and the others to surround him.

The two groups separated. Evelyn counted to ten, then she and her men slipped into the warehouse. Other than last night, she'd never been here before. The weak, lingering light of twilight was of some assistance as they made their way to the stairway. She noted a faint glow of light at the bottom of the stairs. Evelyn started down, the men close at her heels. They were to wait at the foot of the stairs until needed. She pulled her gun from the pocket of her cloak and stepped into the light.

Adrian was tied in the same chair she had been. A lantern on the floor cast a wide pool of light. His gaze met hers, concern flickered in his eyes, but he didn't say a word.

"Lady Waterston," Sayers said smoothly. He stood behind Adrian, a nasty-looking knife in his hand. "How delightful to see you again."

"I fear you have the advantage over me, Mr. Sayers," she said coolly. "I don't recall meeting you."

"You wound me deeply, Lady Waterston. We met at the Spanish ambassador's reception. And we danced at the masquerade. Of course, I was in costume and you had no idea it was me but a delightful dance nonetheless." He paused. "We also nearly met one other time at the British Museum. I delivered the book from Sir Maxwell. I assumed it was a private matter between you and he as I was told to find the lady with the locket that matched the cover." He chuckled. "I never imagined Sir Maxwell to be quite so romantic or discreet."

At once Evelyn realized Sayers had no idea of her connection to the department. And why would he? Adrian had had her name expunged from the records. Best to let Sayers believe she and Max were lovers.

"Discretion forbids me from comment." She forced a pleasant smile. "My husband is sitting right here, you know. How are you, darling?"

"Excellent at the moment." His brows drew together. "Bit of a headache, though. The chloroform, you know."

"Nasty stuff," she murmured.

"That's enough." Sayers glared. "This is not afternoon tea."

"But where are my manners?" Adrian said pleasantly. "I should introduce the two of you."

"As Mr. Sayers has just pointed out, we have already met."

"Ah, but you don't know his full name." Adrian paused. "Allow me to introduce Mr. Emmet Sayers *Hardwell*."

"Hardwell?" She frowned. "As in Sir George Hardwell?"

"Sir George was my father." Sayers smirked. "Which means you are my dear cousin. Oh, quite distant, of course, but we are relations nonetheless. Indeed, I am your only living relative."

Evelyn stared in disbelief.

"Evie, dear, Mr. Sayers or rather Mr. Hardwell has been good enough to explain everything to me." Adrian shrugged as best he could given his bonds. "As he intends to kill me, it seemed only fair."

"How very gracious of you"—she forced out the word—"cousin."

"It seems, darling, your parents did not leave you penniless after all." Adrian's tone was light. "You have quite a sizable fortune in trust that you will inherit on your thirtieth birthday."

"However," Hardwell began, "that same fortune has provided for my father and myself. I had no idea, of course. I thought my family was financially sound. As it turns out, my dear father had been taking money from your trust for, oh, as long as he had been in control of it."

"I see," she murmured. It was most interesting but not of any great concern at the moment. Still, every minute she kept him talking was another minute for Max and his men to surround him.

"I knew nothing of this until my father cut me off a few months ago. Apparently, in his declining years he had developed something of a conscience. That and the fact that he knew he would be found out when you turned thirty, which, I believe, is next week." He heaved a dramatic sigh. "Unfortunately, he passed away that very same night."

"Helped by his loving son," Adrian added.

"Well, I would have hated to see the old man imprisoned for embezzlement." Hardwell shuddered. "He wouldn't have liked that at all."

"What a good son you are," Adrian said under his breath.

"I'm afraid I find this all most confusing." She

shook her head. "I would think then that you'd want to kill me, not my husband."

"Ah, but if I were to kill you first, the inheritance would go to your husband. If I killed him after your birthday, your inheritance might well become part of his estate." He grinned in a most evil manner. The man was obviously mad as well as dangerous. "But if I kill him before you inherit, I can wait as long as I wish to kill you."

"How very clever of you, cousin."

"I thought so," he said modestly.

"You do realize I would not have come alone," she said coolly. "You will not escape this."

"On the contrary, cousin." He scoffed. "I have explored this building thoroughly. I know every entrance, every exit. And I know them in the dark. Once I dispatch your husband, I shall extinguish the light and vanish in the shadows." His tone hardened. "Admittedly, I had originally planned simply to slit his throat and throw his body in the river. It would have been much more expedient that way. But I am thoroughly prepared for the circumstances I now find myself in."

"I am sorry, cousin, to disillusion you but you cannot get away with this."

"Oh, but I can. You see . . ." He lowered his voice in a confidential manner. "Your friend Sir Maxwell heads an organization that is . . . how to explain it?" He thought for a moment. "Let us just say they do not work within the confines of the law. Were I to be imprisoned, even executed, I shall make certain the activities of your lover's organization were made public." He shook his head in a mournful manner. "It would be most distressing to the entire government. I cannot imagine the political repercussions. Therefore, it's in everyone's best interests to let me vanish and forget all about me. Once I am finished here, of course."

There was an obvious flaw in his plan, but the man was too smug or too mad to see it.

"My, you are clever. But you have forgotten one thing." She raised the pistol. "I have a firearm."

He chuckled. "And a charming little toy it is, too. However . . ." He laid the knife against Adrian's throat. "Unless you can kill me with one shot, you will not have the chance for a second."

"One shot, oh dear." She shook her head. "That is awkward."

"At the very least," Adrian murmured.

"Do try to keep still, dear."

"I am trying." A tense note sounded in his voice. Oddly enough, his concern lessened hers and she'd never been calmer.

"Come now, cousin," Hardwell scoffed. "Your hand is already shaking."

She cupped her right hand with her left. "That's better, I think."

Hardwell laughed. "I must give you credit, cousin. You do bluff well." His eyes narrowed. "But as amusing as I find this, I am tiring of this game."

Her gaze met Hardwell's. "Do you trust me, Adrian?"

"With my life, apparently."

"Did you know I am an excellent shot, darling?"

"I do hope so, my dear."

"Even if you could make that shot," Hardwell said, "I daresay you won't shoot the only remaining member of your family."

"Oh, but you are not my family, Mr. Hardwell. My husband is." Her tone sharpened. "And if you do not drop that knife and step away right now, do not doubt for a moment, I will shoot you."

A slow, evil smile spread across his face. His hand twitched and she squeezed the trigger. The shot caught him right above the bridge of his nose. His eyes widened in surprise and the knife dropped from his hand. No more than a trickle of blood oozed from the smoking hole in his face. Odd, she'd thought there would be more blood. Slowly he crumpled to the floor.

Adrian stared in shock.

"Excellent shot." Max emerged from the shadows.

"Are you all right?" Concern sounded in Adrian's voice.

"Quite." She nodded, turned, took a few steps, doubled over, and retched.

And in the end . . .

Revelation

. . . but at the length truth will out.

—William Shakespeare, *The Merchant of Venice*

Chapter 25

"Untie these blasted ropes," Adrian ordered.

"I'm trying," Max said sharply. "But it would go much faster if you would keep still."

His poor wife was doubled over, retching. Not that he was surprised. He'd seen the strongest of men react similarly the first time they'd killed a man. The ropes around his wrists loosened and he pulled his hands free, rubbing them briskly to restore feeling.

Max knelt to untie his feet. His voice was low, for his friend's ears alone. "Hell of a shot, Adrian."

"She saved my life," Adrian said simply. It was, however, an amazing shot, even for him. If asked, he would have wagered she could not repeat it. But these were extraordinary circumstances, and in his experience, even the most ordinary of men rose to the occasion when pressed. Of course, Evie was not now, nor had she ever been, ordinary.

"Done."

Adrian kicked the ropes away and rushed to his wife's side. "Are you all right?"

"You needn't keep asking me. Yes, yes, I'm fine. Better now, really." She straightened and stared at him. "Are you?"

"You saved my life." He yanked her into his arms. "But I'm more angry than grateful. You placed yourself in grave danger."

"My apologies." She glared up at him. "But you obviously needed my assistance, and I was not ready to become a widow." The faintest flicker of amusement shone in her eyes. "A wealthy widow apparently, which I suppose would tend to take some of the sting out of widowhood."

He narrowed his eyes. "I have no intention of allowing that to happen until you are entirely too old and feeble to enjoy being a merry widow. And with that in mind . . ." He released her and gently removed the pistol from her hand. "I'll take that, if you please." He flicked the revolver open and emptied the bullets. "I would hate to be shot accidentally."

She stared at him, then laughed; laughter tinged by the faintest edge of hysteria. "It would be no accident."

"Good to know." He studied her closely. "You're shaking."

"Well, I did just kill my only living relative." Her gaze slipped past him to where Max's men were collecting Hardwell's body and she shuddered. "He was a nasty sort, though, wasn't he?"

"As he had already killed two men, including his father, and fully intended to kill us both, I would say calling him a nasty sort is being kind," Adrian said firmly. He handed the pistol and bullets to Max, who had come up behind him, Miss DeRochette by his side.

Evie's gaze searched Adrian's. "We have a great deal to talk about."

More than she knew. He drew a deep breath. "Then let us go home."

"I'm afraid not." Max stepped forward. "As much as I hate to interrupt this reunion, Miss DeRochette will accompany Lady Waterston to your house. You will ride with me. There are matters—"

"Of course." Adrian smiled into his wife's eyes. "I will join you soon."

Her eyes narrowed. "See that you do."

A short time later they had seen the ladies safely off, and he and Max were in a second carriage. Adrian had been both surprised and gratified that Max had been able to marshal the resources of the department so quickly. But then he'd really never doubted his friend's ability to run the organization.

"I'm assuming you learned more from Sayers, or rather Hardwell, than you revealed to your wife," Max said.

Adrian nodded. "Apparently he joined the department under the name of Sayers to avoid any question of nepotism, even though Sir George had already retired by then."

Max sighed. "His record was excellent."

"And I believe, from what he said, it was legitimate. His references and background, however, were more than a bit fictitious. He discovered Evie had married a former head of the department after he began working directly for you. He admitted he found that rather amusing at the time." Adrian clenched his fists absently. "It wasn't until he had that falling-out with his father over money that he came up with his plan to get her inheritance."

"By doing away with you?"

"By killing me first and then her. It was really rather

an ingenious plan." Adrian sorted through the information in his head. "He thought by taking the file, killing Lansbury, and then me, it would appear whoever was behind it all was targeting the department. It would never be suspected that Evie's money was his real goal."

"Then Lansbury's death was—"

"Nothing more than furthering the impression that this had to do with the department."

"Poor bastard," Max murmured.

"Once I was out of the way, the pressure on him would be lessened." His voice hardened. "And he could take his time to kill Evie. He planned to make her death some months from now look like an accident.

"With her birthday approaching, I was a more pressing problem. Hardwell hadn't quite figured out the best way to dispose of me as of yet. But when he learned I would be meeting her at the Langham, he seized the opportunity."

"He wasn't as clever as he thought."

"His biggest mistake was in thinking he knew everything. In thinking his plan was foolproof." Adrian's gaze met the other man's. "I'm assuming, even if he escaped tonight, he would never have been allowed to live."

"He thought the department would let him go to avoid embarrassment and exposure." Max shrugged. "Which is far easier to do if the threat is eliminated entirely."

Adrian nodded. "He never thought Evie would come to you for help. And why would she? It would be most awkward, after all," he said in a casual manner. "He assumed you and she were lovers."

"So I heard."

"He was quite snide about that. He said he thought sending me the note to join her through you was some sort of game she was playing." Adrian shook his head. "But he never imagined she'd been trained by the department."

"Which is why he wasn't concerned tonight about her appearance." Max paused. "In hindsight, your insisting her name be wiped from the records proved his undoing." He chuckled wryly. "Given her actions this evening, perhaps she is the one I need to return to work."

"Don't even think about it, Max," Adrian warned.

It was odd, though. Upon reflection, Adrian realized there'd been no mention of the department, no reference to him as Sir during the confrontation between his wife and her distant relative. Was it at all possible his secret was still safe? Did she or did she not know he was Sir? With all that had happened in recent days, was it even conceivable that particular point had evaded her notice?

He'd be foolish to assume she knew if she didn't and even more foolish to assume she didn't if she did. Best to let this game play out to the finale. Once again he realized his friend had been right. This was indeed the most dangerous game he had ever played.

And he had no idea how it would end.

He stood in the doorway of the dressing room that connected his bedroom to hers and watched her pace for a moment. Evie had changed into her blue dressing gown, the one that fairly made his mouth water. He took it as a good sign.

He cleared his throat. "Evie?"

Her gaze jerked to his. "Oh, Adrian!" She flew across the room and into his arms. "Oh, darling, I was so scared."

"As was I." He chuckled. "And never more so than when I saw you in the cellar."

"Oh." She paused. "About that." She heaved a heartfelt sigh, pushed out of his arms, and stepped away. "There are things I need to tell you."

He nodded. "There are things I need to tell you as well."

"Mine are in the form of, oh, a confession, I would say."

"A confession," he said slowly. Perhaps it would be best to let her have her say before he said anything he might regret. "Go on."

"Well." She wrung her hands together in an overly dramatic manner. His eyes narrowed. She was rarely overly dramatic. "It's about tonight."

"I assumed as much."

"When I saw that madman was prepared to kill you and I realized it was all my fault . . ."

"Yes?"

"I simply couldn't live with myself if something had happened to you."

"It would have been . . . awkward," he said slowly.

"Awkward?" She scoffed. "It would have been devastating. The guilt alone. And your mother . . ." She shuddered. "Your mother would have made my life a living hell."

"Something to consider, of course." His mother? He was dead and she was worried about his mother's reaction?

"Well, that's neither here nor there now, I suppose."

She waved in an offhand manner. "You're alive and look none the worse for it."

He rubbed his forehead. "I still have a bit of a headache."

"As I did last night when I was abducted and dropped." She scoffed. "You'll be fine."

"I suppose . . ."

"You're alive and that's all that matters." She squared her shoulders. "And I intend to keep you that way."

"You do?" he said cautiously.

"Without question. I will not allow you to be put in danger again." She shook her head in a mournful manner. "And I fear it could happen in the future."

He stared. "I don't understand."

"I know, you poor darling." She paced the room. "This is difficult to say."

"Then it's best simply to say it," he said in a harder voice than he had expected.

Her brow rose. "I shall attribute your irritable mood to the events of this evening. I know I felt rather ill-tempered last night. It's not pleasant to be abducted and dropped, you know."

"My apologies," he muttered.

"Accepted," she said in a lofty manner and continued. "Before we were married . . ." She frowned. "Perhaps you should sit down for this part, darling. It might be a bit shocking."

His jaw clenched. "I prefer to stand."

"I am concerned about your aching head."

"It feels much better."

"Really?" Her eyes widened in astonishment. "I know when I was abducted and dropped—"

"Would you stop saying that?" he snapped.

"What?" Her eyes widened in an innocent manner. "That I was abducted and dropped?"

"Yes."

"Why?"

Because it was at my direction! "It was a dreadful incident and I do not wish to be reminded of it."

"You poor dear. Very well then." She shrugged. "Stand if you feel up to it."

"I'm fine."

"As I was saying." She drew a deep breath and yet she appeared remarkably collected. "Before we were married, I worked as an agent for a government department that, oh, operates for the most part in a clandestine manner."

"Oh?" Was this the moment to tell her he already knew? Or should he just keep his mouth closed?

"I had thought it was all in the past." She shook her head. "But last night I realized that it will never be in the past. Indeed, I fear now my true identity has been revealed. It had been hidden up until now, thanks to the efforts of a truly remarkable man. Quite dashing and adventurous and I must say . . ." She sighed again. "The intoxicating way he takes pen to paper is only eclipsed by his charm in person."

He glared. "And?"

"I know that after last night, you are full of, well, *confidence* in your courage, and indeed, I am most proud of you," she added quickly. "But you have to admit, that in spite of one adventurous moment, aside from your past adventures with women . . ." She shook her head in an annoyingly kind manner. "You're really not an adventurous sort."

He stared.

"And I have come to realize that you might well never be safe as long as I am in your life."

"I am perfectly capable of taking care of myself," he said through clenched teeth.

She continued as if he hadn't said a word. "So, in order to keep you alive and well . . ." She shook her head sadly. "I'm afraid I have no choice but to leave you. Forever."

"What?" Surely she wasn't serious?

"Oh, darling, don't look at me that way." She cast him a pleading look. "This is as difficult for me as it is for you." She paused. "Although I suppose I will be able to turn to Sir for comfort and—"

"This has gone far enough," he said in a hard tone.

"And I much prefer it go no farther." She sniffed back a sob. "Why, when you were abducted practically in front of me—"

"When I was—" At once, he realized the truth. *Adrian* wasn't abducted. *Sir* was.

She crossed her arms over her chest. "When. You. Were. What?"

Damnation! For the first time in his life, words failed him. "Uh . . ."

Her eyes narrowed. "When. You. Were. What?"

He winced. "How long have you known?"

"Only since this morning." She studied him coolly.

"How did you find out?"

"I found my letters in your desk."

"You went into my desk?" Indignation sounded in his voice.

She raised a brow. "I thought you had nothing to hide."

"I don't now," he said under his breath. He studied her cautiously. "Are you very furious?"

"This morning I was furious. Very furious. As the day wore on, I became less angry and more determined that you needed to be taught a lesson."

"At the very least," he said staunchly. She didn't seem nearly as angry as he thought she'd be. Perhaps this wouldn't be as bad as he had anticipated. "The Langham then?"

A reluctant smile tugged at the corners of her lips. "It was going quite well, too. And then, of course, you were kidnapped." She paused. "I do feel bad about that as it was ultimately my fault. Oh, not in the way my abduction was orchestrated by you—"

He cringed.

"But it was my mad cousin who had already killed two men, holding a knife to your throat."

"Not at all your fault."

"I know that. Still . . ." A shadow passed across her eyes and she shuddered. At what she had seen or what she had done or what might have been, it scarcely mattered.

"My mother would have been most upset."

She cast him a grateful smile. "As would I."

He stepped toward her. "Evie."

She held out her hand to stop him and stepped back. "Very nearly losing you put your deceit—all of it—into an interesting perspective. While coming to your rescue, I had time to think." She pulled a deep breath. "I understand, given the nature of the department, the need for secrecy. But I don't understand why that applied to me."

"Once I had met you as myself . . ." He chose his words with care. "I wanted you to, well, want *me*. The man who had an extensive family and a new title and all the rather ordinary responsibilities that went along with it. Not the man who ferreted out information and apprehended villains and lived a life of secrets and danger." He stepped closer. She studied him warily but didn't move. "I was already in love with you by then."

"I used to think we met by chance. It wasn't chance, was it?"

"No." He shook his head. "Your manner had changed and there was concern as to your loyalty. And rightly or wrongly, I saw it as my opportunity."

"I see," she said slowly. "I am assuming you then discovered I had simply grown weary of working for the department?"

He nodded.

"When you married me—"

"I did so because I could not imagine my life without you."

"Aside from matters pertaining to Sir and the department . . ." She met his gaze directly. "Have you ever lied to me?"

"I lie to you all the time."

Shock widened her eyes.

He moved closer. "The last time you wore that bilious green gown with the cream-colored lace and asked me if I liked it, I lied."

"I see." She nodded. "Go on."

"When we went to Lady Lovett's garden party last summer, I said I was looking forward to it." He shook his head in a mournful manner. "I lied."

She bit back a smile.

"When I said you could spend vast amounts of money in a frivolous manner and I would not say a word . . ." He cringed. "It wasn't a lie at the time. Now, however . . ."

She arched a brow. "About nothing of importance then?"

"Well, vast amounts of money . . ."

She choked back a laugh.

He met her gaze firmly. "I lied to you when I let you think I could live without you. That was a lie of omission."

He was within a step of her now.

"I deceived you when I led you to believe that I didn't take what I did, when I didn't trust you, as a serious sin. Or perhaps that was another lie of omission. I'm not sure and it's of no importance now. But I do regret my behavior and I am deeply sorry. I wouldn't hurt you for anything in the world."

"Why did you send me those notes? Why did you pretend to be Sir at the masquerade?"

"Because I am a fool," he said firmly. "Because I find it hard to believe someone like you would choose someone like me over someone like Sir."

She studied him for a long moment. "Do you know what is saving you, saving us really, aside from the fact that I came entirely too close to losing you tonight?"

"My devastating charm and complete and utter honesty?" he said hopefully.

"Not entirely." She considered him for a moment. "For one thing, I have been little better than you in regards to our respective pasts."

"There is that," he murmured. Her eyes narrowed and he remembered his resolve to keep his mouth closed.

"For another . . ." She drew a deep breath. "I know you, Adrian Hadley-Attwater. I may not have known all your secrets, but I know the kind of man you are." There was a slight tremble in her voice. At the same moment he realized his cause was won, he vowed never to hear that tremble because of him again. "And I know that I want to end my days with my hand in yours."

"Then you forgive me?" He pulled her into his arms.

"For all of it?" She gazed up at him. "Not quite yet." She smiled in a wicked manner. "But I will allow you to continue to make it up to me. For the rest of your life, I think."

"I should like nothing better."

"No more lies," she said firmly. "From either of us."

"Agreed." He grimaced. "However, you should know I am considering returning to the department. On a strictly occasional basis," he added quickly. "Probably as nothing more than an advisor."

"Occasionally, you say?"

"No more than that."

"That does sound like fun." She cast him a brilliant smile. "Working together again, you and I."

"You and I?" Caution sounded in his voice.

"I have no intention of permitting you to do so without me." She smiled in a smug manner. "You need me, *Sir*."

"I believe I always have." He stared down at her. "And I know I always will." He pulled her closer against him. "I couldn't live a single day without you, Evie. For the rest of my life I want your hand in mine."

"Oh my." She gazed into his eyes suspiciously. "Which one of you is speaking now?"

He raised a brow in a suggestive manner. "Which one would you like?"

She laughed. "It scarcely matters. Both of you are mine."

"Forever." He lowered his lips to hers, and it struck

him once again that life was indeed made up of endings and beginnings. And he realized as well that for the rest of his days he would face each ending, every beginning, and all in between with the hand of the woman he loved held firmly in his. "But admit it, my love." He brushed his lips across hers. "You like the idea of an adventurous husband."

"Only if it's you, darling. Only if it's you."